THE CLASH OF STEEL.
THE REWARDS OF BATTLE.

Blows. Screams of horses and men. Roland, at Charlemagne's flank, raised his sword to ward off a blow, then ducked as the wood shattered before the onslaught of steel. He thrust the hilt aside. Useless . . .

All his being gone savagely intense, Roland found himself tumbling as his horse screamed and sank beneath him. He rolled and sprang to his feet, then seized a sword from a man caught beneath a destrier's iron-shod hooves. He ducked and flitted . . . Struck, and grinned at the blood he saw spurt from a neck.

How he had waited and struggled for this joy.

CHARLEMAGNE'S CHAMPION

More praise for Gail Van Asten's
THE BLIND KNIGHT:

CHARLEMAGNE'S CHAMPION

GAIL VAN ASTEN

ACE BOOKS, NEW YORK

This book is an Ace original edition,
and has never been previously published.

CHARLEMAGNE'S CHAMPION

An Ace Book / published by arrangement with
the author

PRINTING HISTORY
Ace edition/April 1990

ISBN: 0-441-10287-5

Ace Books are published by The Berkley Publishing Group,
200 Madison Avenue, New York, New York 10016.
The name ''ACE'' and the ''A'' logo
are trademarks belonging to Charter Communications, Inc.

PRINTED IN THE UNITED STATES OF AMERICA

10 9 8 7 6 5 4 3 2 1

For, most especially . . .
G.B.

Shrouded in the mists of time
And in the passing of generations,
A hero is remembered in a song.
A puissant knight,
Progenitor of Chivalry,
Symbol of things most magical
And long forgotten . . .
A single man, who, like every other,
Died . . .

—G. S. Van Asten
August, 1987

ONE

A.D. 772

Eager to continue its run, the stallion snorted impatiently at the tightening of the curb, but halted obediently at the crest of the hill. Astride the beast, his hair silver hued like the frost that lurked near the woods and in the gullies where the sun had not yet reached, the tall man frowned to hear the thunder of approaching horses that pursued him up the long hill. He had no wish to indulge in the distraction of this autumn morning's sport.

Charlemagne . . . They were calling him that now. Great Charles—even though he had been King but four years and had not yet attained his thirtieth birthday. It was the name he had given himself in his own mind, symbol of his determination fo fulfill all the tasks that lay before him. Now, it sounded on the lips of men. All men. He had earned it; yet, he knew, he had made but a beginning.

He glanced back to the company of lords that, upon reaching the upper flanks of the same hill, fanned out and reined in their mounts to await his pleasure. He wanted none of them. He wanted to be alone.

He signaled impatiently to the falconer to relieve him of the hooded bird upon his left wrist.

"We wish thee good hunting, my lords," he told the company in stern dismissal as the man took the jesses of the hawk, then turned his horse away.

"Majesty . . . ?" Ganelon De Maganze called out. Charlemagne touched the stallion's bridle again, then turned in the

1

saddle to look at his Champion. "Surely, Majesty, thou have need for some escort . . . ?"

Charlemagne sighed heavily at the Champion's consternation, and, still frowning, passed his gaze across the group. All highborn men, they were a mixture of older lords and the younger knights of his own creation. Eagerness was reflected on the faces of the latter. They too, he thought, were but a beginning . . . He wanted no one. Yet, it was a small yielding to give their concern and honest loyalty.

Lord Oliver De Montglave nudged his horse forward a little. Newly knighted, he was a youngster of unquestioned honor and valor. But . . . Then, the King caught sight of the raw-boned, beardless, and unkempt boy astride a palfrey at the falconer's flank. His body held defiantly erect, this boy's eyes were firmly downcast, without expectation. His features were composed to a sternness that bordered on the sullen, and were remarkably harsh for one so young.

"That squire," Charlemagne said brusquely, pointing, "shall accompany us. For the rest, do thou be about thy sport!" He turned away, and set his mount to plunge down the side of the hill, through the tall grasses, toward the woods that began below. He had caught the brief look of chagrin on young Lord Oliver's face. And the thoroughly startled look of the boy who had raised his eyes at last.

He heard the boy following behind him as he rode, and the thunder of the other horses as the company of hunters swept away in the opposite direction. He sighed his relief.

Charlemagne slowed the stallion as he reached the first of the trees, then loosed his grip on the reins to let the beast pick it's own way. He knew these woodlands beyond Aix La Chapelle intimately from uncountable boyhood forays. He shifted his shoulders, thrust back the folds of his cloak, savoring the chill of the air, and began to relax at last.

The boy followed unobtrusively, keeping a discreet distance, still astounded by the triumph and distinction of having been chosen by Charlemagne. Squire . . . So the King had called him. But, for truth, he was apart from other such, being more a blend of servant and butt of every jest and contempt. He had another name that defined him before all men. That damned him.

After near an hour of aimless, leisurely riding, Charlemagne stopped his horse by a stream and dismounted, loos-

ing the bridle to let the animal drink. The boy dismounted as
well, and came forward quickly to take the reins from the
King. Eyes downcast once more, he was acutely conscious
of his station and of the fact that he had never been so close
to the King. He led both horses away, and, standing between
them, let the animals browse upon gold and brown vegetation. He watched as the King moved away, strolling upstream
for a few yards before seating himself slowly in the tall grasses
by the water's edge and leaning back comfortably against the
bole of a tree. Then, the boy ventured to crouch down on his
haunches between the two horses to wait.

Carloman, his well loved brother, was dead. Ever frail, that
Prince's health had gone completely as he surrendered to the
bitter damp of the past winter. Now, his half of the kingdom that
had been divided by Pepin's decree, was given up to Charlemagne. I have it all, the King thought. It was at last, as he had
always known it must be . . . And, he had made it perfectly
clear that Carloman's small sons would inherit naught but the
nobility and fiefs he decided to grant them. No more division of
power. This realm must be held in a single fist. There could be
no more such rifts if the western heart of Christendom was to
be kept entire, brought to prevail.

Byzantium was too far away to involve itself, either effectively, or with interest, in the welfare of Western Christendom. As he and the new Pope, Adrian, were fully agreed,
Rome and the Papacy must become the seat of the Holy
Church in the west. Frail, isolated Rome, as yet . . . Charlemagne closed his eyes briefly as he considered the future.

Sons. He grimaced as he thought of his brief and fruitless
marriage to the daughter of Desiderius of Lombardy. Arranged by his mother, the Dowager Bertrada, the marriage
had been a mistake. Beyond his loathing for the sight of the
woman, his relief in obtaining the annulment had been profound. His need, most politic. Now, freed from any familial
obligations toward Desiderius' avaricious disruptions of
Christian unity, he could consolidate his protective stance toward Rome. Next summer, he promised, Lombardy would
be brought to heel, never again to disrupt Frankish unity.

There were too many foes to permit anything else. Charlemagne did not underestimate the Saxons, despite the campaigns of the past summer that had effectively pushed back

their attempts to invade the north and west. Nor were the Saxons the only barbarous and heathen tribes eager to conquer the rich, fertile lands of the Franks.

Little by little . . . Aye. A stew of schemes and foresight. Likewise, his plan to raise an elite corps of noble young lords to champion his cause was beginning to realize fruition. Under the rule of his old friend and now Champion, Ganelon De Maganze, these youngsters, brought to Aix, inspired others with their dedication, would dare almost anything for his favor.

Delicious solitude . . .

Charlemagne shifted comfortably, savoring the fresh breeze that ruffled his silver-blond hair and touched his face. He listened to the birds that sang in the distance, and the sounds of rustling leaves, dying, becoming crisp, releasing their hold on branches and twigs before tumbling gently earthward in this, the early part of autumn.

Who would be the next great knight? he wondered idly. Oliver De Montglave? Possibly. He turned his head to look downstream at the boy who had accompanied him.

"What is thy name, squire?" he asked after some moments.

The boy, after seeing the King settle himself, had moved to the edge of the stream, first to cup water in his hand, then to kneel in the grass and stare at his own reflection.

His thin face was strong jawed. His mouth made a hard slash. His cheekbones were high, and his eyes were large and well spaced. Hazel colored? Nay. They were a peculiar golden hue with overlarge pupils that made them seem near black at times. Oddly cold, expressionless. Unnatural. His face was surrounded by a thick mass of unevenly cut, half-tangled, tawny-gold hair that covered a wide forehead and fell to his shoulders. Beardless still, he noted. Not yet a man. Hateful youth . . .

He started as he heard the King's question, and stood up abruptly. Then, more hesitantly, compelled by the uncompromising stare of Charlemagne's pale blue eyes, he ventured toward the King and bowed deeply. The King's eyes could cut through a soul better than any steel, he thought.

"I am Roland, Majesty." he managed a toneless response. Charlemagne looked away.

"Roland? Is that all?" he asked, staring across the stream. Roland felt a sickened disappointment in the pit of his belly. Had the King forgotten the beggared child, the thief, he had taken from the hills near the fiefs of Montglave far to the south, four years before? Praised for courage instead of punished, the King had willed him to be reared with others of his household, and trained to arms . . .

"Roland the Bastard, Majesty." He answered with a more deliberate tonelessness. Charlemagne looked at him then, scanning the lanky, immature frame, the disarray of unkempt, overworn, discarded clothing. He had been slow to sprout in his sapling years as well, he remembered.

"Sit, boy," he said quietly. "I'll not crane my neck to look at thee." Astonished again, Roland dropped cautiously to sit cross-legged something more than a yard distant. "How old art thou?" Charlemagne asked then, although he knew very well.

"This is my fourteenth year, Majesty." The answer was restrained.

"How were thou got, Roland the Bastard?" Charlemagne pursued, catching both the reactive stiffening of shoulders, and the abruptly lowered gaze as Roland looked down to conceal his expression.

"My father I know not, Majesty." Chill tones. Control overlay violence. "My mother . . ." Roland's lips tightened further. "My mother is dead," he concluded and looked up. Charlemagne caught the flash of venom that slipped across those eyes that were much lighter than Berthe's. His sister . . . He arched a brow in query. "She was a witch, Majesty!" Roland rasped it out. Defiant pride that lacked respect even for princes. Charlemagne looked away to conceal his own expression.

"Aye. We do recollect," he murmured distantly. Then, "And now, thou art a squire in our household?"

"Aye, Majesty."

Charlemagne smiled fractionally, recognizing everything. So like himself, this boy . . . his son. His firstborn and only child. His secret. He inhaled deeply, smelling the blend of sunshine and woodland in the crisp air.

"And, were thou to be made knight, young Roland, what name would thou choose for thyself?" he asked slowly, looking at the boy whose eyes went wide, then wary, then still.

"Roland. Naught else, Majesty." The answer came in an uneven whisper as Roland looked away, giving voice for the first time to his dream.

"Look yonder, Roland the Bastard." The King's voice was

smooth, sure, and Roland followed as he pointed toward the
great oak tree that towered up and outward on the other side
of the stream. Massive trunk. Great, gnarled branches . . .
"Do thou consider the oak," the King continued. "Got of a
single acorn, it grows in solitude. It grows with determined
patience, oft overtaken by other, trailer trees in its sapling
years. Yet, in the end, it grows to be greater than all the
rest, its roots reaching deepest into the earth, its branches
climbing highest to the sun, its wood the hardest, akin to
steel . . ." The King fell silent, and Roland slowly withdrew
his gaze from the tree to stare with mesmerized fascination
into Charlemagne's uncanny, penetrating eyes.

"I too, have a single name now," Charlemagne said then,
very clearly. "Go now. Get the horses," he added softly.

Roland rose to his feet, staring down at his own long fingered hands as he did so, and knew then, he had been afforded a great and rare privilege. He had not been forgot, as
he had thought. Bastard. Witch child . . . Nor had he been
found wanting. Feeling welled up to strangle any capacity for
utterance as he walked back to recover the tethered horses.
He had been afforded a special gift. He was, he understood,
for some mysterious reason . . . beloved of Charlemagne.

Keeping to the distance that was proper for a squire, Roland rode quietly behind the King. Not once did Charlemagne
so much as glance back toward him. Nor did it matter. What
had been given was tightly held inside. Comfortably astride
the gently-gaited, meek-tempered palfrey, Roland, too, savored the solitude and the silence.

As they neared the great, sprawling magnificence of the
castle of Aix La Chapelle, he looked around to see the company of hunters was returning as well. Their horses were wet
and frothy. The falcons and hawks were hooded, and game
hung from saddle bows.

Surrounded once more, his face froze reflexively to its usual
blend of imperviousness. He ignored the thoughtful frown
that Lord Oliver sent in his direction, and did not see the
slight flickering that crossed Lord Ganelon's dark complected
features. Attentive only to the King, he dismounted and made
sure he was ready to receive the bridle of the King's horse as
Charlemagne halted the animal before the portal of the massive stone keep in the inner bailey and vaulted lightly down.

A groomsman leaped forward to do the same for the King's Champion as Lord Ganelon passed his hawk to the falconer, dismounted, then followed the King up the broad, stone steps. Charlemagne paused suddenly and swung around to glance over the company. Roland, busy loosening girths prior to leading the horses away, caught the look.

"That one, Lord Ganelon!" Roland stiffened as he heard Charlemagne's imperious tones. "Roland the Bastard. He is well disciplined. He shall squire us on our campaigns next summer. Do thou attend to it." Roland bowed his head abruptly to conceal the startled widening of his eyes, the violent thudding in his chest, and forced himself to walk away, leading the two horses as if he had not heard.

Of all the rest of the company of highborn youths under Lord Ganelon's rule and tutelage, only Lord Oliver had been so honoured as to squire the King. Nor, for all his deep and long standing hatred of the other, could Roland deny Lord Oliver's worthiness. Indeed, De Montglave had proven himself extraordinary, had won his spurs, and was now a new-made knight of singular prowess and repute.

Totally, intensely preoccupied, Roland's reflexes took over as he set about tending to the two animals he had somehow brought to the stables. Hope was something painful. Could he too, win his spurs . . . ?

In time with the strokes of the brush in his hand, a single set of words repeated themselves over and over in his mind, becoming a pledge. More; an oath.

I will be worthy. I will be worthy. I will be worthy . . .

"Majesty?" Concealing his horror at the King's pronouncement, Lord Ganelon followed as the King erupted into the keep. Charlemagne did not break stride. "Majesty, the boy is undeveloped and too young by far." The King stopped sharply and turned to face him.

"It is a credit to thine instruction, my lord, that we choose accordingly!" Charlemagne returned. "The boy is hard and rules himself well. He will serve." Lord Ganelon frowned, using consternation to disguise the ire he truly felt.

"Majesty. There are others of high birth and great prowess. Likewise, older youths among these select who are more than ready. There will be resentment for this decision that passes over them to one who is not nobly got, or even legitimate . . ." The King's stare had all the warmth of a winter storm.

"Are we to understand, my lord, that these boys take greater pride in the purity of their pedigrees than in the honor of their duty? If so, then there is a grievous error in their training as Christian knights!" Cat nimble, Lord Ganelon leaped to avoid the trap.

"My consideration goes deeper, Majesty. Beyond his common blood and his bastardy, the boy, Roland, is said to be witch got. There is even evidence . . ."

Brows rising slightly above a frigid stare, Charlemagne cut him off. "That cannot harm us, my lord! Do thou forget we are annointed of God to rule His Christian people? No power may transcend that! Put away those foolish, heathen notions. As we have said, so we will do!" An instant later, the King was striding briskly away, toward, then across the great hall.

Tall and supple, intensely vigorous. Elusive . . . Lord Ganelon stood very still, watching the silver-blond head that was unlike any other of his line. Aye. It was no longer possible to know the workings of Charlemagne's mind. Acutely aware of how neatly he had been caught, he frowned as he, too, turned on his heel and strode away to seek the privacy of his own apartments.

The friendship they had once shared had now dissolved into the relationship between liegeman and lord, he knew, as he closed the door to his chamber behind him some minutes later. Old, youthful intimacies were long vanished, and the openly ferocious, ambitious, and compulsively passionate Prince he had known and understood had become a King he no longer knew at all.

Power sat with unnatural ease upon that fair head. All traces of former temper and impulsiveness had likewise vanished. Even in battle. Now, everything had been composed into unrelenting, assured deliberation, uncanny, even intimidating, in its perception.

So it had been since the boy, Roland, was found.

Lord Ganelon never forgot the reports of the man he had sent south to Montglave to examine the hidden cave in the hills where the boy had come from. Where he, himself, had left the corpse of the boy's lunatic mother. Berthe. The King's sister.

The cave was entirely barren, the man had said upon his

return. He had found no rotting flesh. No bones, or rags. Nor any kind of evidence whatsoever that it had known human habitation. More, it was devoid as well, of any beast sign that could indicate its use as a den.

The servant had been dispatched, his throat neatly slit, his body disposed. Lord Ganelon had never forgotten.

And now, he thought, the King moved to elevate his incest begotten son. Incest, that most heinous of sinful lust . . . Yet, there was more at play here than the mere presence of the manifest consequence of that sin. Witchcraft. Aye. He knew it. A true, perverse and insidious witchcraft crept through every corner of this like worms through a dead man . . .

For his office of King's Champion, and for the obligation of his duty, Lord Ganelon had assiduously watched and instructed the youthful elite gathered at Aix. Now, he was beginning to realize the reward of loyalty given to him as well as the King. But . . . Roland the Bastard? He had quietly encouraged the other highborn youths to make life hard for the boy, hoping that Roland would come to learn and accept that his place lay entirely beyond the pale of the well born.

But Roland was something apart. Incredibly fearless, he had a stubborn tenacity that was his truest resemblance to his sire. He took every insult and tumble, every bruise and beating at arms his smaller size and lesser strength generated, then rose up and asked, by sheer, silent persistence, for more.

Nor was he humble as was proper for his station. Instead, he took every defeat with an infuriating, square-shouldered defiance, and a temper that was only barely contained behind a perpetual, grim-faced glare.

Roland was impossibly proud . . .

Beyond that, the plan for rearing an exclusive company of well-born knights to champion the King's cause, and to bring greater unity across the Kingdom, was succeeding well. Hostages become servants to the realm . . . Not since the tales that had come to court of that King Arturus of Mercia in the island of Britain some two hundred years before, had such a thing been wrought. It was said that the half-Roman King had made wondrous gains in unifying the tribes of Britons against their foes. Until he died. Then, the Saxons, Angles, and Jutes had overrun that misty isle once more.

The rest was legend, of course, and filled with splendid magics. The young knights in particular, Lord Ganelon knew, savored these tales of mighty deeds, high purpose, and un-common valor, and sought like glory for themselves.

But . . . His mouth tightened brutally. The boy, Roland, had no right to the same. Even less, for the dangers that were implicit in his very existence. Lord Ganelon frowned deeply. This was the Devil's handiwork, he thought, built upon the incestuous sin of princes to strike at the heart and root of Christendom.

He looked up abruptly, his eyes widening slowly as he stared unseeing in the direction of a tapestry that adorned the far wall. A thought that had occurred so fleetingly four years earlier, when he had withdrawn his sword from that vile, scarecrow body in the cave, returned now, like a blow. Aye . . . Reared, himself, in the Royal household of Pepin, he had known Berthe before she had been so hurriedly wed to Lord Milone. Not long after she and her lord had dissappeared. A tall girl, and proud, stamped clearly in the golden tones of Pepin's blood. So too, Carloman . . . But Charlemagne? He was totally unlike the rest with his silver-blond hair and pallid, cold blue eyes. Unique . . . Like the moon. Not the sun.

Unnatural? Yet, God's annointed. Unholy . . . ?

His own descent, Lord Ganelon thought, was free of such implicit and terrible doubts.

That evening, his duties of service to the highborn lords and knights at supper complete, his own meal gleaned, as usual, from the scraps that were returned to the kitchens, Roland was still too filled with all that had occurred to him that day to seek his rest in his customary place in the hayloft above the stables. Instead, his cloak drawn about him against the chill of the air, he slipped out of the castle.

It was something he had never done before, yet, as he ran lightly up one long hill, down the other side, he felt com-pelled by thoughts of the oak tree that the King had made so important.

Skilled at tracking since early childhood, he veered sharply to follow the dusk-shadowed trail of trampled grass, then plummeted downhill toward the embrace of quiet trees. The sun had sunk behind the high ground. Broad, darkling shad-ows spread slowly to make a potent contrast to the fading amber radiance of the western sky.

His breath made quick puffs of white in the settling chill

as he followed horse tracks, and the sign of broken twigs, bent bushes, and trampled forest floor to seek the stream. Much later, when he found the place, he paused, crouched slowly, and reached to touch the spot where the King had sat. Then, he waded across the shallow, icy water to settle himself underneath the great oak tree itself.

Massively trunked, it reared up, vast and opaque above him. Its branches made a complexly twisted black canopy against the faint light that remained. It was silent. Unmoving . . . Sure.

Roland tucked his legs against him and clasped his arms around his knees. He could feel the rough bark against his back and even, it seemed, the iron density of the wood itself.

The darkness thickened. He heard the sporadic rustlings of night creatures venturing forth. He caught a glimpse of a pair of gleaming eyes staring at him from the underbrush on the other side of the stream.

He felt no concern.

Roland bowed his head and closed his eyes. He began to feel the poised silence that permeated the surrounding woodlands, seeped through the very air. It was as though another kind of life was about to awaken. Aye, he knew. This was the spirit time. The time when witches and goblins and the like, unable to bear the sun, roused from sleep, crept out from their hiding places to roam about through the dark hours.

He heard a soft rustling above him, and looked up to see the ghost pallid shadow of a large owl settle in the branches of the oak. It's great eyes stared down at him with the same undecipherable certainty he had seen in the King's eyes. Eerie, knowing, its stare unblinking. Spirit bird, Roland sensed. Magical and canny. What, he wondered uneasily, did it see? He shifted, drew his cloak more tightly about him and eased back, forcing himself to relax against the bole of the tree.

His mother had shunned the sunlight, he remembered with undiminished hatred. Malevolent creature, she had kept to the dark recesses of the cave where they had lived since he was born. She had toyed continually with the fire kept perpetually burning there. Like a weaving, vicious demon, she had mumbled sing-song chants, incantations he could not understand . . . And curses. How he remembered her curses. How grateful he had been for her death at the hands of the

Dark Lord of Maganze. Monster she was. Not even human . . .

Which made of him a halfling, Roland knew. Got of human seed upon her vile, witch's body. At the root of his frigid determination was the passionate desire to conquer that demon-got part of him and become in all ways, a man. Aye. To rid himself of every vestige of the damning, unnatural things that tainted his blood and rendered him accursed in the eyes of men.

He looked up again. The last traces of daylight that followed the setting sun were gone. Around him there were only variations in the qualities of the darkness. Dense places. Opaque. And a soft-edged translucence to the air that chilled his face, seeped slowly through the folds of his shabby cloak, the neck and sleeves of his tunic to his skin. He did not care. Such discomforts were an unconsidered part of his life.

He moved to trace the fingertips of one hand across the trunk of the great tree. A slow growing giant, the King had said. Could it be the same for him? That had been the suggestion. The penetrating clarity of the King's gaze had seemed filled with knowledge of such matters.

He thought of his own tough, scrawny, thin body with its new growth of hair at groin and armpits. How he hungered for size to come to him with such abundance. Size and power. Thin-limbed, ever hungry, it seemed he never quite managed to get enough to eat. Nor would he beg. Not for anything would he beg.

Charlemagne. A single word to name the mightiest Prince in Christendom. Roland . . . Somehow, the King had made a bond of that singularity. A pact, seemingly, between them.

And, when the next summer came with its wars against the heathen, he would be the King's squire. It was a miracle to have been so chosen. I will be worthy, he thought fiercely. Aye, he knew, he would move the earth itself to prove himself, to bring honor to the King's gift.

"God make me the King's truest liegeman," he whispered fervently into the night. "Let my every endeavor bring glory to his name." God and Charlemagne. They had become inextricably intertwined. Roland frowned in concentration. "And," he added carefully, "if there be witch's power in me, let it be tempered to the King's service. Let it be ruled by the man I will become!"

Above him, the owl he had nearly forgot, blinked once, very slowly, then spread broad wings and took to the air. Roland started a little and looked up to watch. He saw it vanish in silent flight above the trees. Affirmation?

Across the stream, he heard a deeper, stealthy rustling, then saw the gleam of two angry eyes. He stiffened defiantly, one hand going to the dagger in his belt that was his only weapon. The beast spirit growled low menace from the darkness, then turned and slipped away.

Temper, in the guise of a wolf.

Roland's jaw tightened with resolve as he felt the nocturnal silence close about him. Even the giant oak loomed over him with its own potently quiet power. Harbinger of magic. Nay. He would not flee from what he felt. He would bear it through and await the dawn when the witch folk and fairie were compelled to scuttle back to their nooks and crannies. They would not take him, he decided. He belonged to the King. He was human. He was Christian. And, if it was given that he, born of curses and darkness, had to overcome a mightier peril than other men, then his honor was proportionally greater. His reward would be a brighter, richer light. Aye, a brilliant, golden glowing . . .

The night kept its silence. Spirit beasts stirred through the encompassing dark from time to time, repelled, Roland thought, by the very power of his resolve, for none ventured close.

Frost appeared in the air, then settled gently to make a diminutive snowfall upon every leaf and twig. Cold seeped through his clothing and deep into his skin. Roland raised himself to stand against the tree, absolute in the conviction of the special sanctity of this very private vigil.

An eternity later, dawn crept across the tree tops with the first soft greys and blues, slipped down to separate the rocks and water, and every sort of vegetation from the obscurity of the darkness. And, when it was light enough for the first threads of color to appear in anticipation of the rising sun, Roland finally turned to walk with long, easy strides, back the way he had come.

TWO

A.D. *772–773*

The winter was brutal, less for the cold than for the heavy, near continual snowfalls and the fierce winds that made blizzards an overfrequent occurrence. The young knights and active fighting men that abounded in the King's court grew restless and high strung, deprived as they were for the most part of their chief winter sport, and of the fresh meat that was got by such hunting.

The wild game was effectively protected by impassable drifts and impenetrable white.

Roland refused to be troubled by the cold or the winds that sent him to burrow deep beneath the hay to huddle half shivering each night. He was preoccupied with other things that were occurring within him.

It was as though his vigil by the oak had been blessed. As though, now he understood the course expected of him, he was being rewarded with that which he needed for the accomplishment of his resolve. A light scattering of new, golden hair appeared on a chest that widened and deepened of a sudden. Soft down began on cheeks and chin, requiring shaving in the manner of the highborn. Bones that had been, hereto, compact and diminutive abruptly began to lengthen greatly, and, best of all, did not cease their growth as Roland became, at first, lanky. Then tall . . .

How had the King known, he wondered with an awe that gave Charlemagne an even greater proximity to the divine.

14

Limbs that had been but lightly muscled began to swell into
the sleek promise of masculine power. His shoulders widened, their angular bones retreating beneath hard meat and
smooth, tight skin. Thighs and legs became muscular and
powerful, and if coordination was near impossible to find at
times, Roland did not feel resentful. It was simply a matter
of learning again, skills to match the changes in his body.
Changes he had longed for, knowing what they meant.

As with the rest, his face changed also. Large eyes that had
seemed hazel before became more clearly an unusual golden
color now. Set beneath fiercely arched brows, they gleamed
intently from features that were becoming remarkable for their
strength and symmetry. He had a perfectly straight, fine-
nostriled nose. Beneath that was a mouth of elegant shape
save for its eternally grim set. A man's cheekbones were set
firmly above hollowed, muscular cheeks, and a jaw that was,
beyond doubting, assurance of unquenchable strength of will.

Roland was startled to find that the appendages of manhood
grew as well. Stirred and developed their own unsettling, not
entirely controllable life. Most commonly at night, just before he settled into sleeping, Roland would feel the pleasure
twists and hardening of his shaft. A bittersweet keen hunger
that was a potent, driving blend of pleasure and pain. He
began to understand how it was that men were tempted to
use the vessels of womankind. He remembered his mother.

He noticed then the sometimes sly, sometimes open dalliance that occupied many of the young lords. Saw embraces
and occasionally a coupling that was lewd with panting cries,
inelegant posturings. And he hated his own near unmanage-
able response to shapes that had been invisible to him before.
The swell of breasts. The curve of hips beneath the flowing
of a robe. Hair that gleamed like silk, and eyes that frequently
glinted sly assessment at him. And, sometimes invitation . . .

Invariably, he would look away, face stern, defiant of the
insidious and pervasive temptation into vile sin. These women
would not have opportunity to use or subjugate him, make of
him a beast, or bring out that witchling facet of his blood.
Roland's hate was abundant protection against the promptings
of disobedient flesh. More. Without conscious awareness, he
had incorporated into his own being that precept of Holy
Church that equated chastity with high purpose.

Likewise, of a sudden, Roland found that he tumbled less often in practice with horse and lance. That he could take a buffet without loosing his seat, and that the hereto violent and unpredictable movements of a hot-tempered warhorse were natural and smooth to feel.

And with this new success came another. For in practice with the wooden swords that were used by custom for training, Roland began to find his opponents needed more time and greater effort to fell him. Sometimes he would have the opportunity to savor a responsive grunt when, as never before, his own blows found a mark. It would come for him, he knew. It had to come.

Then, at last . . . It was like a dream to stand there, panting with effort, and see the young man before him pick himself up from the packed ice and half-frozen mud, expression startled. Roland's heart pounded in astonishment. Then Lord Ganelon's scathing reprimand slashed across the elated triumph of his mind.

"That was folly, Geoffrey, to raise thy guard so! Thou did deserve the tumble, even from so inept a strike." Inept? It had been unthinking instinct. Roland turned, then froze as he caught sight of Lord Ganelon's face, the expression of dark anger that vanished as quickly as it had appeared behind the gesture of a slight nod. Illusion? Roland hardly noticed that he was felled by a hard blow across the ribs. Or the chuckles that passed around him. Lord Ganelon, the King's most cunning and fiercest knight. A brilliant fighting man— unchallenged Champion.

He picked himself up slowly, reflexively—needing time to capture an elusive but vital piece of information.

"That was a reminder, Roland the Bastard, not to leave thy back unguarded!" Roland stood awkwardly, shifting his feet, all triumph banished by Lord Oliver's dry comment. He scowled. De Montglave's impassive expression became an annoyed frown.

Still panting, Roland balanced on the balls of his feet, poised with softened body as his eyes focused on the other young man who waited with serene confidence. He raised the wooden sword, then with a new remoteness lowered it several inches from that place where he had been taught, pointing it instead toward Lord Oliver's upper belly, just below the sternum. Not the heart direct . . . Not the heart. Instinct. Aye. Such as had felled Lord Geoffrey.

Then he understood with frightful clarity the cause of so much misadventure in his training at arms. He had been mistaught. How thoroughly, how cunningly, he had been taught to misuse himself, and whatever weapon had been put to his hand. Just enough to feel the perpetual clumsiness that came from precarious balance. Just enough to create vulnerabilities where there should have been none.

Weaknesses that had been used against him times beyond counting.

Lord Ganelon had done this, he knew then. And had done it so well that no one, not even himself, had noticed. And, how many times had his efforts to obedience been scorned as incompetent? Ineptness that was inherent in a bastard. How many bruises and scrapes had he endured? And how many times had his lance catapulted him from a horse that was impossible to manage when he sought to strike the quintain?

How thoroughly, under the guise of a tried patience, had he been taught to fail? Roland locked his jaw and crouched. No more. Never again.

His mouth became a slit across his face, as, deliberately, he spat the full force of all his hate, his fury, at Lord Oliver.

It was too hard a buffet, Lord Oliver thought, watching the sluggishness with which Roland picked himself up, and the almost dazed way he stood for a few moments afterward. He'd be a little easier next time, he thought, well aware of his kindness in offering the boy the experience of his own superior skills. He relaxed and, likewise, prepared to savor a game with the misbegotten boy whose surly manners and ill-tempered arrogance never failed to annoy him. Virulently unpleasant this bastard in their midst. A perverse reminder, mayhap, of the right course. Lord Oliver stiffened a little as Roland shifted and raised his sword, startled, despite himself, by the sheer viciousness of the look that came over Roland's face. The boy spat. Lord Oliver ignored the gesture, more interested in the new way the Bastard crouched and poised, a strange blend of temper and thoughtfulness that was entirely unlike his usual rabid attacks. He noted the corrected sword position, then, prepared for Roland's invariable ferocity, lunged lightly in a feint . . .

But Roland did not counterattack in his usual inflamed manner. Instead, his wooden sword held steady, his gaze unwavering, he ducked to one side. Oliver feinted again, a more definitive invitation to engage. Again, surprisingly, Roland ducked aside and, this time, brought his own weapon down across the tip of Oliver's sword as it reached its farthest extension, knocking it aside. Oliver turned his stroke into a powerful lateral swipe and advanced another pair of strides. For the third time, Roland ducked away.

What did he wait for? Oliver wondered.

It went on and on, the others who were gathered in the court slowly setting down their own weapons to form a curious arc about the pair, watching the young knight and the gangling boy who, of a sudden, had grown near as tall. Behind them all, Lord Ganelon watched, dark eyes gleaming oddly beneath features schooled to that specific patience that was reserved for those he trained.

Roland continued in his unusual manner, eyes too steady and face too hard to suggest that his retreats were got of cowardice. He continued to dodge, sometimes backward, most often to the side, then, suddenly, forward. Oliver gasped with surprise as the Bastard's wooden sword came down across his right shoulder with astonishing force. He had not realized the boy was that strong. Quickly, shifting to one side himself, it was pure instinct to engage his left hand upon his weapon and sweep right, smacking Roland hard across the ribs.

He let himself frown as Roland's eyes locked with his, and leaped forward with a low growl that was illusion of temper, into a flurried series of blows. Rapid lunges, sweeps—all smoothly integrated in a manner for which he was acquiring some considerable renown. Roland ducked and dodged, forced now into clear retreat, catching some of the blows, avoiding or parrying others. Still watching with the cold clarity that had come to him of a sudden, learning from each stroke.

Roland's determination was so powerful that he did not feel the blows that caught him across one thigh, on his side, or shoulders, or, once, across the steel squire's cap he was permitted for helm. Nor did he hear the hoots of encouragement that supported the popular Lord Oliver. There was only the other man's sword and the vulnerable places of his body, shielded by a steel hauberk that mere wood could not hope to damage. His own wool tunic offered no like protection.

He found opportunity as one foot slithered in the mire and he dropped to one knee. With all his concentration, he lunged forward just as Lord Oliver shifted his sword to fell him completely, aiming for the other man's throat. Oliver jumped back, and Roland, in imitation of what he had seen, leaped after him, raining a two-handed flurry of blows of his own.

The group around them grew silent with surprise as they watched, and Lord Oliver, with another growl, this time of sincere annoyance, charged through this onslaught with battle-hardened viciousness.

How dare this—half-human—arrogant—ill-mannered—brat even touch him! He had no right . . . Oliver's sword struck again and again, sometimes successfully countered. More often than not, finding a target. How dare this—bastard not surrender, he thought. How dare he stare with those unnatural and distempered beast eyes. This bastard who needed to be taught once and for all who was master . . .

Roland was learning. Rapidly. But it was not enough to enable him to withstand the onslaught of Oliver's considerably greater strength and experience. Some of his own blows landed, and that was a small triumph. Like the sincere anger he saw in Lord Oliver's eyes now, entirely different from the overfamiliar contempt to which he was accustomed.

Flesh, not will, began to yield as hard, buffeting strokes from Lord Oliver's wooden sword caught him across the forearms, about the ribs and shoulders and head, until, unable to help himself, Roland sank to his knees in the icy muck. Lungs raw, still clinging to his own weapon, he tried another upthrust, but Oliver shifted easily and, with a spurred foot, sent him flat on his back. He tried to roll away, but a foot descended on his wrist, forcing his hand to open and the hilt of his sword to fall away. And then Oliver knelt over him, one knee rammed into a chest that heaved for air. Sweat trickled down the stern face that stared at him, and Oliver's wooden sword came across his throat, half crushing it.

"Yield, Bastard!" Oliver hissed. Roland stared back at him, hardly able to breathe, let alone move. The sword shifted from his throat, and now he could hear cheers for Lord Oliver pass through the cold air around him.

"Nay!" he found voice enough to grate. Oliver scowled,

anger flaring to rage. He brought his gauntlet across the side
of Roland's head with resounding force.

"Yield to me, cur dog! Acknowledge thy betters!" He
snarled. Roland stared back through senses that reeled. Out-
maneuvered in skill and strength, he was not yet—he would
not be—beaten. He closed his eyes for a moment. Pain was
seeping across every part of him . . .

He smiled suddenly and opened his eyes, an expression
that Oliver had never seen on him before. Eyes quiet, absolutely certain.

"Never, my lord!" he said clearly. Shocked out of fury,
Lord Oliver could only stare back. Unable to respond, he
stood, his gaze still locked on Roland's face.

Roland turned on his side. Clumsily. Pain flooded through
him now. He gasped, groped, then pulled himself to his feet,
and with excruciating effort bent to retrieve his training sword,
now badly battered. He looked down, still breathing heavily, and hefted the hilt of the weapon. Slowly, he raised his
eyes, his face ashen and hard as he looked around him, then
shifted to face the Champion who instructed them all.

Aye. Roland knew he had read Lord Ganelon well as he
caught the tightening of a muscle in the dark lord's cheek, a
veiled glimmer of response quickly dispatched. Now, the dark
lord knew he understood. Roland bowed, the movement cost-
ing him dearly.

"With whom am I to practice next, my lord?" he asked
courteously. "It is most evident to me that I have much to
learn!" Lord Ganelon smothered a frown. The rest were silent. Oliver's eyes widened at the audacity of the boy, then
sharpened as he caught something remarkable and peculiar
on the King's Champion's face.

"The time for this day is spent, squire!" Lord Ganelon
grated. With a nod to them all, he turned on his heel and
strode back to the keep, cloak swirling about his ankles.

Standing alone, the cold wind biting through his sweat-
soaked tunic, bruised beyond belief, and aching with fatigue,
Roland watched the other young men turn away to form pairs
or groups to find other occupation for the remaining afternoon hours. Not a one so much as looked at him.

He had been—entertainment. Roland inhaled painfully,
keeping his head erect. His isolation was absolute. They were
all his foes . . .

Slowly, with concentrated effort, he walked across the inner bailey toward the stables where he quartered himself.

Oliver, reaching the corner that led to that tower of the keep where his chamber was located, responded to an urge to stop and look back. Friends, companions, the others were rapidly dispersing. But—the Bastard still stood there. Alone . . . He watched the boy walk slowly across the bailey and was startled, of a sudden, to realize that the contempt he had always felt for the Bastard was changed.

Roland had won his respect. Unqualified and sincere respect. Oliver shook his head, annoyed with himself.

"I am mad to feel so!" he murmured dryly. "He is naught but an ill-mannered whelp with no honor whatever!" He turned away and strode briskly to the spiraling staircase that led up to his chamber.

That evening, as he served the knights in the customary fashion at the evening meal, Roland was too grimly preoccupied with trying to manage a body that wanted nothing more than absolute stillness to notice that Lord Oliver did not bait him, but, rather, had undertaken to watch him from time to time instead, his look assessing, curious.

Roland's face showed a swollen purple welt where Oliver had struck him. And when his sword hand held out the flagon in response to Lord Oliver's signal for wine, it was red-grazed and overlarge at the wrist where his mailed foot had trampled. Oliver looked away. He did not need to imagine the rest. He himself nursed more than a few bruises.

It was Roland's unrelenting refusal to yield that kept him fascinated, he acknowledged. Clumsy. Ill-bred, and with little talent for arms. Yet? He stared into his wine cup. Yet—he was brave far above the common.

Oliver, considered a fair-minded and pleasant-natured young man by his peers, was somewhat startled to find himself thinking that, given skill, there would be few better than the Bastard to have at one's back in battle.

"Whyfore so pensive, Oliver?" Sir Florismart of Aquitaine, who shared his trencher, leaned toward him. De Montglave leaned back a little and found a smile.

"I do consider what lies before us this summer." He found an answer. "It comes to mind that our first campaign will not be to the north against the Saxon, but, rather, against the Lombards.'' Florismart leaned forward.

"Thou think it possible?'' he asked eagerly.

"Likely, Floris.'' Oliver nodded at his friend, glad to be diverted from more uncomfortable directions of mind. ''I consider the King's need to safeguard Rome.''

Embroiled in a discourse of strategy, a favorite topic for them both, Oliver did not notice when, sometime later, Roland left the hall to find his way to the rest that awaited him in the stables.

Lord Ganelon had been most ingeniously cunning. Roland began to fully understand in the weeks that followed. He had tempered the delicate, deliberate flaws in his instruction with looks of disappointment—disgust—insidious indications that it was Roland's own size and inherent incompetence that was responsible for his inability to find any prowess at arms. At the same time, he had cleverly fed the contempt of the others, highborn young men who were Roland's elders and betters. Then he had let Roland's own ferocity and willful determination do the rest.

With a new, hard cunning of his own, Roland gave only the appearance of attention and belief to his instruction from that point on. For the rest—to the end of real learning, he watched the better knights with devoted concentration. He learned to pick through the idiosyncracies of individual method. He learned to experiment. And he learned a thoughtful deliberation in his own efforts that was totally devoid of the emotional ferocity that had been his most outstanding attribute before.

Slowly, surely, he began to succeed. Subtle changes that came from attention in the way he sat a vile-tempered horse brought a new tenacity to his riding of the beasts. He learned to hold lance and shield and sword, axe and mace, with a new, ingenious looseness that enabled him to make instantaneous shifts and adjustments. Watching, he learned to see with an analytical clarity entirely independent of instruction or advice from others. A way of seeing that became knowledge of itself, more intimate than instinct.

And he lost that little trust that remained in him.

* * *

The last weeks of winter passed rapidly and melted into a quagmire spring with warmer weather, heavy rains, and deep mud. The first sunny days were welcomed with near heathen abandon as men discarded fur-lined cloaks and quilted gambesons for lighter tunics of fine wool or linen and colorful cloaks. Those who had grown beards for protection during the winter shaved them off.

Roland's own growth had been so rapid that his own attire of undertunic and coarse-woven, heavy wool outer tunic were rapidly becoming too tight across chest and shoulders, the material surrendering in places to the wear of age.

Unconcerned with the problems of his clothing, beyond the restraints of an ill fit, Roland, likewise, had no interest in the frivolity and lightened mood that came with spring. Instead, his entire being was focused on undoing the mis-instructions that had cost him so dearly over the past four years. Even alone, he found ways to practice. Aye, until the rawhide-bound wooden sword danced easily in his hand, until axe and mace flowed through the air. Until he could move any weapon with speed and assurance and absolute clarity of intent.

And for the first time, he began to feel the agility and strength that was developing in him with the changes in his size and musculature. He savored these with the keen sensual pleasure that was with others, reserved for dalliance.

Likewise, he relished each triumph on the practice field. Each blow he managed to deflect. Then, each he gave. The next young man he felled . . . The first knight he unhorsed . . .

Now, when weapons were held at the ready and he faced an opponent, the outcome was no longer assured. Nor were there the familiar grins of contemptuous satisfaction. He was no longer subjected to the insults of being called "Little Rooster," or "Brat." Instead, he was gradually accorded a new and curious distinction, that of being called simply "Bastard," a term suggesting a perversely singular, if reluctant, respect.

Even Lord Oliver, with whom he was increasingly paired, would look at him with cool sobriety. Oliver, who was the best among them. The leader. Beloved of all. Roland could feel the sparks that flew between them. De Montglave, who beat him with inevitable consistency. Roland hated him for that, and for the thrashing and humiliation Lord Oliver had laughingly ordered given to the child thief he had once been.

It became something of an odd ritual between them. Roland, who lay panting and immobilized under Oliver, invariably to hear the other man demand, ''Yield, Bastard!'' To smile slowly and whisper with heartfelt deliberation.

''Never, my lord!''

It surely was the hundredth time, Oliver thought, frowning a little as he raised himself up from the Bastard's prostrate body. He looked up, away from the compelling will in Roland's oddly golden eyes, and saw with surprise that the King was watching them from a rise of steps that led to an extension of the keep a short distance away. Fully armored, his cloak and surcoat shifting lightly in the breeze, crown gleaming from its place on his brow, Charlemagne was a giant among men in more ways than the gift of his height. Oliver's eyes widened as he realized that the King's attention was on the unkempt squire in the process of picking himself up. He glanced toward Lord Ganelon, positioned at the base of the steps, as the King turned and strode away, to see that the Champion had been watching Charlemagne as well.

Had the King seen it all? Oliver wondered, retreating to rest against a wall, watching as the Champion turned his dark gaze toward the Bastard. Oliver's own eyes widened as he caught something in that look that vanished, seemingly, as rapidly as it had appeared. Venom. Aye. Had he not seen the like before? With a shock, he understood that Lord Ganelon hated the boy. Worse. Loathed. He frowned and looked down, caught by this unexpected discovery.

He had always thought Lord Ganelon to be overkind and remarkably, albeit disparagingly, patient with the clumsy, defiant, ill-tempered and graceless boy. But the Bastard had changed during the past months. Aye, since that one day in midwinter. Grown in breadth and height, the Bastard revealed a sudden ingenuity and talent for arms that had never, even remotely, been apparent before. There was a peculiar inconsistency there, Oliver thought, realizing as well that he had not seen Lord Ganelon offer instruction to Roland as he had in the past. Now, he simply ordered the manner of practice, and the pairings.

Something, Oliver thought carefully, was afoot here? But what? And why would the Champion have such a hate for the Bastard? Roland, being below the salt and accursed in his birth, should not warrant any such feeling at all. Any more than was given to others that were bred to serve.

Not that the Bastard was a likable individual, Oliver thought wryly. Entirely without humor, he was prideful past sin. Arrogant. A continual source of irritation in his manner. He turned away, an intrigued curiosity added to the blend of dislike and respect he felt.

Lord Ganelon got to his feet slowly as the King concluded the meeting of his High Council and made his departure for the evening Mass. Face closed and introspective, he made a pretense of studying the maps that were spread out upon the council table before him while the other lords likewise dispersed.

Two wars were to be undertaken through the summer months. The first was to be a campaign against Desiderius of Lombardy who had, of late, become too great a threat to the security of the papal estates to be ignored. The King's position was unquestionably clear. Anointed to protect the chief part of God's earthly realm, he was likewise impelled to be guardian to Saint Peter's successor. Besides, it was now known that Desiderius had undertaken alliance with the southern Infidel who was sprung from the deserts across the Mediterranean . . .

Lord Ganelon frowned as he thought of Charlemagne's failed and childless alliance with Lombardy.

The other war was to be a northern endeavor against the Saxons who persisted in their encroachments through the Rhineland into the northernmost parts of the realm. Charlemagne was resolved to gain foothold in their territory such as would facilitate annexation and put a conclusive halt to their pillaging and heathen ways.

Alone at last, Lord Ganelon pursued the personal reasons for his somber mood. Earlier, the King had given quiet reminder of his intent to use the boy Roland for squire. Ganelon had hoped that Charlemagne would have forgot, or changed his mind. But nay. Instead, the King had murmured quietly when watching the young men in the court that very morning.

"Thou hast done well, my lord. We consider our faith justified. The boy develops well." He frowned. Far better to have chosen Rinalde of Montalban or, best of all, his own

nephew, Thierry of Leon. They were the last of the fledge-
lings who had yet to achieve knighthood, and that because
they were somewhat younger than the rest.

Older by a year than this—bastard. Lord Ganelon's frown
deepened as, abruptly, he turned and strode from the council
chamber. Surely the King must realize that such an honor
given to one so—lacking in worth was grievous insult to better bred and more deserving individuals? And it was worse
for knowing that, of late, he had himself lost all control of
the boy, that all his careful efforts to ensure the boy's place
as outcast and incompetent were come to naught. Moreover,
he had been found out by Roland himself.

And he thought of the witch blood in the Bastard. Equally
disturbing was the Bastard's silence on the matter. There had
been no outcry of foul, nor protest, nor any sign beyond that
single look that Roland knew.

Only silence—unnatural, potent silence.

And Roland was growing, of a sudden, to be a powerful
young man, after the promise of Charlemagne's blood. Or the
other . . . Lord Ganelon closed his chamber door behind him.

Was it coincidence, he wondered, that the King's will and
the boy's abrupt maturing into young manhood were occurring together? Unable to forget that afternoon the autumn
before, Lord Ganelon was inclined to believe it was magic.

He eyed the servant who stood, silently on the far side of
the chamber, awaiting whatever command he chose to give.

"Do thou fetch my nephew, Lord Thierry of Leon, to me!"
he said coldly, and walked across the chamber to seat himself
in a high-backed, ornately carved chair.

It was time to put the seal of usefulness upon his own
bonds of blood.

There was a stunned silence in the hall as the King's Champion, his announcements made, departed into the shadows
behind great stone columns. Stares were exchanged, then all
eyes turned toward the Bastard who stood unmoving, his face
impossible to decipher, with the other servants, holding a
platter of roasted and spiced meats.

"It is insult to us all!" Sir Geoffrey of Anjou broke the
silence first. "Whyfore should the King choose that—ill-bred
boy for squire, when he could have Rinalde. Or thee,
Thierry?" He glanced at his friend. The other two squires

were seated with the knights by virtue of their high station, as both were heirs to considerable demesne. Across the hall, Lord Oliver sat back and sipped wine very slowly. It had come as a surprise to him as well, and he acknowledged an unpleasant feeling of having been slighted in the worth of his own memory of such service. Rinalde of Montalban's face assumed the mottled flush of angry humiliation, for he had been accorded the comparatively demeaning state of service to Lord Oliver, instead of the Champion. Thierry of Leon, all had thought, would be the next to squire the King. Thierry held his head high and glowered, not entirely reassured by the private considerations his uncle had offered him but a short while before.

"Aye. The Bastard is not fit!" he said clearly, signaling for meat. "By skill, or blood—and most certainly,"—his look became particularly scathing as Roland, hard-faced, held out the platter for choosing—"his manner!" Thierry neatly speared a piece of the cooked flesh upon the point of his dagger, ignoring the Bastard. "Worse. For he will do naught, thereby, save bring shame upon the company we are become!" He bit off a piece of meat, then, scowling, turned it out and spat it directly into the front of Roland's tunic.

"Pah! He even contaminates the meat with his filth!" he growled. Roland straightened, his face going very white. Watching from his place, Lord Oliver felt the surprise of a grin tug at the corners of his mouth as he read what was about to occur. Roland stepped forward, raising the tray, then brought the whole down upon Thierry's head, reversing it as he did so to spew meat and gravy all over the other's finery.

"I am Roland!" he roared. "Know my name, for thou will all be honored to utter it one day!"

He was attacked instantly then. The company rose to a man, outraged by this arrogance. Only Lord Oliver, grinning fully, did not move from his seat.

The Bastard fought wildly, of course, but he was outnumbered and overbourne. Puzzled by his own response, Lord Oliver got slowly to his feet and followed as Roland, kicking and struggling, was carried from the hall, out into the rain, across the inner bailey, then tethered by his arms and legs to a hitching rail.

One of them tore his clothing, stripping aside his tunic.

Roland spat defiance. Another, Sir Geoffrey, took the whip that was proffered and raised it.

"This time, thou shall be properly humbled, as befits thy place!" he roared, and struck. Blood appeared instantly in a line across Roland's upper belly. Again. Roland did not utter a sound, but glared back with venomous eyes. Again he was struck, this time across chest and over one shoulder.

A murmur of blood lust passed through the group with the fourth blow, and abruptly, from his place behind them all, Lord Oliver strode forward and placed himself in front of the tethered boy.

"Enough!" he thundered. There was silence as hard young faces stared in astonishment. The whip went slack . . .

"Thou disgrace thyselves with this behavior!" Oliver said coldly. "All of thee resemble naught so much as a pack of halfling wolves growling over carrion! Thou—who are brought to be the King's chosen. To be examples of honor and prowess for the King's service, and for the good of Christendom!" He stared them down. "Should another be ill-mannered, it is not for thee to imitate!" Faces began to flush with angry humiliation, clearly recognizing the truth of this. Some glowered at Roland, helplessly bound and half gasping with pain and fury. "And," Lord Oliver went on with deadly quiet, "if the *King* should choose the Bastard to serve him, who art thou to say him nay?"

Not a one attempted to answer that. Nor did they wish to. More shamed by the contempt and dignity of one they unanimously liked and respected than by any harm done to Roland, they stiffened shoulders and, one by one, turned away.

Manhood was a strange and complicated condition to grow into, Lord Oliver thought, shaking his head as he watched them go, drawing his cloak about him to shield himself from the rain. Then alone in the dusk, he turned slowly to look at Roland who was still trussed and unable to move. Not one among the company had stepped forward to loose him.

Those oddly golden eyes gleamed at him from a face gone drawn and haggard. It was the look of a trapped beast. Lord Oliver drew his dagger and stepped forward. The younger man's expression did not change as his eyes fixed on the weapon. Irresistably tempted, Oliver raised the point to touch Roland's breastbone. Felt the boy inhale sharply.

"Yield thyself, Bastard!" he growled. Roland's eyes flashed upward.

"Never, my lord!" he whispered with hoarse and total honesty. To his astonishment, Lord Oliver shook his head and grinned broadly. Then, with leisurely dignity, cut him loose.

"So much pride, Bastard," De Montglave murmured gently, "will make a most shattering agony for thee!" Gold eyes met his. "For, I fear, thou hast such a mighty distance to fall!" He stepped back a pace, resheathing his dagger.

Roland did not answer. Instead, he stood, now feeling shaken, still astonished by Lord Oliver's service, and at his last dry comment. He found he could not bear to look into the other's face. He busied himself with an attempt to cover himself with the remains of his tunic.

"Come with me," Lord Oliver said suddenly. Roland looked up, startled, ashen-faced. Then did as he was bid, following uneasily to find himself a short while later standing in the entrance of Lord Oliver's private chamber. His eyes widened.

So much luxury! Candles. A bed with rich furs and linen sheets. A chest. Other things . . .

"Do thou stand there like a dolt, or do thou come in?" Roland started at the insulting words offered in the unfamiliarity of a friendly tone. He stepped forward, one hand holding his tunic across the weals on his chest. Lord Oliver turned away and strode across the chamber to kneel before a chest. He opened it and rummaged briefly, then withdrew a fine blue tunic broidered along throat and cuffs with scarlet, an undertunic, a pair of chausses and shoes with cross gartering of the same color. He stood up and held them out. Roland did not move. Instead, he stood wary-eyed, rigid.

"Here," Oliver said pleasantly. "Take these. Such is reasonable attire for one who is chosen to squire the King." Roland's mouth tightened bitterly. He had been correct in his suspicion. Lord Oliver had brought him here to offer another humiliation.

"I do not wish thy charity, my lord!" he sneered. Oliver frowned and strode forward, the taller by a few inches still.

"Fool!" he grated. "I do this for mine own dignity! I do not wish to be seen beside such"—his eyes passed down Roland's frame—"an unkempt, bedraggled beggar as thee! Decent garb might"—he stressed the word—"give at least the

illusion that thou are fit company for us, even fit to ride behind the King!'' He flung the bundle at Roland, who caught
it, then, shamed in a new way under that steady gaze, began
to feel a flush of heat rise up along his neck.

He looked down, heard the other man step back, and found
safety in cold demeanor once more. He raised his head, then
bowed with dignity.

''I will endeavor, my lord, not to bring shame to thine
attire!'' he said icily, then turned and left.

Behind him, Oliver stared at the empty portal and exhaled
violently. Jesu! But Roland was intense enough to rout an
entire army! He shook his head and grinned to himself, eyes
widening slowly.

''Never say it?'' he murmured slowly. ''Could it be thou
hast a liking for him?'' Moments later, he heard his own
resigned ''Fool!''

THREE

It was a far different thing, Roland learned, to ride at the King's flank amid a great army of knights and common soldiers than to listen to scraps of conversation about the previous year's campaigns in the unchanging environment of the castle. Wearing the garb given him by Lord Oliver, Roland kept half his attention on the King's whim and used the rest to absorb uncounted details of the army itself and of the land through which they passed.

Common soldiers, divided into battalions, were flanked by sergeants and lesser knights. In the midst of these was the supply train of provender and weaponry. Before all these, and flanking the King and highest lords, rode the elite company of highborn young knights who were beginning to attain particular renown as Charlemagne's own especial corps.

A squire, Roland knew, was a combination of untried knight and body servant. The latter aspect seemed to be his chief function. Not that Roland felt anything but honored, for the King's person was regarded as sacrosanct. It fell to him to serve the King's meals, to tend to his arms and clothing, even assisting with the intimacies of the King's bodily concerns and grooming. Likewise, it fell to him to attend the King's great destrier as well as the light palfrey that had been allotted for his own use.

And at night, it was his duty to sleep as bodyguard on the ground near the foot of the King's couch.

Roland accomplished all his duties with an honestly respectful silence, and an air of sober maturity that was inconsistent with his actual years. He learned aspects of the King's wishes and habits and grew to anticipate them, able to provide an instant before he was instructed.

And, his service was willingly given, for although Charlemagne only rarely addressed him, Roland could not help but feel that the King never, even for an instant, forgot his presence. He treasured the feeling as he treasured the memory of what had passed between himself and Charlemagne the previous autumn.

Likewise, his position as royal squire was an isolating one. Something else that Roland found himself inclined to relish, for it removed him from the degrading contempt and loathing of the company of knights to which, it seemed, he had become indelibly and permanently bound.

And there were other fleeting times he savored. Short periods, usually in midevening when the King had little use for him, and when the bulk of his tasks for the day were accomplished. Periods of solitude that he used to walk alone, away from the army, oft to seek out a quiet place amid nearby trees.

Then he would think about his hopes. About that which lay ahead, inextricably intwined with another thing the King had said so long ago.

Knighthood. Both goal and portal, it lay before him like an imperial summons.

Crouched thus one evening against the bole of a tree, listening to the sounds of men and horses spread all about him in the near distance, just beyond viewing, Roland stared at the bright points of glowing campfires that were becoming more conspicuous through the underbrush. Oranges, reds and golds against the deepening blue of twilight. He straightened slowly then, aware of an eerie feeling, as though he was being watched. He looked up.

Above him, perched on a branch near the trunk of the tree, was a great white owl. Roland's eyes widened. He shifted abruptly, for it watched him with enormous dark, brown-rimmed eyes, and an intense unwavering resolve.

He had seen this bird before, Roland knew suddenly, going rigid. More clearly brilliant now in the brighter light, it was the same as that pale bird-shade he had seen before, when he had made vigil.

It cocked its head, plumage purest white around eyes that seemed to study him. Its beak was fierce dark and seemed a blend of birdlike instrument and half-human smile, knowing, clever, unnaturally thoughtful.

Spirit bird, it was—Roland stepped back abruptly and crossed himself.

"I am human!" he grated harshly. "I belong to the King. His true liegeman!" He felt a surge of defiance, uncertainty, something akin to fear. The bird continued to stare at him. "Art thou some witch's messenger come to summon me?" Roland whispered harshly. "I am not for thee! Nor for any heathen—thing!" The owl blinked slowly, shifted the tilt of its head, and seemed to smile. Amused. Wry.

Roland glared at it and strode with something greater than his usual briskness back to his place by the King.

Its ranks swelling from musters got from Frankish fiefs, the ever-growing army ascended into the mountains that surrounded the northern end of the Italian peninsula, crossed the Alps by following an old Roman road, then descended into Lombardy.

The King held nightly councils with his Champion and other favored, experienced, and powerful lords whose service was as much for strategy as for battle. Roland, with a wineskin to offer, stood in attentive readiness through these. He kept his head bowed, his thoughts concealed, and listened, learning much on matters concerning the uses and deployment of forces.

Things that were needful for the future, for consolidating his fealty to the King.

He had seen that same snow-colored owl once again. Perched on a branch amid a grove of trees as they rode past, it had ruffled its feathers and stared at him, then taken flight, seeming to vanish in the brilliant sunlit sky. Unnatural, abroad in the daylight hours, with that uncanny gaze that haunted his consciousness.

And it was the same one, Roland was unhappily convinced. Not another of the same kind. Why did it follow him? What did its presence portend?

He sought refuge in vigorous daily prayers that were never answered.

* * *

The first village and castle fell to Charlemagne immediately, overwhelmed by the mere sight of his forces. Encamped there, the King then sent messengers to Desiderius with packets of letters that commanded the Lombard King's surrender, and the relinquishment of all fiefs and vassals.

Roland watched in awe as Charlemagne so easily inscribed the Latin words upon sheer parchment, then sealed the documents with wax and his seal. Reading and writing were skills reserved for the clergy, and, it seemed, princes . . .

"It is not so difficult a thing to master," the King had murmured after passing the scrolls to the knight who was to deliver them. Roland bowed his head.

There was a quickening now in the march-hardened army. A mood of eagerness, even anticipation, that sprang, Roland saw, from the knights and others who were eager to prove themselves before the King. He felt it too, this keening hunger. Fingers itched to wrap themselves about the hilt of a steel sword, rather than around the wooden training sword that was his squire's insignia. Loins and thighs hungered to ride the tempest of a fierce destrier, rather than the meek palfrey that was his mount.

Elation was palpable when Roland saw some seven days later the sinister chill of Charlemagne's smile as he looked up from the single written line that was Desiderius' reply. He waved the travel-weary messenger away, and Roland knew this was exactly as the King had hoped.

"Does he really think to defy us?" Charlemagne murmured, scanning the missive once more. He looked toward Lord Ganelon. "Make ready, my lord," he said quietly. "We march south on the morrow."

Roland gave most particular care to the King's war stallion and armor that night. Oiling, polishing. Checking and rechecking for any weakness in mail or harness.

The army became the broad hand of the King, moving across the land as it swept southward, deploying into the fingertips of his will as it captured villages and manors and the common single-towered castles.

Horses and men made thunder reverberate through the earth as they passed, and battle cries added punctuation.

Keeping to his place at the King's flank, removed from any

battle as the King sat his stallion atop a hill, Roland watched the carnage with a growing hunger to participate. He envied Lord Oliver and the others, astride their destriers, proof perfect of the King's might, wonderful in their daring and skill, inspiration for the common soldiers.

"For God and Charlemagne!" It was a haunting echo in his mind.

And when battle cries died away into the quiet of triumph, the King rode down through trampled and mutilated bodies already bloating in the hot summer sun. Roland stared about him with interest as soldiers passed among the corpses, dispatching mortally wounded foe, stripping bodies by their right of pillage. He was not perturbed by the sight of so much bloodshed, unlike the squeamish palfrey that had to be wrestled into obedient pursuit of the King. Instead, he understood that these dead were the real symbols of achievement. Proof absolute of the King's victory. It was the opportunity to fight that Roland hungered for now with all his soul. He longed to partake of the feast that was battle itself.

Sir Roland, he dreamed, and looked with hunter's cunning for any opportunity, feeling the obedience that bound him to the hocks of the King's destrier. I need a horse, he thought. And a sword—and arms. And garments of my own, not this attire that was given by Lord Oliver. Such things as he would win for himself. The just booty of his own effort. Not charity. Never again, charity.

He did not see that Charlemagne glanced at him once or twice and read that hard-set face, then smiled consideringly as he looked away.

And then, in the harsh mountainous country to the west of the small fief of Parma, Desiderius' army was at last espied. The Lombard King had marched quickly north, abandoning successful forays against the fiefs of Rome, and had encamped his forces along a great high ridge, deploying them to await his foe from a nearly invulnerable and highly advantageous position.

Charlemagne brought his own forces up to encamp upon two opposing hillsides that were neither as high, nor as well defended by such treacherous slopes. Worse yet, these were divided by a valley that became a deep gorge carved by a

fast-flowing river as it bent and passed between the two bodies of the army.

This splitting of forces was both a puzzle and a point of
troubled concern to the lords that gathered at the King's command to council. But Roland, staring out at the vast line of
Lombard campfires on the distant ridge and listening from
his place behind the King, felt a new sense of familiarity. He
understood this harsh country with its sparse gnarled trees,
scattered bushes, its great, brutal outcroppings of rock that
provided excellent concealment, and the rocky, shattered
ground that revealed few footprints.

Evidently, the King was thinking in a like direction as he
spoke with these highest lords who were his generals, pa-
tiently listened, and even solicited thoughts or plans. Roland,
shifting his gaze a little, saw that Lord Oliver, now elevated
to such high rank by virtue of recently proven brilliance, was
looking thoughtfully at him. Then Lord Oliver quirked an
eyebrow as though amused, and looked away.

A combination of plans was brought together and woven
into an ingenious blend of direct confrontation and flanking
entrapment. Most important was the need to draw Desiderius' army down from the ridge where they were secured. To
this end, it was decided to make use of the seeming vulnerability of the gorge that divided the halves of Charlemagne's
army. A force was to be sent down that milder incline in such
manner as to make them seem easy prey. Prior to that, under
cover of darkness, another large force was to be dispersed in
small bands around and behind the Lombard encampment to
wait concealed until such signal was given as to send them
through the Lombard camp to block any retreat from the precipitous slopes under the anterior ridge. Likewise, under cover
of darkness, foot soldiers, archers and spearmen, were to slip
across the river and conceal themselves amid the outcroppings of rock everywhere under the ridge. There, too, this
force would await the Lombard descent.

Charlemagne himself was to be the bait. Eager now and
restless, the lords dispersed, each to undertake the duties that
fell to him. Orders were dispatched through the encampment
to douse fires and to condense in such manner as would de-
ceive the Lombard King into thinking Charlemagne's forces
numbered fewer. Everywhere, there was a quiet, intense
scurrying. Horses' feet were wrapped in skins to mask the

sounds of their passage before the first men disappeared into the night. Men shrouded themselves in their cloaks to conceal any gleam of mail or helm or weapon, then slipped away.

And the King, with confident manner, knelt in brief prayer before seeking his couch for the remainder of the night. Roland, all his tasks fulfilled, set himself in the required place at the King's feet, thinking enviously of those who were to fight on the morrow.

"This time, Roland." He went rigid at the unexpectedness of the King's whisper. "We give thee leave to fight as thou may find opportunity."

"Majesty!" It was an awed and grateful whisper. He heard the King chuckle a little.

"Aye, boy. We know thy appetite!" the King murmured. Roland could not answer. He lay rigid, filled with pure joy, heart pounding in his chest loud enough for any to hear. He stared into the darkness, beyond sleeping now, a slow smile slipping across his features.

As the sun began to emerge behind the Lombard encampment to the east, then rose to touch the gorge with light, Charlemagne, fully armed, his crown clipped to his helm and his banner carried before him, led the body of his younger knights slowly down the long incline toward the river. Followed by several phalanxes of foot soldiers, it appeared that he was bent on singular attack.

Roland, uncaring that he was still armed with his wooden sword and without helm or hauberk, felt a tingling eagerness as he rode his palfrey just behind the King.

Distant cries were heard. The alarm was sounded through the Lombard camp. Then as they reached the banks of the fast-flowing river and thrust their horses into the swirling, stirrup-high currents, the Lombards took the bait and came swarming down the slopes in their masses with loud, triumphant cries, on horses that plunged and slithered to keep from stumbling.

Roland caught the King's boyish grin as he signaled for the advance with the winding of a single horn. Behind the Lombard camp, Lord Oliver whispered to his sergeant. Hands were slipped from horses' muzzles, and as a body, Lord Oliver's force swarmed out from concealment, up the last remaining slope and into the near-empty Lombard camp. Archers notched arrows to their bows. Aimed. Killed. Within moments, there was none left alive in the camp. Lord Oliver's knights and horsemen closed ranks to form a line several deep above and behind the downward-plunging Lombard army.

Roland's eyes found the Lombard King at once. Beneath his banner, Desiderius was swarthy-faced below an ornately crowned helm, unmistakably resplendent in a purple surcoat. Roland used his wooden sword to slap his palfrey upon the flanks and inspire it to greater effort as it plunged through turbulent waters in pursuit of the King's destrier. Then as the first flank of Charlemagne's knights reached the slope of the riverbank and thrust up the steep incline, the Lombards met them, and the battle was enjoined. Men, hidden during the night upon the far slope, emerged from their concealment and moved to attack. Above these, Lord Oliver's horsemen swarmed down from the ridge toward the back of the Lombard army.

The rest was shouting and turmoil and blood. Blows. Screams of horses and men. Roland, at Charlemagne's flank, raised his sword to ward off a blow, then ducked as the wood shattered before the onslaught of steel. Useless. He thrust the hilt from him and sent his terrified mount into a gallop, leaning down to scoop up the first weapon he could garner from a dying man, a lance.

He used it, eyes flitting back and forth, ever conscious of the Lombard King who fought with tenacious expertise. That was the triumph he wanted, Roland knew suddenly. The Lombard King! The head and heart would be his!

All his being gone savagely intense, Roland did not notice that he thrust his horse away from his place at the King's flank to angle into milling men and beasts. He discarded the lance when it broke, then found himself tumbling as his horse screamed and sank beneath him. He rolled and sprang to his feet, then seized a sword from a fallen man. He ducked and flitted. Struck, and grinned at the blood he saw spurt from a neck.

How he had waited and struggled for this—joy.

He caught at the reins of a loose horse, a great grey beast, and swung himself into the saddle with unencumbered agility, then slapped the animal on the rump with the flat of his sword just as an axe swooped toward his shoulder. The beast leaped forward in a great bound that carried him past two knights as his eyes sought and found the Lombard King once more.

He did not feel the sword that sliced across his left thigh. Nor the point that scraped across his ribs. Then he saw the guard surrounding the Lombard King dissipate into the melee as Lord Oliver's men fell upon the rear to shatter the formation of those ranks. Desiderius looked about him, eyes widened, then spurred his horse up a nearly sheer wall of rock, trampling one of his own men as he reached the top, and swung his stallion toward the north.

Roland sliced across the face of a knight with sword upraised to fell him, and knew—knew that the Lombard King was now bent on fleeing the assured defeat that awaited his forces. He rammed his heels into the grey destrier's sides, all his will bent to one single thing.

The grey horse answered willingly, and Roland shot past a foot soldier with a set spear. It was but reflex to swing his sword down, slicing through wrist and wood. He looked up and saw another man join the Lombard King, a small, dark-faced man mounted on a wiry chestnut that was barely visible beneath loose robes of flowing gold brocade. A strange and exotic warrior who wielded a peculiarly curved and flattened weapon as he took position at Desiderius' flank, slicing air and flesh more neatly than any butcher carving meat.

The grey destrier, trained to savagery and nimble maneuvers, swept Roland through milling men caught in encounter with each other, up, onto a rise, just as Desiderius seemed to vanish in the direction of the rising gorge. Hearing shouts behind him, Roland knew that Desiderius' flight had been seen. He glanced back once and saw Charlemagne laying about him like silver death while others charged in his direction.

"Nay. This King is mine!" Roland growled, and beat his beast to bolt northward across ragged, treacherously precipitous ground.

It was the exotic heathen who made it possible for the Lombard King to slip through a gap in the northern side of battling foot soldiers, to melt into the concealment offered by great outcroppings of rock as he sought and found a trail used by wild creatures.

Roland followed, eyes never leaving his prey. Down a slope, up a steep rise. Through flood-battered trees that scraped and twisted, obstructing passage, then across a difficult part of the river where it tumbled downward in a cascading fall from ledge to ledge.

And the sounds of the battle melted away behind him, until there were only the echoes of his horse's lathered heaving, iron shod clattering against stone, his own heartbeat and heavy panting. The grey stumbled, and Roland hit it. Then it was an upward climb, along a precipice that was suited only to goats, sheer cliff on one side, nothing on the other . . .

The grey struggled on, and Roland frowned, for Desiderius had seemed to disappear. Only scraped stone revealing any passage.

Sometime later, the grey nearly spent, Roland erupted onto more level ground, and a heavily wooded place well to the north of both armies. He caught sight of tracks and clenched his teeth in determination. Minutes later, the grey swept him into a clearing, and directly before him, Desiderius sat astride a heaving stallion that dripped froth and blood. The heathen lord was beside him. Roland jerked his horse to a halt and tightened his grip on his sword.

The heathen spoke in some incomprehensible language. The Lombard King nodded and grinned, his eyes traveling down Roland's body.

"A boy, by God!" he said in the Frankish tongue. "Do thou desert? Or come to seek a quiet place for thy final rest?" The heathen spun the little chestnut away from the King. Roland growled and raised his sword, hefting it loosely as he had learned. The unexpected was needed here . . .

"For God and Charlemagne!" he roared and charged, swinging the sword in a wide arc over his head, then, at the last moment, slipping to flatten himself along one side of the grey, shifting his stroke to lunge for the Lombard King's horse's throat. He felt his sword bite deep. The beast screamed and reared, displacing Desiderius' blow so that it sliced into the pommel of Roland's saddle, nicked him on the thigh. Then, the grey, completely spent, stumbled, lurched and fell.

Roland jerked himself free and tumbled to roll in the sod and spring to his feet. Desiderius' stallion floundered and fell also, blood spewing from its throat in a hideous gurgling, eyes glazing. As the Lombard King stumbled in an effort to find his feet, Roland charged, needing the fleeting advantage as the heathen brought his little horse about. He managed, with both hands upon the hilt of his sword, to strike Desiderius' blade away. It sailed through the air, and Roland spun, following the same sweep, to curve his arc up and out to meet the charge of the heathen.

Again, he went for the horse. The sword shuddered in his

grip as it sliced through a foreleg. The little beast described a screaming somersault, catapulting the golden heathen through the air. Roland spun, light-footed, to see Desiderius lunge after his sword. He leaped. Another blow with all his strength behind it caught the Lombard King across the back and felled him. Roland was upon him in an instant, clutching at the helm on Desiderius' head. He looked up and saw the Infidel come toward him, strangely curved blade raised. The heathen's dark eyes met his, and beneath him, Roland felt the King squirm and writhe. He jerked on the head.

"I yield me!" Desiderius rasped. Roland jerked loose both crown and helm, his eyes never leaving the heathen, and grinned. "I yield me!" Desiderius grated more clearly. Words that were pure joy to hear. Roland's smile widened, and the Infidel blanched as, with lightning speed, Roland drew back and brought his sword down with all his strength, completely through the Lombard King's neck. The body convulsed violently. Blood spewed. The head rolled away as Roland crouched and stepped forward, raising his sword to counter any blow from that peculiarly curved weapon in the small man's hand. He growled then, and the heathen leaped to one side, face gone grey. Roland could not know that the Infidel saw not a boy, but a tall man with hard lion eyes that gleamed Shaitan's own blend of scarlet and vindictive fire. He made a sign and turned to flee. Roland lunged, charging in pursuit. He caught at robes with one hand and raised his sword into a lethal arc. But the garment came away as the heathen spun nimbly, then bolted into the trees to vanish in an instant.

Roland stood then, his lungs heaving, sweat pouring down his body. Slowly, his left hand lost its grip on the gold cloth that billowed down to crumple quietly upon the sod. He turned. Near his feet, the King of the Lombards lay in pieces. Roland grinned around his panting.

"For God—and Charlemagne! For—Roland also!" he whispered. Thrashing sounds made him shift again to see the suffering chestnut horse. He strode toward it and killed it. His own horse—aye, it was his own by right now—had clambered to its feet and stood, head down, exhausted. Froth dripped from neck and flanks and its sides heaved. It was useless for the present.

Suddenly, Roland could feel pain. He looked down at himself in surprise, seeing places where his own blood trickled slowly to stain the blue of his tunic across his side, his leg. He felt an almost violent need to rest. Instead, he clenched his teeth and looked about him.

There was no sign of the vanished Infidel. Around him, the trees were silent. There were no birds. No rustlings of any kind.

The air was poised. He was entirely alone.

Slowly, still holding the sword, Roland limped awkwardly to Desiderius' body, bent, and cut loose the back half of the purple surcoat. Then with another scooping movement, he grasped the Lombard King's head by the hair and wrapped it in the purple material. Setting the bundle down on the bloody sod, he reached for the helm and carefully loosed the crown. This he set beside the head. Then, still holding the helm, he shifted back to the rest of the corpse. He knelt awkwardly and with great deliberation, began to strip Desiderius' body of its armor—his now.

Calf length, the hauberk was made of the tightest double steel links. Immensely costly, Roland knew. He took the mail leggings as well, and the gorget. And the gauntlets. And the spurs.

Something he was not yet entitled to wear.

Exhaustion and pain swept over him then, and he sank down to sit on the trampled grass, looking first at the armor. A King's armor—and then at his own blood. Aye, he thought. He had won this for himself. And the iron grey destrier. He closed his eyes to rest awhile.

To yield for a time to wounds that did not matter at all.

Stuporous with exhaustion, Roland dozed as sweat dried, clothing stiffened, and blood congealed in raw cuts and gashes. He did not hear the cropping sounds made by the grey horse that had recovered sufficiently to graze. He did not see the dark thing that plummeted like an illusion from the concealing shadows amid the thick woods surrounding the glade, to vanish behind the carcass of the Infidel's dead horse.

Fluttering sounds aroused him, bringing him instantly to his feet, sword at the ready.

Roland paled.

The white owl, its feathers as pure as virgin snow, perched upon the hip of the dead chestnut horse.

"Mother of God!" he breathed and crossed himself. The

owl cocked its head a little and stared at him, then fluttered lightly to resettle on the dead animal's saddle. It made a distinctive downward pecking movement, then looked back at him, blinking slowly. Roland stiffened, and shifted toward it. The owl cocked its head, seemed to smile slyly, spread its wings abruptly, and took flight.

Roland stared, then flinched as it swooped around his head in a wide arc, veered back toward the carcass, then spiraled up to vanish through the tops of the trees.

Why did it follow him? Roland swallowed and looked at the chestnut carcass. What did it want . . . Or, mean? There was naught here but heathen . . .

Heathen? Roland stared, his eyes widening slowly at something half-buried under the carcass. He stepped closer. Stopped.

It was a sword, he realized with wonder. A dark sword, unlike any he had ever seen, or imagined. He bent to touch a hilt that was as black as ebony and felt like some impossible blend of stone and metal beneath his fingertips. Silken smooth, uncannily cold, it was a wonder to view, for the cross pieces were a pair of wings outspread. Cast, or carved— it was impossible to tell—to incredible detail, they were eagle pinions. And, rising up between them to compose a guard and grip enough for a two-handed span, was the form of a woman clothed only in twisting spirals of hair that wound around her to completely conceal both arms, and thread between her feet to meld with the eagle winged hilt.

Roland shifted and, grasping the hilt with his left hand, set one foot against the carcass. He pulled, then jerked back to keep his balance as the sword came free almost of its own volition.

He poised, his eyes widening further as he stared at a blade that was longer and narrower than any he had ever seen before, ending in a point so fine it seemed, quite simply, to vanish. And heavy . . . He felt its weight as he let the point sink toward the earth, the blade alone equal to his length from foot to sternum. And with the hilt he realized, the sword reached from the ground to touch his collarbone.

He stared at the pommel. Hair so cunningly wrought as to appear real surrounded a face that was stern and perfect, and elfin fine. Eyes stared back at him, blank, dark. Orbs to be imagined, not understood.

Roland dropped his other weapon, brought his right hand up, and shifted his grasp. Like a miracle, the extraordinary hilt molded itself to fit his hand with impossible perfection. Awed, he traced his left fingertips down along the blade and felt another mystery. Cold to the touch, it was a blend of midnight hues and dusky, thunder tones. Blues and lightning silvers slithered in an elusive dance along its length, around the symbols engraved on the upper part of the blade.

This, Roland knew, was a sword that had its own name.

He knelt, uncaring that the movement ripped at the deep gash in his left thigh, and set the sword before him on the turf. He touched the edges of a blade so sharp they could slip through flesh before they were felt, and marveled at its unblemished flawlessness.

And touching, stroking the weapon was a most extraordinary thing. Chill and silken and hard beyond conceiving, it was a seduction of its own. Alive? Or was it a trick of the sunlight that speckled through the trees? Roland frowned as he thought of the white owl that haunted him. Nay. The sword had *not* been there when he butchered the Infidel's suffering horse. Could it be that the spirit bird had brought him to this weapon by some conjuring of its own?

His hand moved again, fingers and palm seating themselves around that miniature female body that melded with unnatural perfection to his grip. He gasped, eyes widening as the strange chill melted into an oddly powerful warmth. Then, he stood awkwardly, drew the sword up, and lofted it high above his head. He felt the sword leap then, as though of its own will, eagerly responsive to his hand. Weight vanishing into an uncanny, buoyant lightness.

He swung then, sending the dark sword into a wide, swooping arc, heard a singing come from the blade. The song of sinister wings. Brutal. Ecstatic. Filled with the same ferocious, hungry joy he himself felt in battle. Heart pounding, and filled with awe, Roland swirled it in another arc before bringing it to rest, point down upon the turf once more.

"What a wonder thou art!" he whispered, loosing his grip to caress the winged cross pieces, the mystery of the woman hilt, feeling every texture, every detail. Steel? Stone? Warm to his touch now.

"Can it be thou art for me?" he asked it slowly, and knew, even as he spoke, how much he wanted her . . . Aye. This sword beyond all swords. Having held her once, he could never bear to be parted from her again. Pure vehemence, like his vows to honor his King above all else. Aye. She must be for him. He could not bear for it to be otherwise.

"Thou art the only woman I will ever touch!" Roland told the sword with absolute sincerity.

It was another hour before the grey destrier was rested sufficiently to be ridden again. Roland spent the time stripping the animal of its battered saddle and accoutrements, rubbing it down with clumps of grass, then resaddling it with the much finer equipment wrested from the Lombard King's dead destrier. Likewise, he put on the dead King's armor, savoring the feel of mail leggings, the weight of the finely crafted hauberk. He donned the gorget and buckled Desiderius' blood-splattered cloak to his shoulders, then girded his hips with the dead King's sword belt. Desiderius' princely weapon rode easy against his hip, yet Roland thought it could not hope to compare with the wonder of the dark sword.

His lips twisted a little. Only hours before, he recognized, he would have thought it a very miracle to gird himself with a sword of such fine damascened steel and jeweled hilt. Now? Comparison was impossible.

He bound the bundle of Desiderius' head to the pommel of his saddle, and the crown with it, then drew up the mail coif and set the conical helm with its engraved nasal on his head.

He glanced about him as he thrust spurs and gauntlets into his sword belt, and bent to retrieve the gold brocade robe of the vanished Infidel. He touched the heavy material that was a marvel of rich texture and design before folding it tightly and affixing it to the saddle. Something for some other, undefined use.

Then he bent and grasped the dark sword. His. Only his. He went to mount. He gasped as the effort ripped his thigh and set it to bleeding again, took up the reins, and turned the weary stallion through the lengthening shadows, back the way he had come.

Back—to offer up his victory to Charlemagne.

FOUR

What had begun as a bloody battle between two equal forces turned slowly into carnage, and then a rout. The Lombards, unable to sight their King after Charlemagne descended upon their rear, soon understood that he had abandoned them and fled the field. Caught before and after between the two arms of a Frankish vise bent on slaughter, they soon lost heart and began to put down their weapons. Common men did so thankfully, eager to preserve their lives. Knights and lords did so with a sullen dignity, angered by the humiliation and betrayal their fealty to Desiderius had brought upon them.

Dragged forth and bound, all had to listen to the triumphant shouts of the Franks, to watch as they gathered around the almost-legendary silver Charlemagne to honor him.

Charlemagne sat astride his tired stallion on a broad, high rock overlooking the river. The stench of animal sweat rose up around him, but he knew, scanning the field of battle, it was naught compared to the sweet rot that would shortly begin to arise from the place.

He watched his men search among the dead for that which was useful or, better yet, valuable, and thought, thankfully, that his own losses had been comparatively few.

"Lord Ganelon!" his voice boomed suddenly across the valley as he caught sight of his Champion. The dark lord swung his lathered bay about and set the animal to plunge down through corpses and boulders toward his King. "There

46

is to be no Christian burial for those who took up arms against the Pope!'' Charlemagne spoke with frigid clarity as the other drew rein below him. "Let them rot. Let their bones be scattered about this godforsaken place!'' The Champion nodded.

"So it shall be done, Majesty!'' An instant later, he was barking orders as his stallion swept him away. The King flexed his shoulders, still studying the field with cold intensity. Then he saw the carcass of the palfrey his squire had been given to use. His mouth tightened against private feelings. Of Roland, there was no sign. No corpse. Nothing. Roland. His . . .

"Lord Oliver!'' he grated abruptly as that young man cantered past, headed for the river. De Montglave looked up startled, and brought his destrier about, his squire, Rinalde of Montalban, doing likewise.

"Majesty?'' Oliver's young face was sweat-streaked and triumphant, Charlemagne noted. With good cause . . .

"Our squire, Lord Oliver?'' the King asked. "We do not see him, and we have use for his service.'' De Montglave glanced about him, frowning. Rinalde's face went taut with knowledge.

"Nor have I seen—my liege.'' Oliver spoke slowly. He looked up. The King's face was remote.

"Give leave, my lord?'' Rinalde addressed him suddenly.

"Aye?'' Oliver said sharply.

"Majesty. My lord.'' Rinalde spoke with some uncertainty. "I did see Roland the Bastard a long while past. He was astride a grey destrier and was beating the beast into full flight with a sword.'' Lord Oliver's face tightened alertly. The King's did not change. "He passed from my view in that direction,'' Rinalde finished, pointing toward the narrowing, precipitous ravine to the north, away from the battlefield. The conclusion was obvious. Oliver's eyes widened as he looked up at the King. Not the Bastard? Yet, the King was alone, and had been so for some time. He followed the direction of Charlemagne's frigid stare and recognized the carcass of Roland's palfrey. There was no body near it.

"Lord Oliver.'' The King's tone was remarkably even.

"Majesty?''

"We will have the service of thy squire then.'' Charlemagne nodded toward Rinalde, who, entirely startled, looked up with open joy.

"Gladly, Majesty," Oliver said, and glanced at Rinalde. Nay. He had not lied on what he had seen.

"Thou hast done well this day, Montalban," Charlemagne said more gently. "We must consider that thou hast won thy spurs in service to thy lord. But, for the present, go thou. Make all ready for us. There is much yet to be done." He nodded toward the Frankish encampment to the west. Rinalde flushed scarlet in pleasure and bowed.

"Majesty!" he breathed. Then, heels clapped to his horse, he set the animal to plunge across the river. Oliver lingered, frowning now as he looked back toward the dead palfrey. Nay, not Roland, the thought came again.

"We will find replacement for thy squire, my lord," the King said in not unkindly tones. Oliver looked up. "One who is worthy to serve so valuable a lord!"

"Majesty," Oliver breathed recognition of the compliment. But his answer was lost as the King spurred his stallion to leap off the ledge into the river in a marvel of horsemanship. He did not move as he saw the stallion bear Charlemagne across, then lunge up the steep incline toward the encampment.

Slowly, he turned his own horse about and rode through the dead and dying. Nor did he find that for which he was so oddly compelled to search.

The shadows lengthened rapidly as the sun slipped behind trees and high ground to the west. Roland soon realized something of the distance the grey horse had brought him in his single-minded pursuit of Desiderius. Husbanding the animal that, being a war stallion, had greater value than most men, he stopped to water and rest it when he could from small trickling brooks that seeped out between the rocks.

The descent was more difficult than the climb had been by far, for downward leaps were impossible along the treacherous precipices. But the grey horse was gallant in its efforts. Cliffs and gorges gradually softened somewhat into that deep rift between the mountains where the battle had been undertaken. It was fully nighttime when Roland found himself riding slowly parallel to the river, toward the battlefield itself.

All was silent. The grey horse trod with wary care between opaque black shapes that were clumped on sloping ground faintly lit by a waning moon.

A sweet stench arose from the dead scattered all about, thickening the hot night air. Roland saw a fox glare at him, then go back to rending meat from a dead man's hand. The morning, he knew, would bring crows and buzzards, and all manner of other crawling things to feast upon the unburied.

Looking up toward the high ridge to the east, Roland saw no glow from the Lombard encampment. Halting his horse by the river and shifting his gaze, he saw the fires of Charlemagne's forces high above him on the other side.

The river was a dark and roaring force to negotiate. Roland stroked the neck of the exhausted grey, knowing it must rest before he attempted the last. Nor did he trust himself to dismount. His left leg throbbed violently and seemed to but hang in the stirrup. Instead, he shifted the dark sword he held at his right side and set it before him across the pommel of his saddle.

Black, opaque, in the night, it seemed more feeling than reality beneath his fingertips as he traced its length with his left hand. Warm yet, and strangely so, aye, as though it were alive. Roland could not fear it. Nor the power, the magic that was implicit in it. Rather, it was as though the dark sword, above, beyond anything he had ever known, belonged to him, had become one with him. To be parted from it now would be unthinkable.

A dismemberment, crippling.

Slowly, sometime later, he moved his right hand and positioned the dark sword to hang beneath the folds of his cloak as he set the grey to the river.

The stallion was trembling with exhaustion and heaving badly when Roland finally reached the top of the southwesternmost hill. Again, he gave the destrier time to rest, and during that time contrived the means by which he could carry the dark sword upon his person. He wound the slim belt for the hauberk over his head and beneath his left arm, then, twisting it, set the dark sword through it, to hang against his left shoulder and side beneath the folds of Desiderius' cloak.

Both hands free, he then took the grisly bundle of the head from his pommel and unwrapped it. Clutching blood-matted hair, he wedged the crown firmly around the brow and held it up for a moment.

"I have a name now," he whispered. "Justly won . . . I am Roland Kingslayer!" The night offered no reply.

He stiffened his shoulders against his own exhaustion and the pain of his wounds, and set the stallion to walk slowly through the shadows toward the perimeter of the encampment, Desiderius' head hanging from his hand against his right leg. The grey horse carried him past guards who started warily, then saw he was alone. Past campfires and common foot soldiers, who, beyond a glance, had no interest in him.

Past lesser knights and, finally, through the camping site of the highest born, the lords and others who knew him, but did not recognize. Who roused from other preoccupation to stride toward him with curiosity and protectiveness for the King.

The grey horse stopped of its own volition in the shadows by the King's banner, and Roland saw that Charlemagne sat before his tent, with others of his highest lords, around a table strewn with parchments. On the other side, flanked by guards, were two other lords, battle-stained and drawn of feature. He stiffened. Rinalde of Montalban stood in his own place behind the King.

He heard the hiss of a sword slipping from its scabbard, and he touched the grey. The stallion stepped forward restively into the full light of a large, roaring fire. The King rose to his feet and stared with frozen eyes toward him.

"Jesu! It is the Bastard!" He heard the exclamation from his right. Other lords rose also, among them Lord Oliver and the Champion.

"He fled," another voice grated. "See. He returns with plunder got from the dead!" Fled? Roland's eyes widened as the King stepped forward, then stood, silent and regal, his gaze a ghastly, frigid conformation. Fled? Nay. Never! And it was Lord Ganelon who strode forward, sword drawn, to seize his bridle. Roland spun the beast sideways to elude him. Others closed in.

"Craven bastard!" the Champion growled. "Get thee down from that beast to receive the just reward thy treachery and cowardice have earned!" Roland sat in sickened disappointment followed by a surge of proud, grinding rage that he should be thought capable of such desertion. He made the stallion rear and strike at the hands that reached for him.

"For God and Charlemagne!" His own voice made a thunder cry across them all as he brought up his right hand and held out the head of Desiderius for all to see.

Stunned silence followed as the grey horse settled. All eyes stared at the gleaming crown of Lombardy. At the head beneath, now grey with bulging dull eyes and half-open mouth through which the tongue protruded, already swollen and black, and at the oozing stump of neck below.

Roland glared at them all, pride and injury keeping him in the saddle, unaware of the changes the day had wrought in his face. Boyhood had vanished. It was a grim-faced man who sat before them all.

"It is Desiderius. Our King!" The stillness was shattered by hoarse outcry from one of the prisoner lords who clambered, ashen-faced, to his feet. Roland stared directly at Charlemagne.

"What does it serve, Majesty, to cut the serpent's tail if the head escapes and lives to grow another?" he said with great clarity. "Now, as God wills, the serpent is assuredly defeated!" It took all his concentration to dismount. To walk without lameness toward the King, then to kneel uncaring of the ripped thigh that began to bleed again. He set the head at Charlemagne's feet. Unbuckled Desiderius' sword and set that down as well. Only the assurance of the dark sword lay concealed against him now.

"How was this done?" the King asked quietly. Roland looked up into eyes that waited, simply.

"My horse was slain. My place lost. I found another beast and saw the King undertake to fly the field in the company of some strange Infidel. I pursued the Lombard King, and when he came to rest, I killed him!"

"Impossible!" Lord Ganelon intervened at once, stepping forward, ire tempered by reason. "Who could believe such a claim from an untried squire! It is not reasonable, Majesty, to believe that a puissant and experienced soldier as King Desiderius should be vanquished by a mere boy!" Unthinking, Roland stood and faced the Champion. Lord Ganelon's eyes passed down his frame. "It was witnessed that the Bastard fled the field alone. Worse, for having got a horse to replace his own, he did not fulfill duty and abide by thy flank as honor requires, my liege, but rather abandoned thee! Nay! I consider that he came upon the King's body and hath contrived this claim to justify the plunder he hath so clearly adorned himself with!"

"Not so!" Roland retorted loudly. "I killed him of my own effort! I have taken only that which I have honestly won!" The Champion's expression hardened.

"It is not thy place, squire," he spoke with frigid contempt, "to speak unless required!" Roland clenched his teeth.

"Where is the rest of Desiderius?" It was Charlemagne who asked, and Roland spun to face the King.

"The body lies in a high grove, yonder, to the north, Majesty. Something better then five miles distant. Likewise are the carcasses of the King's destrier and the Infidel's horse that I also slew." Unreadable blue eyes locked with gold that were too clear for dissembling.

"There are two truths that have the force of witness for veracity." Lord Oliver stepped forward then, his voice quiet with considered reason. "Majesty. It was seen by a number that the King of the Lombards did indeed flee for his life. Likewise, the dead palfrey bears proof of a single thing. The Bastard was torn from his place. Given that he hath this other horse and did not resume his place . . ."

"Thou cannot believe—this—" Lord Ganelon spun to face the younger man. Lord Oliver shrugged and met the Champion's look evenly.

"For justice, I attempt no conviction save on that which is proven," he said with the same calm, looking directly at the King. 'Likewise." His gaze lowered to the head that still lay at Charlemagne's feet. "It is proved beyond the doubt of any that Lombardy is dead. The means by which this occurred? Well—that is speculation for the present." Silence descended once more upon the gathering. Roland stood ashen-faced and rigid, feeling the single thought that was upon the minds of all. The penalty for desertion was a terrible death.

Flaying whereby the skin was peeled slowly from the body after the manner of a hide stripped from a butchered beast, yet without the benefit of slit throat. A slow, agonizing death. Not spurs. Nor the knighthood he craved, or thought he had assuredly won. Nor honor.

"Thou did abandon thy place at our flank." The King's address to him was overquiet. Toneless. Unreadable.

"I sought to give a greater service!" Roland rasped before he could stop himself.

"There is no greater service than to the body of thy King!"

Behind him, Lord Ganelon spoke in fury. Charlemagne's gaze shifted to meet his Champion.

"There is something of compensation by this other service that thou hast wrought on our behalf, we consider. Thou hast brought us proof irrefutable of Desiderius' death." The King went on in the same toneless, awful voice. "For that we are wont to clemency." He was not believed . . . Not believed at all. Roland felt his insides go hollow as the King's words echoed through his head.

"We perceive that thou are adorned, Bastard, with armor and horse that have far greater worth than thine own life, and thereby do choose to give thy body and thy service with all these accoutrements to our valued Lord Oliver De Montglave to use as he sees fit!"

Roland stared, shattered feelings keeping him from either movement or sound. Lord Oliver's eyebrows rose with surprise. Charlemagne's eyes found his. A slight smile passed across the King's lips.

"We have taken thy squire, my lord, and for thy good service will compensate thee with the gift of this—servant, and these other things of value!" To the astonishment of all, Charlemagne bent abruptly and, seizing Desiderius' jeweled sword, held it out to Roland. "Give this to thy master!" he grated abruptly, then spun on his heel and strode away to disappear inside his tent.

Roland stood unmoving, staring at the sword in his hand. Not even a squire then. He was something worse than common now. Degraded.

"Guard thy back, my lord!" he heard Lord Ganelon murmur to De Montglave as he passed by. "The King's justice needs careful stewardship!"

"I will, my lord!" Oliver chuckled. Roland swallowed. All about him, he heard the sounds of lords and knights departing for their various places in the encampment. Then, slowly, chin jutting and mouth a frozen slash, he turned and held out the sword with its jeweled scabbard and hilt. Lord Oliver stepped forward and took it.

"Bring the horse and come with me!" he ordered tersely after a moment. He strode toward his own tent some distance away by a small brook.

The wound in his thigh throbbed agony. Every other cut and bruise pulsed raw and exhaustion seeped across him with the same desperation as this other, hideous—defeat. Roland turned slowly. Not for the world would he be seen to limp. He caught up the reins of the grey and followed Lord Oliver. Master. Foe. Hated. So bitterly hated, more than ever for this.

Charlemagne took the crown of Lombardy that young Montalban held out, then looked up.

"Do thou see to the burial of the King's head," he ordered quietly. "Find a priest to give the absolution of prayer likewise."

"Majesty." Rinalde bowed and left the tent. Alone, Charlemagne studied the jeweled diadem for a moment, then set it down. He knew, with absolute conviction, that Roland had indeed done as he had claimed. It was in the boy's eyes, in the new hard manhood of his face.

He was safe, for the time given to De Montglave.

In another place, not too distant, Lord Ganelon felt his own satisfaction drain to thoughtfulness. It was better by far if the King had been disposed to fulfill the prescribed law and destroy the Bastard. Make of him an example. How neatly Charlemagne had slipped between the lines of proof and speculation.

And however well he associated with young De Montglave, Lord Ganelon was keenly aware of that other's rising power. Nor was Lord Oliver easily managed. He was too lucid by far, with a nature perhaps overprone to generosity. Reared to the scholarship of ancient heathen writings by a grandsire of like temperament, he was of an ordered, rather than passionate, disposition. Lord Ganelon frowned.

Given to such a one, he recognized, Roland was assured a better safety than in any other service. More—Roland was now removed from his own jurisdiction.

"I do not envy thee the King's gift!" Florismart of Aquitaine murmured to a thoughtful Lord Oliver as that other seated himself slowly on the soft turf near the campfire. He passed a wineskin. "Thou hast a very wolf for squire now!" Oliver raised an eyebrow and drank, then looked across the clearing to where Roland now attended his horses. Orders given, yet obeyed without acknowledged response beyond a sullen glaring. He swallowed the welcome beverage.

"Squire? Floris," he inquired slowly, raising his brows.

"What then?" Oliver shook his head and grinned ruefully.

"Thou said it. A half-trained wolf!" he murmured, drinking again. "Sweet Jesu! I do swear that my belly hath found my backbone! What has thy squire got for us to eat?" Florismart glanced toward the tethered horses.

"Nay. I would not trust his cooking, either!" He grinned. "Here." He passed a fresh, stone-baked loaf and a roasted joint. "Yet, I consider thou did speak for him?" Oliver bit into food at once.

"I spoke what I saw. No more," he said without interest. "Enough. I starve!" Wine and food and the fire blazing heat against the chill night brought a mellow contentment to a day of triumph for them all. It was a time for nothing more complex than to savor the simple joy of being alive . . .

It was much later when Sir Florismart slipped away to the rest of his own tent and the attention of his squire that Oliver looked up again toward his horses. Clean now and contentedly munching fodder, they were set for the time. But the Bastard? He shifted to see Roland standing rigid and glaring, gaunt pale, and still encased in armor behind him. Oliver grimaced, aware of his need for body service. Equally aware that he might be better doing for himself than to use . . . He got to his feet and headed toward both the Bastard and his tent, stopping abruptly in front of Roland.

"That mail needs cleaning," he said quietly. "And mine own." The boy's expression did not change. Nor did he respond. Oliver frowned. "A simple 'aye, my lord' will suffice to prove thou are not deaf!" he said sharply.

"Aye, my lord." Toneless.

"Thou will disarm and bathe me now!" Oliver said crisply and strode through the flap of his tent to the welcome glow of its comfortable interior. The advantages of family wealth. He heard the other behind him and turned. Then chuckled. "Do thou think, Bastard, to give decent service in all that armor?" he asked, reaching for his helm and discarding it. Roland scowled. Oliver laughed. "Verily, thou will rust to permanent rigidity before thy duty is done!" Roland glowered even more deeply, his pallor more marked. Oliver unclasped his cloak and set it aside. Then his sword belt, his eyes never leaving the other's face. That ashen hue . . . "Here. I will help thee. Then thou may serve me," he said and reached out. Roland jerked away and Oliver's eyes widened as he stared at the dark thing that had been hidden beneath the blood-stained cloak. "What is that?" he demanded, stepping forward. Roland stared back, suddenly wary. He was property, now. "Mother of God! It is a sword, I consider," Oliver said slowly, staring at eagle wings, and darkness, and a human-formed hilt. "How art thou come by this?" Roland's mouth moved, but no sound came out.

"How art thou come by this thing?" Oliver barked now. Roland went rigid and stared past him.

"It was upon the carcass of the Infidel's horse that I killed!" he grated little more than a whisper. "I took it." Oliver's stare traced down a blade of impossible length and unnaturally dark purity, then up past an inscription that was akin to Greek lettering . . .

"Durandal . . ." he murmured translation and looked up to the astonishment of an almost hungry expression in the Bastard's eyes.

"My lord?" Roland rasped.

"Durandal," Oliver said slowly. "It is the name inscribed upon the weapon." Then, "Pass it to me!" Likewise, he noted the possessive reluctance with which Roland detached and proffered the unlikely sword. He gasped in astonishment and withdrew his hand instantly. It was like touching ice! Nay. More bitter chill than that . . . Yet Roland held it easily. He reached for it again, but could not bear the frozen pain that shot up his arm.

"What is this unholy thing thou hast got?" Oliver whispered. Clear gold certainty met his stare.

"It is a sword, my lord," Roland murmured with a softness such as Oliver had never heard before. "Durandal—as thou have said." And still he held it.

"Remove that armor, Bastard," Oliver ordered then, acutely aware of the exact angle and distance between himself and his own weapon.

Roland obeyed. Slowly, still clinging to the dark, unnatural sword that came to his shoulders, he removed cloak and gorget and hauberk, then the mail chausses, but as though with great difficulty. When it was done, he straightened awkwardly, his pallor now moistened by a cold sweat. Oliver looked at him, recognizing the torn garments, seeing sliced cloth and flesh along the ribs. Then the great gash in chausses and thigh into which welled fresh blood. He understood. The armor had been put on later. After, as Roland had indeed rightly claimed, he had killed the King of Lombardy.

Even now, he stood with that same unquenchable, defiant pride.

"Go now . . ." Oliver said very gently. "Attend to thyself."

"My lord?" Roland's face went wary.

"Thou are of no use to me dead of poisoned wounds," Oliver intoned dryly. "Thou have cost me a good and loyal squire, Bastard, and I intend to have replacement in thee!" Roland scowled and shifted. "Nay!" Oliver added tersely as Roland moved to set down the dark sword. "Keep that clumsy great thing. I want none of it!" Roland straightened, clutching the weapon possessively, yet clearly amazed. Oliver frowned. "Mark me well. Do thou keep it hid from view! I will not have the taint of witchcraft mar my name or my honor!" he growled, exhaling slowly moments later when Roland had vanished into the night.

Typical of the Bastard, he thought wryly, to depart without so much as simple acknowledgment. Slowly, he set about the business of discarding his own armor and soiled clothing. Then, he sank into the comfort of soft furs with a thankful sigh.

"Nor," he murmured a last resolution before his eyes closed, "will I be baited by thee, Roland, into losing my temper!"

The morning brought brilliant sunlight and astonishment with it as Lord Oliver awoke, then roused to instant alertness. His armor was cleaned and oiled. His surcoat and other garments tended. Likewise, the armor of Desiderius. Pulling a cloak about him, Oliver strode from the tent and looked toward the horses. Still there, fed and watered. He turned around, then saw the Bastard lying on the ground by the side of his tent. Unkempt and filthy, Roland lay like the dead, like a lover, half over, half clutching that peculiar sword. And his thigh wound, for all the dried blood and dust about it, was pink and clean, already healing. Oliver grinned and prodded with bare toes. The Bastard jerked to wakefulness.

"I am hungry!" he announced and strode back inside the tent.

FIVE

Victory over the Lombards was finalized by word of the ignominious death of their King, and Charlemagne ordered a
southward march toward Rome as he undertook permanent
consolidation of his triumph and the redisposition of Lombard fiefs. The pace was almost leisurely, due to the large
number of prisoners that, bound together and on foot, had
yet to be dealt with.

There were minor skirmishes along the way. Short, bloody
battles with small groups led by rebellious men who either
did not yet know of Desiderius' death or were reluctant to
accept Charlemagne as their King. The King's elect force of
young, highborn knights fought most of these. Hungry for
glory, for their King and themselves, they were unquenchably
fierce, even joyously so, and they fought brilliantly under the
rising leadership of Lord Oliver De Montglave.

For Roland, it was a bitter time. Caught by his own private
unbreakable fealty to the King, and given by Charlemagne to
Lord Oliver, he kept his service to De Montglave with an
exactitude that none could question, yet with a cold-faced
reserve that revealed he felt no honor in it. Likewise rigid in
his adherence to his place at Lord Oliver's heels, he found
himself becoming acutely aware of every friendly glance and
word that Oliver received. Even the elusive Charlemagne
treated De Montglave with an openness that marked any conversation with his rising favorite.

Lord Oliver, who was so pure and unstained in honor. Oliver, who was loved for his beauty and for a cheerful humor and generous nature incomprehensible to Roland . . .

Oliver—who only three years his senior, had always, easily, beaten him.

For himself, it was worse than during the years spent at the King's court. For most, he was not seen to exist. He was a mere shadow made to menial service, and for naught else. And if his presence was noted upon occasion, it was to make him the butt of gibes or insults to which he was not allowed to respond.

And Lord Oliver was the worst of them. De Montglave did not treat him with the same degrading manner of scorn as the rest. Instead, Roland felt, he was more cunning by far in the manner of his reviling, appearing unpredictably kind and stern by turns.

The sterner aspects, Roland well understood, for he was accustomed to succinctly uttered orders. But the other behavior, the self-interested generosity was such as a proud man might bestow upon a dog, and the other, goading remarks that attacked his pride—were intolerable.

Bones that Lord Oliver found useless were given him. He could not be grateful for the gray stallion that Lord Oliver found too inexperienced. Nor the discarded clothing he was forced to wear so as not to disgrace De Montglave's pride in his wealth. Nor, least of all, for the dark sword that was his own from the first, and which he kept hid under a cloak, suspended from an especially contrived baldric that held the hilt between his shoulder blades. It was an ingenious modification that accommodated both Durandal's great length and her uncanny leaping answer to the touch of his hand.

Worst of all were the times when he was alone with his lord. De Montglave, relaxed and complacent in his achievements, would look at him in a deceptively companionable manner and offer conversation in easy tones such as he used among his peers. Roland knew better than to be drawn out. He husbanded his distrust and responded in monosyllables, if at all. And waited for the chuckled gibe that was invariably given.

And, being no longer squire, nor yet considered soldier of even the commonest sort, Roland found another facet to his anger and humiliation. He was not permitted to flank his lord in any battle. Instead, he was relegated to stay with the baggage, or the recovering wounded, forbidden even to attempt to fight.

Alone at night, cradling the dark sword against him while others slept, Roland stared into the darkness and felt all the sheer desperation of his soul well up into pure and savage appetite for battle. It was a flavor, once tasted, that he craved above all else.

Fingers slipping around the sensuous curves of the hilt of Durandal, across the meticulous feathering of the cross pieces, and along the blade that was impossibly sharp, yet did not cut him, his kinship with the sword deepened, for it was as though she too was honed and waiting.

Like his own flesh, she had become as unthinkingly indispensable to him as his limbs, his senses. Yet she was a greater mystery. A wondrous harbinger of unimagined potential.

He would close his eyes and lie there, feeling the power that glided more smoothly than silken fabric along her, against himself.

Thunder that rumbled sweetly in the distance. Tempests awaited. He had but to get to them.

Charlemagne brought his great army to halt on the border between Lombardy and the papal states. There, in a countryside ravaged by Desiderius, he established a more permanent encampment and, with Adrian, who came north from Rome itself, set about the establishment of a permanent government and order for the newly conquered territory.

With the King and the Pope, and the high lords preoccupied with matters of state and law, the rest of Charlemagne's forces welcomed the respite and set aside their arms from all but nominal duty to savor midsummer pleasures. Prisoners, dealt with by various means, were dispatched or melted away to become part of the populace of Lombardy once more.

The young lords, likewise with time on their hands, spent companionable hours in vigorous sport or in jovial tests of skill at arms. Or at night, in pursuing other kinds of pleasure to be found with common wenches and the like. Girls, who were to Roland demons of entrapment for all their weaker bodies and beguiling looks . . .

Bound perpetually, it seemed, to Lord Oliver's heels, Roland began to see the full extent of his exile as he came to understand the broad reach and depth of the camaraderie that

existed between all the young, highborn knights. He also
came to understand the depth of friendship that existed between Sir Florismart of Aquitaine and Lord Oliver. Like
brothers, they shared meals and conversation, sport, and even
wenches, which meant that Roland's service was often required to include Florismart as well.

Sir Florismart freely voiced his opinions, and his contempt
for Roland's surly, coarse-bred manner. Bent on managing the
silence with which he bound his anger, Roland did not think to
notice that Lord Oliver did not participate in these insults, but
would, rather, find ingenious ways to distract his friend.

Or, with equal frequency, would dismiss Roland for a time.

Roland put these hours of welcome solitude to vigorous
use. Astride the grey destrier, which, though young and inexperienced, was a horse of great heart and willingness, he
sought private places where he would not be seen as he practiced both horsemanship and with the dark sword.

Durandal. Creature weapon, who made wonders when
loosed and held aloft. Who split the air with a resonant
hum of power, and who leaped to each arc or stroke with
predatory nimbleness.

Roland learned that which could not be taught. With Durandal in his hand, he learned a new kind of reach that extended far beyond the norm for a sword. He learned to meld
himself with each swoop or lunge, and he learned a different,
ingenious balance that accounted for the dark sword's impressive range and unique power. He discovered as well, the
skill of redirecting the sword's flight, almost lustful surges of
unison with her as she leaped toward prey—any prey.

Saplings were sliced more easily than with the finest honed
axe, and when he aimed for the bole of a large tree, Durandal
lunged toward it with a ferocity that was purest reflection of
his own determination, slicing into and slipping out of the
wood again with a fluid ease impossible for any natural sword.

And when, to teach himself to bear the hardest of blows,
Roland sent her blade against stone, he learned that even rock
surrendered to her might. Shattered or split, as Durandal's
hum of appetite became a singing resonance of triumphant
power.

Nor did the edges of her blade ever chip, or dull by so
much as a thought of the mind. Welcome, magic . . .

Then, slowly, Roland came to realize that he had not seen

the white owl since the finding of the dark sword. No longer
did he ever feel the watchful spirit consciousness that had
perturbed him before. Only silence and normal rustlings.

Could it be, he wondered, that the white owl had fulfilled its
purpose? For Durandal seemed to have been wrought for him.

He did not know, when the dark sword was in his hand, that
the stone blank eyes of the woman hilt changed to gleaming
perception.

"Our business here is concluded for the time. All is secured as well as may be . . ." Charlemagne sighed and relaxed in the saddle, letting his destrier pick its way across a
meadow toward a dip into woodland. "Now we must go
north. Word comes to us of Saxon raids. God's blood! But
they seem to spring from the very mouth of Hell in endless
quantity, these heathen!" Beside him, on a white horse, his
face partially shaded by the wide cowling of his cloak, the
Pontiff nodded.

"Aye," Adrian said slowly. "God wages eternal war with
Satan for the souls of men. Still, Lombardy is secured for
Christendom now. Thou hast wrought well, Charles. Desiderius had much involvement with the Infidels of the Hispanic
peninsula, we have learned of late." He inclined his head
toward the wiry monk, also with his hood drawn over his
head, who rode at his flank upon a dun mule. "And now his
hold is broken beyond repair."Charlemagne glanced briefly
at the other priest, roughly attired in loose brown robe and
sandals, face concealed by both hood and humbled aspect,
and thought of another mentioning of infidel. He shifted to
scan the countryside that shimmered under the blazing summer sun.

Reaching a rise, he brought his destrier to a halt at the crest
beneath the shade of a stand of trees.

"It was never so simple as spreading furs upon a stone
floor, this dispersing of God's enlightenment!" he commented dryly.

Adrian met his gaze. "What would be the worth in that?"
the Pope countered gently. Charlemagne smiled fleetingly.
They understood each other well, he and this new Pontiff, he
thought. But Adrian was no longer looking at him. Instead,
he stared in the direction of an elusive triumphant ringing
sound in the distance. "What is that? we wonder," Adrian

murmured. Both saw the grey horse that grazed some distance away in the rocky meadow below.

A few yards beyond, the figure of a man was apparent, wielding something long and dark against one of the many boulders in the area.

Again, the figure struck, and again, they heard that eerie clarion ringing.

Adrian met Charlemagne's eyes. "What manner of man is it, we wonder," he murmured, "that battles the very earth?" With that, he put heels to horse and sent the white palfrey galloping down the hill toward the figure. Charlemagne followed, and the wiry monk coaxed his mule to a peculiar amble.

Sighting them, the man figure quickly slipped the weapon against his back and strode the few steps needful to recover his grey horse. Intent on flight, it appeared.

"Hold!" the Pontiff called out, and the shabby young man, half-mounted, desisted. Charlemagne's face went stern as he recognized . . . He drew rein beside the Pope.

Roland paled beneath sweat sheen as he recognized the gold and white of papal robes. He bowed.

"Verily—little more than a boy!" Adrian's well-modulated voice revealed curiosity. "How art thou named, child?" Afraid to look at the King, yet acutely aware, Roland warily looked up into the shadowed face of the Pope, caught at once by wide, generous grey eyes.

"Holiness," he managed. "I am Roland—the Bastard. Servant to Lord Oliver De Montglave," he added. Adrian nodded and continued to look at him with far too much interest.

"What weapon hast thou, Roland the Bastard, that thou must use to battle stone?" he asked. Roland hesitated, glancing at the King who appeared to show neither remembrance, nor interest. Then, reluctantly, he drew Durandal from her place at his back and held the dark sword horizontally before him, hilt in his right hand, the extraordinary blade resting upon the palm of his left. He bowed his head and flushed.

Behind the Pope, the wiry monk also looked upon the dark sword, then he shifted to stare at the Pope with an unusual intensity well concealed by the shadows of his hood.

"Unusual weapon . . ." Adrian murmured fascination. "But I know little of swords and the like." His voice cleared, and he raised a hand to make the sign of the Cross over

Roland's head. "May God in His wisdom bring thee, Roland
the Bastard, to a like and unusual accomplishment on His
behalf," he intoned solemnly. "God bless thee through Our
Savior, Jesus Christ."

"God's will be done!" Roland whispered fervent gratitude
for this generosity and felt the hilt of Durandal shift a little
within his hand. "For God and Charlemagne!" he dared, and
looked up. The Pope smiled and nodded, and Roland watched
as the white palfrey carried the Pontiff away, the King and
the other beside him, as they disappeared over another rise.

The King—who did not even look at him. Roland swallowed and looked down at Durandal in his hands. Brilliant
intonations of blue lightning slithered along the blade, and
he started at the frown on the elfin face above his hand.

"Whyfore should thou mislike a blessing such as were His
Holiness' gift to us?" he addressed the sword without thinking. The expression did not change. Roland frowned in
turn. "Lord Oliver said thou art a heathen thing," he said
more sternly. "But thou are given to serve my will, and I am
sworn to Charlemagne! Know that, for it will never change!
God will surely bring us glory to such intent!" He looked up
to stare at an empty horizon . . .

"Jesu," he whispered hungrily. "But why must it take so
long?"

Some half mile distance from where he had left the tall
boy, Adrian slowed his horse to a walk and glanced at Charlemagne. That most renowned of princes looked particularly
grim and closed-faced.

"That is no common squire, I'll warrant!" Adrian said
slowly, looking ahead once more. "And if I am not misled
in my thinking, he hath uncommon size for a boy of fifteen—
a certain lengthiness, as though he hath of late begun to come
into manhood!" Charlemagne regarded him sharply. Well
aware of this, Adrian continued to stare ahead. "He hath the
coloring of thy sister, Berthe, as I recall. God rest her soul!"
he added deliberately.

Charlemagne's face whitened and grew very harsh. "How
could thou know?" he grated, glancing back to the monk
who was prodding his mule to catch up, too far behind to
hear.

"God hath endowed me with the gift of fastidious mem-

ory!'' Adrian crossed himself. ''Blessed be His Name!'' He
looked at the King's drawn face. ''Art thou so haunted by thy
sin, Charles?'' he asked softly. Charlemagne did not answer,
but stared ahead for a time. Adrian waited.

''Aye,'' the King whispered at last. ''I have got no other
sons. No legitimate heir.''

''God help this Bastard Prince thou hast wrought, then,''
Adrian commented quietly. Charlemagne looked at him, eyes
widening a little. ''He hath much love for thee, I consider.
It was apparent.''

''He is uncommon willful!'' Charlemagne growled.

Adrian smiled ruefully. ''As thou were, I do remember,
when his age!'' he remarked. ''And—without Bastard to mar
thy name.'' A tinge of color swept across Charlemagne's hard
cheeks as he received this reminder of his own youth—the
confession he had brought before the priest Adrian had been
then. There had been no penance, nor absolution.

''Berthe is dead?'' Adrian asked in the same quiet tone.
The King nodded.

''With her lord,'' the King whispered.

''The boy does not know?'' Charlemagne's silence was
affirmation.

''It is a miracle, then, that he is not lost,'' Adrian murmured thoughtfully. ''But then, God's ways are ever mysterious. I have oft thought that the common path is not for
favored men. Nor is God's intent with them of an ordinary
disposition.'' Charlemagne's eyes met those of Saint Peter's
heir. Adrian, he realized, would reveal nothing of what he
knew. Of what had passed between them. Gently, the older
man raised his right hand and made the sign of the Cross
over the King with particular elegance.

''God give thee peace, my son,'' he said earnestly. ''And,
a most—clear—knowledge of His will.''

A.D. 773—774

It was a rested and eager army that marched north through
the mountainous parts of western Lombardy, then back across
the high passes of the Alps, down into the Rhone Valley.
From there they traveled north through the rolling meadows

and wide stretches of hardwood forest that marked that part of the Frankish realm.

Midsummer passed. Fledgling birds left their nests. The season's crop of new born wild creatures grew to resemble their elders. The green of trees and shrubs and grasses lost their verdant freshness and became mature as the first hints of the coming season slipped into summer's rich fulfillment. The odd leaf withered upon a branch. Seed appeared on tall stems to ripen in the sun. There was fruit to be plucked in passing. Wild grapes and berries . . .

Reaching the high country from which the Rhone were sprung, the army marched straight toward Aix La Chapelle. The signs of late summer harvest were apparent as they passed small villages and larger manors. Cows were fat with well grown calves. Sheep were indistinguishable from lambs, and all the strips of planting revealed the first incursions of the harvester's scythe.

Rumors of Saxon pillaging grew increasingly commonplace as Charlemagne moved his forces into the lower, gentler lands near Aix La Chapelle, then, with barely a halt, swung them east to confront the great Rhine river.

Encamped upon the shores of the river as autumn made its first appearance, interweaving gold with green, the army confronted the task of felling trees and lashing them into great rafts that, when put into the river, were to form a great, floating bridge. Then, in a slow stream of its own, men and horses and baggage were moved across the river to establish a guarded base upon the eastern shore.

Marching east, the work of the Saxon raiders became obvious along this northern periphery of Charlemagne's realm. Villages, cautiously passed, revealed charred ruins and bloated, crow picked corpses; mute testimony to the savagery that had occurred. Livestock was gone, taken, like anything else of value, for booty. Women also . . . The aged, the men, and the children had all been slaughtered. Some gruesomely crucified to trees or the remains of buildings.

Roland had found the long days and weeks of the northward march to be a welcome relief from serving the more idle requirements of his lord. More, the hope of war, of opportunity, lay ahead. But, having reached the northern frontier, he found things very different from his first experience of the encounter between two great armies.

It was strangely sobering to sit astride his fit, grey horse and stare about at the destruction that had been unleashed upon essentially defenseless people, and yet to see no other evidence of the foe. To feel the growing temper of Charlemagne's men from witnessing so much outrage as they salvaged where they could. And where they couldn't, they buried the dead.

Listening carefully, he learned from the talk between Lord Oliver and his boon companion, Sir Florismart. There were the Saxons from the east, the Danes from the immediate north, and a newer, even more savage type of barbarian from the frozen wastes near the northern edge of the world. Vikings. Allies through their worship of the same heathen gods. Saxon and Dane sought plunder as well as conquest. But the Vikings sought conquest through complete destruction alone. Like wolves, they were fond of night fighting. Like wolves, these berserkers roamed about in small, elusive packs . . .

Roland, at Lord Oliver's flank, stopped his horse to stare at the ruins of a monastery set against a nearby, forested hill. He stared at the single, mutilated body tangled in the remains of a coarse, brown robe that lay on the path toward it. Half dismembered. White bone jutted through butchered flesh. All that remained of a monk given to peace and charity and worship. Roland stiffened abruptly realizing that Lord Oliver was staring at him, rather than the corpse.

"I pray, most earnestly," Lord Oliver said very quietly, "that thy heathen weapon will consent to draw blood from its own kind!"

Roland went rigid, eyes glittering.

"It is governed by a Christian hand, my lord!" he retorted immediately. "I am a Christian man!"

De Montglave continued to look at him with unwavering calm. "Do thou claim so, Bastard?" he asked mildly. "It is a point of question!" With that, he spurred his horse to the gallop and lunged away, barking orders to his men. Roland had no option but to follow.

He did not see the concerned frown that accompanied Sir Florismart's glance in his direction.

As Charlemagne directed, the army swung east, riding along the hills and heavily forested high ground that was the southern border of the plains and coastal lands to the south of Daneland. Keeping the advantage of high ground and using the forests for partial concealment, the King moved firmly into Saxon territory. He dispatched men to scout the foe and, upon learning something of their positions, split his forces into two great bodies to form both flank and pincer around encampments and settlements discovered to be south and west of Daneland.

The first battle was little more than slaughter as Charlemagne pushed north with one branch of his army beyond the perimeter of his own battered frontiers. Christian knights and soldiers descended with brutal ferocity upon a Saxon village set on a hill in marshy country. Surrounded by a palisade of wooden stakes and half moated by treacherous swamp, it was clearly a permanent settlement.

Nothing deterred Charlemagne's forces. Archers bombarded the village with fire arrows that soon set straw thatch roofs aflame. Great beams were brought to bear on the outer walls, making openings for eager knights on destriers trained and willing to trample and strike.

The defenders, sorely outnumbered, had little chance, and it was a short, deadly battle.

Roland, bitterly resentful of the order that had relegated him to wait with the supplies, ventured from that place as soon as the outcome was assured, and soon found his lord. De Montglave and Sir Florismart sat their horses, swords still drawn and bloody, near the King as survivors of the battle were herded together in what had been the center of the village. Women and children for the most part, Roland saw at once. Some old people, few young men. Moving to flank his lord, Roland saw Lord Oliver nod acknowledgment as Charlemagne's order rang out across them all.

There were to be no prisoners. Not even the children. Foot soldiers began at once, with short lances and daggers. Screams and wailing cries pierced the air as bodies tumbled one by one.

Roland stared at one soldier as the man seized a babe by the heels, wrenching it from its mother, then smashing it against a post, blood and brains spilling out . . .

"Ah, Sweet Jesu!" Lord Oliver whispered strangely and swung his horse about, face gone ashen pale. "I have no stomach for such as this!" Roland stared at him in astonishment, entirely distracted. Oliver caught his look and met it grimly. "Does this please thee, Bastard?" he grated.

"It is war," Roland offered simply. Then Lord Oliver was beside him, glaring furiously in a way he had never seen before.

"War, Bastard?" De Montglave snarled. "Needful or nay, this is not war! Battle is one thing. But this—this is butchery, and I am not so distempered as to find either honor or satisfaction in such as this!" Roland's face hardened reflexively, and this seemed to anger Lord Oliver the more. "It is that lack of such fastidiousness, Bastard, that declares thee common!" he growled and thrust his horse past Roland, away from the massacre.

Roland followed, filled with pure hate.

Sir Florismart exhaled in relief as the Bastard departed Lord Oliver's tent, his duties complete for the night.

"He is a viper, that one!" He turned to his friend. "I would not trust the safety of my meanest hound to him, let alone give my person to his service!" Oliver sighed and leaned back against his furs. Sir Florismart pursued it. "It is evident that he hates thee. Why do thou bear it, Oliver? Surely, it would be better to give him elsewhere, or dispatch . . ."

"Nay, Floris," Oliver said firmly, then sipped mead. He looked at his cup and shook his head. "Nay, Floris," he repeated more softly. "He is mine . . ."

"That one? I will dispute it, Oliver. He is wild, or worse!"

"I grant the tiresomeness of his manner . . ." Oliver began.

"I fail to understand this peculiar tolerance thou hast for him," Florismart said sharply. "In any other it would not be bourne. Thou, who may have thy pick of worthy servants, better by far than . . ." His eyes widened suddenly, and he went on more slowly. "I grant his looks, but I had thought . . ."

"Correctly, Floris!" Oliver said firmly. "I have no such appetite, my friend. That which we knew once, thou and I— it was a part of boyhood ignorance long past discarded!"

The other flushed a little, his face abruptly vulnerable. "So I was given to understand."

"It is truth," Oliver said very quietly. "I know thy preference, Floris. But that has naught to do with friendship."

"I had thought . . ."

"Because I am fastidious in my wenching? That I have another interest in Roland?" Oliver shook his head. Drank again. "Nay, Floris. I confine my appetite because I do not wish to sire a flock of bastards." His friend frowned. Oliver spoke firmly then. "He is my servant, and that is all."

Florismart subjected Oliver to a penetrating stare. "Yet," he said slowly. "I consider that there is some reason that thou do persist in this unnatural tolerance of him?"

Oliver shrugged. "He does as he is bid," he said noncommittally, drinking once more.

"Barely!" Florismart retorted. "Nay, Oliver. I am not persuaded."

Oliver glanced at him for a moment, then looked away. "Consider this then, my friend," he said very softly. "Mayhap it is possible that the Bastard was unjustly used these months past. That he did accomplish that which he claimed, and sought and killed Desiderius of Lombardy."

Florismart stared. "Never say so!" he exploded. "That is impossible, Oliver! He hath not the skill." He frowned, then laughed by turn. "Thou have grown fanciful."

Oliver shrugged, then smiled agreeably. "Mayhap. 'Tis certain that he serves as useful reminder to the full scope of Christian charity!" he said lightly, grinning ruefully at his friend.

"Pah! What philosophical rot eats thy wits now?" Florismart muttered disgust.

Oliver, still smiling, sank down amid his furs and closed his eyes with a long sigh. "Does it matter?" he murmured.

His friend studied him for a time, then settled down to his own rest. Like others, he had a profound, if sometimes bewildered, admiration for Lord Oliver's almost scholarly, fastidious attention to the finest particulars of honor and justice. The Bastard must be some other exercise in the same, he decided at length.

SIX

Harsh autumn winds and cold gales blew in from the northern seas. Leaves turned red and gold, then brown, and tumbled from the trees. Green shrank back toward the earth, leaving grasses and the like to stand, rumpled and straw-colored. Chill fogs swirled through the low places, across the marshes and through gullies and valleys, bringing damp and bitter silence—and ague.

Charlemagne led his forces north, like a knife, along the perimeter of the Saxon territory, wreaking havoc and butchery upon one settlement and village after another, determined to drive the heathen back. But the Saxons themselves became elusive, melting back into the wild, unpassable places as though they had never been. The King hunted leaders, chiefs and princes. But none was to be found. Only old men, old women, and the youngest of children. Nowhere were there armies to confront in honest conflict.

And torture served only to wring minimal information from captives that were later killed for expediency's sake.

Reaching the grey sea to the south and east of Daneland, Charlemagne marched his troops south, sealing the winter bulwarks he had established in the high forests where his attacks had begun, for the winter.

With a nominal escort, he departed to attend to affairs in other parts of his realm, leaving the whole to the command of Lord Ganelon.

"Do as thou are able," he instructed his Champion, "to establish our dominion here. In the spring we will return with reinforcements and fresh supplies."

Under Lord Ganelon's capable rule, war was continued in neatly executed forays that put pressure upon the next lines of Saxon habitation.

Then the night raids began.

Shielded by darkness, small predatory bands of heathen came to pick and harry at the flanks and rear of Charlemagne's army. A sudden, isolated death scream was enough to send all to instant readiness. More often, killed silently, a body was found here or there, in the morning. Sometimes, a dead horse. Fires erupted among needed supplies, or within the compounds of hastily built, defensive fortifications.

With aid from their Viking allies, Saxon retaliation grew increasingly brutal and unpredictable. Yet, of the foe, there was still no sign. No sign at all.

Only the howling of wolves in the distance, eerie, singing cries that wafted like melancholy spirit voices upon the wind.

Or bird calls, fey and soft, that could not be natural.

The first frosts came to lace the trees and mist the ground with silver delicacy, pressaging the winter snows to follow. Roland, given to guard his lord during the dark hours, found another frigid bitterness in the looks that were cast toward him. Christian men now saw heathen things in him. They became wary with new suspicions, and hungry to attack and destroy the magic they seemed, of a sudden, to perceive in him. Only the cloak of Lord Oliver's protection shielded him. But he could not be grateful for it.

Losses grew. Supplies diminished as winter encroached. Hunting and foraging became essential risks.

"Haaarrrgh!" Sir Florismart put spurs to his horse, shouting as he lowered his lance and charged through the undergrowth in pursuit of a large boar. Lord Oliver, with a grin of delight, set out after him, riding recklessly at an angle that would bring him ahead to turn the beast. A squeal was heard. And another, indicating a whole herd of wild pig. Lord Ganelon likewise pursued with a triumphant shout, with his nephew and squire, Thierry of Leon, at his flank in hot-passioned determination to keep pace with the hunt.

Roland, burdened by the lead rope of a pack animal carrying the carcass of a large doe, brought along to carry such other game as was found, could not hope to keep pace. Still, he prodded his grey to drag the pack animal into a trot as he followed the crashing sounds and eager cries through the woods.

Frost chilled the air, and cold branches stung as he swept through them, down a steep bank, across a small stream, to lunge up, through heavy undergrowth toward a clearing some distance ahead from whence came the echoes of high-pitched squealing and triumphant shouts.

Around a high bank—Roland jerked on his horse's bridle as he caught a gleam of something brilliant to his left. Then a face. He ducked as an arrow hummed past to lodge itself in the bole of a large tree to his right, and looked again. Aye—a face. Bearded and framed by a steel helm adorned with hawk wings on either side. Another arrow nicked his stallion and set it to plunging. It was instinct to drop the lead rope and reach for Durandal.

He set the grey to bolt up the bank.

Saxon, or Dane, or Viking . . . it mattered not. The group of hunters had been discovered by foe concealed hereabouts. The dark sword hummed with a predatory keening as he swung her and set the grey to charge down, straight into the underbrush where he glimpsed another face.

Around a tree—and the man took flight.

Suddenly there was a great shout. Roland understood and abandoned his chase, spinning the stallion to charge toward the rest.

The lords, dismounted to bind the dead boar and the sow that had also been speared, looked up and raced for their horses, taken entirely by surprise as heathen swarmed down upon them from the underbrush where they had been concealed. Barbarians with axes and longswords. Then horsemen on great shaggy beasts.

Roland erupted down a bank and charged across the flank, bellowing.

"For God and Charlemagne!" He swung the dark sword with all the savagery of his soul. She danced to bite through a back. Through a helm. Shattered a spear. She sang keening, triumphant lust as she cut through an arm. Roland brought his stallion around in a series of well-practiced kick-

ing leaps that trampled and smashed those about him who
were afoot.

The boar forgotten, Lord Oliver and Sir Florismart found
their horses and leaped up to flank each other and hack about
them with the desperate ferocity of the badly outnumbered.
Lord Ganelon and his nephew formed another pair close by.
Horses squealed and kicked as barbarian swords nicked flanks
and sides. Roland, apart from the rest, felt himself become
a whip of urgency and blood lust as he half guided, half
followed the wonder of the dark sword that sliced with im-
pervious ease through flesh, or hides, or metal. Find the
head—find the head—and the body is easily vanquished! It
was the single clarion summons that drove him as he spun
the grey about, and saw an elusive figure emerge from the
trees high on the steep bank on the far side of the stream. A
giant, grinning man on a monstrous horse of gold, began to
charge down upon the lords.

Roland roared at the grey, and it bolted past the beset
Christian knights, leaping bodies, then reached the stream.
With absolute clarity, Roland brought the dark sword back
and jerked, sending the grey across the stream in a gigantic
leap that carried them well onto the opposite bank, directly
in the path of the gold monster, which leaped . . .

The grey screamed and crumpled, blood spewing forth
from between its ears as the giant jerked his longsword clear,
seemingly unaware of the long gash Durandal had made
through his deerskin-clad thigh. Roland jerked himself loose
from the thrashing dead animal. Found his feet as the gold
horse landed in midstream, then turned. He crouched and
grinned, Durandal vibrant in his hand, his eyes locked with
the venomous grey stare of the giant.

With a roar of rage, the giant set the gold horse at the bank.
It snorted and leaped. Roland jumped to one side, half sliding
in the mud, bringing Durandal up in a fierce lunge.

Like his will, she leaped, straight for the giant's ring-plated
body, exposed by his upraised arm, and struck, with all Roland's strength behind her, through steel, and ribs. He jerked.

Out again, into an arc. Roland ducked a large hoof and
slipped on wet leaves, his next blow lost in a tumble that
brought him down to the edge of the stream. He grunted,
found his feet, and leaped upward. But the giant's face fell
in astonishment as blood gurgled in his throat and bubbled

forth from his mouth. His longsword was easily dodged as it fell from nerveless fingers. The gold horse stopped as it felt its rider go slack, then fall.

Roland howled triumph and lunged for the beast. He grabbed the bridle and swung himself astride the great monster. The horse squealed in temper, bucked. But Roland pulled its head up and roared again, then set it to lunge down toward the other heathen.

They turned, and some, seeing their lord was fallen, cried out. Others noted the golden-headed boy, heard the unnatural violence of his shout, and saw the dark sword. They felt the presence of magic, and fled.

Lord Ganelon, with a roar of rage, gave brief pursuit, then gave it up, for as quickly as they had come, the barbarians were vanished.

The gold stallion bucked and squealed savagely as Roland forced it, with a blow from his fist, toward the group of lords. Then as abruptly as it had begun, the horse's fit ceased, and it stood, heaving and quiet. Panting, Roland looked up to see Lord Ganelon and Lord Oliver bring their horses together. Sir Florismart sat grey-faced and rigid, his left side covered with blood that trickled down. Roland stared grim-faced at Lord Ganelon who was breathing heavily in the silence amid the scattered heathen corpses. Slowly, under the Champion's dark scrutiny, he slipped Durandal from view in her place at his back. It was Lord Oliver who spoke.

"That was well accomplished, Bastard," he said, then glanced at Leon. "Thou also, lad. And we have the meat besides!"

"Well said, my lord." The Champion exhaled agreement, looking about him with a frown. Sir Florismart gasped painfully and bent slowly over his pommel. Lord Oliver paled and lunged to catch his friend.

"Nay—Floris!" he called out. "Haste. We must get back."

Lord Ganelon gave Roland a dagger look. "What ails thee, Bastard?" he snarled. "Do thou need reminder to thy duty?" He spun his horse about to lead the way, sword still drawn. "Thierry, hitch the meat to that pony and follow."

Roland, scowling once more, clenched his teeth and brought the ill-tempered gold horse to flank Sir Florismart's other side. He caught the knight, as Sir Florismart wobbled

toward him, and held on. Lord Oliver's eyes were startling
with fear as he looked up. Roland looked away.

He cared not, he thought, if this one among so many who
despised him was to die. They were all enemies.

The encampment reached, aid was soon brought to carry
Sir Florismart to Lord Oliver's tent. De Montglave barked
orders with uncommon ferocity, and Roland, after tethering
the horses to the attentions of others, went into his lord's tent
to give whatever service was required.

Stripped of armor and clothing, Sir FLorismart lay amid
the cushioning of soft furs, breathing with great rasping awk-
wardness. Lord Oliver himself held linen pressed to his
friend's side.

"My lord?" Roland inquired tersely.

Lord Oliver did not look at him. "Here. Use this and bind
the arm. He bleeds to death and we must prevent . . ."

"Nay!" Florismart said with remarkable clarity, his eyes
turned to his friend. "I am a dead man . . ." He gasped,
then coughed violently, blood oozing from the corner of his
mouth, then closed his eyes, panting in exhaustion, a film of
cold sweat gathering to make his fair hair cling to his forehead.

"Not thee . . ." Lord Oliver's voice rasped. "Floris?"
Roland knelt and reached to press a linen pad against the
wound that had half severed Sir Florismart's shoulder.

"Fair Oliver . . ." The dying man's eyes opened, and he
found strength enough to lift a hand and lightly touch Lord
Oliver's cheek for a moment, before it sank back down. De
Montglave's face was ashen, haggard—his eyes terrible.
"Thou cannot—know how well—I love thee," Sir Florismart
whispered. Roland stared, hard-faced.

"Floris . . . ?" The knight blinked, stared at Roland for
a moment, his brows flickering as though puzzled. Then he
coughed more blood. Roland went rigid under that peculiar
look, but Sir Florismart shifted his gaze to his friend.

"I think I understand why . . ." he managed, eyes widening slowly as they found Roland's face again. "I caution
thee . . . He—he is not human." Then he arched painfully,
gasped, and stared at nothing. "I had not thought—it would—
darken so!" His voice was a husky rattling now. And Roland
felt the blood drain from his own face as he froze. Not hu-

man? "Pray—Sweet Jesu and all the saints—to intercede for the—absolution of my soul—and the forgiveness—of my sins. Oliver . . . ?" The last was a thread that became lost in a gurgling rattle, then faded into silence. The knight's body went lax, and Roland crossed himself, watching as the last traces of color fled Sir Florismart's face to leave behind a marble complexion. Then the mouth slowly opened. The eyes were blank, void, the soul most clearly gone.

Lord Oliver, to Roland's astonishment, reached for the body and drew it into his arms, held the head against him, and hunched into open weeping.

"Floris, God keep thee . . ." Roland jerked to his feet, then slipped away unnoticed. Beyond the intolerability of witnessing such open grief, something inside felt raw and miserable and terrified. A dying man's words . . .

"I am a man . . ." he whispered desperately to the darkness of a cold night much, much later. "I bleed. I hunger. I will die like the rest. Bastard got or nay, I am a man. I have a soul." He waited.

But the night was still. Not even a breeze stirred the frozen air as snowflakes tumbled lightly from opaque black skies to settle like silver mystery on all around him.

It was a silence of absolute clarity. Not even a whisper from some saint, or the Savior, to affirm a faith that was infinitely more fragile than Roland's fealty to King Charlemagne.

The next morning, Roland stood with stone-cast features behind his lord as the body of Sir Florismart, cleaned and clad in his finest attire, was gently lowered into the grave that had been dug with much effort in the frozen ground. A priest's voice spread simple blessing upon the body and soul of the dead man, and over the company gathered about. De Montglave was the one to kneel and set Sir Florismart's own sword in his stiff white fingers before the first earth was dropped to cover the body.

Too deep for wolves, Roland thought, and looked up to see Lord Ganelon staring at him. Studying him. Roland met the look. The others disappeared to attend to the essentials of grim winter warfare. Lord Ganelon's gaze shifted.

"I am given to think, my lord Oliver," he said with slow regret, "that—had thy servant sought his place, such a gallant and noble knight would not be lost." Again? Roland clenched his teeth and stared at distant trees.

"Nay, my lord," he heard De Montglave's equable voice. "We were thoroughly beset. Though we must grieve, I consider we must think ourselves blessed. God took only one and hath preserved the rest. The boy did well enough. As did thine own squire." His voice shifted to sincere enthusiasm as he turned to consider Thierry of Leon. He smiled. "In fact, my lord, I do think that young Leon has truly won his spurs." That youth flushed his pleasure as Lord Oliver inclined his head courteously and strode away.

Shoulders braced, Roland followed. With his grey horse now dead, he realized grimly, there would be less opportunity than ever to prove himself. Not that—as it seemed—any endeavor of his would be acknowledged for its true worth. If at all.

"I have not yet dismissed thee, Bastard!"

Roland froze as his hand reached for the tent flap. He turned, frowning, because he had left nothing undone. "My lord?"

Lord Oliver did not look at him, but continued to recline as he had for some time, sipping wine, staring with fixed and grim sobriety at the flame of the tallow candle that lit the interior of the tent.

"Over there." De Montglave pointed toward his arms. "That armor I got with thee. Fetch it here." Puzzled, Roland did as he was bid and stood before his lord holding hauberk and leggings, gauntlets, helm and coif of priceless craftsmanship. Lord Oliver studied the things, then looked up.

"Do thou arm thyself with these, Bastard," De Montglave said quietly. "I give them to thy use. Likewise that other horse thou hast got."

"My lord?" Roland's eyes widened in astonishment. Then he glared in suspicion. De Montglave returned his gaze to the wavering flame.

"Thou will fight with me in battle from this time forth," he said tonelessly. Then, on a drier note. "Do I dare to trust thee capable of keeping thy place?" Roland could not respond. Instead, he stared and felt something like a shudder pass through his frame.

Lord Oliver looked up. "Well . . . ?"

"Why—my lord?" Roland managed.

Oliver arched one neat brow and met his look. "I am given to remember that thou hast a modicum of training at arms," he said dryly. "There was some evidence of it yesterday. Nor am I given to waste any, even somewhat capable man during the hard winter war that lies ahead!" Roland felt his face freeze. "Hast thou naught to say, Bastard?" De Montglave demanded after a moment. It was Roland who looked away.

"Nay, my lord!" he said in a hard voice.

"Go then!" Lord Oliver grated, frowning. Roland spun on his heel, then stopped by the entrance to the tent as De Montglave's voice caught him once more.

"Do thou serve me ill in any way, Bastard," he growled lethal promise, "and I will flay the skin from thy body myself!" Roland scowled and did not either turn or reply. Instead, with a deliberate breach of courtesy, he strode from the tent into the night.

Even bastards had a sense of honor.

In the worsening weather that followed, Lord Ganelon moved the army continually as he guarded the northern frontiers of Charlemagne's realm, resorting to every effort to keep Saxon, Dane, and their allies thrust back, to prevent them from using the potential winter respite to replenish themselves.

Battles were fought with unrelenting frequency, as hereto unseen heathen forces emerged with berserker ferocity from blizzard and thicket, crevice and drift, to engage the Christian army and drive it back. Other villages fell, their stores seized. Captured horses were slaughtered, oft as not, for meat. Hunting had become nearly impossible. Hunger became a grim threat.

Lord Oliver De Montglave revealed his continued grief over the loss of his friend with an unrelenting determination and savagery in battle that soon brought him heroic, near legendary renown. There were none who did not willingly, even eagerly, serve the puissant and gallant champion he had become. And, as a result, Roland found that in some ill defined fashion, opportunity had, at last, come to him.

Ignored by all, Roland's entire being focused on the fighting he was now permitted to do with a single-mindedness that excluded every other thought, or doubt, or feeling. He conquered the monstrous, vile-tempered gold stallion with equal dedication, and relished the sweet weight of the armor he now constantly wore. And, above all, he savored the virulent, lethal magic of the dark sword, the death songs of her arcs and lunges that reflected most perfectly his own soul.

He kept his place behind, and then after a time, beside Lord Oliver, both because of the dictates of an honor that could not be bent, nor broken, and because of his own, unrelenting dedication to the single goal of besting the other man by any means short of the direct confrontation that would brand him traitor.

And, between them during the infrequent times of reprieve, there fell a new and bitter silence. Not even the most curtly given orders would draw from Roland any acknowledgment beyond a brisk, hard nod of his head. Anything else was not responded to at all, and Lord Oliver himself abandoned any nicety of address.

"I do marvel, my lord," Roland overheard Lord Ganelon remark once, "that thou are willing to trust thy back to such serpent glarings sufficient to arm that sullen heathen thus!" Lord Oliver had not glanced back. Instead, he had responded casually.

"He serves, my lord! 'Tis better to use Satan's perversity against his own heathen devils, I think, in these times of trial." Overheard by more than one, it became another fathom in the well of Roland's bitterness. Beyond the ambiguity and disgrace of bastardy, there were rumors sprung up around him concerning other, unnatural aspects of his origin. Fed by the sight of him in unadorned mail upon the heathen gold horse, and by the single, awful weapon that he carried, even common foot soldiers drew away when he strode through their midst. Some crossed themselves. None offered speech, or sustenance of any kind.

Roland's stewardship over his silence and isolation became absolute.

Winds and wolves howled together through the harsh time of midwinter, sirens and sisters to heavy snowfalls and bitter cold. And if Charlemagne's forces were oft confined by blizzard conditions, so too were the heathen. Battles often became little more than skirmishes, or ambush and counterambush, all draining of lives and resources. Supplies diminished further.

Losses grew. Lives surrendered to frostbite and hunger, to wounds that festered beneath unchanged garments that could not be removed for the cold, and to war direct.

Wolves, emboldened by corpses left behind after each encounter and by bodies abandoned because it was impossible to dig graves for so many in the stone-hard ground, came close to the camps at night, sniffing the fresh meat of tethered and wary horses, suspicious of the seasoned men and fires that guarded them.

Compelled to hunting and foraging for meat and fodder, both sides preyed upon each other. Roland relished these little battles, seeking to kill more foe than any other man, roaring out the battle cry of them all. And while others hunted hare and deer and the like, he hunted the grey wolves for pelts as well as meat. Then, with his chain mail concealed beneath wolf furs and with a cloak of the same, he became a thoroughly savage sight.

So too, thought the Saxons who were fortunate enough to escape him after any given encounter. They learned to dread the very sight of him, this vile Christian lord who rode at them with the most terrible, dark, singing sword, who smiled as he killed. Was he Fenris the Wolf? Or, more likely, Tyr, the son of Odin? One of their own gods, manifest to turn against them . . . ? It was not possible, they speculated, for such a one with eagle-fierce golden eyes, to be a follower of this peculiar and meek southern god who hung in death upon a tree.

And, for those who followed Lord Oliver to witness the savagery of the Bastard, it seemed as if he was indeed, some perverse limb of Satan wreaking havoc upon his own.

Spring came at last, with warming weather and melting snows. Cold rains washed down hillsides, and ice-covered marshes became treacherous, impassable quagmires. The frontiers were held. And Lord Ganelon marched his worn army south to rendezvous with the fresh forces and supplies brought up by Charlemagne.

Grasses erupted, verdant and lush. Trees thickened and turned green. Wild flowers appeared like blessings, scattered across the countryside. Great flights of birds, duck, and geese were sighted as they flew north. And with knowledge of their hard-won triumph, the massive army, recovered and strengthened, marched north and east once more. This time, to conquest.

Fighting continually they pressed back the frontiers of Christendom, and began to claim the rich, heathen lands for godly men.

Then finally, the Saxons came with their first offers of truce.

"But surely, Majesty, we should continue, for we are well able?" Lord Ganelon asked fiercely, one hand upon a map spread before him. "These proposals of peace are but a ploy to gain the time they need to regroup and summon more allies from the north." He stared at the King who stood a little distance from him. Lost in his own thoughts, Charlemagne shifted a little, turned his clear gaze upon his Champion.

"We do not dispute their intent with thee, my lord, for we are given to conclude the same. Nonetheless—we have other considerations that must be balanced in the scales.

"Word has come to us of another demon that rears its head to the south of the Pyrenees. There is a new King of Saragossa called Marsilla. Likewise, we are given to know that he gathers a great army from all parts thereabouts, even from Africa where these worshippers of the devil Allah are arisen to an abundance second only to grains of sand in the desert from which they are sprung! That, my lord, is our other concern." Lord Ganelon nodded. He understood very clearly. Charlemagne continued, "This Emir Marsilla means to gather himself and march north to the conquest of our more fertile lands, bringing infidel ways and the worship of this false prophet Mohammed to overrun our lands." Lord Ganelon frowned now as well. North and south, there were serious foes at each of the two farthest borders of the realm.

"It is a sobering concern, Majesty," he acknowledged slowly. "The Basques and Gascons of the mountains thereabouts cause sufficient disturbance as it is. Yet they are Christian, and a much lesser problem. It is not certain that they would ally themselves with these Infidels."

"Aye," the King inserted briskly, "for all we have the loyalty, and person, of Roger of Roncesvalles among our company! Listen well, my lord. For thus, we propose to do.

"We will make truce with the Saxon for the present. More.

We too will use such respite well.'' Charlemagne paced restlessly now. Lord Ganelon watched him. ''We propose to build
strongholds along this new perimeter that is won, and garrison them well. From such position, we consider that it matters little which side breaks the peace!'' Charlemagne's eyes
were very clear as he met those of Lord Ganelon. The Champion smiled. Offered a slight bow.

''Of a certain, Majesty!'' he said softly. The King turned
away.

''To such end, we give thee full command of this frontier,
my lord. And, to facilitate thy duty to our will, we entitle
thee to higher post. Champion thou has been, Ganelon de
Maganze. Now thou are made our Lord High Councillor.''

''Majesty!'' Lord Ganelon breathed. Charlemagne smiled
slightly.

''Thus, thou are empowered to dispose our justice, in our
absence,'' he clarified. ''A fitting recognition.''

''Of a certainty, Majesty. I am awed!'' Lord Ganelon
bowed deeply and held himself thus for a moment, frozen by
Charlemagne's next dry comment.

''Awed? We know of none less prone to such emotion as
thee!'' Lord Ganelon straightened, his face carefully smooth.
But the King was no longer looking at him. Instead, he stood
very still and stared with unreadable gaze past the sunlight
that brightened the entrance to his tent. To the troops beyond.

''To thy careful stewardship and service, we will leave Lord
Roger of Roncesvalles. He is capable.'' Charlemagne went
on. ''But in need of opportunity to prove himself. In his
place, we will take Lord Oliver De Montglave.'' Lord Ganelon's face tightened. ''He is southern bred, and of loyal
people well endowed. His brilliance will serve us well.'' Like
a scent upon the air, Lord Ganelon thought, this sudden conviction that he was, in the guise of elevation, more tenuously
placed than ever before. With De Montglave gone—and the
Bastard . . . His mind moved quickly. Carefully.

''Majesty?'' He strode to face the King. ''I consider that I
may have something to offer that may be of considerable worth
to thine endeavor against this southern threat.'' Charlemagne
looked at him.

''Say it.''

''Of my wardships, Majesty, I am guardian of the great fief
of Bordeaux, until the infant Lord Huon comes to sufficient

age. The castle there is a mighty construction, and fitting rich. I consider to give its use to thee for a court that is better placed against these southern Infidel than Aix La Chapelle.''

The King nodded. ''We accept.''

Lord Ganelon found a smile, then let a more fragile expression slip across his features. ''One more thing I would ask of thee, Majesty?'' The King inclined his head. ''I would ask that my squire and nephew go south with thee to serve. He has grown well and learned, and, I think, is due to win his spurs. I would prefer, however, that the accolade does not come from me, but from some other hand.''

Charlemagne smiled genially, then. ''A little thing, we consider, Ganelon. Gladly given!'' Lord Ganelon bowed with immaculate precision. ''Leave us now,'' the King said gently. ''I will give young Leon to De Montglave's care.''

''Majesty!'' Lord Ganelon bowed again and slipped from the tent. It was exactly what he wished. Thierry had learned from him much more than war.

SEVEN

A.D. 774

Unlike the iridescent gleam of marble that made the great castle of Aix La Chapelle seem enchanted from a distance, the stronghold of Bordeaux rose up, stern and grey, as unmoving and permanent as a granite cliff against the purest blue of bright summer skies. Rare among castles, it was much more than single tower and wall. The great keep was buttressed by an adjoining array of secondary towers, and the whole was surrounded by high, impenetrably thick, crenellated walls.

Unmoving power. Lord Oliver drew rein as he emerged from the woods to give himself a few brief moments to view the castle across the meadows. It was, likewise, testament to both the wealth of the fiefs thereabouts with their lush fields and abundant harvests, and to the strength of the lords who resided there, rulers of this considerable domain in the very heart of Christendom.

There were no lords now. Duke Servinus was dead these pair of years past. And Oliver could remember clearly when his lady, the Duchess Alice, had come to court to give widow's duty to the King and seek the dispensation of his will.

She was regal, he remembered, with an uncommon beauty in her brown eyes and raven gleaming hair. And with the child heir beside her. His lips flickered ruefully. He had almost forgotten—what now felt like sapling time when he had conversed at length with her. And more. A mutual folly.

Private things, long put aside. But he had gained new understanding of the foibles and weaknesses of others. Floris, and his ways. He had been a good man for all of that. Oliver shifted in his saddle to look back behind him. Young Thierry of Leon served him now as squire direct. Young? Nay, they were near enough of an age. Yet Leon had something of uncertainty about him. A malleable type, Lord Oliver had concluded rapidly. But competent.

He sighed a little, face tightening as he considered his other—burden. The Bastard. Hard-faced and more remote than ever, Roland sat his great brute, holding the lead ropes of the pack horses that Oliver had relegated to his care. Nothing—nothing at all provoked even so much as the semblance of human civility from that one.

Oliver frowned in the annoyance that even the sight of the Bastard now invoked, and nudged his horse forward. Burden? Aye. That was true enough. The weight of responsibility for that one was becoming too much to bear!

Men at arms, alert upon the battlements with longbows at the ready as they rode across drawbridge and through portcullis, were the mark of a cautious and disciplined household, Oliver noted, glancing about him to see other indications of efficiency.

And the Duchess of Bordeaux stood upon the steps that led to the main keep, watching them. A proud figure in maroon skirts, the breeze stirred the cream of her veil to make a bright cloud against the somber grey of the stone behind her. One hand moved. An order was barked by the sergeant at arms, and Oliver suppressed a smile as he brought his stallion to a halt exactly halfway across the bailey.

He dismounted and passed his reins to Leon, then walked toward the steps, stopping at the bottom of them to bow with exquisite courtesy.

"My lady. I am De Montglave, sent by our liege lord, Charlemagne."

"My lord. I bid thee welcome." Firmly spoken. He looked up and felt a sense of shock. She was the same, he thought as she moved with remembered grace down the steps toward him. Yet she was matured. Sober in a different way. Smooth, pure features, and eyes that held things that had naught to do with youth at all.

"The King has sent me to bring thee word of his arrival here a sennight hence." Lord Oliver found refuge in completing his errand. Her eyes widened.

"Bordeaux is honored, my lord." Her voice was deep.

"There is more, my lady. It is the King's will to establish court here for a time of unspecified duration. I am sent to give such service as will enable all to be made ready for the King's accommodation and to such end." She looked at him.

"So be it, my lord. All will be made ready." She turned to the sergeant, a burly man of middle years who had moved closer with the air of one given to more than dutiful protectiveness. The Duchess was loved by her people, Oliver realized as she spoke softly to the man. He saluted crisply.

"My lady!" He strode away. She turned back to face Lord Oliver.

"Come, my lord, and have refreshment after thy journey. My steward will arrange quartering suitable for the King's emissary. And for thy servants . . ." Her gaze passed to the others.

"My thanks, my lady." Oliver glanced toward his squire and paused as he caught the look of venom on Roland's face as he stared rudely at the lady of Bordeaux. "My squire may reside with me," he said. "The other. He is best quartered with the horses!" The Duchess gave him a surprised look, then turned and, with a light sweeping of skirts, led the way into the interior of the keep.

"As thou will, my lord," she murmured. Oliver followed, suddenly aware of how remote she seemed to have become.

This impression was enhanced by the cool, unassailable dignity of her manner during the few days that followed. Though rank and duty sat him beside her in a place of honor during each evening feast, Lord Oliver found her conversation designed strictly to draw him into talking of himself, of campaigns and court and such things. For herself, she was unrevealing. And for the most part, his days were too filled with attention to the duties of preparing the way for the King to give much consideration to other things.

Remembered intimacies seemed incongruous now. Until, but a pair of days before the King's arrival, Lord Oliver came upon her seated upon a stone bench in a beautifully constructed arbor beside the keep, wherein were planted all manner of flowers and herbs. Needlework lay untended beside her.

A small boy with very dark hair and his mother's eyes rushed to stand before her, toy sword outthrust. She murmured something and the child bowed with great dignity.

"My lord . . ." Oliver smiled as he responded in kind. "I bid thee good day, my lady. My lord. Thou are Lord Huon, I consider . . . ?"

The child nodded. "I am, my lord." Another child toddled up at a precipitous run, stopped, and landed abruptly on his rump in the turf a little before Oliver's feet. Oliver's smile widened, and the yearling boy looked up to stare with eyes the color of summer seas. Soft tawny hair . . . Lord Oliver felt his amusement fade and dropped to one knee as the lady rose to reach for the child.

"Nay, my lady!" he said abruptly, and reached for the boy who smiled with delight and used small fingers to touch the fascinating gleam of the gold brooch that pinned Oliver's cloak to his shoulders. The boy cooed something undecipherable. But it was the smile—the look—the coloring. Oliver set him down carefully, shocked to his soul. Slowly, he rose to his feet and stared at the Duchess. She did not look at him, but busied herself collecting the child while the seven-year-old Huon watched them both.

"My lady . . . ?" Oliver felt the dryness of his mouth. She glanced at him, then turned away. "My lady Alicia . . . ?" Was that his own voice pleading? Oliver wondered. She stopped and faced him again, her gaze as composed as ever.

"This is my second son, my lord," she said deliberately. "Girard De Guienne." The name. It was the family name of the House of Bordeaux. Oliver swallowed. "I think thou must tire of women and children, my lord," she said as he stared, frozen. "This is a pleasant place. Do thou stay. I have other duties to attend." Then she was walking away, one child beside her. The other on her hip.

Nay? It could not be dead Servinus' seed! Oliver felt strangely hollow as he moved slowly to the forgotten scrap of embroidery. He picked it up and fingered it, then stared in the direction she had gone. The small boy had exactly his own coloring—and she had only the one child, that time past. Had she been early in pregnancy or . . . ? He had to know. Very slowly, Oliver folded the incomplete, yet exquisitely, embroidered kerchief into a neat, compact square, and slipped it into the front of his surcoat just above his waist. Then he turned and strode from the arbor to find relief, in other strenuous tasks.

He had to know.

But the Duchess of Bordeaux proved remarkably elusive for the day and a half that followed. Finally, with a feeling of desperation, Oliver sought the privacy of the tower steps that led to the chamber she had moved into as part of accommodating the King's intent to stay at Bordeaux. It was not too distant from the chamber he had been accorded, but well away from castle traffic.

There for more than an hour, he waited, leaning against stone, watching the last blue evening light melt away into the darkness of nightfall. Finally, he heard footsteps and a rustling and saw the glow of a tallow lamp. He stepped forward as she appeared on the landing a flight below.

"My lady?" He said it softly.

She started, and raised her lamp. "My lord! What doest thou here!"

"I would have private conversation with thee, my lady." Oliver moved a step closer, until he stood directly before her.

She found dignity at once. "Surely, my lord, there is no matter so pressing that it cannot await the morning . . ."

"The child," Oliver broke in. "Girard . . ." He could not bear to say the last name somehow. And his voice hoarsened. "He is—he is not got of thy late lord . . ."

She stared at him, face paling. "My lord!" She began to seek refuge in ire, but Oliver leaned closer.

"He is mine, I think," he whispered.

She looked down, away. "He has a name," she countered.

"But he is mine . . . ?" Oliver waited then. She inhaled deeply and stood very straight, her face changing as she struggled with her answer.

"Aye . . ." she barely whispered at last. Then, looking up at him. "He has a name, my lord, for it was his fortune to be born long before he was due." Oliver paled slowly as his eyes locked with hers. He felt somehow humbled as he realized what it had been like for her.

"Then he is blessed in his mother," he said very quietly. Her expression softened.

''The house of Guienne is much reduced,'' she said firmly. ''I am steward of both that name and great estate, and I must guard the honor of both with vigilance and fortitude. I will have Lord Huon come into his estate entire.'' Oliver nodded. He understood completely. ''Girard,'' she added very gently, ''will have a portion thereby.'' She searched his face, then passed on, and within moments had vanished from view.

Slowly, perturbed by feelings to which he was unaccustomed, Lord Oliver made his way to his own quarters, there to spend the night in restless brooding.

It was a restlessness that stayed with him during the first morning hours when, upon breaking his fast in the great hall in the company of the Lady Alicia, he found her manner discreetly softened toward him. Like early morning sunglow, there was an aura of warmth that hung upon the air. Something particular, and vastly different from his memory of that fleeting, nervously heightened encounter of before. Oliver sought refuge in amicable banter, and ordered his horse. Hunting, he knew, would provide both the release of activity and some needed solitude for further thought.

To his pleasure, the Duchess walked with him to the bailey, little Lord Huon striding with profound dignity beside her and, behind, her tirewoman holding the hand of young Girard.

Girard . . . his son. Part of himself. He inhaled deeply and caught the brutal frozen look on the Bastard's face as that other stood, rigidly holding his stallion and the bow and quiver he required.

Oliver took these and slung the bow upon his saddle pommel, then slipped the quiver over one shoulder.

''Prepare the kitchens, my lady, for I vow we will have fresh venison tonight!'' he said blithely as he mounted.

''Of a certainty, my lord!'' The lady smiled. Oliver began to respond with raised brows, then caught the hungry way small Lord Huon stared at his horse.

''I think thou wish to ride,'' he said very gently. The child nodded.

''Aye, my lord!'' he said fervently. Oliver smiled. Remembered, and understood.

''Then, I think, while I attend the King here, I may find

time to teach thee such," he said with sincere kindness.
"Horsemanship is best when mastered early."

"Thou are too kind, my lord," the Duchess responded.
Oliver shook his head, still looking at the delight in Huon's
dark eyes.

"Nay, my lady. It will be a pleasure." Just then, Girard
broke from his nurse's hold and bolted forward. Oliver jerked
his horse back, but the child veered and went, arrow true, to
clutch at Roland, who stood nearby.

Roland froze, and the small child stared up at him,
beamed delight, and crowed, "Fairy!" Roland jerked back,
appalled, but the child clung. "Heee . . . Fairy man!" he
sang out. It was pure reflex to reach and sling the child from
him, growling revulsion. The infant skidded across the court
and began howling.

Oliver did not even realize he had left his saddle until his
leap bore Roland to the ground and struck him a stunning
blow across the side of the head. "Bastard! Thou dare!" he
roared, and struck again as Roland writhed under him to twist
onto his back. "Never again! Seneschal!" Roland glared and
struggled to breathe as Lord Oliver's fist bore down upon his
windpipe. He heard the order and felt himself dragged up to
stand, caught by men and held.

He locked his teeth and met the fury in Lord Oliver's eyes
with all his long accumulated virulence.

"I will bear no more from thee!" Oliver roared, stepping
forward to cuff the side of Roland's face with ringing force.
"No more will I bear the disgrace of thy rabid manner! Nor,
upon *any* condition, will I bear such as thou have just done
from either man or beast under my rule!" Roland snarled
fury and tore himself loose from the men who held him,
found the dark sword, and, with lightning speed, drew it into
a down-sweeping arc that brought the humming, deadly point
to touch Lord Oliver's chest. De Montglave did not move a
muscle. Golden eyes locked with blue, and Roland tensed to
finish it.

"Do thou think to kill me with that witch's instrument,
Bastard?" Oliver's tone made Roland stop. "I tell thee, thou
are not fit, even for my murder!" Pricking De Montglave's
bliaut, the point went no farther as Roland paused unable to
draw his gaze away from the other, caught by a scathing
contempt that had naught to do with hatred at all. Dagger-

sharp in penetration, it was knowledge of himself. Nor was
there the faintest trace of fear in Lord Oliver's clear gaze.
Slowly, he removed Durandal's point from De Montglave's
chest, then slipped the weapon back into her usual place. He
stood rigid and glaring, brittle with a defiant pride that must
never be surrendered.

"Kill me then, and have done with it!" he grated. Oliver
continued to stare at him.

"Nay, Bastard!" He spoke with a deliberate gentleness,
entirely belied by the look in his eyes. "I would not be so
kind to one so devoid of charity as thee!

"Collar this dog!" he ordered briskly. "And chain him
somewhere beyond my sight. Then, when the King is come,
do thou give him to serve the King's horsemaster! If he fails
in that, then it is my order that he be put to tending swine!
Take him away!" With two strides, Lord Oliver found his
horse and swung himself up, turned the animal toward the
drawbridge.

Thierry of Leon, astride his own animal, exhaled in tension
and confusion, then followed. He knew what sensible course
his uncle would have taken. But this? It was peculiar.

Equally peculiar was Lord Oliver's response, sometime
later, when Thierry broached the matter of the gold horse,
the armor and weapons that had been given to the Bastard's
use. De Montglave stared at him for a time, then remarked
coldly that it was none of his concern.

And the Duchess of Bordeaux, after watching the strangely
arrogant acceptance with which the unusual young servant
allowed himself to be taken away, found herself puzzling over
something that went far deeper than the obvious animosity
that existed between Lord Oliver and his bondsman.

Roland made no protest whatever as he was caught by
the arms, his wrists bound behind him, and bourne across
the bailey to the smithy. One man attempted to draw away
the dark sword and jumped back with a startled howl to stare
appalled at scalded fingers. They were rough then, fearful.
Roland locked his teeth as he was forced to bend and submit
as an iron collar was riveted about his neck, a long chain
attached. He ignored wary mutterings as he was bourne once
more across the bailey, and stood with impenetrable defiance

as his chain was fastened to a stout post under the eaves at one end of the stables, against the outer castle wall.

Left alone, he found the corner, and continued to stand braced against it, staring at nightmares such as surely could not trouble other men. Disgrace was palpable in the binding of his arms, in the collar that hung against his neck, and the chain that made a heavy loop to the oak post. But worse, far worse, were the echoes of a deeper horror in the memory of a small child's declaration. Clothed in innocent fancy, it was a sinister accusation . . . Nay. More. A condemnation that was filled with all the terrors of possible truth.

Suggestions of realities far more tangible then the hated hearsay of his purported witch blood.

Much later, when Thierry of Leon came with food and water, and to loose hands gone numb from binding, Roland did not move. He stared, withdrawn and cold, at Lord Oliver's highborn squire.

Thierry stared back for a moment, thinking that his lord was a fool not to dispatch the Bastard once and for all. Then, feeling himself mesmerized, frowned and strode briskly away. He had seen a look like that before in the golden eyes of a wild eagle. Incalculable, unrelenting ferocity.

In a man, it was enough to give any pause.

Roland did not see Lord Oliver directly again. But, true to De Montglave's word, he found himself, a pair of days later, after Charlemagne's arrival at Bordeaux castle, brought to the King's horsemaster as a servant. Collar and chain were struck away, and he was put at once to the familiar tasks of tending destriers, palfreys and sumpter beasts. Nursing his bitterness, he kept silent and absolute obedience to his new master, and wondered when it would be that Lord Oliver would come to collect the gold destrier and valuable armor that remained untouched where he had put them.

Not even the dark sword, concealed beneath the cloak he wore despite summer heat, was his own. He dreamed of fighting Oliver . . . of killing. Slowly.

And for the rest, he kept himself entirely aloof from the abundant populace come with the King to transform Bordeaux castle from fief to royal court. Knights, lords, ladies— foot soldiers and servants of all sorts. He was exiled totally from them all. It seemed more impossible than ever to con-

ceive of winning for himself a place—a place that transcended
the perpetual damnation of his bastardy, of that other dreaded
witch blood.

Alone in the council chamber, Charlemagne was preoccupied with the maps and lists spread across the great table
before him. Anticipating the growing strength of the Infidel
in the Hispanic peninsula south of the Pyrenees, and aware
of his need to maintain his campaigns against the Saxon to
the north, he bent to the task of compiling lists of his own.
Summary assessments of the resources and strengths of his
southern fiefs that extended from the Atlantic into the Italian
peninsula, all increased since his father's time. Abruptly
aware of the peculiar sensation of being watched, the King
looked up to see a man standing by the door on the far side
of the chamber. He frowned and straightened, for he had not
been aware of any intrusion . . .

"Well?" Charlemagne demanded, his eyes passing across
mail armor, white surcoat with a simple crucifix embroidered
upon the breast, and cloak. The other, a brown-haired man
of wiry frame and only moderate stature, strode forward and
bowed with remarkable gracefulness.

"In the Name of Christ, I bring greetings from His Holiness, Adrian, heir to the throne of Saint Peter, to Charlemagne, King of the Franks, and God's earthly sword!" The
man straightened, his voice unusually melodious. "I am Turpin, a Bishop of Navarre, sent by Adrian to serve." Charlemagne frowned a little, disconcerted by large brown eyes of
impressive clarity and a youthfulness that appeared on second
viewing to be entirely misleading. Lines of mischief and experience creased the smaller man's eyes and mouth.

"A priest in the garb of a knight?" he queried. Turpin's
eyes gleamed and his mouth flickered into a mobile smile.

"The Navarrese are a rough people in their faith, Majesty!" he declared with a slight shrug. "They need frequent
reminders that God's strength surpasses their own!" Charlemagne chuckled.

"Well said, my lord Bishop!" he acknowledged. Turpin
seemed to read his mind and answered the next question before it was voiced.

"I have much knowledge of the movements and affairs of
the Kingdoms of Spain, Majesty. And, having given such

knowledge as I possess to His Holiness, am dispatched to thy service for the safety of Christendom." Charlemagne nodded, then sat back in his chair, relaxing to pursue his growing interest in this unusual man.

Turpin stood before him with the patience given to the sworn religious, and answered all that was put to him, openly and fully. Indeed, Charlemagne found, the Bishop knew a great deal. More. He found himself impressed by a clear-witted intelligence and a mind that revealed itself to be uncommonly perceptive and ingenious, if of a somewhat irreverent disposition. This Turpin, he concluded, could be a most useful man.

The King sat silently for a time, digesting what he had just learned of the Emir Marsilla, the precarious northern Christians, and the totally new information concerning an alliance with the vastly powerful Emir Blancandrin of Cordoba. Even from Africa, the Infidel swarmed . . .

"They are a pestilence, these Infidel," he said slowly, at last. "Like flies that overrun a carcass!"

"And like flies, they breed prolific, begetting maggots to infest the world, Majesty!" Turpin commented.

Charlemagne looked at him, noting the bland tone. "Thou do not seem unduly perturbed, we perceive?" he challenged.

Turpin smiled, shrewd eyes meeting his own. "Long ago, my liege, I learned to place my trust in Our Savior. Why should I fear the Devil, who is so much less, for all he attempts?" the Bishop countered evenly.

Again, Charlemagne was compelled to laughter. He stood then, convinced. "Aaah, Turpin!" he said. "We have much need for the like of thee!"

"That is why I am here, Majesty." The smaller man offered simplicity and another bow. Charlemagne nodded acknowledgment and moved to pace restlessly while he considered other things the Bishop had mentioned. Matters more complex than the strategies of armies that were building to the south. Information that explained, in part, more of the nature of these Allah worshippers, and their devotion to such conquest as their faith drove them to undertake.

"It would seem there is a unity of faith among these southern Infidel such as may not be found among the northern tribes . . ." he muttered eventually.

"Just so, Majesty," Turpin responded. "The power of a

single divinity is infinitely greater than the same dispersed among many. Consider, my liege, that the intent of these Infidel is vastly different, also. They do not simply seek warmer climes and more fertile lands, but rather embark upon a holy war of conquest for their God and his prophet, this Mohammed.'' Charlemagne turned to look steadily at the other man. Turpin continued, ''They are given to willing sacrifice for their cause, and, like good Christians, are happy to surrender their lives for their faith.'' He smiled a little. ''And, being as they are, my liege,'' he added slowly, ''they pay stern attention to all signs and mysteries. For all their fanatic unity, they are strangely fearful.''

Charlemagne moved closer and frowned. ''What wily mischief does thy mind consider, my lord Bishop?'' he demanded. Turpin's smile widened, his large pupiled eyes gleaming.

''Simply this, my liege. Knowing what I have just said, it is true that one man may evoke more threat to them than an entire army. Given the right man!'' Charlemagne's frown deepened. Turpin continued, ''Consider, Majesty. Were there to be a single, particular man to lead thy forces against these Infidel, he must be such as would invoke terror in them. A hero arisen, as it were. Impenetrable, and puissant beyond the common, vested with, as they would perceive it, something more than human powers.''

''A champion . . . ?'' the King said slowly.

The Bishop nodded. ''Just so, my liege. A Christian lord arisen and acclaimed above any other among his own.''

''Such a man would, of a certainty, inspire those who follow,'' Charlemagne said slowly, thinking of the brilliance of Lord Ganelon who was now Lord High Councillor, no longer his personal Champion. That office had yet to be filled. ''Thy council is well taken, my lord Bishop.'' Turpin bowed again. ''We have no such man at this time . . .''

''Seek and thou shall find!'' Turpin quoted softly.

The King quirked a silver brow. ''Just so!'' he remarked dryly. ''Do thou remain at hand, Turpin of Navarre. We will have further conversation with thee.'' Charlemagne nodded dismissal. The Bishop bowed, and the King watched him depart, striding across the council chamber with an unusual lightness of step. Indeed, his passage was inaudible save for the soft rustle of his cloak and surcoat. Remarkable for a man

in full armor. With such capacity for silence, Charlemagne
thought, it was easily understood how this unusual priest was
so well informed.

Ideas fermented during the days that followed as the King
explored even more fully the agile wits of his new liegeman.
Then, perceiving a certain wisdom in the advice that had been
offered, he pursued it. Let the Emir Marsilla know that Christendom was united and powerful along its southern front. It
was wise to brew legends to disturb heathen complacency.

A new champion. One sprung of the young elite of knights
so carefully reared, for this very intent, it seemed.

And so, it was proclaimed across the land that a great
tourney would be held. And that the victor, proven against
the best in Christendom, would be the new King's Champion.
Likewise, the new Archbishop of Rheims and Paris, would
ennoble and sanctify this office with God's blessing to the
triumph of Christ over all foes.

Word spread outward from the court at Bordeaux to be
greeted eagerly by Christian men. Beyond the frontiers, it
spread into heathen lands where any knowledge of the powerful King of the Franks was shrewdly studied. To the south,
half-Christian Basques, the Navarrese, and the Asturians
stirred restlessly, wondering what this could portend for them.
Charlemagne's thoughts and presence were clearly turned in
their direction.

Farther south, in Saragossa, the emirs Marsilla and Blancandrin made note, but were not unduly perturbed. The
Franks were a crudely ignorant and barbarous people, they
knew, unclean and self-torturing in their worship of the
Prophet Jesus. A pest to be removed from the ordained direction of the will of Allah.

"Oliver?" His name, softly uttered in the quiet of the arbor
with its abundance of vines, herbs, and flowers, startled him
completely, and Lord Oliver spun around to see his sister
standing but a little distance from him. "The Lady Alicia
said that I might find thee here," she spoke again. Oliver felt
color heat his neck. Made a ward of the King, by their failing
grandsire, Aude had been brought with Charlemagne to Bordeaux and incorporated into the intimate household of the
Duchess.

"I come here sometimes," he said softly.

She nodded, moving closer, a delicate girl with his own coloring and astonishingly long, thick lashes. She smiled. "So I am given to understand by the Lady Alicia!" she murmured.

He felt his flush rise toward his ears. Shrugged. "It is a quiet place for meditation, and I have much to consider these days," he told her. "How fares it with thee?"

"Very well. Lady Alicia is kind and wise." Aude studied him, and Oliver smiled his gratification at the admiration in his sister's voice. "Thou hast undertaken to teach Lord Huon riding, I understand?"

"Aye." Oliver could feel her curiosity. "He is a fine boy, and without a man to father him." He thought of the scrap of embroidered cloth he still had. Never mentioned, nor yet returned, he knew that Lady Alicia understood it was in his possession.

"Kind Oliver," Aude murmured. "I pray to God that I will be given to such a lord as thee." He embraced her then, slipping an arm around her shoulders, kissing her veil where it touched her brow.

"God help me, fair Aude. I will not let it be otherwise!" She smiled. They were fortunate, he knew, in their rearing, to have been given such devotion as their grandsire had bestowed upon them all—his brother, this gentle girl, and himself. He had not seen his brother in a long time. But then, he knew, being the elder, it was duty that bound the heir to the greater portion of the fief of Montglave and to their grandparent's side.

"Thou are changed, I think." Aude stepped back. "Grown handsome, even magnificent!" Oliver shifted uncomfortably.

"And thou are become a jewel!" He gave it back. She blushed. "A prize for some worthy lord to treasure!"

"Will thou fight in this tourney, Oliver?" she asked him then.

He looked at her, expression sobering. "Aye." He met her look. Saw anxiety. "I am war-trained now." He offered reassurance. "And I would win that place that is the prize."

"King's Champion. Aye. I have heard thou are favored above others for it." She looked at him, eyes gone enormous. "I think thou wish more than the honor?" Oliver felt heat waft across his face. He shifted uncomfortably.

"Aye," he said shortly.

"The Lady Alicia?" Aude probed, her expression enchanted. "She is lady of one of the greatest fiefs in the realm."

"It is true," Oliver admitted. His sister smiled radiantly.

"Thou love her, I think!" she said in delight.

He swallowed. "It would be a great match, if I were King's Champion." He half whispered that which he had come to. "What am I now, save a knight, and a younger son with little to inherit?" He felt no resentment against his brother for that powerful difference between them.

Aude touched his arm. "She loves thee as well, I think. The Lady Alicia—" she said softly. "I have seen her look." At fourteen, and new-come to womanhood, his sister would be preoccupied by such, Oliver thought ruefully, experiencing a surge of pleasure at the same time. "She is fortunate. I pray it will be so for me!"

"Are thou so certain then?" Oliver felt surprised by her tone, as though it were already accomplished, this new dream that had arisen to disturb his sleep and keep his waking hours uneasy. She nodded.

"I am," she murmured. "God keep thee safe for it, Oliver." She slipped back, gave him a particular smile, and vanished from the arbor. He stared after her. What did women talk about in the privacy of their solars? he wondered uneasily.

Imagination brought an image of the two, his sister, fragile and romantic, and the other, Lady Alicia, who was mother of his son that he could not claim, save by this effort that hung on the Fates and the will of the King.

Bordeaux, he knew well, was a wardship of Lord Ganelon as well. More likely he would countenance an alliance only to one of his own blood.

And his influence with Charlemagne was profound.

"I will be King's Champion!" he whispered fervently, clinging to that which his sister had said about his lady.

EIGHT

Endowed with an uncanny talent for silence, Turpin, now Archbishop of Rheims, was not noticed as he stopped in the shadows of the beams that supported the roof of the stables to watch the tall youth who was grooming his own war stallion. His dark eyes gleamed in recognition as the shabby boy smoothed the animal's pure white coat to immaculate perfection with a rag. At sixteen years he was not yet fulfilled . . .

"My horse enjoys the skill of thy hand, I see," Turpin said mildly, stepping forward. "He does not attempt to bite, as is his usual wont! Uncharitable creature!" Roland, thoroughly startled, spun around at once. The stallion stamped, snapped, and flattened its ears. Turpin moved to stroke the animal's neck, and it settled at once. Beasts knew. "What is thy name, boy?" he inquired in the same tone, considering the hard, symmetrical face before him, the gold eyes, and the overabundance of shoulder-length, neglected hair that might have been an unusual blend of gold and amber.

"I am Roland." Roland bowed stiffly.

Turpin continued to look at him, brows rising ingeniously. "Just Roland? Thou are a squire, surely, to tend destriers?"

The youth's face tightened further, if that was possible. "I am Roland the Bastard, my lord," he said without tone of any kind. "I am groomsman to the King's Horsemaster. Not squire."

100

Turpin shifted lightly. "Whose Bastard art thou?" he pursued and saw the way Roland's mouth tightened to a grim slash.

"I am not highborn, but am got of some man's seed upon the body of a witch!" Venom shadowed this answer. Turpin nodded.

"Not a common origin, to be sure!" the priest said dryly. "And I am Turpin of Navarre, likewise unusually got! Now I am the King's Bishop!" A slight shrug of one shoulder removed any possibility of pride from this remark, and Roland stared, reddening a little, caught by a hesitant discomfort, fascinated by this unusual priest and his interest.

"What do thou will of me, my lord?" he asked in an effort to close off intrusions into private things.

Turpin smiled. "To know thee a little!" he said promptly.

Roland went rigid and looked away from clear, large brown eyes and unfamiliar intimacy of conversation. "There is naught more to know!" he said harshly. "What task do thou will of me, my lord?" Roland heard the slighter man chuckle.

"Then thou are more unusual than I had first thought, Roland the Bastard!" he said equably. "It hath not been my experience in all my encounters with the souls of men to find one devoid of content, yet housed in a man's body!" Roland scowled, shifted back. "Come now, hedgehog! Do thou fear my interest so much?" This last was gently asked. Roland flushed and glared as he looked back into eyes that were over large—innocent seeming at first, then dark and clever. He saw how lines of laughter deeply creased the skin about them. The Bishop was not young, he knew suddenly, feeling the compelling quality of that gaze. "Is it so much danger to thee to offer thy soul's confidence to one who is sworn to keep silence and listen? I am given to serve divine will, not men's." Turpin's voice was smooth and gentle.

Roland bowed his head. "Aye, my lord," he confessed. "It is so hard."

"Aaah! Then thou hast learned the first strategy of war, young Roland." Roland looked up, startled. "Which is to husband thy defenses!" He swallowed as the smaller man moved a step closer. "Then, thou must establish a good vantage point from which to strike!" Turpin said quietly. "Aye, thou hast seen the face of war. It shows in thee . . ."

Roland suppressed an urge to flinch. "It is all I know!" he heard himself say.

Turpin nodded a little. "Where hast thou fought?"

"In Lombardy." Roland was abruptly conscious of the white purity of the Bishop's surcoat that covered his mail. Like . . . ? "In the north, this winter past," he went on. "With Lord Ganelon, against the Saxon who seek to invade the northern frontier."

The Bishop nodded, almost as if he knew. He cocked his head to one side. "Aye," he murmured. "I have heard of the Bastard. Thou were not raised to common soldiering." Then, more clearly, "Thou would become a knight, I consider?"

"I am a Bastard!" Roland grated harshly.

Turpin's gaze was unsettlingly perceptive. "So—knowing war and little else," he murmured. "Thou are uncommon bred. Is it to be wondered at, young Roland, that thou must tread an uncommon path, and thereby arrive at an uncommon destiny?" Roland stared, caught and held by the profoundly suggestive words so softly uttered. He paled suddenly, recognizing the same large pupils and colored irises that he had seen in the white owl that had haunted him. This man—priest—wore white as well.

"What art thou . . . ?" he whispered.

Turpin was not at all disturbed by the question. Instead, he smiled. "Is it not more significant to ask, what art thou to become, Roland Kingslayer?"

Roland froze, his face paling. That name that he had given himself, whispered once to the night air an eternity ago. Twice earned. Desiderius and the Saxon Prince who was never spoken of. It was part of his disgrace. "How do thou know of that?" he rasped.

The Bishop's smile widened. "I observe. I listen," he commented mildly.

"I was overambitious. I left my place . . ." Roland grated bitterly.

Turpin shrugged. "Mayhap, it is, rather, that thou hast an instinct for another wisdom of war," he said slowly. "Thou hast understood that the unexpected is the straightest path to victory."

"So I perceived at the time . . ." Roland whispered, vulnerable now.

The Bishop nodded, his gesture birdlike, Roland thought.

"And rightly. Uniquely bred and reared, thou may perceive by instinct things that are not given to men made to walk a more ordinary course at all. Do thou consider that thou are, mayhap, caught less by true disgrace, than by the fear and envy of other men who would wish such accomplishment for themselves?"

Roland's eyes went round with amazement at this. It had never before occurred to him. "Nay . . . ?" he breathed.

Turpin continued in a tone silken with cunning. "Mayhap, it is for thee to prove thy true worth beyond the questioning of any man whatever."

Roland swallowed. Those dark eyes that read him, knew him—saw as only a man of God could be given to do. "How?" he breathed. "All I undertake becomes as ashes. Better death than this—perpetual damnation!"

"A unique place for a unique man?" Turpin murmured. Roland stared. He felt as though he was poised upon some precipice. "Could thou, I wonder, become King's Champion?" Tumbling . . . Not for the world would he have expected what was ringing through his mind.

"King's Champion?" he rasped. It was a dream. "The tourney?" He hardly saw the nod of the Bishop's head. De Montglave's place . . . So it was already said. "But I am not a knight." De Montglave.

"King's Champion and knighthood! They are the same." Turpin's voice echoed softly. "Do thou win the one, the other is not even of consequence!"

Roland swallowed. Reality was brutal, different . . . "I have not the right . . ."

The Bishop's look was wry. "That small matter did not stay thee before!" he said dryly. "Whyfore should it now?" Truth, perversely twisted.

Roland bowed his head. Inhaled deeply. "I would be the King's good servant . . ." he whispered the vow that ruled him. He flinched as a remarkably fine-boned, uncallused hand touched the sleeve of his tunic.

"The King has servants aplenty!" Turpin remarked in the same dry tone. "He too must walk a path not made for other men. He needs a Champion now. A man who knows war better than his own mind. A man to whom brilliance is an instinct, not a studied effort—Roland Kingslayer!"

Roland looked up. "I have naught to lose . . ." he whispered.

"Nay. Thou have not."

The other inclined his head in serene agreement. "Why . . . ?" Half-formed question.

The Bishop smiled, his eyes mysterious. "Have I not said, young Roland, that I am given to serve divine will, not men's?" he asked mildly, then turned and walked away.

Roland stood unmoving. He saw, after a time, that his hands trembled as much as his soul. Was this the manner in which God had chosen to answer so many hours of desperate prayer?

King's Champion . . . ? It was a beacon in the darkness of his life.

Eager people flocked from long distances to witness the glorious and festive event that would display the prowess of all western Christendom, that would determine God's particular favor in the person of the one to become the King's new Champion. Knights came, and other lords. Wealth was displayed in brightly colored tents and brilliant banners that sprang up in the meadows about the grey permanence of the castle of Bordeaux. Shields were fresh painted. War stallions groomed and conditioned to burnished hues. Wagers were gayly offered and taken. Geoffrey of Anjou was favored, and Roger of Roncesvalles, who had fought so brilliantly with Lord Ganelon during the beginning of the year and was now come down from the north to participate. Others too. And above them all was favored Lord Oliver De Montglave, who, beyond being proven brilliant in battle, was loved by all for his open nature and generous disposition. If any was worthy to be a Champion of Christ, it was felt, then assuredly it was he.

And Roland, vanished beneath the obscure tasks he was given, knew a sense of unchanging fate. The rest was simply waiting—waiting for the single course that lay before him, unafraid of the death that failure would assuredly bring, bent only toward the dream that glowed fire-bright and hot in his mind. Likewise, he waited for De Montglave to take the gold horse and the armor that were rightly his, husbanding only, in the night while others slept, the dark sword. He sat in the hay of the stable loft, staring into the darkness, caught between prayers that were beyond expression and the sheer, vibrant assurance that was to be found in the feel of Durandal as she lay, dark, moody and silent, across his knees.

De Montglave . . . Part of the fire in his mind was the will to vanquish the nemesis of that name for all time. De Montglave, who did not bother with the gold horse, or the armor after all—hated for humiliations wrought a thousandfold.

De Montglave, whom he had never even come close to beating in battle.

And when it was the night before the day beyond which Roland could perceive no future at all, he found the armor of Desiderius and donned it. Mail leggings and hauberk, coif and gorget, belt and gauntlets. And, on his head he set the helm that, with its broad nasal, nearly obscured his features. Without even the simple, unadorned color of surcoat and shield, he was anonymous. Naught save nameless steel. It was fitting, he thought as he affixed his single weapon to her place at his back. Then, upon sudden impulse, he rummaged for and found the golden robe that he had kept from his encounter with the Infidel.

Gold and steel, I will be, he thought, and set the garment about his shoulders in the manner of a cloak. He saddled the monstrous stallion and slipped away from the castle to find concealment in the nocturnal solitude of a grove of trees on a hill overlooking the meadow where the tourney was to occur.

The night passed serenely. Another vigil . . . And when dawn came to slip blue glowing across the stillness, Roland mounted the gold horse and rode it to the edge of the trees, there to wait upon the perfect moment, unquestioning in his ability to recognize it.

"Into Thy hands, I give my destiny, Oh Lord!" he whispered the single prayer. Wise priest, who had seen so clearly . . .

In the first bright glow of a morning brilliant enough to seem a blessing, Lord Oliver stood very still as his squire bathed, shaved, and dressed him, then proceeded to put him into full armor. His finest . . .

He had seen her briefly, the evening before. Moments only, but intense, vivid enough now to seem as though they were still occurring.

"My lord?" Her eyes were warm enough for drowning.

"My lady?" He had bowed politely, glad that no one else was about the entrance to the tower where he was quartered. Her hand came out, and in the palm lay a small golden crucifix, most exquisitely fashioned, with small rubies gleaming blood scarlet upon each limb.

"May God bless thine endeavor, my lord," she whispered. "I would offer this small token . . ."

Oliver had stared, suspended and reverent. Taken the Cross and the chain in which it had nestled and set it about his throat. Then he had knelt and, taking her hand, kissed the palm with all the feeling in him. "My lady—for thee," he had managed to murmur response. He could still feel the fleeting delicacy with which her fingers had ruffled his hair.

"I had not thought to meet so good a man," she had murmured, then slipped away . . .

"My lord?" Thierry's voice shattered the memory.

"Aye."

"All is ready, my lord."

Oliver took the gauntlets the other held out, then smiled with a brilliance that startled his squire, every nerve in him tingling, eager. "Good!" he said gayly, savoring the feel of the Lady Alicia's crucifix against the skin over his heart. Leon gave him a surprised look, and Lord Oliver's smile widened into a broad grin. He clapped a hand on the younger man's shoulder.

"Fighting is not difficult, Thierry!" he told the other gently. "There are a thousand things in a man's life harder to contend with! Do thou fetch my destrier now . . ."

"My lord." Leon bowed a little and slipped away. It was impossible not to revere Lord Oliver, he thought. I would be like him. I would be like him . . . And yet, he was confused. So much he had learned from his uncle . . .

From his solitary vantage point, Roland fingered the reins of his stallion's bridle slowly as he watched crowds gather about the jousting field below the castle. There were horses everywhere. Whinnies and squeals that carried in the breeze were audible above the unrelenting hum of myriad human voices. And then there was the winding of a horn. He squinted and saw Charlemagne, astride a great dappled grey destrier, ride the length of the field, reach a high dais that had been set for him. Moments later, the King was seated upon his throne, and beside and below his right hand, in Bishop's robes of purest white, another slight figure stood, uttering blessings that Roland could not hear.

The gold stallion snorted and pawed impatiently, as eager as he. Kindred creature . . . Roland touched the curb.

"For this day, I name thee Veillantif." He whispered another pact as he watched a seemingly endless parade of mounted lords, and highborn knights ride across the field to give salute to the King, then disperse, to assemble in two companies, one at each end of the field. Roland's mouth twisted into a hard smile.

It was to be the melee, then. Count Geoffrey of Anjou on the one side. Lord Oliver De Montglave on the other. No rules, save honorable victory.

His heels nudged the gold horse, and it plunged restlessly, ears flicking. They were all his foes. Again, the horn wound, and thunder rumbled in the earth as stallions charged en masse from either end of the field. Lances lowered, and colors melded into cracking sounds and thuds as knight found knight.

The battle was enjoined.

"Now!" Roland whispered, and released the coiled power of the stallion to sweep down from the hill, his right hand finding the hilt of Durandal, his mouth softening in a strange joy as he felt her leap in his hand, sing a sinister hum as he swept her in an arc over his head.

"Haaargh!" Bellowed will roared from his throat as the gold horse bolted toward startled spectators who melted away to avoid being trampled. A barricade was easily leaped. "For God and Charlemagne!" It was thunder from his own throat, Roland realized vaguely, as he shifted weight and set the stallion to charge into the midst of the fray. Awed silence overtook eager shouts of support for favorites as all eyes turned to the strange, anonymous knight, whose gold cloak spread like wings across the flanks of a stallion of the same color. And who was, it seemed, near unarmed. No lance, or shield, or mace . . .

Only a strange dark sword.

And Durandal swooped through the air, like a scythe bent on harvest as the gold stallion plunged against one destrier and knocked it away, then charged on. Steel, leather, flesh.

Lances shattered, and Roland's body became a whip of purpose as he leaned to slice through a shield. Death or triumph, that was the sum of it now.

A stallion skidded into the ground, its neck nearly severed, and a man cried out as a leg snapped when he hit the turf. Roland became a strange blend of beast and man and blade. He did not feel the lance tip that ripped his mail coif and scraped against his neck, nor the sword that came down upon his bridle hand to smash steel links into forearm muscles, as others began to turn from their own encounters to confront this new, unknown, golden knight that had charged into their midst, so clearly bent on besting them all.

It went on and on. Horses screamed and trampled sod and fallen men. Squires raced from the sides to help the vanquished from the field, to tend wounds, and to save highborn lives too well needed to be wastefully spilt. The more than hundred who had begun were soon reduced, and thinning continued as encounters became more enduring and individual. The champions, those puissant beyond the rest, were soon visible. Gloriously skilled in horsemanship and weapons of all kinds, they were watched with awe, with suspense.

Only the golden stranger with his peculiar sword seemed as fierce as they, his great legged beast lunging and spinning, bolting forward, his sword indiscriminately eager. Fifty were twenty—than little more than ten.

Roland catapulted the gold stallion across the field, leaping a carcass, and brought it to a plunging halt some distance from the rest. Durandal poised in his hand. De Montglave. Anjou. A few others. He could see them clearly.

"For God and Charlemagne!" he roared, and raised the dark sword. He waited. Fighting eased, and they turned to face him, these others. He made the gold horse rear and swung Durandal in challenge. To a man, they brought their horses together to form a wall before him. These were the best. Roland grinned.

They came at him then, those who were left, charging to surround him. Roland brought his horse at an angle across them, then made the great horse leap high, straight over the nearest gap, its hooves catching man and beast beneath to splatter them as it soared across the top. It stumbled a little on landing, sides heaving. Roland jerked it up to spin it on its hocks and charge the turning line of knights. The middle, this time—then he abruptly veered to the right, barreling between two men, his sword disarming the first, then swooping down to sever leather harness and backbone of the second man's horse. It screamed and somersaulted. He veered again and found the flank of yet another, Durandal's point slipping under shield and through mail as though there were no obstacle at all.

He did not feel the blow that shattered the steel covering his own left shoulder, only the sudden numbness that made it seem he had lost an arm. The reins fell from nerveless fingers, and the stallion wavered as he caught a glimpse of Lord Geoffrey of Anjou. But the gold horse knew its business and charged of its own volition. Roland dodged another blow that struck his left side hard and, ducking along the stallion's side, brought the dark sword's point up to send Lord Geoffrey's sword spinning from his hand. He could not find his arm to straighten. He jerked violently and recovered his seat, and brought the stallion about, to pause, heaving and lathered.

There were five remaining—Lord Oliver De Montglave danced his own lathered stallion forward, the others seemed less eager. De Montglave . . . Roland, grim-faced, set the dark sword across his thighs as a chant began and rose from uncounted throats.

"De Montglave! De Montglave! The Champion De Montglave!" Roland found his left arm then, a thing that dangled uselessly. Covered with blood or sweat, he could not tell the difference as he stared at Lord Oliver. He scowled as De Montglave saluted the crowd, then held out his hand for the single lance on the field that remained intact. He took it as it was offered, and the other four yielded to him. De Montglave raised his shield and set the lance. "For God and Charlemagne!" he bellowed in a voice that somehow held a lilt of gaiety, and charged. The crowd roared. Roland touched his stallion's sides and spun the beast, swung Durandal over his head. It was between the two of them now . . . at last.

The gold horse leaped a carcass, and Roland ducked to avoid the lance tip, barely in time to avoid being spitted. He felt a shuddering as De Montglave skillfully shifted the point to catch the cantle of his saddle, ripping away the girths. Clinging to Durandal, he felt himself tumble and smack into hard sod.

The crowd roared, "De Montglave! The Champion!" Roland jerked up, found his knees just as Lord Oliver thundered toward him, this time with lance tip lowered as to scoop. Roland found a foot, and swung, twisting awkwardly to bring the dark sword down across the lance just as a flailing hoof caught him in the ribs and felled him again. The lance shattered. Lord Oliver dropped it and brought his stallion about into a series of striking bounds as he drew his sword. Roland, unable to breathe, jerked awkwardly to his feet. He stumbled and ducked as Lord Oliver swept past him, just missing a blow that would surely have sheared his skull, helm and all. Gasping, he brought Durandal around in a horizontal arc and lunged. The sword sang as she bit through the destrier's off foreleg, severing it. The horse screamed and went down. Lord Oliver leaped clear, rolled, and found his feet. Then, still gasping clumsily for air, Roland saw the other man discard his shield and take his longsword in both hands as he prepared to advance.

Roland shook his head to clear his eyes that stung from blood and sweat, set his feet, and raised the dark sword . . . Poised. And suddenly, forcefully, knew something absolute.

Nay. Not with Durandal. It could not be achieved with her, this victory. He lunged back and Lord Oliver's sword point swept across the space where he had been. The crowd was chanting now, in a rhythm that was another, lusting kind of heartbeat. Roland lunged aside once more, and in one hard thrust, sent Durandal away from him, to plunge, point down, into the sod. He saw De Montglave pause, astonished as he scanned the debris of the field for some discarded weapon and found one.

"Thou are a fool, Bastard!" Lord Oliver said clearly, advancing to the cheers of the intoxicated crowd who scented triumph for their favorite. Roland ducked backward. Three steps, four. Five. "Do thou yield?" Lord Oliver shouted, sword poised. Roland took another step, his eyes never leaving Oliver's face, dipped, groping for the weapon he had glimpsed, his hand closing about a bloodied hilt. He grinned, raised himself to crouching, and set the weapon before him, left arm swinging like some useless piece of excess baggage.

"'Never, my lord!" he roared back. "I would not defeat thee by unfair advantage, that is all!" Lord Oliver's face tightened angrily, and he struck nimbly. Roland ducked again, deflecting the blow with the common blade. Aye, he had to acknowledge as he was pressed steadily backward, De Montglave was skilled indeed. Brilliantly agile, mixing one type of blow after another, forcing desperate defense.

Roland slipped around the rump of a fallen horse, then lunged to stand upon its flank, bringing the steel of his blade down in a swerving, lightning stroke, such as he had developed with the dark sword, to catch Lord Oliver on the shoulder, just as the other's weapon slammed into his useless arm. He jumped forward with a growl, teeth bared, and brought his blade into an upthrust that skidded at an angle across Lord Oliver's downstroke, down its length, to pierce the mail that covered De Montglave's sword arm. Lord Oliver stumbled and recovered his grip with his left hand, but Roland, possessed now, risked all, and caught him again, knocking De Montglave's sword away with a single sweep that used all his strength. One last kick, and he felled the other with a foot. Pounced, and set himself astride Lord Oliver, the damaged blade of his sword pressed to the other man's throat.

Heaving breaths made winds that raced harshly to and fro, accompaniment to the galloping of heartbeats. The rest was silence. The crowd did not stir by so much as a whisper as they saw their favorite fall.

Roland heard none of it. He stared like some unrelenting bird of prey into sea-blue eyes—hated eyes in a hated face. He savored the moment so long dreamed of. But Lord Oliver, face streaked with sweat and grime, breath gulping, stared back with unblinking calm.

"Yield, my lord!" Roland rasped loudly. Lord Oliver continued to look at him with serenity, his lips moving to form a slight smile.

"Yield!" Roland grated all the passion of his soul, and pressed the blade closer until a thin line of blood appeared at the other man's throat. "Yield to me!" he demanded.

Lord Oliver's smile widened. "Never, Bastard!" he managed with eerie cheerfulness, his gaze never wavering.

Clear. Pure. And without any hatred at all.

It was his right . . . It was his hard-won right. Vengeance justly given for so much endured. But Roland felt his hand withdraw the sword, thrust it away. Felt himself jerk back, away from De Montglave. He found his feet to stand very still, appalled by the realization that he could not kill this man. So noble a man.

Noble? From whence came this bewildering internal conviction that stayed his hand, overruled his will?

Awkwardly, Roland turned slowly to see uncountable staring eyes focused on himself who stood alone upon the field.

And then he found the King.

Charlemagne stood tall and silver regal, eternal somehow, high upon the dais. And to his right was the Archbishop Turpin.

The golden stallion came to him, saddle broken and askew, still held by breastplate, crupper, and rump harness. Roland walked with feet gone strangely clumsy toward the dark sword. He recovered her, slipped her against his back, and turned to walk with concentrated effort toward the dais. Pain swept across him from some broken place, and he looked down to see his left hand dangle, blood coming from under his mail to stain the gauntlet. He reached for the flaccid thing and tucked it into his belt, then drew the gold brocade cloak more closely about his shoulders to conceal it.

Whatever he was—whatever he had done, it was in the King's hands now. And it was astonishingly simple to let his knees buckle as he reached the foot of the dais and looked up . . .

"For God and Charlemagne!" he whispered hoarsely, then forgot all else as he saw the look in the King's eyes. Recognition. Then something far different from the icy penetration that was Charlemagne's most common aspect. Elusive. Mistlike and grey-soft. Warm. Charlemagne was pleased, he understood as the King stepped down, closer, tall in silver mail and purple robes. His own sword drawn, point held down.

"Thou make a prayer of a war cry," the King said softly, raising the sword. Roland did not move, but felt light touches upon his right shoulder, incredible agony in his left. "Sir Roland." Charlemagne smiled. "Arise, Sir Roland," he said quietly. "Thy triumph is beyond remarkable."

Roland stood obediently, shocked as he understood what had been given with such feathered delicacy. No more than a whispered moment, and he was made a knight.

And then he heard the Archbishop's voice, rich and melodious as it carried out to all who were gathered there. "This day, for our liege lord, Charlemagne, and for Christendom, a Champion was sought from among the highest and best in the realm. And, on this day, we are all given to witness the wonder of God's will. For, out of some silent place, He hath brought one unknown to all, and has invested this man with such triumph as to declare him Champion before all Christian men. So, thereby, has God made clear His will!''

Roland glanced upward and saw the elegant hand that was passed across him in the sign of the Cross. Holy benediction. Compelled, he crossed himself likewise, and heard a rising whisper gather in the crowd, spring into a thunderous acceptance. He realized then, with sheer incredulity, that he was King's Champion. That he had won this high place that was, somehow, less real to imagine now than the death he had otherwise understood to expect.

It was instinct to draw out the dark sword again and hold her forth. Roland heard his own voice call out, ''By God's will, my life is given to my liege lord, Charlemagne!'' And then, he heard his answer, a roaring from the crowd that was approval such as he had never known before. He slipped Durandal from view, then stepped back to find himself surrounded by people he did not know at all. Drawn away, through the enveloping haze of pain to walk toward the castle.

He must not fall, he knew. Not now.

Thierry of Leon found Lord Oliver standing by the carcass of his destrier, blood from slitting the beast's throat dripping from his sword.

''My lord . . . ?'' It did not seem possible that De Montglave had been beaten. Lord Oliver turned to him, blood on his throat, and elsewhere, face drawn, closed. He held out the weapon, and Leon took it.

''Minor hurts only,'' he said, and looked away to stare with unreadable face toward the man with the gold cloak who strode away from them all toward the castle, soon to vanish amid a profusion of people. Thierry frowned angrily. He knew very well who it was.

''How can it be that the Bastard . . . ?'' he began in scathing tones.

Lord Oliver turned on him. ''Enough!'' he barked. ''I will hear not one word!'' Then he was gone, striding briskly away. Thierry stared in astonishment, then, remembering duty, followed.

Somewhere beyond the pain that he fought to control, it was strange to find himself in the chapel, receiving sacrament and blessing. Then in the great hall, seated at the high table near the King's right hand, staring at food he could not eat. Wine he had not strength to reach for. Only will kept him erect as he washed back and forth in a sea of pain that kept perfect time with his efforts to breathe. Roland rediscovered his left arm, still tucked in his belt. He could not move it beyond a feeble twitch of fingers. But he could feel the moisture beneath his mail. Sweat had dried long since. This was blood, coming from the shoulder concealed beneath his cloak.

And later, he managed to walk where he was guided, to a tower chamber that had been prepared—for him? He stared at rich furnishings. At clothing of the finest stuffs and richly embroidered. At the servants who called him "my lord" and tried to touch—to help.

"Nay. Go," he heard himself say hoarsely, and found a place where he could stand by the narrow window as they left him. He leaned back against the stone, locking knees. Knowing that if he moved another step, he would fall.

He must not fall.

It was night, now, he knew vaguely, staring out at the darkness. He groped weakly with his right hand, managing to loose the baldric that held the dark sword and set her beside him, propped upright. Then his helm. Jesu, but it was heavy. He let it fall and clenched his teeth against the clanging of metal on stone as it tumbled away. He pushed back his coif and reached to unclasp the cloak, but there was no strength left, and he gave it up. He leaned back and let the wall hold him. He could feel the blood now, trickling down slowly along his arm, along his ribs and back, soaking mail and the clothing that lay beneath. He found the wound, a gaping pit of mangled flesh and steel links from the hauberk, then gave that up as well. He had not the strength to tend himself. Only to endure, to feel the blood that drained away. And to smile vaguely at the thought that he was dying after all.

He had but to wait for it to come. So cold . . . So cold . . .

Ill rested from preoccupation with his own thoughts, his minor wounds tended, bathed and dressed in fresh attire, Lord Oliver found himself, a little after dawn, soberly rapping against the door to the chamber above his own, now given to

Roland's use. He heard no answering response, and needing to resolve that which troubled him, he opened the door and glanced about the room. At first, seeing the untouched bed, he thought the chamber deserted. He stepped inside, then saw a figure standing, half hidden by shadows, against the wall in the alcove of the single, narrow window on the far side. It was the—nay, Sir Roland now.

Oliver's eyes widened in surprise as he stepped farther into the room, for Roland did not seem to hear him. Nor had he removed his armor from the day before. Only the helm, which lay carelessly discarded on the floor. Had he stood thus the entire night?

"I bid thee good day, Sir Roland," Oliver offered politely. Roland did not move, but continued to stare out the window. Oliver's lips quirked. "Bastard!" he said clearly.

Roland's face turned toward him, shadowed, save for eyes that gleamed with unnatural brilliance. "My lord?" Coldly whispered.

Puzzled, Oliver shifted a little closer. "I sought thee out, Sir Roland, to pose thee a question for which I have not been able to resolve answer."

Roland looked away. "My lord?" he whispered tonelessly, his profile uncompromisingly aloof.

This is folly, Oliver chastized himself, but asked, "Why did thou not kill me as thou were entitled to do?" He heard the other inhale sharply. Roland did not answer, but continued to stare through the window. Oliver pursued it. "I would have slain thee, I think," he said mildly, then, in a drier tone, "I was enraged enough for it. An overcommon condition in my experience of thee!"

Still, oddly, Roland did not look at him. The answer came suddenly, rasped out in harsh tones. "Thou hast said it, my lord. Who am I to murder thee, proven valiant and unquestioned loyal to the King!" Shocked, Oliver stared at the other man, all humor vanished as he absorbed the statement, began to understand, as he had understood that time, an eternity before, Roland's honest claim to the death of Desiderius.

Honor—that was as profound as his own. Concealed, perhaps, beneath a brutal courage and an abrasive granite demeanor. He had never before thought Roland capable of generosity. He stepped forward, for it was clear enough that

Roland would not look at him, and he understood that as well.

"My name is Oliver, to thee," he offered. "Shall I consider that we will fight beside each other now, and never again as foes?" He held out his hand, stopping to stand to Roland's right, and saw Roland's mouth move a little in a face gone grey and haggard. "It hath been a bitter course for thee, Sir Roland," he said gently. "I have seen that much. Thou hast had my respect this long time past." His lips quirked. "As squire and servant, I concede, I would not inflict thee upon even the bravest man. But, God help me, there is no other I would rather have beside me in battle!"

Roland turned his head slowly then, to look at him with eyes gone wide, stark, before they fell to Oliver's still outstretched hand.

"What is this, thou offer me?" he whispered.

"It would seem to be friendship." Oliver grinned, stepping closer still, for Roland was unusually reluctant to move. "Mother of God! What is this . . . ?" He sobered at once at the sight of the blood that stained the gold of the cloak that covered Roland's left shoulder, hid half his body. He reached out and drew the cloak aside to stare at the rest. Mangled shoulder. Broken mail imbedded in the mess. Bloody arm held by Roland's belt. And the blood—so much blood—that had seeped through clothing and hauberk, down his left side and leg, even to form a small pool on the floor. Clearly, Roland had been badly wounded.

"Art thou mad, man, to neglect thyself so?" Oliver demanded, appalled.

"Nay!" Roland grated harshly, head leaning back against the stone, eyes closing. "Leave it . . . It will heal!" Oliver's breath exploded from him.

"Do thou think so?" he retorted. "And will thou stand there until thou have finished bleeding to death? I know thee! Thy pride alone will assuredly kill thee!" He reached for the other man. Caught him under the right arm.

"Nay . . . " It was a barely whispered protest, then Roland crumpled into complete unconsciousness.

NINE

Bellowed orders brought aid. Thierry of Leon, who had been about sundry matters in the chamber below, came to stare in amazement, then fled to fetch the Lady Alicia and her herbs and unguents, brazier and cautery. Oliver himself set about the business of stripping away the damaged armor and the soiled, shabby garments beneath as Roland lay unconscious and breathing faintly on the stone floor of the chamber.

"By Our Lady, he hath lost enough blood for two!" Oliver looked up to see the Lady Alicia as she bent down on the other side of the lax figure. "It is a miracle that he still breathes!" She caught Oliver's look. "I was accustomed to attend my lord," she murmured, then issued orders to her women and bent to the task of cleaning away blood and grit. It was one of the things he loved in her, Oliver thought as he probed the mace-broken shoulder for steel links—her strength.

Blood continued to ooze as Oliver searched deeply mangled flesh to discover the wonder of entire, bright, almost silver-gleaming bone beneath. If Roland survived, he knew then, he stood some chance of recovering, in time at least, most of the use of his arm.

If Roland survived . . .

"Bring me the iron," he grated and held out his hand, then bent to sear the bleeding places. Roland gasped once, but did not otherwise stir, and the stench of burning meat filled the chamber. Oliver stood at last and set the iron in the brazier, breathing deeply as the Lady Alicia and her tire-women completed the tasks of binding linen about the shoulder and upper arm, applying unguents to the other minor cuts. He raised his eyes and caught the look on young Thierry's face then.

Pure resentment.

Old hatreds . . .

"It is finished, my lord. He should be got to the bed." Lady Alicia touched his arm.

"Aye." Oliver looked at her. "I am grateful for thy care."

"It is gladly given, my lord," she told him. "I will see he is attended as is needful. The bandages must be changed often. I fear the fever is begun already." Oliver nodded, bowed as she left, and turned to his squire.

"Do thou help me get him to that bed," he said, bent, and carefully grasped Roland's lax upper body. Thierry caught him up below the hips, and between them, Roland was easily laid amid clean linens and soft down pillows, covered to the waist with furs. Aye, the lady had the right of it, Oliver thought as he touched Roland's brow, felt the fire that had begun, despite the almost waxen pallor, and looked up to see his squire frowning a peculiar blend of puzzlement and acute dislike.

"I do not understand this, my lord," he said.

"What, Leon?" Oliver seated himself carefully on the foot of the bed. The other exploded.

"This! Thy care of this man—this—witch-got Bastard!"

Oliver began to frown. "Sir Roland," he corrected icily, but Thierry did not hear.

"I have never understood thy tolerance of him. Now, it is beyond bearing to see thee attend to him so. He hath usurped thy place by witchcraft . . ."

Oliver stood. "Nay, it was fairly won," he said with chill quiet that the other ignored.

"Better to let him die!" Thierry growled furiously. "Then thou will be King's Champion as is right, my lord!"

"Silence!" Oliver snarled. Thierry stiffened, thoroughly startled, and stared at De Montglave with widening eyes.

"After all this time in my service, Leon, do thou still have so little understanding of my honor?" Thierry paled, then began to flush. The gentleness of Lord Oliver's tone was worse than any ranting would have been. "Nay. I see thou hast not . . ." Oliver continued. Thierry glanced furiously at the unconscious Roland.

"It *was* witchcraft!" he insisted sullenly.

"Nay, Leon!" Lord Oliver's voice was hard now. "It was courage. Rare courage. I consider that thou would not have attempted to undertake such as he did yesterday?" Thierry's flush deepened at his own angry resentment of this truth. His mouth tightened nastily. "I have instruction for thee," Lord Oliver continued. "Do thou take such belongings as are thine, and thy horse. I dispatch thee now to thine uncle's service . . ."

"My lord!" Thierry stared, flush fading.

"Aye, Leon! I will not have the service of one who is given to such poor knowledge of my honor. Nor, for that, could thou expect to win thy spurs from me. Lord Ganelon will welcome thee, I consider. Go!"

White with humiliation, Thierry did not even bow, but spun on his heel and strode from the chamber.

Lord Oliver loosed temper in a long sigh and turned toward the bed. Whether it would be received or nay, his offer of friendship had not been lightly given.

The Duchess had been correct. Fever had begun, and now it grew steadily into a fire that consumed flesh, inflammation that was the most usual and deadly consequence of any wound. Roland lay very still for a time, then stirred to restlessness, and seemed to rouse briefly to stare with brilliant golden eyes at things that were not apparent in the quiet solitude of the chamber.

Lord Oliver did not leave him, but gave such attention as he could. Attempting to cool the scalding brow with cold water, keeping Roland covered when the other thrust back the furs with unconscious reflexes. Holding him when his fingers sought bandages and tried to rip them away.

And when the Lady Alicia came again with her tirewoman and his sister to dress the wound anew, Lord Oliver was astounded to find himself needing all his strength to confine Roland's sudden, violent, raving struggles against her touch. When the bandages were changed, and Roland's body cleaned of putrefaction, and he was laid back to lie in exhaustion, Lord Oliver breathed in relief and met his lady's eyes.

"I will send refreshment, my lord," she murmured. He smiled a little.

"It would be most welcome, my lady," he murmured. Nor did he see the way his sister stared at the face of Roland, unblemished and marble-seeming amid so much golden hair spread across the pillows.

But it was the Lady Aude who came with tray and flagon sometime later. Who set these upon the table in the room and moved to stand by the bed. Lord Oliver, thankful for bread and cheese, cold meats and wine, poured himself a goblet and drank, then paused to stare at her.

"Will he live, Oliver?" Aude asked softly.

"I do not know," he answered honestly. " 'Tis rather soon to be sure. Yet, I do not perceive the streaking of poisoned flesh that comes before death." She reached out to touch Roland's brow, and he stirred restlessly. She turned then, and Oliver saw her look with a sinking in the pit of his belly.

"He is beautiful, this knight," she murmured. "Like a God . . . "

"Aude!" Her eyes met his, clear and undissembling.

"Do thou remember that statue of Apollo, Oliver, that grandfather found?" He swallowed. Her gaze dropped to her hands. "So I have dreamed . . ." she murmured, and left him staring after her. Nay, not this one, he thought painfully. He is not for so gentle a maid as thee. He is hard and violent, this Roland.

Roland's fever worsened, and when the bandages were changed again, Lord Oliver was hard-pressed to hold him as he arched himself, and thrashed, and cried out against the incoherent and bewildering nightmares of delirium that possessed him. He tried to jerk away from the vile taloned hands of evil witch women who reached for him. Whose touch was agony . . . He hacked away at Desiderius, trying to separate his head, bloody and blackening with rot, which stared and would not loosen . . . And he tried to flee the white owl, with its strange Bishop's robes over ruffled feathers, that peered at him with unblinking, eerie, knowing eyes.

"I do not belong to thee . . ." he shrieked once. "I am the King's man. I am not a witch . . . I am not a witch . . ."

Still holding hard, Oliver met the shocked look on the Lady Alicia's face, then shifted his gaze to his sister, Aude, who stared with molten-eyed sympathy.

"I will tend him from this time forth, my lady," he told

them all. The Duchess inclined her head in understanding as
Roland tossed his head and clawed at the fresh bindings about
his shoulder.

"As thou will, my lord," she said. Roland lunged then,
and occupied with holding him, Oliver did not see the Duchess and her women depart.

"I am not . . . a witch," Roland rasped harsh protest, and
subsided into shivering as fever consumed him. Oliver exhaled abruptly and eased his grasp to settle on the edge of
the bed. He understood, he thought. He understood much
more than he had before.

Roland's fever flowed in waves that drove him to frantic
delirious raving, then to violent bouts of shivering in the
strenuous hours that followed. The King came once to stand
and gaze upon the stricken Champion, his gaze incomprehensible as ever, the Archbishop Turpin with him. Lord Oliver crossed himself as the priest made the sign of the Cross
and murmured a musical blessing. Charlemagne met his eyes
as he looked up.

"We will not forget, my lord," he said quietly, then turned
away to leave. Oliver bowed and stared for a moment at the
door that closed behind his vanished Prince.

Charlemagne, he knew, loved courage as well.

Nay, he thought later as he changed dressings once again.
This could not persist. No man could bear much more and
live . . .

Weaker now, Roland's breathing was an awkward rasping.
His skin had become peculiarly translucent. Illusory.

"I grow fanciful," Oliver murmured in recognition of his
own growing fatigue, and settled himself to doze lightly in a
chair by the head of the bed, one hand reaching out to rest
against Roland's hair.

"Durandal . . . ?" he heard the other whisper, and closed
his eyes against the candlelight that softened the night with
shifting fireglow. Only Roland, he thought ruefully, would
mistake the touch of a human hand for the bloody caress of
a sword . . .

Dawn brought little relief to Oliver's self-imposed vigil.
Roland was weakening steadily. Dry-hot, he tossed his head
back and forth in perpetual restlessness. Nor would he be
still enough to take more than a sip of the watered wine that

Oliver held to his lips. He murmured sometimes. Unintelligible things—and his eyes would open briefly, to stare without recognition.

The deadly red streaks and swelling and the stench of poisoned flesh begun to decay did not appear in or around the wound. Yet, as the second night descended to the rumbling echoes of approaching thunderstorms, neither did the fever abate.

For Oliver, now feeling his own exhaustion as a palpable aching, it became the simple completion of a duty begun with his offer of friendship. Roland, surely, would not live much longer. . . His breathing was little more than an uneven whispering, and his restlessness had faded to sporadic twitchings. The unnatural hue of his face had become more pronounced, and tension and pain showed in his furrowed brow and taut, partly opened mouth. He wore the look of one who would die hard, Oliver thought as he sat and listened to a sharp cracking of thunder and the rumbling that followed to reverberate through the very stone about them. It was a bad night for dying. But, he thought, watching Roland's face, at least he would not die alone.

No man should have to die alone.

Across the chamber, in the corner where she had been set, more opaque than the shadows that concealed her, the woman hilt of the dark sword stirred. One arm, hereto invisible beneath waves of carven hair, emerged to point toward the window, diminutive fingers curving to beckon . . .

Lightning cracked the air apart, and a sudden gust of wind screamed through the unshuttered aperture, gutting all the candles on the table. Thunder reverberated and even the stone shuddered. Oliver flinched inadvertently as another bolt of lightning seemed to strike the very tower itself. Roland writhed suddenly, with renewed violence, arching. . . He screamed, an eerie keening at one with the next deep bellowing thunder, and clawed at covers and unseen things. Oliver, fully roused, lunged to seize the other man and hold him still, recognizing crisis. Roland gasped and struggled with extraordinary strength, cried out again, some incoherent defiant sound—then, of a sudden, went lax and panting against Oliver's chest.

"Mother of God! Praise be!" Oliver breathed aloud, forgetting the violence of the storm as he felt Roland's face, the drops of moisture that were gathering on his skin. Impossibly—the fever had broken, and he felt a foolish grin tug at the corners of his mouth. "Thou are not so easily killed as I had thought!" he muttered. "Thy insufferable stubbornness, no doubt!" Roland groaned as lightning split the darkness once more, from some farther distance. Abruptly, his eyes opened. His mouth stirred, dry tongue across parched lips.

"Thou!" he rasped in amazement and stiffened.

Oliver's grin widened. "Aye. Myself!" he acknowledged.

Roland swallowed, eyes still gleaming as he stared in open-faced wonder. "It was thou who—kept the witch women away . . ." he said faintly. Oliver's smile vanished. Roland sighed, closed his eyes, and went limp as he tumbled into the honest sleep of healing.

Witch women? Oliver did not move for a time. The rumbling thunder faded gradually to disappear behind the steady sounds of falling rain, and the lightning lost brilliance, becoming distant and erratic flashings of light.

He knew of the truths that were present ofttimes in the dreams, even delirium, of men. He was puzzled by Roland's peculiar statement, and the even stranger gratitude that had seemed to accompany it. Slowly, he lowered the sleeping man into the pillows, feeling cooling skin and sweat. Exhaustion made his senses reel. Vigilance was no longer needful, for it was clear enough that Roland would live. Oliver gave it up and sank back in the chair to almost instant slumber.

Roland winced occasionally as Oliver changed the bandages about his shoulder the next day, but otherwise made no sound. Likewise, he had silently accepted food and drink, only struggling to sit up with determined effort.

"It is clean and shrinking, God be praised," Oliver commented. "I consider that it will heal well and quickly, do thou have a care." He finished strapping Roland's upper arm to his ribs and stepped back.

"Why do thou do this?" Roland asked suddenly.

Oliver looked at him. Smiled a little. "Someone must!" He shrugged.

Roland shook his head and looked away. "Nay," he whispered. Oliver sighed inaudibly and moved to pour himself a goblet of mead from the flagon on the table. He drank slowly, with pleasure.

Roland shifted himself with great effort and no small discomfort, his face hard. "I hate this weakness!" he growled.

Oliver grinned and seated himself comfortably in a chair by the table. "That is evident!" he said. Roland did not look at him, but stared toward the window with focused attention.

"I think, thou did not leave me through the whole of it, my lord!" Roland said roughly after a moment. Statement or question . . . It was acknowledgment of a sort.

"Nay," Oliver responded agreeably. He drank again and set the cup down, and added a drier note to his voice. "It took a strong man to hold thee in thy fevered ravings! So, I flatter myself, I am!"

Roland was silent for a time, and watching him with interest, Oliver was content to wait. "I am—unused to kindness!" he grated at last.

Oliver's eyebrows rose. That, coming from Roland, was a monumental concession. "Aaah. Well!" he said smoothly, smiling broadly. "That, as I perceive it, Sir Roland, is a problem in charity!" This time, Roland turned his head to look at him. Oliver went on, "Charity is a perverse virtue, for giving may easily be done without nick or blemish to the pride! But, receiving, which is the other side of the blade . . . Aaah! That does require another, humble sort of generosity!"

Roland frowned, his eyes wary as he remembered his astonishment at Lord Oliver's offer, a little before he had lost consciousness a few days before. "Thou mock me!" he growled.

Oliver straightened and leaned forward, his face gone intently serious. "Strangely, Roland, I never have!" he retorted clearly. The other continued to stare at him with taut-featured reserve, but did not respond.

Oliver stood, abruptly restless. "I concede, I have learned to counter the burdensome weight of thy unrelentingly intense ferocity with some sharpness of wit!" he said acidly. "And I have used the same in an effort to be generous with thee, despite the hazards of attempting to scale that mountainous, granite pride behind which thou conceal thyself, for I have long admired that particular and unusual courage that is thine!" He exhaled abruptly. Roland looked away, jaw hard. "More. I gladly recognize the rare prowess that courage hath

brought thee! My honor is not a small, mean thing to be-
grudge another man his well-earned brilliance, nor even to
resent honest victory over me! Nor do I neglect to remember
that thou may have slain me as thou were entitled to do.
Indeed, knowing thee, as I expected!" He shook his head.
"Thou who are become better in battle than any man I
know, who killed the Lombard King and took his head?"

Roland jerked around at that. "Thou know of that?" he
grated, eyes wide.

Oliver paused, then nodded. "It was evident. I saw thy
wounds. And thy bitterness," he said quietly. Roland's jaw
hardened at the memory. "Pride, like charity, is perverse,"
Oliver added more gently. "Thou art a man of honor, for all
thy savage manner and countenance. I have never been thy
foe, Sir Roland. Not like others." Roland looked away again.
Annoyance flared as Oliver made a last attempt to breach that
impenetrable expression. "Indeed," he drawled, turning toward the door. "I commend my own good courage for the
times I have, with full knowledge of thy distempered hatred
of my person, entrusted my back to thee in battle, this winter
past!" He reached the door and grasped the latch, pulling the
heavy oak door open.

Roland's voice stopped him. "Noble Oliver." It was said
without sarcasm of any sort. Oliver spun about, amazed. Roland's face was more open than he had ever seen it, and for
an instant, he saw admiration, before the other looked away.

"I have no experience—of friendship," Roland said in a
voice gone soft. Oliver did not answer at once. He nodded a
little, recognizing another, even more monumental concession. He found a rueful smile.

"Nor am I given to love wisely, I consider!" he murmured.
Roland looked at him. "That is the chief beauty of friendship," he offered gently. "It is not a lonely condition!" With
that, he left.

It was Sir Roland now. A name without a house of origin,
but instead, an office that while it was achieved had yet to be
fulfilled. King's Champion . . . Defender of the King's honor
. . . Acutely sensitive to the potent implications of this, Roland was uneasy on another account, as he found himself
incorporated into a world that, previously, had vehemently
held him to its periphery. Needing the single reassurance of

his own strength, Roland pursued his own recovery with ha-
bitual belligerence, declining aid, moving the mangled shoulder and arm despite violent waves of pain, bandaging and
cleaning the wound himself.

Likewise, he was uneasy to find himself quartered like a
rich man, and with property from some unspecified source.
There was richer clothing for him than he had ever seriously
imagined owning, and an abundance of it. New arms and
armor, and a shield with a plain gold surface. New accoutrements for the golden horse.

"Where are my own garments?" he asked Lord Oliver on
his first day out of the bed where he had lain, overlong, it
seemed.

"Burned, thankfully!" The other man grinned.

Roland frowned suspiciously as he fingered the broidered,
fine green wool of a new-made tunic. "Then, from whence?"

Oliver spread his hands, lips still quirked. "Nay. Not from
me. I do protest innocence!" he retorted. "Perhaps the
King?" Roland looked startled, then knew it must be so. He
dropped the matter by broaching the difficulties of clothing
himself.

It was likewise strange to find himself amid the company
of the highborn, seated at the high table in the great hall for
each evening feast, his place now among the highest of all.
It was a new experience to be served, instead of serving, and
unobtrusively, he sought to imitate Lord Oliver's easy manner, though in his own more sober, self-contained way. Cour-
tesies that came with natural elegance to the other man were
for him fraught with effort.

So it was as he moved among the other lords, face cold as
ever, and stern, meeting looks that were sometimes accept-
ing, sometimes admiring. More often concerned and suspicious. He had won a place, he understood. He had yet to
prove his fitness for it.

As he recovered, it seemed strange to realize the near constant companionship of Lord Oliver. Oliver, who was loved
and sought after by all, whose openheartedness and shrewd
intelligence and gift for laughter seemed to leave good-
naturedness in their wake. Oliver, who drew him inexorably
toward the company of other, primarily young men, where
he took some small part in discussions of horses and arms,

or hunting, or strategy and such interests as preoccupied them all.

Oliver, whose very apparent friendship did much to breach any chasms of resentment against him for the office that many thought rightfully belonged to De Montglave. Still, Roland knew, he had much yet to prove.

And Oliver, who was equally popular with women, it seemed. Who spoke to them with a gentle, particularly warm and gallant courtesy that was entirely alien to Roland's feelings. And these highborn women, with their fine attire, and deadly large doe eyes, were everywhere now, no longer a remote hazard. Roland felt each curious or thoughtful look, or smile, with greater clarity than he would have noticed the loosed arrows from longbowmen at twenty paces, and sought refuge in remote expression and eyes that did not seem to notice, a frigid manner that was easily read.

Roland waited in the shadows of one of the pillars that supported the ceiling of the great hall as Oliver had requested, aloof from the rest who drifted into groups for conversation after the evening's feast. His shoulder pained him, and he could feel his own exhaustion. He frowned. It took too long, this healing. Surreptitiously, he slipped his left hand through his belt to provide support, then exhaled in relief as he saw Lord Oliver stride toward him from across the hall.

"The council is to assemble a few days hence," Oliver told him quietly, "as I understand, to plan strategy against the Infidel who rise up in the Spanish peninsula to the south." He sighed deeply and glanced about him. "The new Archbishop, Lord Turpin, has been in private council with the King these past weeks. He comes from the Pope and knows much of those realms beyond the Pyrenees. Something of this new and ambitious Emir of Saragossa, by all account. Thou will attend the council, of course." He added, "Maps and charts are being readied now."

Roland inhaled sharply. "I know naught of such charts or documents," he admitted after a moment.

Oliver gave him a penetrating look. "Nor much of councils, I consider!" he inserted dryly. " 'Tis of little import. Listen with care, and thou will learn all thou need to know. For the rest, there are not many who read or write. Myself—I had the fortune to be reared by my grandsire, a scholarly man after the manner of our King. I learned from him, and would gladly teach thee what I know.''

A muscle in Roland's hard cheek tightened as he looked away. ''I thought such was the province of holy men. Priests and the like . . .'' he murmured.

Oliver smiled. ''Not always!'' he said. ''Well . . . ?''

Roland looked at him. ''I accept, and gladly,'' he managed in a husky voice that revealed his long habit of total independence.

Oliver grinned. ''Good . . . '' he began, and saw the other man's face harden.

''My Lord Oliver . . .'' Softly uttered. Oliver turned to see the Duchess of Bordeaux and his sister, her eyes downcast.

''My lady?'' he offered warmly, and bowed, reaching to kiss the hand she held out to him.

''I am come to thank thee for thy particular attention to my son.'' She smiled as he straightened. ''He thrives under thy tutelage and example, my lord. And, I am given to know that this very morning, he galloped his palfrey without a tumble!'' Reluctantly, he released her hand and smiled as well.

''Lord Huon shows heroic courage, my lady,'' he told her gently. ''He has aptitude. More. I do enjoy the experience, my lady, for it anticipates the welcome condition of fatherhood that, God willing, will be mine someday!'' The Lady Alicia flushed a little and looked away. Roland went rigid under her interested gaze.

''Sir Roland.'' She held out her hand. ''I am glad to see my prayers for thy recovery answered.'' Roland managed a frigid and minimal bow, and swallowed, unable to utter a sound. ''It was a most fearful injury thou sustained,'' she offered smoothly, then, with a slight hesitation, removed her hand from such awful proximity.   •

''My—lady!'' Roland rasped clumsily, sketched another bow, and strode away. Better the battlements than this . . .

Oliver stared after him, frowning, then turned to salvage something from this hideous breach of courtesy. ''I pray thy charity for my friend, my lady,'' he managed. ''He is better accustomed to address the point of a sword than the gentle dignity of a lady!'' Lady Alicia smiled, her eyes twinkling with amusement, clearly unoffended.

It was the Lady Aude behind her, gazing in the direction

that Roland had vanished, who spoke. "He is shy, I consider!" she murmured very softly.

"Come, Aude, we have much to do before we seek our rest!" The Duchess took command. Oliver bowed as they left, and straightened to exhale almost audibly.

Shy? Roland?

"Mother of God!" he spluttered softly. Shook his head. "Oh, Aude!"

It was infinitely more comfortable, despite the arm held by his belt, to be astride the gold horse once more, riding out with Lord Oliver the following day to indulge that other's passion for falconry. Hills and woods, open meadows and brush, were welcome after so much new experience of people and court. Roland raised his face to the fresh warm breeze and savored the feel of it ruffling his hair. He glanced at Lord Oliver, who rode easily, his left arm held out in practiced steadiness, the hooded peregrine perfectly balanced despite talons and jesses upon it.

Some five miles southeast of Bordeaux castle, Oliver drew rein upon the crest of a hill overlooking a gentle meadowed valley beyond. He breathed deeply and turned to Roland who brought his horse to halt alongside.

"It is a pity thou are not yet able to manage this," he said, glancing at Roland's relaxed face and right hand that held the reins. "I have another bird."

"Nay. I am content."

Clearly it was so, and Oliver dropped his reins to stroke the bright speckled plumage of the falcon. "She is a valiant creature, my Valkarie," he said softly. "I like to loose her to find what she will. I never hunt her with others, or with dogs." He looked up. "I raised her from a fledgling." Roland nodded. He understood. Oliver loosed the hood with its crest of bright feathers and unwound the jesses. Held out his arm. "She always considers before she takes flight," he added. Roland watched.

Neat and quick, the falcon opened her wings to the breeze yet continued to cling to Lord Oliver's glove. Sleek, fierce against the bright sky. Dark, Roland thought, like Durandal's wings. He shifted in the saddle. The bird's eyes were clear, deep brilliant as she turned her head and seemed to stare into his own with unblinking ferocity. Canny wild eyes that knew . . . Roland had an unsettling lurch of feeling that he had been recognized, then Oliver moved his arm and the falcon took to the air, fluttering upward until she became a mere speck against the cloudless blue sky.

They both stared after the bird, following her wide, soaring arcs on wings outspread to embrace the thermals, jesses trailing. Nay, this was not the same as his previous experience, Roland acknowledged as he listened to the falcon's poignant, solitary cry echo across the air. There was no multitude of lords and others. No grim attention to the managing of blind hooded birds for their masters, ever at the frail, tempered call of the falconer. Just himself and Oliver—and the one peregrine. And silence, of a sort.

The falcon swooped with a single cry, then soared upward in a spiral to hover as a dark speck poised in one place, far, far above them.

"I have often wondered how it is they see . . ." Oliver said softly.

"Very clearly," Roland murmured unthinking reply, eyes never leaving the falcon. Oliver glanced at him, and the bird plummeted then, truer than any arrow, to a point more than a hundred yards beyond them, to vanish amid tall grasses. Oliver nudged his horse's sides and trotted down the hill toward the place where the bird had disappeared. He used no lure, Roland noted, following, halting his horse and remaining astride as Oliver dismounted and went to retrieve the falcon and her prey, a small partridge.

Jesses fastened, he did not hood the peregrine at once, but stood, instead, holding the partridge and allowing the falcon to feed from it.

"I mislike to do my hawking as others, in a company," Oliver said slowly, watching the bird tear and gulp meat. "The beauty of it is lost then. It is not the prey, or the hunting. It is the bird itself." He looked up, and Roland nodded. Their eyes met in a moment of pure understanding, then Oliver discarded the few feathers and scraps that remained of the partridge and walked to his horse to mount with a singular gracefulness that did not disturb the peregrine's balance in the slightest.

The falcon cocked her head and stared. Roland reached out, as though compelled, and touched her sleek plumage uneasily. Those eyes—what did she see . . . ? Again, he had that eerie feeling of being recognized.

"I am surprised. It is not like Valkarie to accept a stranger's hand," he heard Oliver say. Or was it that he understood that look, something so wild as to be fraught with a unique power of its own. "I have another young bird I would gladly give."

"Nay!" Roland cut him off, withdrawing his hand to find the reins. He watched Oliver fasten the falcon's hood. "I would but set it free!" he grated harshly and swung his stallion about, set it to canter up the hill, back the way they had come.

Oliver stared after him for a moment, surprised, then intrigued. He spurred his own mount to catch up, wondering if he understood.

Roland—who could never be entirely predictable.

TEN

A.D. 774–775

"I reiterate." Lord Gerard of Rouscillon spoke with vehement conviction. "By far the most prudent course at this time, Majesty, is to continue to fortify and garrison the Saxon March. Thereby, the truce may be enforced next year, and the frontier is assured. Lord Ganelon may then, this winter, march south with such forces as can reasonably be removed. For the meantime here, Majesty, thou may assemble an army and gather such provender as is needful for an arduous campaign in suitable places just to the north of the mountains. Then, with the coming of spring, I do propose a march south to take Navarre and secure the mountains . . ." Charlemagne sat quietly at the head of the table, his attention apparent only in his slight frown. To the King's left, the Archbishop sat with negligent ease, his keen brown eyes watchful and alive with interest. Duke Naimes De Baviere, likewise an older man and a very experienced soldier, leaned forward.

"Majesty, I must endorse Lord Gerard's good sense, for his plan is most practicable. And we must have Lord Ganelon . . ." A rippled murmur of agreement passed through the lords gathered at the table. Roland frowned. Apart from the others, he stood against the chamber wall to the right of the King, unable, as he had been for the past two weeks, to seat himself amid the rest of such auspicious company. And, as Oliver had suggested, he had listened assiduously, and

132

learned, assimilating information and opinions with increasing preoccupation. Likewise, to Oliver's silent surprise and willing cooperation, he had become engrossed at other times in the study of maps and lettering sufficient to learn to recognize place names and such symbols as were used to define boundaries, rivers, coast lines, mountains, and plains.

Nay, he thought now. Not this way.

"To pursue Lord Gerard's direction a little further, Majesty," Duke Naimes continued in a modulated, deliberate voice. "With Navarre and the Pyrenees taken, it would be wise to plan, at this time, to fortify the mountain passes, and by this means secure the realm and hold the Spanish March against these Moorish Infidel and, at the same time, minimize the cost in men and resources . . ."

"Aye!" another lord broke in. "It is a good plan that does not forget the Saxon or Dane, and considers the tribes of Avars and Slavs that also grow restless to the east. Given strategic placement for such fortifications, minimal garrisons will be sufficient to secure the passes. And the mountains are impassable in winter." Roland felt his own teeth clench. It was too much talk of defense.

"Do thou think so, my lord?" De Montglave drawled clearly, his eyes keen. "I do recall an ancient history of one Hannibal of Carthage who brought elephants out of Africa and across those same mountains in winter to the very gates of Rome! Nay, my lord, I consider thy optimism imprudent!" The other man scowled, and Charlemagne, with rare expressiveness, shot Lord Oliver an appreciative look as he sat back with a sigh and began drumming long fingers slowly on the surface of the large map before him.

"And so," the Archbishop Turpin murmured softly, yet with remarkable clarity, "like Hannibal, the Emir Blancandrin rises out of Africa! And Africa is vast indeed!" Unable to keep silence anymore, and understanding the priest's meaning, Roland strode forward to stand at the foot of the council table. He sketched an impatient bow that ignored the startled glances of those who had virtually forgotten his presence.

"Majesty, this is all defensive parleying!" he grated. "There are fortifications along the western coasts, yet they do not prevent the Vikings who come from their land far away across the sea from raiding and destroying year after year!

Likewise, what does it serve to secure the mountains when the Infidel may plot and grow stronger still in their untouched southern holdings!'' His eyes sought the King's unreadable gaze. "Is Christian might to begin this war like a wolf cornered against a cliff?" There was annoyed murmuring in response to this.

"Mad raving!" someone muttered. The King, by contrast, relaxed even more in his chair, and Lord Oliver smothered a grin as Roland grew rigid and scowled. Lord Gerard of Rouscillon leaped to his feet, also scowling darkly.

"Majesty! I do protest Sir Roland's inexperienced and youthfully emotional outburst!" he shouted hotly.

"I would be an idiot not to realize the hazards of such ponderous and cautious plans as I have heard proposed, my lord!" Roland hissed his scathing retort. "Were these Moors a pack of wolves against which thou propose to defend thy flocks, why then—as I am given to understand—by the time thou hast prepared thy holding pen, they will have had time sufficient to multiply and rear another generation to increase their threat!" He shook his head and shifted restlessly. "Nay, Majesty. This is not sufficient enterprise! Taking Navarre will not even threaten the growing might of these Infidel. Nor put any halt whatever to the ambitions of their princes!" He began to pace, wild and taut with vigor, save for the clearly injured arm held by his belt. "And to wait, Majesty. That is the height of folly!" Voices swelled into a furious cacophony to fill the hall. Roland stopped pacing and stood, feet apart, glaring. Only Oliver's face was calm. The one man who understood him, he realized with surprise. Friend. The Archbishop studied him with penetrating cunning, and the King?

Charlemagne's eyes gleamed with curiosity. Slowly he rose to his feet. "Silence!" he roared, more frigid than an arctic gale.

He was obeyed, in an instant.

"Are we surrounded by so much cackling poultry to make such disturbance at the growlings of a new fox in thy midst?" Charlemagne asked quietly. Then, in icy tones, "This is our council of foxes and wolves! Each man here hath a place earned of particular merit, or skill. But it is our will that decides the course of Christendom." The lords regarded Roland with controlled anger, but none countered the King's reprimand. "Thou art a new voice to be heard, Sir Roland,"

Charlemagne said clearly, reseating himself. "And, beyond this tempestuous display, it is apparent thou hast something important to offer! We are curious and will hear thee out."

"Majesty!" Roland whispered in a tone of gratitude. Then he frowned and began pacing like a caged beast once more. "Majesty, as I have said, it is folly to wait and, by waiting, to plan no more than a defensive strategy that may do no more than deter the foe! Such position suggests weakness to my mind, and would rather incite these Infidel princes to even greater effort against thee in the conviction that there is little, in effect, to bar the path of conquest." He glanced at the Archbishop and saw Turpin give a slight nod of approval. He continued in the same sternly determined tones. "And it hath been established that conquest is their intent!

"To leave the Infidel's power unblemished, without curb or restraint sufficient even to force parleying for treaty, is of itself invitation to unrelenting conflict! Nay, 'tis better to assert thyself now and bridle these Moorish lords before they have come together with their armies."

"Majesty!" Lord Gerard broke in, standing, his face mottled and furious. "We have not sufficient forces gathered to loose an army upon the Infidel at this time!"

"An army is not needed!" Roland's voice sliced across the other man's speech. His eyes glinted. "Do thou take the queen bee, my lord, and thou hast the hive! Nor does it take an army to conquer by such fashion, my liege, but, rather, a hornet is more effective!"

"Thou are mad, Sir Roland!" Lord Gerard growled. There was a murmur of agreement, and Roland glowered, his right hand going for the dark sword at his back. She hissed wickedly as he brought her through the air and held her, point first toward the company as he advanced upon them.

"Nay, my lord!" he grated harsh retort. "Rather, I am the hornet, and this is my sting!" He looked at the King, his voice becoming passionate as he lowered Durandal's point to the stone floor. "Majesty, loose me! Use me to strike direct at this Emir Marsilla who, even now, attempts Navarre! I need but a few to ride with me . . ."

"Majesty!" Lord Gerard leaned toward the King, fists clenched in temper. "This is not strategy, but rather the vanity of one untried in war who seeks to glorify himself to the cost of us all!"

"Aye, my liege!" Duke Naimes stood now, with others whose voices rose in outraged agreement.

Again, Roland cut across the cacophony. "Not so, Majesty!" he snarled hotly. "The wolf doth not announce his presence, but hunts with stealth and silence, unknown until it is too late!" Eyes turned toward him then, and voices stilled. "So, too, this wolf would hunt with his pack, seeking to disembowel the foe. Nay, Majesty, the single glory I seek is Marsilla himself or, failing that, such members of his house as would serve for hostage!"

"Unnatural!" Lord Gerard whispered audibly. "Impossible!"

"Ingenious, Majesty!" the Archbishop said smoothly, rising for the first time, his dark eyes gleaming, a smile lurking about the corners of his mouth. "And fitting, for these Infidel have a great fear of such demons as they call Djinn. Likewise, they revere their lords. Aye. It is not unwise, I consider, to fight Djinn with Devil!" Charlemagne gave him a penetrating look, and Roland saw Oliver's lips flicker with amusement as he nodded slightly. "Or so they will believe," Turpin went on in the same even, melodious tones, one hand fluttering a little, "for such is their faith!" Angered lords subsided into their seats, and Charlemagne sat back in his chair, eyes shifting to Roland, who stood under that intent scrutiny with his entire body braced, surprised by the Archbishop's support.

"Aye. 'Tis the Devil himself, conspiring such . . ." Lord Gerard muttered. "We need the wisdom of Lord Ganelon!" Turpin looked at him and crossed himself with singular elegance.

"Blessed are the faithful!" he said with bland reverence. "I do not seek to question divine will, but to understand and serve its course! From among great lords and proven knights, this man hath been raised to singular prowess and victory. To the south of Christendom, Satan raises his head and summons his demons against the might of Christendom. Is it to be wondered at that divine will should also raise a shield to the protection of the sword of Christ that is our liege lord, Charlemagne?" So gently uttered—Turpin's words were met with a constrained silence. The King shifted and stood, a smile crossing his mouth briefly.

"Such is the will of the sword of Christendom!" Charlemagne said firmly, still looking at Roland. "We will embark upon both courses, seeing inherent compatibility in the plans.'' He looked at Lord Gerard. ''For the spring, we will so prepare.''

''Majesty.'' The other stood and bowed deeply. But Charlemagne looked again at Roland.

''And for the present, we will loose this wolf to hunt among Infidel sheep! God's will shall manifest itself in the result!'' Roland felt himself exhale in relief and gratitude.

''Majesty!'' he breathed and bowed in turn.

''My liege?'' He straightened as Lord Oliver stood then, and looked at the King.

Charlemagne turned a little. ''My lord De Montglave?''

''Majesty, I would become a wolf with Sir Roland. I fancy such hunting as he proposes to do!''

Again, Charlemagne smiled. ''So be it, my lord.'' He looked at Sir Roland once more, his expression unreadable. ''Go now, Sir Roland. Prepare thyself. God and the good Archbishop shall go with thee!''

Roland stared in surprise, then bowed deeply, missing Turpin's like gesture of acceptance. He straightened, smiling a gleaming combination of eagerness and conviction. ''Majesty!'' he offered reverently, startling them all with a tone that implied he had been given great riches rather than near-certain death. He turned on his heel and walked away, slipping the dark sword into her baldric among the folds of his cloak.

''Majesty?'' He heard Duke Naimes behind him. ''Surely such enterprise should be delayed. Sir Roland hath but one arm?''

Roland spun about, still smiling. ''I have but one sword, my lord!'' he retorted clearly. ''One hand is sufficient to wield it!'' Then he left them all.

The first suggestions of the autumn to come emerged as a well-mounted and armed troop of a hundred carefully picked knights rode down along the banks of the Garonne River, then south, across the wild passes through the high mountains of the southern border, almost directly north of Saragossa.

Each man chosen, or volunteered, was fully armored and rode a good destrier. Likewise, each carried his own supplies and essentials, thereby eliminating the hindrance of pack animals. For the same reason, food was hunted rather than carried, and each man was a veritable arsenal, armed with longbow and abundant quivers of arrows as well as the usual weapons of the highborn, lance, shield, axe, mace, dagger, and sword. Only Roland, riding at the head of the company with Lord Oliver beside him, dispensed with most of these, being fully armored astride his gold horse, with bow and quiver slung against his saddlebag, and naught else, save for the dark sword that he often held across his thighs. He was also the only one to ride without some blessed and sacred relic upon his person, a vial of blackened Martyr's blood, or Saint Augustine's molar, or the finger bone or lock of hair from some other holy and blessedly revered personage.

Instead, the Archbishop Turpin rode his conspicuous white stallion beside him like some reminder of God's warlike interests in this undertaking . . .

Autumn was firmly entrenched as the company left rugged, snowcapped peaks behind them to descend through ruddy and gold woodlands where leaves had begun to tumble and litter the ground, and rode down into the harsh, arid land between Navarre and Aragon, a land filled with boulders and ravines, dust, and clumps of rough, knife-edged grasses, low shrubs fit for goats and little else.

It was little. wonder that the Infidel turned avaricious eyes toward the lush fertile lands and the abundance of the Frankish north, Sir Rinalde De Montalban commented once.

And Roland led them on, discreetly riding for the most part, at dawn and dusk, keeping to terrain that offered the greatest concealment. Aye, he thought, staring with fierce-eyed penetration at all about him, we have become as wolves . . . And we shall come out of the darkness, like demons, to strike, like the northern heathens, with fire and terror. Impatiently, he brooded and stroked the lethal promise of Durandal's dark blade. Impatiently, it was Roland who slipped from whatever camp his company made, to search the surrounding land for prey as he led them westward into the borders of Navarre, past small, impoverished villages whose livelihood was precariously eked from herds of tough, lean sheep and goats to other scattered hamlets farther south where evidence of the Infidel Marsilla's interest in conquest became apparent in the devastation of the land.

* * *

They were encamped in a small, deep gorge that was flanked on one side by a high and precipitous ridge and on the other by undercut stone belied by the faint trickle of a small stream. Most of the company was asleep, huddled in cloaks and furs against the sharp chill of the dry, late autumn air. Roland looked up and glanced about, seeing the dim, dark shapes of men, barely visible about the embers of neglected and diminutive fires. Horses snorted occasionally, occupied with consuming the grasses that had been gathered for them, the grain that had been carefully pilfered, and the Archbishop's white stallion was a grey shade in the darkness.

Oliver lay beside him, face serene, eyes closed in absolute peace. Something, Roland thought uneasily, that he could not attain. His face tightened, eyes narrowing as he thought he saw the gleam of something a little beyond the encampment where stone rose up like a wall to the south. He stiffened, drawing his feet under him as the—grey, nay—white object slipped down as though floating against the sheer precipice to vanish.

Roland frowned, and a moment later, from the same direction, he saw the Archbishop Turpin striding lightly toward him from the tethered horses, tossing back the brown cloak that was his single concession to the blatant white of his attire. Buoyant of stride, he slipped nimbly, silently among sleeping knights, approaching purposefully, eyes gleaming in the darkness, pupils enormous.

Roland noted the priest's unerring tread, and then he reached him and folded himself gracefully onto the ground before the dying fire, his cloak billowing like crumpled wings on either side of him.

"Aaaah!" The Archbishop sighed deeply as though fatigued and leaned forward to lightly touch Lord Oliver's brow. "He sleeps with the profound peace of one who is confident of his soul's safety, thy lover!" Turpin remarked, settling back, both hands at rest in his lap.

"Lover?" Roland growled, eyes widening for an instant before he glared at the priest.

Turpin cocked his head a little, expression unperturbed. "Is he not, Sir Roland?" he asked. "Some say so, for it is a wonder, this—friendship that hath sprung up of a sudden between thee when, but recently, it was surely apparent that thou were bent on mutual slaughter!"

"Nay!" Roland snarled in outraged indignation. "That is heinous and mortal sin!"

Turpin smiled a little. "There are some undeterred by such consideration," he remarked dryly. "And it hath been noted likewise, thou elude the company of women with the agility of a wild hare!" He shrugged a little as Roland felt scarlet heat rise up his neck, flare across his face. "Not to put too fine a point on it, but such conclusion was not without its own logic. A Roland for an Oliver, they say!"

"Then let them say it for a better reason!" Roland said. "I would not have my honor so blemished, nor his. And if I do not bear the company or use of women, then that is my affair!"

Turpin's eyes probed his own. The priest smiled of a sudden. "Then thou are more chaste than I!" he commented softly. "Do thou husband thy virgin estate, Sir Roland, for it is known that the pure and chaste are blessed with especial favor and given to singular accomplishment." He made the sign of the Cross over Roland's head as Roland glanced down uncomfortably. "So is manifest the direction of divine will." Roland looked up, eyes widening as he understood. Could it be so—and because . . . ? "But this is not the main point on which I sought thee out," Turpin continued, his tone firmer.

"My lord?" Roland managed.

Again the priest cocked his head, mischief in the depths of his eyes. "It would appear thou are uncommon favored, Sir Roland, for, verily, such highborn Infidel as thou seek do ride toward us, come from Saragossa and on direct passage to Pamplona."

"What is this?" Roland hissed, leaning forward, every nerve alert, eyes glinting, all else forgot.

Turpin smiled. "Such lust!" he noted. Roland scowled. "As I have said, something near half a day's ride from here, and to the west, a fine prize awaits thee! One of the most powerful among these Spanish Infidel in the person of Lord Aelroth, who is the firstborn son of the Emir Falsaron and, by blood, nephew to both the emirs Marsilla and Blancandrin." Roland's eyes sparkled and his lips began to curve into a vicious smile. The priest continued, "This Lord Aelroth, in company with his sire, Lord Falsaron, marches to secure Pamplona for the Infidel Marsilla by treaty got with threat of force. Do thou bridle thy passion, Sir Roland!" Turpin added sharply as Roland's smile expanded into a wicked grin. "They ride with three thousand, and I do not consider that they will tumble readily into thy bloody embrace!" Roland stood and stared, as though transfixed, into the darkness.

"Will they not . . . ?" he whispered hungrily, dismissing entirely the stated odds of thirteen to one. "Will they not!" Then suddenly he frowned and turned to the Archbishop. "How is it that thou hast learned all this in what can be no more than a brace of hours?" he grated violently. Turpin stood with unruffled calm.

"I am not given to uttering untruths, young Roland!" He shrugged a little. "Consider this information got from the gift I have for divine vision!" Roland continued to stare into those remarkable eyes, his frown shifting in quality.

"I am the King's Champion," he said slowly, "yet still I am a bastard witchling, which makes of me a two-fold creature. What, I am wont to wonder, beyond God's Bishop, art thou?" Turpin smiled wryly. He shook his head a little, as though amused by Roland's intensity.

"Suffice it to say, Sir Roland," he said calmly, "that in this instance, I am no more than thyself, an instrument of divine purpose!" His look became more penetrating as Roland's frown deepened. "I am the message. Thou are the means!" With that, he made the sign of the Cross in blessing and bent lightly to set a miniature version of the benediction on Lord Oliver's brow. "I bid thee good night," he said softly, straightening to stride away. Roland watched until the Archbishop finally disappeared into the shadows on the far side of the camp. Then, slowly, he reseated himself beside Oliver, who stirred sufficient to shift position.

"I think thou are not a priest at all . . . " Roland murmured to himself. "I think—thou may not even be a human soul . . . "

Instincts, and illusions . . . He shook his head to clear it for other, far more important matters.

How to best odds of thirteen to one . . .

In the darkest hours of a moonless night, fire erupted as though outflung by some powerful sorcery to ignite the brush and shrubs about the Infidel camp. Driven by erratic, shifting gusts of the night wind, it swept down upon them with ravaging appetite. Small, fleet, desert-bred Infidel horses screamed and rolled their eyes, jerked loose from tethering lines and milled about, trampling men and supplies in their panic as the flames rose high and leaped greedily toward them, accompanied by billowing clouds of bluish, suffocating smoke. Gone beserk with terror, they screamed and stampeded in a wave through the fire to vanish into the night, leaving destruction and chaos in their wake.

And then, out of the fire, a demon of a man appeared. Mounted on a great monster of a horse whose color showed it to be wrought of the same fire that roared toward men and tents and supplies alike, he was swathed in gold, his eyes blazing venom. And in his hand was a dark sword that sang hideously, even above the cries of men, and the crackling of flames, its keening hum the sum of chaos as it brought death to any in its path.

He was a Djinn—or Shaitan come out of the darkness, a horde of like demon warriors at his flank. A sorcerer, or so the Moors believed, who sliced a path of rapid and unrelenting destruction toward the Emirs they sought recklessly to protect, harvesting life more easily than a scythe could cut wheat.

Routed from tents of beacon magnificence, the lords Falsaron and Aelroth were barely able to bring up scimitars to their own defense before these weapons were shattered by the swooping dark sword of the Djinn, and they were seized. Half stunned, they were jerked up to hang across saddlebows like so much venison as the Djinn with the dark sword brought his horse and demons about, and thundered away, to vanish into the embrace of the fire, into the night.

Lathered, heaving horses stood, legs braced and thankful for the halt. Men, likewise, exhaled relief and wiped dust and sweat from their faces, cleaned bloodied swords, and eagerly drank stale water from their wineskins. Roland, his horse behind him, strode to a rise among the boulders strewn across the craggy ground and leaped up to stand, feet apart, undiminished, frowning at the horizon to the south.

"My lord . . ." he called out, hearing someone pass behind him. "What are our losses?" Rinalde of Montalban, in the process of dismounting, completed the move, then led his exhausted destrier closer.

"Three dead, Sir Roland." He removed a gauntlet and

wiped a hand across his mouth to clear his lips of dust. "Several wounded, but none too seriously." Roland nodded, his gaze shifting to the west for a moment, before he turned to face the other man.

"Good," he said softly. "And the Infidels?" Sir Rinalde grinned. It was such expression as one equal gave another, Roland noted at once. Acceptance . . .

"Four. Three died, but the heathen princes are healthy, and all are trussed like chickens for slaughter!" Montalban said cheerfully. Roland smiled a little then.

"So" he murmured. "We have two to question!" Then, more clearly. "We will rest here until the horses are recovered, my lord." Montalban nodded. "Who among us knows the Infidel tongue?"

"The priest, Turpin, as I do recall. 'Tis said he is from these parts," Rinalde answered promptly, then watched as Roland grinned this time and strode away toward the prisoners, calling for the Archbishop. After a moment, he followed, curiosity piqued.

Hideous, terrorized screams of agony faded into awkward rasping moans that rent air gone completely still. Sickened by what seemed an interminable process, Lord Oliver swallowed hard against the bile that rose violently in his throat and glanced at the two Infidel princes. Slighter than the Franks, begrimed and wiry beneath a tangle of rich, loose attire, bound to complete immobility, their swarthy complexions had become a peculiar shade of grey. The eyes of the younger Lord Aelroth glittered black loathing . . .

Oliver shifted as moans faded to spastic gasping. The second heathen was dying now. At last. It had gone more quickly with the first, dismembered with clear brutality, one finger at a time. Then the hands. Then other parts. Oliver looked at the priest who had stood beside Roland through the whole of it, murmuring translations. Now the Archbishop was silent, his wily face uncommon stern, and his look strangely threatening as he stared at Roland's unnatural sword, still held some three feet above the naked, spread-eagled remains of the man in the dirt before them both.

"It is done. There is no more to be got from him," he heard the priest murmur. Then Turpin turned and met his look. Oliver had a sudden impression of complete understanding, even approval, as Turpin swung away. Roland slowly lowered his sword, until it almost touched the ruin he had so slowly made of the dying man's belly.

"Leave the carcass here!" Roland grated. "Let the Infidel lords meditate upon it!" He swung away and strode to his horse, seizing wineskin and ration pouch from the pommel of the saddle before taking another few steps to some boulders where he seated himself. Without quite understanding why, Oliver followed and watched as Roland wiped gore from the dark sword's blade with a corner of his surcoat, resheathed it, then reached into the ration wallet for dried meat. He chewed vigorously as he stared at the corpse with an unsavory combination of eagerness and concentration.

"Mother of God!" Oliver gagged, his own face going ashen as he bent to retch up the acid contents of an empty stomach. "Aaah, Sweet Jesu!" He sat down abruptly on another rock.

"Truly, the combination of thy appetites is terrible!" Roland stopped eating and looked at him in surprise.

"Hunger is natural enough after so much effort," he began, his voice sharpening under the sheer revulsion of Oliver's look.

"After that?" the other demanded harshly.

"This is war!" Roland retorted, frowning. He glanced at the two remaining prisoners some fifty yards distant. "Or rather, the beginning of it."

Oliver continued to stare at him. "God keep me from ever committing such—untroubled bestiality as thou have just done!" he said brutally.

Roland met his look, but his face hardened. He continued chewing deliberately, swallowed, and looked away. "Being got as I am, my lord," Roland said icily, "I am not endowed with the fine sensibilities of such nobility as is thine!"

"Pah!" Oliver scowled dismissal. "That is but excuse! Nobility is as much a condition of the will as of the blood. And it is plain enough thou are not common bred!"

Roland rounded on him. "Nay. I am not!" He scowled. "I am a bastard witchling! And I do not forget it for an instant! I have even been given this unnatural sword to serve me! Know this, my lord. All I am, and all I do, is given to a single thing—the service and triumph of our liege lord, Charlemagne!" He looked away and continued eating with predatory ferocity.

Oliver was silent for a time, temper evaporating. Finally he exhaled with slow deliberation. "Thy singularity hath been noted!" he commented dryly. Roland looked at him, a little warily. "I consider," he went on slowly, "that destiny may be perceived in all this. I could never serve the King as thou are clearly meant to do."

Roland's face opened then. He did not respond, but glanced down at the remaining piece of dried meat in his hand, then, deliberately, put it back in the ration pouch. "Strange," he murmured, not looking at Oliver, "of a sudden, the sight of food sickens me!" He inhaled sharply and looked up, staring to the south and west with eagle keenness. "It will be snowing in the mountains," he said. "A hard return. I will have this Infidel Lord Ferragus to whom the Emir Marsilla gives Navarre and Pamplona, next!"

Oliver smiled a little and shook his head.

"I do not doubt it!" he murmured.

ELEVEN

A.D. 775

Charlemagne, enthroned in the great hall of Bordeaux castle, did not move by so much as a fraction as Roland, slightly to the fore of the company of returned knights, drove the two Infidel prisoners before him, then thrust them forcibly to their knees some six feet before the dais. He bowed deeply and gestured inclusively with one hand.

"Majesty. That which we were dispatched to do is accomplished. Into thy hands are delivered these two Infidel princes, the emirs Falsaron and Aelroth, both of the blood of the Emir Marsilla of Saragossa." As he spoke, the Archbishop Turpin strode silently from his place among the ranks to stand by the King's left hand. As Roland finished, he bent and murmured. Charlemagne, expression unchanged, inclined his head and stood.

"We are indeed well served, Sir Roland." His voice boomed out like measured thunder across the great hall to touch every member of his court, and he raised a hand to beckon slightly. "As befitting his office, we give custody of these two princes into the safekeeping of our Lord High Councillor, Lord Ganelon." Roland felt an unpleasant jolt of shock and stiffened as he saw the dark lord stride forward. Old foe—private enemy, and the man who was perversely responsible for honing the tenacity of his will to brutal strength.

Lord Ganelon bowed to the King and, with guardsmen

flanking him, took the two prisoners. Face stern, responsible, Roland noted as the dark lord inclined his head courteously, but otherwise unreadable, save for eyes that were deep like some witch's brew quietly fermenting into purest venom.

"Sir Roland, do thou come forward." Charlemagne's voice caught his attention, and Roland stepped forward to stand at the foot of the dais. His eyes widened at the slight smile that flickered across the King's hard mouth, then he bowed his head. He felt Charlemagne's hand settle on his right shoulder and knelt. The King spoke again with penetrating clarity.

"From the dust and fabric of Christian souls is sprung this Champion, and given to God's puissant duty, ennobled by singular accomplishment, we do likewise accord recognition.

"Do thou arise, Lord Roland, and receive from us the gifts of the fiefs of Brittany. We do endow thee with the duty and holding that is the Count of Brittany, Lord Prefect of the Breton March!"

Roland looked up, hardly aware that the King's hand had left his shoulder, eyes widening with a blend of awe and surprise. Charlemagne's eyes met his for a moment as he stood. Obedience that was unthinking—he had not thought beyond . . . Yet the King's eyes held a mystery of knowledge.

Roland bowed, incapable of speech, and reached for the King's hand, pressing his lips to the back, to the seal ring.

"I am thy man, body and soul," he managed to rasp. Charlemagne smiled fleeting acknowledgment as he straightened, then turned to face the rest of the company, faces that reflected either understanding or approval.

Save for one. Roland stepped down from the dais, caught Oliver's grin, and felt his friend's hand upon his shoulder. Beyond the rest, Lord Ganelon's face was fleetingly seen just before the dark lord left the hall.

He saw hatred there.

Amber light flickered from sconces set along the stone walls of Lord Ganelon's private, if temporary, quarters in Bordeaux castle. It was supplemented by a pair of time candles set on either side of a large table littered with maps, a bowl of dried fruit, and a flagon of wine. Behind the table, Lord Ganelon sat at attention, his fingertips delicately touching each other as he considered the Infidel prisoner before him, and the silent, guardian formality of his nephew Thierry near the door.

Dark heathen eyes that watched, expression contained by a will that was as determined as his own.

"Lord Aelroth, heir to the Emir Marsilla, and nephew to the Emir Blancandrin, son of the Emir Falsaron, now our— guest. There are empires awaiting thee!" Lord Ganelon said quietly in the Moorish tongue, rising gracefully to his feet and moving around the end of the table to stand directly before that richly robed, slight young man who stood proudly before him, for all his hands were bound behind him. Aelroth's eyes narrowed to counter his surprise at this knowledge of his tongue.

"Allah be praised. So I am!" he responded deliberately, in flawless Latin. The swarthy-featured Frank's eyes flickered. "I had not thought it likely for a Frank to know our language." He arched a brow. "Indeed, experience hath given me to know the northern Franks as a brutish and uningenious race." Lord Ganelon's features tightened, his responding stare assessing, as he reached for his dagger. The Moorish Prince did not even glance at it.

"And among us, my lord," he commented dryly in the heathen tongue, "thy people have a like repute!" He reached behind the prisoner and cut the Infidel Prince loose from his bonds. Aelroth moved his elegant, uncallused hands before him at once.

"Such courtesy!" the Infidel murmured, reverting to his own tongue. Lord Ganelon frowned, and from his place by the door, where he was given to steward the privacy of this incomprehensible intercourse, Thierry watched in wary confusion.

"Thy father . . ." Lord Ganelon began.

"Who art in chains!" Lord Aelroth cut in, coldly misquoting.

"The Emir Falsaron," Lord Ganelon's voice hardened, "and thyself are now held by our liege lord, King Charlemagne, Defender of the True Faith, as hostage to the intents of thy uncle, the Emir Marsilla of Saragossa." Aelroth's lips described a sardonic smile. His eyes gleamed in anger.

"As we were not—butchered with others of our race by the Christian Djinn with the dark sword, it was not difficult to conclude such intent!" Lord Ganelon's eyes narrowed.

"It is presumed, likewise," he said sharply, "that thou hast value to the Emir." Aelroth met this with a shrug, eyes flitting about the chamber, clearly unimpressed by his surroundings.

"Do thou wish to ransom us then?" he inquired smoothly. " 'Tis ironic, for I had thought followers of the Nazarene prophet were professed to disdain gold and such gifts as are given to men by Allah, His Name be praised!"

Lord Ganelon frowned at the contempt of the younger man. "It is the King's wish," he said in a hard voice, "that Marsilla disperses his forces, and that the Emir Blancandrin retires back across the sea to the land from which he is sprung!"

Lord Aelroth gave him a slanting look, then smiled. "Two small lives for so much?" he murmured smoothly. Then, on a harder note. "We too know the worth of martyrs, my lord! Allah is the One God, and Mohammed is his prophet! My revered uncle"—he made a slight and graceful gesture of obeisance—"is one of the faithful and will bring enlightenment to the western world. Sacrifices to such a cause are to be expected!" He shrugged again.

"Charlemagne is likewise a devout prince, champion, and guardian of the True Faith!" Ganelon retorted. Aelroth met his look. Dark gazes locked—melded—and became understanding.

"Then, the course of destiny is a matter for divine interpretation,"Aelroth said. "And men are but the instruments of its execution. Yet." His look hardened again, still locked with Lord Ganelon's. "I have understood that the followers of the Nazarene Prophet Jesus forswear all traffic with Djinn and the like. And I cannot honor thy liege lord's claim to just cause, nor consider him an equal and honorable foe when he summons Shaitan to his aid!"

"Who?" Aelroth caught the hard flicker of the Frank's eyes. He had touched a raw cord, he knew.

"I refer to the man with the lion's hair and the eyes of Shaitan, who is neither natural, nor human in battle. The Djinn of the Dark Sword." Aaah. It was unmistakable, the gleam of recognition and venom in this powerful Frankish lord's eyes. He continued, "This Djinn, who rises high in the eyes of thy—Christian King!" He turned away a little. "My lord Marsilla, who is devout, even holy, can only be reaffirmed in the justice of his intent to bring the light of Allah to these northern realms when he is given to understand thy Christian Prince is governed by Devils that draw him from honest practice of the teachings of the Prophet Jesus, whom he also reveres.'' Ganelon could not control the tightening of his mouth. Aelroth looked at him directly. "And thou, my lord," the young Infidel Prince sliced neatly with the scimitar of his wits. Drew blood. "Who understands how to be a king beyond the desecrations Shaitan wreaks upon honor?"

Lord Ganelon scowled and turned away, recognizing how accurately he had been read by this wily heathen, who could not be more than twenty-five years. He glanced briefly at his nephew still standing at attention, who could not have understood a word of this conversation. Ganelon inhaled sharply, realizing the potential that brewed so clearly between himself and this ingenious heathen Prince. He sought his chair and reseated himself, indicating with one hand that the Infidel should do likewise.

Roland, now Count of Brittany . . .

"Let us learn the intricacies of each other's mind more closely," he said with steel deliberation. Lord Aelroth found the comfort of a cushioned chair with regal grace. And from his place by the door, Thierry's brows tightened in a slight and very puzzled frown.

A few days later Roland felt compelled to seek the rarified air of solitude and the clearheaded sanity of Lord Oliver's presence upon the battlements. He flexed his shoulders as though against the exhaustion of unfamiliar burdens as he stepped through the tower portal and caught sight of De Montglave some distance from him. The air was bitter chill as it swept along frigid stone crenellations, and sheltered mounds of frozen snow lingered in the places the remote winter sun could not touch. Roland drew his cloak more closely about him. Oliver did not move, but continued to stand, staring outward, toward the east, a half-rolled parchment hanging from one hand. Roland trod lightly toward the other man and stopped against the parapet a stride to one side of his—aye—friend.

"I am disconcerted to be called my lord . . ." he began unevenly, facing the wind. "These vassals who come to give fealty to me, their new-made lord . . . I know naught of these fiefs, nor of the intricacies of my duty . . ." His mouth tightened in characteristic defiance. "Never have I felt so clearly, this—rootless—witch's bastardy that got me!'' Oliver turned, features strained and preoccupied, yet caught by Roland's confusion. ''War, I know,'' Roland whispered. ''Then, everything is clear.''

Oliver continued to look at him. ''It will come to thee,'' he said after a time, shifted the document in his hand and began to roll it up with controlled deliberation. Roland caught the strange edge to Oliver's voice and shifted. He saw the other's pallor and unusual strain.

''I too must learn a new duty,'' Oliver said quietly, staring out to where the sun touched frost and snowbanks on a white and umber countryside. Roland straightened. ''My grandsire and my brother are dead. Now, their duties and fiefs come to me.''

''Lord Oliver, Count de Montglave! None could be more worthy!''

''Nay!'' The hard edge of Oliver's voice surprised him completely. ''Thou misunderstand. I have in no way sought this. I am not as thee—possessed by such singular and overwhelming combination of ambition and honor! I loved my brother and wished him well of his inheritance, and my grandsire, likewise, from whom I learned much! Now this . . . This dual death that hath the stench of foul contrivance about it! I cannot be glad of what comes to me from it!'' Roland stared. Oliver looked away, pain and control at war upon his face, eyes gone liquid in honest regret. Oliver— who could weep.

Roland swallowed hard. ''Forgive me . . .'' Roland was astounded to hear himself murmur. ''I have no knowledge of familial love.'' Oliver looked at him again. He reached out and set his hand upon Roland's fur-clad shoulder. Strange touch—fraught with feeling things. A portal.

Deep blue eyes locked with gold, and Roland swallowed again, feeling something surge hard and painful inside him. He knew it was a common feeling, at that moment. Oliver moved closer, setting his other hand upon Roland's other shoulder, gaze softening.

''God is kind . . . '' he murmured very gently. ''For now I have another brother with whom to walk the path of life.''

Roland nodded. ''Aye,'' he said. It was a different, vulnerable commitment of the soul, this feeling of another's grief as though it were his own. ''Aye. Thou hast . . . ''

The embrace that followed was simple, natural affirmation of what was, in truth, a vow.

Restlessly unable to occupy the chair in the council chamber that was now his by right, Roland stood in his accustomed place apart from the rest of the company gathered about the vast oaken table. Remote, although in a different way, the King sat back in his great, ornately carven chair, gently stroking the curve of a dragon arm with the fingertips of one hand, listening with brows gathered in a frown that none could decipher.

Roland frowned as well, caught by the details of discussion that moved from lord to lord, and something more. Undertones—a thread woven through the fabric of the whole debate with subtle ingenuity, a misdirected emphasis on difficulties to the north with the Saxon tribes now held securely at bay, and a peculiar reluctance to encroach upon those southern strongholds where the Moors gathered like a tempest brewing.

Roland's feet shifted a little in confined response to the tension that shimmered through him as he listened. It all came from one man—Lord Ganelon. The Lord High Councillor, who had charge of, and traffic with the pair of hostage heathen princes, who could weave words to entangle men in much the manner of a fisherman throwing nets in the water, letting others do much of his persuading for him, simply directing them from time to time with the appearance of a troubled and conscientious mind.

Nay. Roland thought of the looks he had seen in the Infidel eyes. Treaty was but a ploy. Navarre and Catalonia were not to be secured by such.

He stepped forward.

"Majesty!" His voice sliced through that of Lord Gerard of Rouscillon. "This will not serve! 'Tis but the winding of linen about an unclean wound to conceal the festering poisons that will brew beneath with even greater force! I cannot believe the lives of these two Infidel princes were sufficient to do more than dissuade the Emir Marsilla's intent. Of a certain, I cannot conceive that this Blancandrin would be convinced thereby to yield sufficient to shift himself back to Africa with so much already secured by him in Spain! Nay. These Infidel must be met and conquered. They must understand the might of Christendom transcends their own before honest parley can be undertaken . . .''

Lord Ganelon rose gracefully to his feet, his face set in tempered thoughtfulness. ''Majesty,'' he said smoothly. ''My lord of Brittany is young and brash''—Roland scowled—''and his instinct is sprung from singular focus. The greater concern encompasses the entire realm and must ascertain a course that will not drain all of the resources of Christendom and thereby undo what hath been wrought for the protection and security of those other frontiers.

''I do not refute the might of the Infidel, having been brought, of late, to a greater knowledge of its direction and extent. Rather, I seek to temper that knowledge to permanent and constructive end. These hostage princes will secure for us a treaty that will hold the Pyrenees.''

''And leave those Christian lands of Navarre and Catalonia to Moorish rule . . . ?'' Roland cut in. ''Nay, my lord. It will not serve! Would thou yield already to this Infidel Ferragus to whom so much hath already been promised by Marsilla?'' Lord Ganelon's eyes flashed surprise, quickly veiled. His lips tightened as he reseated himself.

''I have heard of this Ferragus,'' another lord interjected. ''The Emir's Champion. 'Tis said he is a giant man and shields himself in sorceries that make him invulnerable.'' Roland leaned forward a little, his eyes searching the King's.

''And would thou credit one of such repute to be so easily appeased by the simple gift of the city of Pamplona? Nay! Why else whould Marsilla set such a man there, save for his future intent to northern conquest? Nay. Would thou secure a treaty for those same fiefs, and thereby conserve thy resources and men, there is another way.'' Charlemagne's eyes seemed to gleam a little. He leaned forward, fingers still at last.

''What do thou propose, my lord?'' he asked softly. Roland straightened and relaxed, his certainty absolute.

''Why this, Majesty. Let Champion meet Champion upon the field of battle! Let the dispute concerning Navarre and Catalonia be resolved thereby, and such treaty negotiated from the result of such contest. As the Emir Marsilla must have conviction in this Lord Ferragus' repute for sorcerous invulnerability, so too he will readily accede to this proposal, guided by the conviction that he will win the contest and those fiefs thereby!''

"This is madness!" Lord Gerard began.

Roland rounded on him. "Nay, my lord!" His voice dropped. "It cannot be, for I will have this Lord Ferragus' life!"

His eyes glided fiercely from man to man, seeing questions upon the faces of some who were not wont to dismiss the possibility of his triumph, doubts and refutation upon the faces of others.

"Majesty?" Lord Ganelon spoke then. "Such arrogant presumption is sure invitation to disaster, and so the Emir Marsilla will perceive it! Of a certain, he will accept such a challenge. Why would he not? This Lord Ferragus, of whom I have likewise learned, is by witchcraft made invulnerable!

"Only by like sorcery could he be vanquished." His eyes turned to lock with Roland's. "And should such—accident occur, then what of thy own repute, my liege? For who would then forget that God's anointed steward of Christendom hath summoned the Devil to his service!" He leaned back. "Some there are who do not forget that Lord Roland is witch-bred," he added softly.

Silence poised, congealed—and, for Roland, struck like a blow beneath the heart. He sought the King's face with his eyes. Charlemagne, whose blue-eyed stare held the lofty spaces of vast skies, such as eagles knew who were made for soaring.

Slowly, Roland dropped to one knee, his gaze still locked upon that of the King. He touched his breast and loosed the passion in him. Something beyond himself . . .

"However I am got, all I am—flesh, and soul, and wit—is given, aye, even joyously, to the service and glory of my liege lord, Charlemagne, for I know him to be, as other men cannot attain, most clearly—the Prince of Christendom!"

The King stood then, rising from his chair, tall and proud. Stern and perceptive. Mysterious and powerful. Roland's fervent declaration of the depth of his fealty hovered in the air before them all.

"So be it," Charlemagne said softly, after a time. "God alone can determine whether a long and arduous, or succinct and easy war lies before us. But Lord Roland hath perceived the truth around which, my lords, thy debating hath skipped and danced. It is a war that may not be denied, nor delayed, but must be met. The southern flank of Christendom must be secured.'' His frigid gaze scanned the company, pausing to linger upon the brow of the Lord High Councillor. ''Do thou prepare. We will march south with spring, our armies at our flanks. More. We propose this challenge to Marsilla that he may know our trust in the True Faith. Let his Champion meet our own upon the field of battle, there to undertake single combat for the fiefs of Navarre and Catalonia. And—for the outcome, let the strength of honest men's prayers summon the course of God's will!''

Roland stood again, hardly aware that he did so, watching with the rest of them as Charlemagne strode from the chamber with brisk confidence. Bowing, likewise with the rest, as guards held open great doors, then closed them behind the vanished King.

Face schooled to calm, Lord Ganelon clenched a fist about his anger beneath the concealing folds of his cloak.

Rounding a corner of the keep on the balmy morning of a late winter day, heading toward the arbor where he knew Oliver was wont to go, Roland broke stride, then froze in the narrow arched corridor of winter vines and trellises. A woman came toward him. Small, her form concealed beneath a deep blue cloak, she looked up and paused, then stopped. Roland felt himself press back into the tangle of sleeping roses about him as he recognized Oliver's sister, the Lady Aude.

The girl did not pass on as his yielding invited her to do, but rather drew closer by a pace, held out one small, delicately lethal hand.

''My Lord of Brittany,'' she said softly. Roland jerked a bow of sorts, but she was not deterred. Instead, she smiled and stared at him, a slight flush touching her cheeks. Roland stared back, feeling astonishing degrees of terror shift and nudge, then paralyze his innards with ice. Her eyes were molten, treacherous seas, searching through the very soul of him, finding that vile fear. He swallowed. Her smile became more delicate.

''Now I understand how it is that my brother loves thee so well!'' she murmured with seductive conviction. ''God bless thy endeavors, gentle lord!'' She flushed scarlet and fled. Roland felt his own suspended breathing.

Gentle . . . ? He . . . ? It was a word incomprehensible to
him. He shuddered, then shook his head to clear it. Women—
they were witches, every one of them. He spun toward the
arbor and jerked aside once more as the Lady Alicia swept
past him, the younger of her sons held up about one shoulder,
waving one short arm. He inhaled sharply and caught sight
of Lord Oliver in the middle of the hibernating arbor, one
hand slowly falling from a return wave.

Roland strode forward and stopped again, startled by the
determination on Oliver's face. He spoke, "I thought to find
thee here . . ."

Oliver quirked a brow and gave a rueful smile. "Aye. I
come here often. Much that I care for may be found here!"
he said wryly. Puzzled, Roland jerked to look in the direction
of the vanished Duchess. He was well acquainted with Lord
Oliver's especial interest in the fledgling Duke Huon. He
looked back, his confusion apparent.

Oliver grinned. "I will trust to thy discretion, Roland, and
share with thee this source of my delight!" He stepped closer
until he stood within arm's reach. "She will have my suit,
my lady," he said very softly, with a kind of intimate glad-
ness such as Roland had never heard before. He inhaled
deeply, slowly then. "Now that I am full endowed with my
brother's inheritance, it will be a good match. Bordeaux and
Montglave. Both fiefs of great wealth. It but remains to put
the matter before the King, and I consider he will favor my
suit in this even though Bordeaux is a wardship of Lord Ganelon of Maganze."

"Thou intend to wed—the Duchess?" Roland said slowly.

Seeing the look on his face, Oliver grinned. "Aye, thou
dolt! I would. Why else would I stand here, my heart hanging
upon my sleeve?"

Roland stared. "Thou love—this lady?" He breathed in
enlightenment, a blend of astonishment and revulsion.

Oliver's look sharpened. "Aye. Strangely, I do!" he said
more crisply. "Best of all, 'tis a mutual affection that offers
much promise of contentment for the future." His voice
dropped. "And, I have a potent wish to play father to her
sons, the younger being got of my seed, and therefore my
own . . ." Roland's eyes widened. "There is not a soul beyond us three, thou, my lady, and myself, who knows the
truth of that. Nor would I have it known, for my lady hath

secured for him both name and lineage. Still, I would parent what is mine, and provide . . ." He looked intently into Roland's eyes. Slowly the other nodded, far too well acquainted with the consequences of bastardy.

"The information is secure with me," he said tersely. "And that which—I give to thee, I offer likewise to thy child."

Oliver smiled then, with singular warmth. "Thou content me well. So I had hoped," he said softly. "I do wish for thee a joy like to my own in thy own wedding and begetting . . ."

Roland went rigid, face gone battle-hard. "Nay! Never!" he growled distaste.

Oliver frowned. "It will occur," he said slowly. "Duty compells the begetting of heirs to the surity of thy fiefs, and whyfore should not a shrewd and happy alliance be sought?"

"Nay!" Roland growled again. "I'll not be bound—to some woman!"

Oliver's eyes widened. "I sensed . . ." he murmured slowly. "And I have thought thee uncommon abstaining! Or, is there another reason for such churlishness about this happiness that I contrive?" He stepped closer by a stride, searching Roland's features.

"I keep aloof from bestial lusts, and vile congress with women!" Roland grated, looking away. "Nor will I be entrapped to the same. Nay. There is but one I am content to touch! She is all I will ever know of that!" His right hand came up and sought the strange woman hilt of the dark sword. Fingertips caressed fleetingly before he let his hand fall. Oliver's frown deepened as he perceived the extent of his friend's profound capacity for passion and the contradiction of its direction.

"Thou are virgin!" he said at last.

Roland shrugged, met his look. "Not an uncommon condition!" He dispensed with the matter. "Enough of this! I sought thee out, thinking to ride awhile and consider this matter of the Infidel."

"Aye!" Oliver exhaled. "So be it!" He smiled ruefully, shook his head, and began striding from the arbor. Impenetrable Roland!

TWELVE

A.D. 775

The sun glared brutally as it shone down upon tan-colored earth and scattered patches of grassland, made lush by the winter melt that flowed down from the mountains to the north. The great army of Charlemagne camped on high ground with the snowcapped peaks of the Pyrenees to their back. To the south and west lay the walled grey city of Pamplona, and before it, on the far rise of the valley, was encamped a combined force of Navarrese and Moors.

Unlike the obvious cohesion among the Franks, it was apparent, even across the shimmering haze, that the Navarrese were disunited, gathered in individual battalions, each under the banner of its respective lord, near lost from view amid the vast and colorful array of the Infidel horde whose crescent banners rose up high above the whole.

Eager and battle-hungry, Roland kept to himself save for the occasional, silent presence of the Archbishop Turpin, or the equally watchful companionship of Lord Oliver. He paced restlessly or rode, in the manner of a lion on a leash, eyes scanning the foe or the terrain, preoccupied with details, his sense of purpose profoundly clear.

Potent and sinister, heathen drums made low booming thunder as the foe shifted, grouped, and advanced toward the rise in the middle of the valley to make an arrowhead of men, a rippling wave of bright shields, spears bristling in between.

158

Behind this advance were horsemen by the thousands whose prancing mounts made the earth tremble with another kind of thunderous rumbling.

At the apex of the Infidel spearhead, a giant of a man rode astride an iron-grey destrier, his face dark beneath a silvered helm, a peculiar double-curved scimitar glinting as he held it aloft, a mighty, double-bladed, long-handled axe in his other hand. Roland's fist tightened about the lance he held, with the King's banner fluttering aloft from its tip.

"Ferragus!" he hissed. Charlemagne glanced at his Champion.

"Marsilla means to contrive beyond his acceptance of our challenge!" Charlemagne said coldly, meeting Roland's equally hard gaze, barking brisk orders to the lords flanking him. Roland's horse caracoled restively, its ears twitching in response to the pricking of its master's spurs.

"Does he so . . . ?" Roland grated, his lips curving into a brutal smile beneath the nasal of his helm. He spun the golden stallion, Veillantif, about, lofting high Charlemagne's banner. "Now is the time! Haaaarrrrgggh!" And in an instant, man and horse were catapulting down the hill, arrow-true toward the apex of the Infidel force led by the heathen Ferragus. Despite himself, Charlemagne felt his eyes widen.

"Rash young fool!" he heard Lord Ganelon murmur beside him.

Charlemagne raised a hand. "Hold!" His voice thundered the single order. Ganelon eased his grip on his bridle. A brilliant, futile suicide. He glanced to his left, past the King, and saw De Montglave lounging in his saddle, a lopsided grin upon his mouth. He frowned and stared ahead at the plummeting passage of Lord Roland, at the royal banner that flew smoothly, falconlike, toward the Infidel now ascending to the crest of the low hill in the center of the valley. Then Lord Roland reached the crest of the hill himself and brought Veillantif to a plunging halt. Incredibly, to a man, the heathen stopped likewise. Even the insidious music of the drums was stilled. Slowly, Lord Roland's lance dipped and pointed directly to the breast of the giant Lord before him who seemed twice his size. It was the sorcerer Ferragus.

"Ho! What is this? A royal flea sent of some barbarian Prince?" Ferragus grinned, his voice rumbling audible thunder as Roland moved his stallion to a plunging halt some twenty yards before the giant of whom he had heard so much.

"Nay, heathen! Fist rather, sent to squash the beetle that doth infest this land!" he hissed back. "Or had thou forgot the challenge that hangs between princes?" Again, he lowered the point of his lance until it pointed toward the Infidel's silver-plated breast. White-rimmed eyes gleamed in a black face and the giant's grin widened to reveal sharp, evenly pointed teeth. He relaxed in his saddle, scimitar set comfortably across his steel-plated thighs. He laughed again, and Latin rolled from his tongue.

"Aaah, little man. Who are thou to challenge me!"

Roland let the sounds die away. Then he spoke very quietly, "I am fate! I am Roland Kingslayer!" He nudged the stallion into a series of bounds, reins taut, as the animal described an arc, bent and plunged Charlemagne's banner into the sod, letting his shield fall from his arm at the same time. Then he straightened and grinned, right hand seeking Durandal, feeling her leap to his fingers. His eyes found those of Ferragus, no longer smiling, but rather curious.

"Come!" he purred. "Embrace the irrevocable!"

Giant and grey horse plunged as one. Axe and scimitar became a shimmering series of spirals in the air. Roland raked the gold horse's sides, drawing blood. He ducked and struck, Durandal humming with power, with temper that focused, like his own. He felt a great shudder pass through his body as Durandal screeched across the scimitar, deflecting it, then bounded away from the giant's left shoulder. Laughter and mockery followed him as the gold horse bolted past, then gathered and spun on its haunches in response to the raking of a single spur. Again, they charged and met, and Roland caught a sudden glimpse of scarlet in strangely black eyes as he parried the scimitar and brought Durandal down against the haft of the axe.

This was no ordinary man, he knew then, no mere oversize warrior, taller than himself by near a pair of feet, but a lord of strange knowledge and skills, the like of which was beyond his experience. Again, he swung the stallion about and felt the woman hilt of Durandal seem to writhe and harden in his grasp as he abandoned the bridle and brought his other hand up to clutch the hilt. The stallion bolted forward, neck snaking low. This time he scored, slicing across the grey destrier's haunch.

It screamed and stumbled, yet remained upright as the giant wrenched it about. Roland whipped his own prized beast clear of a blow intended to decapitate it, then vaulted clear as the giant loosed himself from the dying grey as it crumpled to the dust. He did not hear the awed hush that descended upon the Infidel forces. He rolled and sought his feet, bringing Durandal before him, her blade purest obsidian now, blue lightning flashing along her length.

The giant laughed and moved, unnaturally light, with his body of metal plates that resembled an insect's casing. Then he advanced, scimitar twirling and swooping, axe describing another kind of arc. Roland lunged and parried.

"Come to me, little man!" Ferragus rumbled glee. Roland did not waste breath to answer. Instead, he struck another blow that made an eerie, outraged screeching as it slid across the giant's breastplate.

It was duck and dodge and strike after that—an effort of relentless concentration.

He did not know that to a man, the Infidel and Navarrese loosed their grips upon their weapons, all thought of pending battle forgot, awed and compelled by the persistence of the Frank against one who was known to fell his foes with little more than a glance. Nor was he aware of the stillness that had likewise settled over the armies of Charlemagne assembled along the high northern hills that defined the valley. Only a light breeze ruffled cloaks and horses' manes and tails. Every man was intent upon the contest between this—unnatural pair.

Roland could feel the power that slithered through Durandal, the rage that gathered and leaped like an extension of his will, to take a nick of steel from the giant's scimitar, or to dent, or to scratch that unnatural armor. Sweat poured down his face and stung his eyes, slithered in rivulets down the leather gambeson beneath his chain mail hauberk. His lungs heaved for air, and still he fought on . . .

Teeth clenched, and so intent as to be unaware of the rents that appeared in his golden surcoat, or the shattered links in his armor, he did not feel the cuts and bruises that appeared on arm, or thigh, or along his side. Instead, he watched the giant's black face, seeing that arrogant grin fade slowly. Then, a puzzled look appeared. And when he saw sweat on that dark face, trickling like rivers across black granite, Roland grinned again, for he knew that Ferragus was indeed mortal.

He fought on, hunting all the while for some weak place in that incredible armor.

His muscles screamed and shuddered for strength. His heart pounded agony. All he could manage finally was to cling to the dark sword and follow where she led.

But Ferragus was tiring as well. He no longer used both weapons together. Then as if by mutual consent, they stood some twenty feet apart, weapons lowered, breathing in great racking gulps, staring at each other . . .

Not a soul watching moved, even then.

"Thou do well, stripling, for one who battles with a God!" Ferragus managed to rumble between gulps of air. "But now—I consider—it is time for thee to die! Prepare thyself!" Roland raised Durandal.

"God indeed!" He grinned and lunged, and, aiming for the giant's eyes, jerked to one side to receive a glancing blow across the back, instead of the edge that would have split him open. He slipped and skidded on one mail-covered knee.

"Die, Frank!" Ferragus snarled, enraged at last, and struck. But Roland found his feet and spun away.

He did not die, or even yield much ground. Shifting constantly, he moved around the giant, compelling the other to hunt for him as he searched and prodded, ever seeking the single, fatal flaw that he knew beyond conviction must be the key to Ferragus' mortality.

The impartial sun beat down upon them both. Exhaustion slowed them. Both grew clumsy, aim erratic, stumbles more frequent. It seemed to Roland that Durandal's singing was the impatient stabbing of spurs against the bloodied flanks of the exhausted warhorse he had become. Her power was unabated, growing even, while his heart and lungs and muscles could not seem to keep pace.

Then he lost his footing and went down upon one knee and elbow, to feel sheer agony slice across his left hip. He jerked, and fell. Rolled, and pulled himself half upright, and saw Ferragus looming over him, scimitar and arms upraised for the finish.

Suddenly, he saw a dark place, mere flesh, beneath the

juncture of the giant's arm. There . . . There . . . He jerked and, with all his remaining strength, brought Durandal up, point first, and sent her into flight just as Ferragus, with a roar of triumph, brought down his weapon. He heard the sword scream as he twisted under the blow to follow her. Then, on both knees and one hand, he saw the giant pause—lose his grip.

An astonished look came over Ferragus' face as steel plates clanked and folded, his weapon fell into the dust. Then, slowly, blood spewing from his left armpit and trickling from his mouth, Ferragus fell in the manner of a tree, thudding into the ground beside Roland with enough force to make it shudder. Roland blinked and stared, lungs heaving. He scraped sweat and grit from his eyes, aware of a peculiar feeling of amazement. Then he jerked the dark sword loose, using her to clamber awkwardly to his feet, and hobbled a pace to stand over the dying man.

On his back, the black-skinned sorcerer changed color slowly, becoming a strange, uncanny shade of grey. His large, white-rimmed, black-centered eyes looked up toward Roland, meeting that tawny golden gaze, then they widened as though with awe.

"Thou! I know thee!" the heathen rasped in an urgent tone. Roland felt himself go rigid. "Thou art indeed—a God!"

Roland gasped, what blood remaining in him draining from his face. "Nay!" he snarled. "Thou'll cast no spells on me at this time of thy demise, Ferragus!"

But the giant continued to stare up at him, smiling now, eyes become black pools of knowledge. He gasped and bit back agony, then became serene of feature once again. "Nay, my lord"—softly, reverently whispered—"that I could not do . . ." He coughed blood. "What mortal sorcerer could hope to pit himself against such as thou? I did not recognize . . ." His breathing became an awkward contorted rattling. His last whispered threads sent the ice of conviction through Roland. "I did not—recognize thee—Lord of Eagles . . ."

And the heathen's face went still, eyes glazed, void, stone grey as ashes upon some forgotten hearth. Spirit vanished, the rest was clay.

"Nay!" Roland whispered, shuddering as he stared at the corpse. He glowered. It was the final delusion of a heathen mind embarked upon its passage to Hell. A last attempt to cozen another soul into treading the path of the damned . . . His fingers clutched tightly about Durandal's hilt, he stood for a moment, still panting, and felt the first waves of pain and exhaustion. He glanced down at himself to see the strange reassurance of his own blood.

Then, with what strength remained to him, he sought the gold destrier and struggled to seat himself in the beast's high-pommeled saddle. He resheathed the dark sword and found the King's banner, jerking the lance loose from the sod that held it. He had not enough strength left to loft it. Instead, he found his voice.

"For God—and Charlemagne!" His call resounded in triumph across the poised silence of the valley as the golden destrier shook its head, then lunged forward to bear its lord back up the hill toward the King.

Roland barely heard the answering thunder that came from every Christian throat.

Many hours later, within the sheltering privacy of the small tent he shared with Lord Oliver, Roland, stripped of battered armor and torn, bloody clothing, yielded to his exhaustion, allowed his knees to buckle, and sprawled with a thankful sigh upon the thick furs he used for bedding. He closed his eyes and let himself go completely lax, uncaring of the pain that seemed so much less than this incredible weakness, as Oliver, beside him, began to tend to cuts and bruises with fastidious care. He sighed again, savoring the way his cheek nestled against the soft pelts, the sweet air that touched his clean, naked skin. He reached out with a last effort to touch fingertips to the hip of the woman form on the hilt of the dark sword beside him.

Another breath of the cool, fresh air of nightfall, and with its slow, exhaling release, Roland surrendered to the haven of sleep.

Oliver dabbed at the last of the dried blood that had congealed about the deep cut across the upper part of Roland's left thigh and buttock, then reached for the poultice he had prepared, setting it firmly in place. He shook his head a little and, aware that for the time being there was naught else he could do for the other man's welfare, settled back to sit upon his own sleeping rugs. He reached for wine and, sipping del-

icately from the skin, studied the way the late evening sun
melded with the firelight of a lamp to cast a warm, clear glow
across the perfection of Roland's body.

His friend was much changed, Oliver thought, settling back
to savor that pleasant sensuality of comfortable weariness.
Taller now, by several inches, his face, of late, had lost the
look of boyhood, and had begun its final maturing. Roland,
he acknowledged, had become uncommon beautiful with his
strong, crisply defined jaw, his nose of flawless straightness
and neatly refined nostrils, high, clear cheekbones and gracefully arched brows. His thick, loosely curling hair gleamed a
mixture of amber fire and golden brilliance where it tumbled
down the nape of his neck. Oliver grinned fleetingly. Quiet
now, at ease in sleep, Roland's beauty was remarkable, not
concealed beneath the fierce hard expressions that marked his
wakeful self. Yet Aude had seen . . . Oliver sipped again
from the wineskin, rolled the fluid in his mouth, and swallowed. Roland shifted to his side and Oliver lunged forward
to steady the poultice on his hip. A deep wound, but clean.
He frowned, sensing something odd, yet unable to discern
exactly what it was . . . Aude . . . ?

Something. He glanced again along Roland's body, and
thought of a sudden of that other wound he had tended sometime before. Slowly, he leaned forward to study the shoulder,
where that hideous, near crippling wound had been.

Where there should be the slight puckering and white
streaking lines of resultant scarring.

But there were no scars. Instead, the skin of Roland's
shoulder was as smooth and unblemished as if it had never
been touched.

Nay, nor was there any trace of blemish on the leg where
another deep wound had been received when Roland had returned with the head of Desiderius a seeming lifetime ago.
Oliver exhaled violently and shifted back, examining the
shoulder once more, staring at the purity of it.

Scars. They were an unconsidered and commonplace consequence of being a fighting man, and Oliver well knew the
several his own body bore. But Roland . . . ? Save for these
new injuries incurred in the incredible battle with the Infidel
giant Ferragus, he was without blemish.

It was not natural, Oliver thought. He frowned. And yet—
why should he think that Roland was entirely unaware of this?

His eyes followed the line of Roland's arm to the long-fingered hand reaching out with a lover's delicacy to touch the diminutive woman form of the hilt of his witch sword Durandal. A hand more in keeping with the image of a jongleur's or a harpist's . . .

And the small head of the woman hilt of Durandal was turned a little, giving the impression that she stared at Roland's sleeping, youthful face out of featureless, obsidian eyes.

Oliver shook his head and stared at the half-consumed wineskin.

"Thou, my lord," he muttered to himself, "have achieved that condition of addle-pated fancy known as staggering drunkenness!"

On the other side of the Christian encampment, Thierry of Leon sat alone amid tall, sharp-bladed grasses, resting quietly as night fell, content to do no more than stare across the horizon toward the place where the sun had slipped out of view off the edge of the world. The sleep his uncle had dispatched him to eluded him. Instead, he was plagued by a troubled unease.

A festering uncertainty about himself—and other things.

At his uncle's flank, he had seen, as the sun attained the pinnacle of its arc across the sky, how Lord Roland, returning upon the conclusion of that incredible and interminable battle with the legendary Infidel giant, was swept from his horse onto the shoulders of triumphantly shouting knights, and bourne in rare honor to the King, having brought unparalleled honor to them all.

Beside him, he had heard Lord Roger of Roncesvalles murmur, "The Bastard uses witchcraft to rise above us all. 'Tis Satan's work, this day!" He had begun to nod agreement, then stopped to stare as the Count of Brittany was lowered to his feet, then limped clearly exhausted, tattered, and bloody, to drop to his knees before the King. Lord Roland had loosed his helm and thrust back his coif, and Thierry had been totally startled by the look of passionate devotion upon his face.

"Not for all the world," he had heard the Champion's fervent declaration, "would I fail thee, my liege!" Lord Roger had heard it too, and muttered some venomous expletive into his ear, but Thierry had been too startled by his own realization of the depth of Roland's honest love for the King to attend. And Charlemagne had smiled and had raised his Champion up with his own hands . . . Thierry stared at a blade of grass that he had unthinkingly plucked and was now twisting between his fingers.

It had been a moment such as minstrels sang of—pure— with honor. He had felt it clearly, beyond the deeply entrenched habit of hatred that the very sight of the Bastard, now Lord Roland, invoked.

And that jolting imbalance had lingered within him as he attended his uncle through the remainder of the day. Lord Ganelon had spent much of the afternoon with the higher lords in council with the King, warhorses held nearby, and arms and men at the ready, alertly attentive to the silence that came from the Infidel about Pamplona. More than once, his eyes had been drawn to Lord Roland who stood, haggard, in defiance of his own exhausted and wounded condition, in unswerving duty to his place at the King's flank.

Further, he had noted how, when emissaries from the Emir Marsilla came, Lord Ganelon seemed as ignorant as most of the rest of the Infidel tongue, leaving such translation as was needed for that briefly held discussion of terms to the Archbishop Turpin. Yet he had used it fluidly, fluently, in the several secretive and protracted conferences he had held with the hostage Lord Aelroth at Bordeaux. Thankful for the darkness now punctuated by campfires, Thierry discarded the mangled blade of grass and plucked another.

Likewise, he had been dispatched in the early evening to summon Lord Pinnabel of Sorence, his uncle's newest favorite, to private conversation beneath the concealment of Lord Ganelon's tent. Thierry, dismissed with a smile, had been surprised to find himself lingering for a few moments beyond the closed tent flap. Listening intently. Hearing softly uttered discourse in the same heathen tongue both lords claimed a complete incomprehension of in public . . . Thierry frowned.

Lord Pinnabel, elevated by his uncle's endeavor and purported to have come from Italy, though his origins were elusive, was a heathen-looking man. Slight of frame and dark-complected, for all he professed the True Faith.

Not unlike the younger hostage Prince.

What was the truth imbedded in his uncle's sly traffic with these men? Thierry looked up and shifted to stare at the dark shadows that defined Lord Ganelon's tent. Then he stiffened, catching sight of a shrouded figure in a dark cloak as it slipped with only the faintest rustling from the flap of the tent. The Lord of Sorence, Thierry knew, and sat up, all senses alert.

The slighter man strode briskly away, past campfires that punctuated the darkness, and without thinking, Thierry slid to his feet and followed quietly, to where other Moorish hostages, surrendered by Marsilla that afternoon, lay in tightly bound clumps upon a stretch of uneven ground. Eluding guards, the shadow of Lord Pinnabel became near invisible as he slipped to the farthest side of the group, then shrank down into their midst. Thierry, too, stopped and crouched down low, watching intently.

A little later, Lord Pinnabel reappeared and began strolling back through the camp in a path that differed greatly from the way he had come. Thierry would have followed, but his eyes caught movement, sounds that were concealed behind the chuckled bantering between a pair of guards. One of the prisoners got to his feet, then melted into the night.

Slowly, uneasily, unaccustomed to stealth, Thierry made his way back to his former place in the grass beyond his uncle's tent. He sat down again and stared at it. The night breeze seemed to waft uncertain odors of treachery.

"Blood or nay . . ." he murmured a long time later. "I'll not have my own honor compromised!"

THIRTEEN

A.D. 775-776

Lord Ganelon was given custody of the Navarrese and Infidel hostages given up by Marsilla, and the task of ordering the newly acquired demesne of Navarre. Wielding power second only to the King's, it was left to him to secure the territory and to dispatch clergy to convince a people prone to be fragile in their faith. Further it fell to him to subdue the rebellious and scattered Basques who were now caught between the pincers of the great northern Frankish kingdom and its new southern acquisition.

Marching eastward, the rest of Charlemagne's massive army moved to the precarious frontier between Navarre and Catalonia. The Emir Marsilla had refused to relinquish Catalonia, vanishing with all his forces into the night before additional parlance could be undertaken.

There, the army paused like a lion crouching watchfully on high ground to consider its prey. There too, Charlemagne received oaths of fealty given by rough, impoverished Christian lords of small holdings scattered across the northern reaches of Catalonia. Southerners melted away into the hills and dry country to await what lay before them all.

The summer months slipped by like dust blown by fleetly darting winds across a barren landscape. Then autumn, then winter.

Charlemagne moved eastward to sack Barcelona on the coast in a protracted series of bloody battles. Then, unable to press south to Valencia for the strength of the Moors, he turned west to cut a swath across the upper heart of the Spanish peninsula, leaving an arc of conquered fiefs just south of Navarre and Pamplona where Lord Ganelon now ruled.

Bitter winter brought some sort of balance as fighting was forced to yield to biting cold and howling winds, drifting, treacherous snows, and hard-frozen water supplies. Charlemagne settled back to consolidate his grip on the territories he had won and to prepare for the next forward thrust.

For Roland, upon awakening from the sleep following his triumph over the heathen giant Ferragus, it was as though the world had blossomed into a brilliant and colorful panoply. The old names of Bastard and Witchling were no longer uttered in stealthy whispers or implied in sidelong glances. They were even forgotten as he was accorded all the honor due a King's Champion of such puissant and unquestionable valor. Like the warmth now apparent in the King's penetrating stare, honor enveloped his name.

And with honor—and war—everything was clear.

The months that followed were a time of growing power, both as a consequence of the light of the King's favor and of his own, now unquestioned, brilliance. His thoughts on matters of strategy were no longer given reluctant attention, but were eagerly sought. And, throughout the King's army, there was a steady growth in the numbers of men who were eager to follow where he led, confident that behind him they were assured of triumph.

He was Count Roland now. Or, the Champion. Increasingly, he was vested qualities beyond those of other men. His purity was marked, for it was soon apparent that he kept himself aloof from all congress with women, seemingly free from such sinful and debasing appetites. His beauty was also cause for comment, doubtless sprung from that blessed chastity given to one favored of God. Golden-haired, eagle-eyed, supple and relentlessly vigorous; he was, beyond question, rare. Even the lethal singing of the dark sword Durandal seemed to be a part of his uncanny instincts and daring in battle. Men caressed their own weapons thoughtfully, understanding that peculiar intimacy between a knight and his sword. No longer did any think it strange that Count Roland should have any but such a remarkable weapon.

Another facet of worth was found in his devoted friendship with the equally revered Lord Oliver De Montglave. Lord Oliver had become the embodiment of all the finest, most discreet aspects of honor and generosity. His wily, even-tempered, and cautious understanding made a perfect counterpoint to Count Roland's volatile disposition.

The sly phrase "a Roland for an Oliver" took on a new, proud meaning.

From the bond between these two, a direction emerged for those other proud, young lords who rode in the King's service. Between battles and other duties, during the long, bitter winter nights, tales were spun around campfires, or in the halls of conquered keeps. Fantasies of great prowess, of distant lands and magic, of fair maidens and rare horses, and of wonderful deeds for all. Tales that jongleurs wove into a lyrical tapestry of shared confidence and glory.

A.D. 776

Spring and early summer brought hard battles against renewed Infidel strength that had used the winter to draw upon the unfathomable well of Africa. With brutal determination, Charlemagne penetrated to the harsh mountains and high, arid plateaus just to the south of Toledo, then found himself contained in a bloody balance of power. Like some monstrous and unmoving dragon, the power of Blancandrin breathed unrelenting waves of destruction, yet, for the present, that Emir could not be reached.

Then from the north, word came from messengers astride overdriven horses of raids from the heathen Vikings along the western coasts of Normandy and Brittany and Bordeaux, and of another Saxon uprising far to the east. The time for compromise had come . . .

Messengers were dispatched. Highborn emissaries were sent to Blancandrin and Marsilla to talk of truce between the two faiths.

They were returned. Decapitated and desecrated, their bodies bound to trembling, shattered horses. Frigid with rage, Charlemagne paced his fury at this, then, understanding the peculiar Infidel point of faith that forbade the use of the unclean left hand for eating, ordered that the hostage princes,

Aelroth and Falsaron, be deprived of their right hands and returned. Likewise, he slaughtered other captured highborn Infidel men, hostages, taken in the progress of conquest. These too were sent to the two emirs.

The war continued then, but differently. It became more spasmodic, confined to sortees along new frontiers, while each side gathered itself to brood upon strategy and consequence while weighing the other's strengths.

Charlemagne stayed with his armies through the summer, then as autumn brought the assurance of continued stalemate, and winter's promise of relative quiet, he marched north to Bordeaux, flanked by a nominal guardian force and a selection of the elite corps of young peers. Secure in Pamplona, Lord Ganelon was reaffirmed in his jurisdiction over Navarre and Catalonia, and Lord Roger of Roncesvalles was dispatched with him to tighten the King's fist about the rebellious Basques, to secure the northwest coast of Spain, and to keep open the northern mountain passes to France. The newly conquered southern heartland fiefs were given to the administration of the experienced and shrewd Duke Naimes.

A.D. 777

"Aaaah!" Lord Roger exclaimed in contentment, sipped wine and settled back in his chair to savor his meal. "I confess, my lord, that I relish the prospect of a few days of such comfort after the blizzards in the mountains!" To his right and between them both, newly knighted Sir Thierry of Leon saw his uncle nod and smile amicably.

"I am reassured to know there will be no disturbances there!" he said pointedly. Lord Roger looked up and, setting down his wine cup, reached to spear another piece of roasted mutton with his poniard.

"And I, my lord, would be better content to know an equal stability to the south!" He bit into meat, shifted and frowned a little. "It bewilders me that the King did not leave Count Roland with Duke Naimes to guard the new frontier." Surprised, Thierry sought refuge in his own eating.

Lord Ganelon responded at once. "How so?"

Lord Roger swallowed his mouthful and shrugged. "Duke Naimes is an old man," he said brutally. "Such a puissant lord is the Champion is surely of better use where the very sight of him throws the Infidel into disarray!'' Thierry felt every nerve alert.

Lord Ganelon shifted to face the other man more directly. ''Count Roland's reputation begins to surpass the believable,'' he said smoothly. Thierry knew that silken, predatory tone. ''And the King seems intent to favor him.''

Lord Roger gave the older man a sidelong glance, then stared out across the hall to the hearth fire in the middle. ''I cannot like him, for he lacks social grace entirely, and is crude and arrogant!'' he said bluntly. ''But in battle? Aye, I would follow him to Hell itself! He can scent the manner of victory even as fighting is begun, and with greater shrewdness than a bloodhound come across prey!'' He sipped again from his cup. Fair assessment, Thierry thought, and saw his uncle's knuckles whiten about his own goblet. ''In battle, he fights as one possessed. There is nothing he will not undertake,'' Lord Roger went on, staring toward the fire, and his own memories of the past year. ''The Infidel call him a Djinn, which means Devil, as I understand it.''

''Mayhap, being Satan's children, they are well able to recognize one of their own?'' Lord Ganelon proffered softly.

Lord Roger stared at him. ''Speak thy mind, my lord,'' he said.

Lord Ganelon grew contemplative then, dark eyes fixed upon his wine cup, brows knitted in a frown of consternation. ''We are blessed, after a fashion, my lord. Consider— Christendom grows in strength and territory, spreading the Truth, and the Word of God, under the rule of God's clearly favored Prince, our liege lord, Charlemagne.'' Lord Roger inclined his head in understanding and agreement. Thierry was wary, and sought refuge in continuing his meal. ''But, as God endeavors through man, so too Satan is likely to contrive greatly as well.''

''It is only sensible to presume so,'' Lord Roger commented.

Lord Ganelon inclined his head. ''I am concerned for the safety of our liege lord, and for the realm,'' he continued in the same troubled tones. ''For he raises up this Count Roland to high estate, giving him nobility and glory, and may, thereby, be vulnerable to Satan's seduction. For it doth seem to me that Lord Roland enjoys both favor and uncommon prowess through most unnatural means." Lord Roger's eyes widened. Lord Ganelon's fingers left his cup as he sat back in his chair and reached to negligently dissect a pullet's leg. "Do thou not remember, my lord," he inquired, neatly slipping a morsel of meat between his teeth, "that Count Roland's lineage is unknown, beyond that he was got of some vile, inhuman witch? I saw the creature, and slew her to save the King, enough years ago for it to be long forgot." Thierry listened, attentively, mistrust for his uncle growing by the moment.

Lord Roger stiffened, face opening like a flower to be plucked. He leaned toward the older man and spoke slowly. "I knew he was bastard. But I have not thought on the matter this long time past. Yet?" Lord Ganelon relaxed farther in his seat, eating with elegant delicacy. Lord Roger continued, "His devotion to the King's interest is a passion apparent to all, and he seems to enjoy the blessing of particular friendship with my lord the Archbishop Turpin who often elects to fight at his flank. I am persuaded that God's favor may be revealed through the same."

Lord Ganelon frowned, dark eyes impossible to read. "Aaah! The good Archbishop. There is another mystery to resolve!" he murmured.

Lord Roger frowned in confusion. "I do not understand. He is a priest sprung from this land hereabouts and, favored of the Pope, given to serve our liege."

Lord Ganelon's hard eyes gleamed. "Not so!" he contradicted quietly.

"What then?"

"That is the mystery," Lord Ganelon said carefully, abandoning his meal. "I have made inquiries of this priest, who, coincidentally, came to the King's service but a little before Count Roland won his place as Champion, and claims to be Navarrese." His tone shifted. "Yet, even among the priesthood, none have heard of such a man." Thierry almost strangled on his mouthful, frozen by astonishment. "And," Lord Ganelon went on, "to the matter of His Holiness' recognition of the same—the Pope was strangely inconclusive, recalling not a bishop, but a monk who was dispatched as a courier, bearing letters to our liege."

"Nay . . . ?" Lord Roger breathed, staring into Lord Ganelon's eyes. The other sighed deeply.

"Hence, in part, my consternation," he murmured, and crossed himself. "I fear the sorceries that are implicit between these two. How else could Lord Roland have triumphed over the powers of Ferragus or come unscathed through so many battles?" Thierry's stomach knotted as he thought of the giant's head, still impaled upon a lance above the city gates not too distant. A skull now, the flesh had slowly melted away. Even the crows had seemed reluctant to pick at it. Lord Roger exhaled sharply and sat back, to brood upon this information.

"Insidious," he murmured a long while later, and crossed himself. His eyes locked with those of Lord Ganelon in a moment of purest understanding.

"Such is the Devil's way," Lord Ganelon murmured, inclining his head. Thierry abandoned the pretext of eating and reached for his wine cup. This was not the first time he had shielded himself behind the appearance of gross appetites. Staring at the surface of the table, he saw not wood but spider webs of cunning.

Lord Ganelon, whose continued traffic with the Infidel was a secret that was given to him to guard. Lord Roger was the newest fly to become entangled in the skeins of this incomprehensible plotting. He looked up, hearing the faint echoes of dismal howling as the winter wind swept around the thick stone walls of the keep in Pamplona where they sat. Smoke from the hearth fire spiraled restlessly upward in misty cords toward the soot-blackened beams above. Weaving—like the confusing suggestions of treachery.

He heard the stern uttering of his name and spun to meet his uncle's frown.

"Where are thy wits? I posed thee a question!" Lord Ganelon said sharply. Thierry stared, then, of a sudden, grinned.

"I was thinking of the wench I've found to bed tonight!" he said cheerfully. "One appetite dispelled—" He glanced at Lord Roger. "I fear I need to uncover another!" Roncesvalles laughed. Lord Ganelon's hard look spoke contempt. Thierry widened his smile, still looking at Lord Roger. "Shall I contrive her a sister, my lord?" he inquired.

Lord Roger nodded in enthusiasm. "Aye!" Lord Ganelon rose from the table. Thierry avoided looking at his uncle and embarked on a lurid description of possible "sisters" that set

Lord Roger roaring with laughter. Privately, he felt himself cringe. I am become my uncle's fool, he thought.

Frosted breath made plumes from the horses' nostrils in the cold, still air as Lord Oliver abruptly changed direction and brought his stallion and the pack horse he led to a halt on one of the high bluffs that banked the east side of the Garonne. Behind him, Roland drew rein also and watched as his friend shifted in the saddle to stare across the frozen river toward the distant grey shadow of Bordeaux castle. Content to wait apart, Roland was acutely aware of Oliver's pensive silence, and his own bewildered unease at his friend's brooding fretfulness since their departure from the castle but two hours before. Roland nearly started when Oliver suddenly spoke.

"Strange. I have come to love this place," he said slowly, still staring at the pristine quiet of frost laden trees and a snow-covered landscape. "I had never presumed to envy my brother's inheritance, and now that it has come to me, I have no particular devotion to it beyond duty. But here I find myself most greatly content, and wish to put down my roots." He shifted his horse to look at Roland. "Pray God," he added fervently, "the King accepts my suit for the Lady Alicia!" Roland did not respond. Oliver gave him a penetrating look. "Come," he said after a moment. "We have many miles before us, and much to do before we reach Aix in the spring!" Roland nodded and let his golden stallion lunge forward to lead the way.

North—to Brittany. To the fiefs that were his, that he had never seen, and that he knew very little about, beyond the spoken reports brought to him during their eight-week sojourn at Bordeaux. He heard the other horses snort behind him, and the metallic sounds of armor muffled by heavy furs as his stallion slithered down a treacherous bank and made for the woods ahead.

He frowned, drawn from his thoughts of responsibilities to his fiefs, back to that time shortly after their arrival from the south when Lord Oliver had set his petition before the King. Charlemagne had listened without response, and Roland, standing some distance behind his friend, had seen the King's eyes shift to him. He remembered a peculiar apprehension at

the assessment in Charlemagne's eyes. Then the King had
addressed Lord Oliver.

"My lord, we commend thy honest petition and answer
thee according. We will have time to consider the matter and
shall give thee our decision in the spring when we are at
Aix." Oliver, Roland remembered, had bowed his head, then
his body.

But De Montglave had become very open in his courtship
of the Dowager Duchess after that, and was often as not to
be found attending to her in some manner or other. More, he
had been equally open on the matter of his liking and attention to her two sons. The King had shortly after taken the
young heir, Duke Huon, into his own household to begin his
training as a page.

Roland had been glad to preoccupy himself with less person-
ally unsettling matters concerning the safety of the borders of
the realm. Other young lords, likewise brought north with the
King, were dispatched to the north and east, there to attend to
the details of fortification and administration needed to safeguard against any further uprisings of the rebellious Saxon tribes
so recently brought under the King's dominion. Roland's duties
lay with his own fiefs of Brittany, the coast that had been brutally
raided by Viking marauders in the past summer, and needed
both replenishment and fortification. Lord Oliver's fiefs, secure
and peaceful in the eastern heartland of the realm, needed no
such consideration and, aware of this, Charlemagne had dispatched Oliver to assist him. Roland turned his face to the biting
clarity of a new winter breeze and inhaled deeply as he put his
stallion to the canter.

Aware of how little he knew of his own vassals and fiefs,
and knowing that the next months would immerse him in the
same, he was glad of Oliver's company. He glanced back at
his friend whose horse plunged in the wake of his own stallion's tracks. Then he looked forward, becoming preoccupied
once more.

Since the battle with the giant Ferragus, and through the
course of the subsequent campaigns, they had become insep-
arable, he and Oliver. Twins. A pair. Not kindred tempera-
ments, perhaps. But a balanced and lively counterpoint of
dispositions from which sprung a combined brilliance with
strategy and in battle.

But Roland found himself thinking of shared times in Spain.

Private times, when they quartered together, or tended each other's nicks and cuts, or shared bread, or slept. There too the brotherhood between them was apparent. Begun and nurtured, it had grown to something rich with unstated understandings and mutual respect. Nay—more profound—a deep and abiding love.

Roland's fist tightened upon the reins, his features becoming stern as he looked ahead, putting aside the confusion of unaccustomed vulnerabilities, for the more tangible winter landscape. Love, that was for him singular. Unfamiliar. And compelling.

Not so for Oliver, he thought. Oliver, whose natural generosity of spirit and kindness enabled him to liberally bestow affection on many others. It made Roland acutely aware of the brutal hardness of his own internal self. But this passion for a woman? The Duchess. Roland could not get past his own loathing, and the grim terrors that were at its root, to understand that at all.

Forcibly, he turned his thoughts to the business that lay ahead of him. The months of winter to come would be filled with many miles of arduous riding as he traveled through the lands that had been given to his rule. He would visit each inland holding to learn conditions, populace, and fortifications. To secure . . . Then he would follow the wilder parts along the coast of Brittany where Viking marauders came to pillage, to plan for defense.

Roland put his stallion to the gallop and charged up a steep hill that led from the remains of a fishing village toward the woods on the other side of the bay. Reaching the peak, he drew the animal to a halt and slackened his grip on the reins as he looked about him. The mists and the sea made everything a secretive, grey quiet. Even the gulls that soared overhead were silent upon the damp, cold wind. To his right, the land rose sharply into ruggedly lacerated and wooded terrain. Gnarled and weather-stunted trees and bushes made a black, linear tangle of dead seeming vegetation; stark contrast to the surrounding sea mist.

It was desolate, this westernmost part of Brittany.

"I begin to understand why the King gave me this fief!" Roland said quietly as Oliver brought his horse to a halt beside him.

"How so?"

"It will take a bastard witchling to hold it!" Oliver opened his mouth to retort, then closed it again as he realized that the self-description had been uttered in a peculiarly quiet, meditative tone. Roland sat his beast in a relaxed manner, looking about him as though he had not uttered a sound. "I like the wildness of this place," he murmured after another few moments had passed, then shifted to look at Oliver.

"It is that—wild!" Oliver offered dry-toned agreement. A thought struck him as he too looked about him. "I am given to wonder at these persistent heathen marauders that come from the frozen seas. Surely, there is less than nothing to plunder here?"

"And yet they return. Year after year," Roland added softly. Oliver glanced to the west and became practical.

"Which we will not do unless we seek shelter for the night! There remains little more than an hour of daylight."

Roland nodded. "I will build my own castle hereabouts when the war against the Moors is finally won," he said, and, nudging his horse's sides, set the animal to plummet down a treacherous path between upthrusting rocks. Oliver did not have time to respond. He jerked on the lead of the pack horse as his own mount made to follow.

The golden stallion reached the bottom of the gorge and grunted as it half leaped, half plunged through a short stretch of salt bog and bramble, then thrust its way uphill into heavy undergrowth and black, gnarled, bare trees. Roland ducked branches and held up one mail-covered arm to guard against briars, barely able to see the way before him.

"Jesu!" he heard Oliver exclaim behind him. "What possessed thee to undertake this direction?" He did not answer as his horse struggled its way uphill, then slithered down another brutal gorge.

The stallion leaped boulders, shattering silence as it thundered into even thicker undergrowth. Roland could see little ahead of him and let the beast find its way. Up another hill he nudged the stallion forward as it crested the rise, then scrambled down to lunge through another wave of the thorny undergrowth, to erupt into a small and level clearing to one side of yet another well-concealed gorge. He brought the horse

to a halt beside a small stream and lowered his arm to stare
in amazement.

Set against a backdrop of sheer rock half overgrown with
vines, yet sheltered from the sea wind, stood a partially
crumbled, partially overgrown building of pure white stone.

"Truly this is a ruin of another kind!" Roland murmured
as Oliver drew rein beside him, then stared likewise, eyes
widening in astonishment. He glanced at his friend, their eyes
locking for a moment, then turned back to absorb the details
of the rectangular structure. Great columns that had been
thrice the height of a man thrust up toward the grey sky, most
broken and tumbled to lie in pieces amid the debris of many,
many winters. A few were still entire, one pair still supported
a cross beam of the same white stone around which was
wound a tangle of vines, revealing that at one time the structure had been roofed. Nudging his horse forward, Roland
crossed the small brook and rough-grassed turf, halting again
much closer. The columns had been set to surround a court
that was raised above the level of the ground by half-buried
stone steps. Overgrown by a meshwork of vines and dead
leaves, much of which was decayed into soil, suggestions of
smooth, intricate stonework were delicately revealed in
places. Slowly, Roland dismounted and left his horse to walk
toward the place.

Up the few steps, through a pair of broken columns, he
trod carefully between fallen pieces of lintel, then stopped to
scuff debris with one mail-shod foot. The floor beneath was
made of a multitude of small fragments of multicolored rock,
a mosaic such as he had seen to be popular among the Spanish Infidel. He looked up as Oliver came to stand a little apart
from him, staring likewise.

The whole structure seemed to erupt from the very face of
the cliff beyond. Suggestions of a flawless white surface without portal of any kind was concealed beneath a flowing abundance of thick vegetation. Something was built into the
surrounding bedrock. Other buried structures, doubtless more
pieces of shattered lintel, lay around.

"What manner of construct is this?" Roland asked.

Oliver continued to glance about him. "It does appear to
be the ruin of an ancient temple to some heathen God," he
said slowly. "From Roman times, I consider. I have seen

some of the like about Rome and in other places. They were greatly given to symmetry and the use of marble.''

"Here? In this godforsaken place?" Roland asked.

Oliver smiled. "I confess myself surprised as well"—he shrugged—"but am reminded that the Romans ruled much of the world in those past ages." He glanced about him, scanning the cliffs. "This will serve well enough for the night, I consider. We will at least have shelter from the wind, and there is some grazing for the horses."

"Aye," Roland murmured, turning to tend to practical matters.

Three horses snorted contentedly in the fading chill blue twilight. Relieved of saddles and harness, their grain rations consumed, they browsed with determined preoccupation on the dried grasses of the small clearing. Against the cliff face, partially sheltered by overhanging granite next to the ruined temple, the two lords settled comfortably amid their furs before a blazing fire and ate of the provender they had brought with them. Bread and cheese, dried meat, sharing a wineskin as well. They put aside weapons and removed helms and coifs in unstated acceptance of the quiet, secret isolation of the place.

Bellies filled, and comfortable in the radiance of the fire that lofted bright orange sparks into the unmoving air, they talked together, sharing their thoughts about the wars with the Infidel Moors, strategy and the like. After a time, Oliver reached to rummage through one of the packs and extracted a lyre.

"It is peaceful here," he said softly. "Enough of war! I would conclude the day with a song or two!" Roland shifted closer as Oliver settled the instrument on his thighs and began to lightly pluck the strings with elegant fingers. Roland had listened to De Montglave a few times before, at first with astonishment at the contradiction between his own knowledge of the other's warrior capabilities and this other skill that was found in some men who knew nothing of arms. But then, part of his private awe of Oliver was for the breadth and scope of the other's knowledge. Almost mysterious, these scholarly attributes.

The darkness and the breezeless silence made a harbor of sorts in the clearing. Oliver looked up to search the sky, the faint shadows of cliff and woods and undergrowth lit by the fire.

"Nay. Not words," he said softly. "Just melody." Plucked strings sent delicate sounds into the air, harmonies and pure, isolated notes. Roland watched and listened, and felt surprise as he acknowledged a sudden wish to have a similar skill. It must have been revealed on his face, for Oliver spoke suddenly.

"Shall I show thee how it is done?" Roland stiffened with discomfiture and sat up from his half sprawl. "It is not so difficult," Oliver continued in the same easy tone, moving closer and holding out the instrument. Roland took it gingerly. "Sometimes, for me, it is a way to listen to the voice of God," Oliver said softly. "There is purity in the music, and beauty likewise such as must be reflected in His voice."

God? Roland thought. Nay. God was pure and empty silence. Inaudible. Undetectable. He said nothing and listened as Oliver continued to talk, showing him how to understand the instrument, then reaching to set his fingers upon the strings, guiding him to pluck them and make sounds. Pure— aye. Clear and smooth. He probed and pursued this unfamiliar use for his hands, listened to each note he found, and the sequence. Clear, yet soft-edged—weaving together like . . . He stopped abruptly and thrust the instrument toward Oliver. Like—magic.

"Nay. It is not for me!" he grated roughly at the surprise on Oliver's face.

"I do not understand? 'Tis plain enough thou hast the talent for it."

Roland shook his head. "It is not for me!" he said vehemently.

Oliver gave him a long look and put the lyre away. "Very well . . ." he said slowly. Roland exhaled audibly, and Oliver looked up, startled by his own recognition of the other man's fear. "I still am not able to understand?" he tried gently. Face taut, Roland looked away. Oliver waited.

"Thou cannot know," Roland whispered at last, "how much I fear the witch blood in me!" Oliver's eyes widened, and Roland looked at him, golden eyes haunted and vulnerable. Roland . . . ? Then the expression vanished behind the more familiar, impenetrable hardness. Roland looked down at the hands that lay across his knees. "Thou?" he said in a soft, peculiar tone. ''Thou are not cursed as I! Rather, thou are blessed. Honor and virtue are worn by thee more easily than any other garment!'' Oliver went scarlet as Roland looked at him with a new and penetrating passion. ''By thy friendship, I too can know some sense of that same purity!'' Oliver swallowed.

''I consider—thou exaggerate!'' he managed. Roland shook his head, his gaze unwavering.

''Nay,'' he said with unqualified conviction. ''It is a knowledge as sure as the love I bear thee!'' Oliver met that look, his breathing paused, and he saw himself for a moment reflected with uncomfortable brilliance in the other's eyes. Saw too, within the intensity itself, passions that were, in others, sexual. But in Roland, as yet untouched by such experience, they were astonishingly innocent. It was the innocence, and the powerful implications of potential within it, that made him look away into the darkness.

'' 'Tis a mutual feeling,'' he said carefully, after a time. ''Nor, I think, a bond such as is usual among men.'' His lips quirked at a subtle irony. ''Mayhap it is that we are balance, each for the other—thy ferocity—my—virtue!'' He smiled. ''I do not question, but trust to the future that God intends!'' He met Roland's look and sighed, then comfortably settled down into his furs, indicating his wish to sleep. ''Now, anticipating a hard day's ride, I intend to rest according!'' he added pointedly.

Roland nodded and looked away, hands still draped over mail-clad knees. ''It is a wonder to me,'' he pursued aloud, ''thy faith. It is not so for me. I listen, and I pray—and I am answered with silence. Or worse. Sly hints of things sorcerous and magical, perceived by that witch blood in me.

''Only in battle am I clear-witted and sure of the way.''

Oliver frowned and shifted to settle his head on one arm, caught by a deeper sense of understanding. It was, in part, explanation for Roland's incredible courage and ingenuity in war, and, likewise, in part, explanation for other, less admirable attributes. Aye—fear. Deep-rooted fear.

''I consider thou make too much of this unnatural heritage thou seem perversely bent to cleave to!'' he commented at last. Roland did not answer, and slowly Oliver allowed his eyes to close, his consciousness to melt away.

Later, Roland looked at his friend as the fire sank steadily toward its embers. Oliver's face was soft with peacefulness. Untroubled, pure humanity. He shifted and, drawing his own furs about him, settled himself to lie beside the other man.

Then, he too slept . . .

And, from her place, propped upright against the granite precipice barely a pair of yards behind the sleeping men, the dark sword seemed to shift tones, becoming more opaque than the surrounding darkness. The woman hilt moved a little, her head turning to stare with brutal-eyed ferocity at Lord Oliver. Virulent, unblemished hate . . .

The fire, neglected, consumed its remaining fuel while bent, elusively flickering shadows danced like spirits against shattered, near-luminous, ruined columns. Then, it sank slowly into embers that glowed faintly orange in the darkness.

And the dark sword stood for a time, still against the granite wall. The diminutive face of the woman hilt laced disquiet with shifting flavors of temper as her eyes continued to focus on the sleeping men.

Then Durandal moved from leaning, to poise unsupported in the air, tip just touching the ground. The woman form shifted sinuously, loosed hands and arms with languorous sensuality from their place of concealment in the hair that hung like some luxurious filament garment about her. And, as she did so, the eagle wings of the guard folded slowly, then melded into the blade. The dark locks that trailed about her form shifted, flowed, and merged with the hard, lethal blade. The woman form raised her arms above her head and, like a mirage, grew with her hair, absorbing the blade until her neatly arched feet touched the place on the ground where the point of the sword had been.

Then she stood, exactly the height of the sword, the darkness of her form and the garment of her hair like the midnight reflection of a starlit night upon a lake of total stillness . . .

FOURTEEN

In silence, the dark sword woman Durandal frowned still. Then, stern-faced, imperial, she moved restlessly, her darkness melting like a nocturnal sea mist to reveal other hues of flesh and hair, softening to paler tones, exquisite blending of lavenders and silver blues that managed to embody all the qualities of cold.

Across the debris that covered most of the ground, she moved. Disturbing not even a single dead leaf or fallen twig, she walked across the winter resting, up the steps of the crumbling, ancient temple, across the detritus covered mosaic floor of intricate and ancient design, moving toward that place where the temple joined with the natural granite of the concealed gorge. She paused beside the jagged-edged remains of a broken lintel and stared at the rivers of tangled vines grown down from the precipice above to cover the temple's juncture with the cliff, flowing beyond to spread over fallen pieces of columns and other marble structures, spreading outward in woven, wooden ropes to reach across the temple floor, and wind their various ways upward again around those few columns that were still entire.

Her expression shifted then to some frigid blend of bitter pain and steel resolve, and she moved forward through the hinted paths between the vine-covered rubble to a spot near where the temple floor rose up to become another kind of surface. There, briars and vines met and intertwined to tangle like an impenetrable web. Her fingers reached out with light-ning filaments gleaming along the skin and grasped briars and the like, tugged them aside to reveal part of that which lay beneath.

On an oblong of moon-gleaming stone lay the statue of a recumbent man as unblemished and white as the slab of which he might have been part. Seemingly imprisoned beneath the meshwork of brambles, he was flawless of form and perfect in repose. Durandal touched fingertips to frozen eyelids, moved along the brow where a simple carven fillet held a scattered wealth of curly locks, down a nose of perfect straightness to lips bow-curved and colder than ice. Her face changed again to reflect determined power and ageless en-durance, and her voice whispered across the night like the distant echoes of a storm brewing upon an unseen horizon.

"It will not be much longer—this waiting. A little time— a little time. But a moment in all the ages I have endured . . ."

The statue did not respond as her fingers caressed the molded perfection of one broad, muscular shoulder, shifted down to the hand that clasped a lyre, then withdrew in rec-ognition of futility.

She turned away, caught by sounds from the clearing.

One of the sleepers murmured and shifted restlessly, softly uttered troubled and incoherent noises. The shadow woman melded with the hues of the night and shifted across the dark-ness to stand once more behind Roland.

He stiffened fleetingly, eyelids closed, and flung aside part of the fur lined cloak that covered him, then went limp in exactly the same pose as the statue.

Durandal watched him with eyes of obsidian and lightning, hearing his slow breathing and the faint thunder of his heart-beat. Mortal flesh that clothed . . . Deep within—incalculably potent—it grew. He grew . . .

Slowly she darkened, arms vanishing into the filament hair that was her only garment, wings slipping forth as her feet withdrew, body melting upward to become the form of the dark sword once more.

Dawn was a translucent melting into another grey chill day. Sea mist hung quietly in the air, making it thick, moisture condensing a drop at a time to drip from vines and tree branches and stone, softening any possible crackle of brittle debris.

Awake before his friend, Roland sat huddled in the cloak he had managed to discard during the night through some restless folly, attempting to dispel the chill that had permeated chain mail and the clothing beneath to make his skin feel brittle. He frowned at his own unease as he broke his fast with a scrap of bread and a piece of dried, spicy meat. Appetite uncertain, he remembered eerie dreams of the past night.

Unsettling images . . . The ghost of a woman, face exquisite with power, form unclothed save for nocturnal rainfalls of hair, herself shadow-seeming and stormy-hued with magic . . . Standing over him. Watching with eyes that held all the turbulent passion of a thundercloud filled with lightning as yet unleashed. And her hand that came toward him seemed to touch with awful clarity, fingertips reaching to define some shell of incredible cold . . .

Himself? Feelings unimagined, yet profoundly clear. Being bound in unmoving layers. Stonelike. Or, divided somehow. Peculiar contradictions of being frozen to total and perpetual immobility, and yet, by contrast, free in another fashion, sensate in all familiar ways.

He abandoned further attempts to eat and looked toward the ruin of the ancient heathen temple. White stone was reduced to magical soft suggestions of substance in the heavy mist that overhung the gorge. Only the dark intertwining vegetation had any clarity, like the trees that made grey, engraved shadows about the whole. He stood, restless, and reached for the dark sword, girding her to her place at his back. Then, seeing Lord Oliver stir, he strode across the damp cold sod, up worn steps, and paused to stand in the center of the temple court.

A silent place . . . His eyes were drawn to that peculiar, largely concealed place where the temple joined with the cliffs, to the overgrown rubble that lay before it. Slowly, he picked his way toward it, ignoring briars that snagged on mail and cloak, and stopped abruptly before—the figure of a naked and sleeping man reclining upon a slab of the same, pure white, unblemished stone. Partly concealed by a meshwork of briars, the form was clearly complete and perfect in every detail.

A statue, Roland thought with wonder, staring at the youthful sleeping face and locks of shoulder-length hair bound by a narrow fillet upon the brow. Perfect of form, even beautiful, the very detail made it seem . . . seem? Real.

His eyes traced along a strong jaw, the column of the neck, broad shoulders and arms that slipped beneath the vines, one to rest a hand upon the abdomen, the other clutching a lyre of the same flawless stone.

Unable to resist, he reached out to touch a surface of silken texture. Bitter cold . . . He traced fingers across the upper arm, along a collarbone and throat to touch lips that were hard and soft at the same time. Flesh—like a corpse.

He withdrew his fingers at once and swallowed, his face ashen.

"What is this thou hast found?" He heard Lord Oliver at his side, and started. He could not answer. Oliver did not look at him, but stared with untroubled interest at the figure. "A statue . . ." he said slowly. "And wondrously made! It is a marvel that it is not damaged." He touched briefly, then looked at Roland, eyes widening at the other's pallor. "Art thou troubled by it?" he asked bluntly. Roland's expression was answer enough. He looked bewildered, then shook his head. "This must be the image of the God of this temple," he said slowly, looking back at the figure, eyes fixing on the lyre. "Apollo, to judge from the instrument he holds. The Romans were most fond of that divinity." He moved back as Roland exhaled relief. Oliver, whose humanness brought the world to simple clarity once more.

"Aye," he murmured.

"Come then," Oliver said, striding back the way he had come. "We've a long day's ride ahead."

"Aye," Roland murmured once more, glancing back at the figure. Uncanny—flesh caught in some incomprehensible and lifeless rigor. Waiting . . . He fled.

"Aye! Let us be gone from this accursed place!" he near shouted, half leaping down the temple steps to stride toward his stallion. His own mount ready, finishing the task of binding their baggage to the pack animal's back, Oliver looked around in surprise at the vehemence of Roland's tone. He had slept soundly in the relative safety and quiet of the place.

"I consider," he said with careful deliberation as Roland brought his horse close by a moment later. "That the only witch blood in thee is the brewing of an overused imagination!''

Roland hefted saddle and reached to tighten girths. ''Aye!'' he said after a brief silence. The single word was exhaled like a sigh of relief. He smiled briefly, and Oliver grinned response, shaking his head ruefully as he mounted. Roland finished bridling his horse and mounted as well. Reaching for the pack horse's rope, Oliver turned his mount about and set the beast toward the woods. East—toward Aix La Chapelle.

At Roland's back, the diminutive face of the dark sword shifted fractionally to glare with venom at De Montglave.

Summoned to Charlemagne's presence, Roland stood a little behind Lord Oliver. Before them both, the King sat comfortably loose in a chair a little to one side of a great oak table littered with documents. On the other side sat the Archbishop Turpin, quill and ink pot by his right hand. More startling than the King's unusually relaxed manner was the presence of the Duchess of Bordeaux and, beside her, Oliver's sister, the Lady Aude De Montglave. Both women stood, gazes lowered, by the far side of the chamber.

''My Lord De Montglave.'' Charlemagne spoke in a tone that was as relaxed as his carriage. ''We have considered the petition thou brought to us and will give thee our answer now. Bordeaux, being a great fief and with a young lord to inherit, has been in the guardianship of one of our most trusted liegemen, Lord Ganelon. Any disposition of the same must be done with reason and foresight. We have elected to grant thy wish to wed the Lady Alicia, Dowager Duchess of Bordeaux, and, in accordance with that, do likewise assign thee such following duties as will serve the interests of both ourself and the future of Bordeaux!'' The Lady Alicia looked up, her face gone radiant, Roland saw. Oliver, too, grinned in a manner not unlike some halfling boy. ''We have removed Bordeaux from Lord Ganelon's wardships and do now bestow the same on thee.'' Charlemagne continued, ''We are confident of the honor that will safeguard its rightful heir, young Duke Huon, to such time as he may undertake rule of the same.''

''Gladly, Majesty!'' Oliver half breathed, eyes meeting his lady. Roland began to smile uncertainly, acknowledging his friend's happiness, until he saw that the King was studying him intently. He stiffened and felt his stomach knot.

"In conjunction with this dispensation." Charlemagne straightened somewhat, his eyes still on Roland. "It is our wish, Count Oliver, to bestow the hand of our ward and thy sister upon Count Roland of Brittany." Roland felt his breathing stop for a moment, the blood drain from his face. Nay. Nay! But the King's voice continued, clattering across horrified wits. "Thereby will be established an enduring alliance between thy houses, my lords!" And there was naught he could do about it, Roland thought slowly, turning a little to stare at the Lady Aude.

A female Oliver, slight and graceful, her face was turned to him, eyes luminous, color flaring in her cheeks. She, he saw with revulsion, was well delighted. He glanced at Oliver who had turned to look at him with sober penetration.

De Montglave looked away and bowed to the King. "I rejoice, Majesty, in thy gift," he said softly.

Roland bowed tersely as he should, but could not voice a response. Straightening, he saw total determination in the King's eyes and felt even more trapped. "Thy will be done, my liege!" he managed to grate, and spun on one heel to stride from the chamber, his cloak swirling like some wild thing about his ankles.

Time enough to deal with Roland later, Oliver thought, looking at the combination of surprise and delight on his sister's face. He sought the Lady Alicia's eyes, instead, and found all he wished for there. He strode toward her and, bowing, reached for her hand and pressed his lips to the back.

"My contentment is secure with thee!" he murmured. She smiled and relaxed.

"Go now!" Charlemagne spoke abruptly. "We have other matters to attend!" Oliver flushed, then used the perogative of the betrothed to set his lady's arm through his and draw her away. The King smiled briefly.

"My lord Roland is very shy!" He heard Aude's murmur as they reached the hall beyond the chamber and turned to look at her.

"Aye, he is that, little one!" he managed after a moment, trying to overlay his fear for the blindness of her infatuation with calm.

* * *

Alone, save for the Archbishop Turpin, the King settled back in his chair and frowned, aware of the large, birdlike eyes that watched him.

Power that needs be shifted so smoothly as to seem to glide like fate toward the inevitable. The Lady Aude was well dowered and impeccably bred. Beautiful and devout and virtuous. Most suitable. But Roland's response was unexpected. Stonecold withdrawal—that gave credence to his reputed chastity.

"We have been most careful in this matter," he heard himself mutter.

"Of that I am aware, Majesty." Charlemagne met the Archbishop's dark eyes.

"He will come to terms with it when he is wed!"

Turpin shifted one shoulder, unconvinced. "Destiny is not a thing contrived even by great Christian princes," the priest said very softly.

Charlemagne's eyes narrowed as he searched the priest's wily, confident face. "Are we to consider ourself warned, my lord?" he asked tautly.

Again, Turpin shrugged, unperturbed by the frost in the King's gaze. The very quiet of his reply suggested a different manner of authority. "Given as I am to the hearing of confessions, I am fortunate to know aspects of the human soul not apparent in any public display. Likewise, I perceive thou are compelled by the silent dreams of a close-held heart." Charlemagne stiffened reflexively, but the priest did not seem to notice, his large brown eyes intently affixed on a candle that flickered on the table. "Lord Roland is got beyond the pale of Christian men, for all his love of thee, and he is a man who must answer the summons of his blood beyond any, even royal, contriving!"

Charlemagne's eyes narrowed farther and he leaned forward.

"Explain, my lord!" he ordered brutally.

Turpin's eyes widened then. "Majesty, 'tis common enough known and, to Lord Roland most especially, that he is witchgot and a bastard besides!"

"Fairy tales drawn of old resentments!" Charlemagne muttered at once.

"Nonetheless, my liege, a man is composed more of his beliefs than of the flesh that houses them. Count Roland's singular brilliance is for war. On other things, he is known to be uncommon abstaining, even to complete innocence."

Charlemagne closed the fist of privacy about old, deep-seated knowledge and settled back deliberately in his chair.

"Then there will be no bridals until this Spanish war is concluded," he said after a time. Turpin nodded, almost imperceptibly.

Oliver braced his shoulders uncomfortably as he caught sight of Roland farther along the battlements of the keep of the great castle of Aix. The other man stood leaning against the parapet, his cloak shifting about his ankles as the wind caught at its folds, staring out at a stark landscape threaded with the first hints of spring green, all brightened by a cold drizzle. Two weeks had passed since Roland had found himself betrothed, and for the whole of that time, he had kept to himself, becoming remote and elusive. Oliver thought of his sister's quietly expressed feelings and hopes, all the more powerful for the innocence that underlay them, and his mouth tightened. He inhaled sharply as he approached the other man.

"Roland?" Oliver shielded himself from the worst of the weather by pausing behind one of the crenellations. "We have not spoken together for many days past." Roland glanced at him, face stern, eyes glinting.

"What is there to speak on?" he demanded, anger festering. "Thou hast intimated to me before on the matter of marriage. I did not heed it, like a fool, and now I am bound by the King's own command to this woman!" He shifted to face Oliver. "Thy own blood, my lord! I consider thou hast known of this, even to have contrived the same!"

Oliver drew himself up, glaring back. "Nay, my lord!" he retaliated. "The King's will hath no influence of mine. I would not bear to see so gentle and innocent a maid as my sister given to one so churlishly disposed as thee!" Roland stepped back a pace, eyes glinting in rage. "Thou are an ingrate, I consider!" Oliver went on. "Aude is young, and beautiful. Her lineage is proud, and she is well reared to Christian obedience and housewifery! More—she thinks thee a very God! Husbanding her will be no gruesome task, I do assure thee! Unless thou are not man enough for it?" The insult hung in the air between them, and Oliver realized his hand had gone to his sword hilt.

Roland's face went ashen. Then, of a sudden, he stepped back another pace. "Thou know what manner of man I am!"

he said with unexpected quiet, and looked away. "Nor will I raise even a finger to defend myself against thee." Oliver exhaled abruptly and deliberately removed his grip from his sword hilt. Roland did not move.

"Nor would I be brought to quarrel over this," Oliver conceded. "But I care for my sister and will not see her misused." Roland looked away once more. "Having known her since her swaddling days, I will not see the dove she is become rended by an eagle such as thou!" Roland swung about suddenly, his expression haunted.

"Why do thou call me so?" he demanded harshly.

Oliver was entirely disconcerted. "What?" He frowned.

"An eagle!"

Oliver stared his confusion. Then shrugged. "It was an apt analogy, I consider. Thy ferocity is of the same ilk! What is this about . . . ?" Roland did not answer at once, but searched his face with aggressive golden eyes. "What is this about?" Oliver repeated, aware that he had been drawn from the subject of his chief concern.

"So I have been called before!" Roland half whispered.

Oliver frowned, entirely at a loss, then shrugged. "Mayhap 'tis the color of thy eyes!" he attempted to quip. But Roland's face grew more stark.

"By Ferragus as he died!" Roland grated. "He claimed to recognize"—his voice shifted to an uncertain whisper—"that I was a God. Lord of Eagles, he called me!"

Oliver swallowed as he met Roland's look, aware of the import of a dying man's words, feeling as though he were caught, if fleetingly, in some tormented vortex within Roland himself. He shook his head abruptly, clearing his wits, aware that this connected in some skewed way to Roland's betrothal to Aude.

"Nay, Roland," he said firmly. "Thou put too much credence on it. Ferragus was heathen and given to strange belief! It was some last fantasy to justify thy triumph, I do not doubt!" Roland's eyes were watchful, not convinced. Oliver inhaled deeply and thrust down his own uncertainties and doubts. He took a forcible grip on good sense.

"I think," he said with determination, "thou spend too much time alone and brooding on such, and by that brooding ferment a potent brew of overindulged superstition. Thou would do better to spend thy time among people and practice

other normal interests as becomes a man. Jesu! And I listen
to thee, even I am given to half believe! Nay, it will not serve.
It will but drive thee to madness in the end! For myself, I am
well content to my duty, and to savor every joy that God
chooses to bless me with. Do thou likewise!'' Roland's expression closed. Oliver frowned a little and grew firmer still.
''I trust to my sister's sweet and devout disposition to soften
thee to better humanity!''

It was a warning, Roland knew. He nodded a little and
looked away. ''I will face that when the wars with the Moors
are concluded,'' he said reluctantly, clearly thankful for the
delay. Oliver released a silent sigh. He knew that Roland had
turned his mind completely to the southern campaign.

''Nay. Stay. I may require some service of thee!'' Sir
Thierry's hand abandoned its reach for the iron bolt to the
door of his uncle's private chamber.

''Very good, my lord,'' he murmured, turning, reluctant
to move farther into the chamber. His answer was not acknowledged by even so much as a nod. Lord Ganelon stood
in rigid sternness, as he broke the royal seal that bound the
documents Thierry had just delivered to him, unfurled the
several scrolls, and began to read with eyes that flitted like
dark beetles. Thierry watched as his uncle's brows closed into
a frown.

The first document, then the second. Lord Ganelon's face
paled slowly, his features growing taut. Then the third. A
hideous wave of purplish hue swept up across Lord Ganelon's
face and his fist closed to crumple the scrolls, knuckles showing white. He looked up, and Thierry stiffened against an
urge to flinch at the fury on Lord Ganelon's face.

''Royal writ of decree!'' he growled. ''Mother of God, but
it goes beyond tolerance!'' He flung the crumpled documents
down upon the table on one side of the room.

''He hath given the whole of this southern campaign to
Count Roland!'' Lord Ganelon snarled furiously. Thierry
swallowed. ''And I—I am bid to honor this commission with
an oath of fealty and service to this same—ill-got bastard
witchling! I—I, who have served with honor and sacrifice,
and am now reduced to meaningless entitlement. Lord High
Councillor! Pah!'' He began pacing. ''Such hollow distinction as is given to old men incapable! And he hath disposed

of Bordeaux. My wardship to tend! Given to the stewardship
of De Montglave by this marriage to the Duchess! What sorceries are spun between those two? By God's Blood, it is an
unholy alliance, for the Count is now betrothed to Lord Oliver's sister!'' Frozen by the door, Thierry prayed earnestly
that his face showed the faint surprise he felt, not his appalled
horror at his uncle's grotesque rage. But Lord Ganelon did
not seem to notice him at all.

''It goes too far!'' he snarled, still pacing. ''It goes too
far! Charlemagne whose blood is less pure than my own!
Who betrays that very throne that is God-given to him by
these acts!'' Thierry's stomach lurched at this scalding treason. Eyes gone black bored into Thierry's from a face harsh
and mottled with uncontrolled temper. Then, of a sudden,
Lord Ganelon turned and found a chair by the table, and
seated himself, drumming fingertips on the smooth oak surface.

''I see thou are appalled as well!'' Lord Ganelon said in a
greatly moderated tone. Thierry managed a nod. Lord Ganelon breathed violently, his fingertips making a restless tat-
too of noise, face resuming its normal color as his eyes flitted
to the documents, then to the hearth fire across the room.

''I will see an end to it!'' Lord Ganelon whispered after a
time, his scowl unrelenting. Thierry did not move, and slowly
Lord Ganelon turned his head to study the young knight.

''Aye . . .'' he said slowly, eyes going from temper to cunning, voice colder than an ice storm. ''I have service aplenty
for thee!'' Thierry felt his eyebrows rise, and realized his
expression was being misconstrued. Lord Ganelon smiled
nastily. ''Even thou will not bear to see beloved Christendom
seduced into Satan's hands! I have taught thee well, for all
thy frivolous and inattentive ways! Now thou will become fit
to be my kin!'' Thierry knew better than to react to the insult.
Lord Ganelon looked away and continued speaking, slowly—
deliberately.

''On the morrow, thou will depart my service. Find me in
the morning and take from me the letters I will prepare. Thou
will then ride to the King and give the same into his hands.
No other, mind.

''Of these documents, one will state that I am in all things
his loyal servant, and do gladly give my service to the Champion's use!'' Thierry felt his stomach clench. ''Another will

express my—relief at the marriage of Lord Oliver, which re-leives me of duties I have not the time to attend, being pre-occupied for the King's interest here in the south. The third will affirm my loyalty through the gift of thy own service to Count Roland!'' Thierry's eyes widened.

"Just so!'' Lord Ganelon's tone was sardonic. "To him, I give thee, my beloved nephew, to serve in battle and such other as he requires and expressly to guard him from harm! Aye. I know thy hatred is like unto my own!'' Lord Ganelon's tone became determined. "But thou are well taught to dis-semble. Do so now. Give the appearance of such devoted loyalty as I require and send word to me of *all* information thou may obtain by getting Count Roland's trust. I will give thee a man to squire thee. He will serve as messenger!''

"My lord!'' Thierry managed. His uncle nodded, eyes still fixed on him.

"Serve me well, and there is undreamed of reward for thee,'' Lord Ganelon said softly.

"My—lord . . . ?'' Thierry breathed.

Lord Ganelon smiled his confidence. "I know thee well,'' he said gently. "Nor do I forget my own blood! Go now.''

"Aye, my lord!'' Thierry thrust himself from the chamber with a vigor he knew his uncle would misread. Down a half-lit corridor and a stairwell to some place of silence and sol-itude. A barren and shadowed corner.

Then, sickened to the core, he stopped and leaned back against the cold, damp stone, raised his face and gulped air. One hand went to press against a stomach gone sour and painful, even as he knew he would do as bid. He closed his eyes . . .

"What am I become?'' he whispered to the air. "What am I become . . . ?''

The question hovered in the shadows, like the ghost of things that had once, in a boyhood near forgot, been brilliant clear . . .

FIFTEEN

A.D. 777–778

Worn down by the tensions of a quiet but uneasy winter, and a spring that had become simply defensive in strategy against a new onslaught of unpredictable Infidel raids, the armies of Charlemagne welcomed Lord Roland, Count of Brittany and King's Champion, with great fervor upon his return to the southernmost frontier. Flanked by others of the peers who had gone north with the King, leading substantial reinforcements, he seemed the very symbol of renewal as the armies loosed themselves from winter watchfulness into a panoply of vigor and motion. Even the ageing yet resilient Duke Naimes was glad to relinquish his responsibilities to the younger man.

Resplendent, clearly visible in his characteristic gold cloak, Roland undertook to cover his hauberk with one of the pair of exquisitely embroidered, scarlet surcoats that had been the Lady Aude's parting gift to him. Astounded, he had stared in awe at the wonder of an ingenious and elegant interweaving of the arms of Brittany and of the King. He had swallowed helplessly looking down at the slight girl who had, clearly, wrought this for him. She had smiled incomprehensible delight at his reaction, and he had managed some half-mumbled courtesy. Now, Roland flung himself, body and soul, into the single kind of endeavor he understood above all other as plans were brewed over nocturnal campfires, and strategies considered . . .

The western frontier must be secured, a task facilitated by the scattered populace of largely Christian folk under leaders of minor significance. Then they would march south, across a hundred and fifty miles of treacherous mountains to wrest Cordoba from the powerful Emir Blancandrin. From there, it was a relatively short distance to the sea, and the remaining Moors would be confined to the east, removed from their access to the resources of Africa. Then, like locusts, the Christian forces would surround and consume the land, taking for the True Faith this last of Infidel strongholds. Marsilla would have to surrender, or die.

A simple, orderly progression of schemes that proved much harder to execute. The Infidel were everywhere. Time and blood were spilled like coins across a marketplace as one pitched battle after another was fought. Towns were besieged and leveled. Booty of all kinds seized.

Summer brought heat and drought. Sweat and shimmering, relentless mirages to delude the mind. The fires of burning towns melded with the scorching sun, shimmering like the corners of Hell. Flies by the millions swarmed over the bloated and rotting corpses, the carcasses of horses, left in the wake of Roland's determination to triumph for his King.

And with the hard-won miles of progress, the Infidel became increasingly elusive. With their fleet horses and cunning uses of bow and arrow and firebolt, they were brutal thorns that stung and bit into the flanks of grim Christian intent.

It was sheer will, Sir Thierry thought, that brought victory after victory to Charlemagne's army until, in mid-autumn, they stood encamped on the high bluffs that nearly surrounded the north side of the exquisite city of Cordoba. Thierry accepted the rations his squire held out and, crouching down on his haunches in the windblown, dried turf, began to eat. He shot a look of acute dislike at the wiry little man who had been given to him, as the squire undertook to tend to the horses, then shifted his gaze elsewhere. Some twenty yards to his left, near a precipice that tumbled down to the valley below, Lord Roland sat his horse and stared toward Cordoba. The city gleamed pure, near white, beside the sluggish flow of the drought-depleted river, and beyond it lay fields and vineyards, the whole glowing ruddy in the late afternoon sun.

But Thierry had little interest in that now-familiar view. Instead, he watched Count Roland. The golden stallion swished its full tail and gnashed its teeth against the bits, spewing froth about as though annoyed at being held to stillness. The man astride it, his surcoat bloodred, golden cloak blowing in loose folds about him, sat alertly as he scanned the valley before and below him with predatory intensity. Beneath the nasal of his helm, Lord Roland's mouth was set to sternness, and his eyes gleamed as they considered that which lay ahead. His fingers moved restlessly, caressing the flat surface of the blade of the mysterious dark sword that lay across his thighs. The weapon rarely left his grasp now, Thierry knew. His touch was slow, strangely sensual, as though he were in some exclusive communion with the thing.

The Djinn of the Dark Sword, the Infidel called him. Thierry looked away to reach for the skin of watered wine that the squire had set beside him, and drank. He settled himself to cross-legged comfort and studied the ground before him with eyes that did not see it at all.

Nay. Count Roland was not the same at all, he thought, as the baleful, arrogant boy he remembered and had hated. The realization of that had struck him upon reaching Aix La Chapelle in mid-spring with the packet of documents from Lord Ganelon upon his person. The King had accepted his uncle's seeming goodwill and had sent him to Count Roland who was preparing to march south.

The first shock was Count Roland's height, nearly as great as the King's. Thierry had been surprised to find himself the shorter man. Count Roland had looked at him with a memory of old feuds, but had not commented until Thierry had completed his explanation for his presence. Then, disconcertingly, Roland had continued to study him silently.

"I see thou bear little resemblance to Lord Ganelon," he had said suddenly. Thierry had been surprised.

"Nay, I have my mother's look," he had managed to reply. Roland had nodded as though satisfied about something.

"I remember thee as skilled at arms, Sir Thierry," he said then. "Thy service is welcome."

"My lord!" Thierry had bowed. Lord Roland had turned away, and that had been the sum of it, beyond orders.

Nay, Lord Roland was not the same. Largely solitary of disposition, remote save for the companionship of Lord Oliver, and, on occasion, the Bishop Turpin, he had become a man of profound and confident power, of absolute dedication, and a conspicuous, brutal sort of honesty. Thierry watched as the Archbishop, garbed in his inevitable white, rode up to set his horse beside Count Roland's. Whatever was said, he did not catch, but he saw Lord Roland give an answering nod and, with the other man, dismount.

The two then led their horses away from the precipice, toward where Thierry sat. Drinking again from the wineskin, Thierry swallowed surprise as well when the Champion paused a few feet away and scanned him with appraising eyes.

"Thou are without injury, I am glad to see," Count Roland half murmured, then passed on to the place a little distant where he shared camp with Lord Oliver. Thierry thought further, frowning a little as he drank more of the vinegary contents of his wineskin. For all his power and resources, Lord Roland was wont to be remarkably unencumbered. A single pair of packs carried all the goods he seemed to require, furs for sleeping, clothing, bow and quiver for hunting. Little else. Thierry thought of his uncle's need for far greater luxury. Nor was the Count seemingly interested in adding to his property. He took no booty for himself as others were given to do when battles were won.

Bitter victories all, Thierry thought, that had brought them to the gates of Cordoba. He bowed his head and studied the sod by his feet. Won more by sheer will than anything else. He knew why, of course . . . Cryptic messages were dispatched to his uncle at sporadic intervals. He drank again, hearing the threads of conversation that passed between Lord Roland and the Archbishop who had settled themselves near an outcropping of rock close by. Acid coiled in his stomach, and he thought bitterly of what he had become as he listened closely.

"He sleeps, my lord." Roland nodded toward the small pitched tent a little to his right. "The leg heals well, for which God be praised. I have sworn to deliver him entire to his lady!"

Turpin nodded as he shifted to lean back against stone. "I am glad to hear it," he murmured, then looked up, large brown eyes searching. "I know thou love him well . . ."

Disconcerted, Roland reached for wineskin and the ration

pouch he carried. "More than any other soul . . ." he whispered after a moment. "He is more to me than a brother."

Turpin smiled. "A Roland for an Oliver!" he quoted softly. Roland shifted and bit brutally into some dried meat that he had taken from the pouch. "Be not discomfited, my lord." The priest continued, " 'Tis much admired in thee, and hath set an example that is emulated to good effect! But that is not the matter that brought me to seek thee out." Roland looked up. "I have word, my lord, that the King rides south to join us for the conquest of this city."

Roland swallowed, and his eyes gleamed. "Good!" he said bluntly. Then, "We must take Cordoba and keep it undefiled for our liege. It will serve as a stronghold for the coming winter." Turpin nodded. Roland frowned, his attention focused. "I have studied it at length. Cordoba is most shrewdly built." His voice dropped a little as he looked toward the precipice. "Our numbers are badly reduced, and there are so many wounded. These Infidel are like locusts that seem to know our every move." His mouth tightened, as he was caught up in wondering yet again how to preserve his forces and still successfully take the brilliantly fortified city in the valley below.

"A single man can slip through a crowd unseen," he heard the priest observe casually. "And, to that, I have more for thee, my lord. Blancandrin is fled with the greater part of his forces and gone to Marsilla at Saragossa."

"Nay!" Roland went rigid and stared at the priest. "When?"

Turpin shrugged. "These few nights past, as we approached." Roland's frown deepened. "There is but a small garrison left. Cordoba is, to all intent, abandoned."

"Why?" Roland whispered slowly, then stiffened to search the priest's ingenious face and large brown eyes. "How is it that none of the scouting parties have discovered this, yet thou know of it?" he demanded.

Turpin made a ruffling movement of one shoulder. "Is it not sufficient to utilize such as my particular gifts bring thee?" he countered. "Thou hast not hesitated before!"

Roland met the look in Turpin's calm eyes. "I am given to a certain awe for that—gift of sight that is thine!" he retorted. "But I would harness the Devil himself were it for the King's interest!"

The priest grinned and shook his head. "And I," he murmured dryly, "must likewise be in awe of such—irreverent and determined arrogance!" He stood and inhaled deeply. "I do not intend, as thou, to spend the night battling frost and cold. I seek the comfort of warm rest, anticipating that the morrow brings hard effort." He made the sign of the Cross over Roland's head. "God bless thee, my son!" He made soft benediction and, turning, strode lightly away, the white of his cloak swirling warm and orange as it caught the light of the setting sun. Roland watched him disappear through the mass of camping men, then bent his head to frown in concentration as he finished his meal.

Farther away, Thierry of Leon settled himself in his own furs beneath the shelter of a small tent, and thought wonderingly of what he had overheard, and of the last message he had dispatched to Lord Ganelon ten days before. Strange . . . He would not have thought there were enough sound men left to take Cordoba. Why would the Emir have fled? Understanding was like attempting to stare at the water in a well where only the surface gleamed. The water lay there, impenetrably dark. Unmeasurably deep.

Much later, alone, upon a rise well apart from the Christian army encamped on a plateau on the mountainside below, a white figure stood amid a small dense grove of wind-gnarled olive trees. He was still for a time, staring thoughtfully out toward the distant, quiescent, pearllike gleam of Cordoba in the moonlight.

Moonglow made silver hues between the opaque shadows of the night, and the figure reached to touch an olive branch— and frowned . . . He shifted restlessly, like a bird ruffling feathers that were not comfortably disposed. The night wind caught at the folds of his cloak and set it to furl like silver wingtips about his ankles.

After a time, he raised his face to stare at that newly waning orb, and the twinkling constellations scattered across a black and serene firmament. In a face both youthful and ageless, his eyes were dark pools of clarity. He sighed, and mischief flickered at the corners of his mouth.

"Nay, maiden," he murmured in a tone that melded with the breeze that rustled through the olive branches about him. "I think it will not all come to pass as thou will have it!"

* * *

To the surprise of all who had steeled themselves for the bloodiest encounter of the campaign, Cordoba was easily won, a sign of divine blessing. A nearly abandoned city of some common folk and a nominal Infidel garrison who were willing enough to accept the True Faith, it was a place of great beauty and vast treasure. Brilliant, spacious, high-arched palaces dominated the city. Composed of granite and marble, they were miracles of architecture, ornamented with colorful mosaics and abstracted, exquisitely patterned carvings. Elegant pools and fountains, these bore quiet testimony to the wealth, skills, and power of the Moors who had fled.

Likewise, there were incredible supplies of furnishings and textiles. Precious woods, silks, and brocades, ornaments and utensils of silver, or copper inlay, or gold, and myriad other such near unimagined luxuries. More importantly to the army that was to winter there, Cordoba's granaries and storehouses were well filled. Aware that the King was on a southward march to rendezvous there, Roland sternly issued orders against pillage and looting. Cordoba would be presented intact, like the jewel she seemed to be, to his liege.

Charlemagne's arrival coincided with the blessing of a brilliant sunny early winter day. Riding before the highest of his lords brought from Aix, he was flanked as well by substantial companies of men, brought as reinforcements from the north.

The King's eyes gleamed and a suggestion of a smile lurked in the corners of his mouth as the gates of Cordoba were flung wide to the accompaniment of a thunderous roar of triumph from the Christian men behind the walls. A company of colorful knights erupted through the gates and galloped toward him on stallions whose leaps and snorts and kicking hooves were pure expression of their exuberance. He drew rein and watched, his smile widening as the company fanned out on either side of the unmistakable scarlet and gold of the Count of Brittany.

"They are fine, are they not, Ganelon?" he murmured in a tone that reflected old intimacy. Slightly behind and to the right of the King, Lord Ganelon found an answering smile.

"Aye, my liege." Then the company brought their horses to plunging halts in a semicircle before the King. There was a deep resonating cheer as, to a man, they bowed from the waist.

"God hath never assembled so great a company of Champions to His service as thee!" Charlemagne's voice rang out in full-throated praise over them all. Young faces smiled beneath nasaled helms. Boys no longer, they were battle-hardened and vigorous with the blossoming power of full young manhood and experience. Still smiling, the King nudged his horse to gallop and charged through the midst of them toward the welcoming pearl of Cordoba. The peers, filled with pride at the King's praise, swung their own animals about to gallop behind him.

As he fell back to lead the rest into the city, Lord Ganelon's expression showed only watchfulness.

Charlemagne established himself in the palace that surely must have been the Emir Blancandrin's own, and a court of sorts was soon in place about him. Smaller, without the scholars and others that were entrenched at Aix, it was a warlike court with qualities of energy and purpose as could be thought to resemble a pride of hunting lions.

Councils were a daily occurrence, held with Charlemagne and, for the most part, the older, experienced lords. The Lord High Councillor figured strongly in these assemblies, his shrewd capabilities and sound advice, his assiduous and unrelenting energy on the King's behalf, gaining for him even greater power and respect.

Fierce arguments were waged before the King concerning the strength of the foe that remained and were now concentrated in the north and east under the Emir Marsilla at Saragossa. Costs were assessed, and the balances of power. How to secure the southern coasts. When to march on Marsilla for that final encounter. The odds of triumph, and those administrative details that would make of Spain a Christian realm entirely.

Some lord, it was proposed, well known to all, and of unqualified loyalty to Charlemagne, could be made King of the Spanish peninsula. Given to rule newly endowed fiefs and to bring total Christian enlightenment to a populace uncertain in its faith, he must be, likewise, Charlemagne's vassal.

Emperor was the new word murmured privately as eyes studied the silver King. And it was whispered that the Lord High Councillor was the most fitting man for such great and privileged responsibility as the ruling of Spain.

Count Roland and the younger peers attended these councils with variable frequency. But, unlike the rest, he kept himself apart and did not speak. Instead, he watched and listened with stern attention. At other times, restless with winter inactivity, he took troops out into the lands beyond and to the south of Cordoba, skirmishing and fighting to secure the southernmost seat of the King.

"We cannot rest against these Infidel now," he told Lord Oliver once. "The King's triumph is not absolute until we have Marsilla's head!" Oliver had nodded agreement and gladly accompanied his friend. Restlessly eager to dispose of the time that lay between him and his return to Bordeaux. And the lady and child that awaited him there . . .

A.D. 778

The bitter cold and freezing rains of the southern mid-winter brought an unexpected surprise, for, upon one brutal morning, sentries espied a company of ten riding down from the hills, along the half-frozen river's edge, toward Cordoba. Conspicuous in white attire, they were heathen-garbed in those loose robes that the Moors were wont to wear. And the leader was the only one mounted, riding a white stallion of remarkable delicacy.

Apparently unarmed, though this was impossible to determine with the shrouding robes of the Infidel, they were escorted watchfully to Charlemagne's presence. Charlemagne sat enthroned and garbed in purple and gold and watched as the ten approached, then bowed, and dropped to their knees to touch brows to floor in the Infidel manner of obeisance. Only the leader, his white garb shot with silver thread that sparkled, kept to his feet. A slim man with dark-skinned and hawklike features, he stepped toward the King's throne and, with exquisite grace, extracted something from the folds of his outer robe and held it out. An olive branch, still with green leaves upon it.

"I am Blancandrin, Emir of Cordoba and Tangier," he said in flawless Latin. "I give greeting to the glorious Christian King of the Franks who is known throughout the world as Charles the Great, from Marsilla, Emir of Saragossa and Valencia, and uncounted lands beyond the sea!"

Charlemagne stood. "We welcome thee, my lord!" he said, and Lord Ganelon stepped forward to take the olive branch, bowing low to set it at the King's feet.

Blancandrin offered another graceful, yet distinctly imperial bow and stepped back a pace or two. "I am come as embassy to talk of peace between us, for the Emir Marsilla hath commissioned me to put such petition before thee," he said in the same liquid language. Charlemagne stepped down from the dais, in courtesy, his eyes gleaming a blue contrast to the dark pools of Blancandrin's own. The two exchanged steady looks, and Charlemagne slowly inclined his head, clearly willing to listen. Blancandrin spoke again.

"My lord. The wise and valiant King Marsilla, who is a prince beloved of his people for his great philosophy and generosity and for his justice, hath been beset by strange dreams and visions of late, and is most troubled in his soul, and hath come to understand that these are given to him of divine will.

"He hath sought council with the greatest of his lords, and with scholars, and hath sent me to bring to thee word of these visions. He hath seen the waning of the Crescent, and hath seen, likewise, a great and winged golden angel come to him and take from him the crescent blade, and touch it to make of it a Cross. And with this, brilliant light abounds and the Cross casts not shadows, but bright colors at his feet. Such is the vision of my lord . . .

"Troubled, the Emir Marsilla hath sought understanding, and hath prayed for long hours—and hath come to know that thou, Charles the Great, Lord King of Christendom, are in truth the champion of the True Faith." Charlemagne shifted a little, inclining his head.

Blancandrin offered a graceful touching of brow, lips, and heart, then continued, "My lord the Emir Marsilla, who loves his people as a father loves his children, grieves for the suffering wrought of these wars and seeks Christian priests to instruct him in the ways of peace. It is his wish to be baptized in the Christian faith at the font at Aix La Chapelle!" A ripple of indrawn breath went through the assembled lords. "I am bid to offer thee, my lord King of the Franks, by token of such faith, gifts of my lord Marsilla's wealth. Great treasures of gold and silver. Beasts beyond price and jewels. And, further, he offers to pledge to thee the sons of highborn houses for hostage, and for instruction in the faith of the Cross. Among these, even I am come to give my own son, Lord Jurfaleu.

"And, with his baptism into the light, Lord Marsilla will declare homage to thee and all service according to such oath, for he is a great lord, and beloved for his jurisprudence, and would hold his fiefs as thy true and honest vassal!"

Silence followed this lengthy and elaborate speech that was a declaration of surrender, a suing for treaty. Charlemagne stood very still for a time, searching the eyes of the slighter man before him, then, inclining his head, he returned to his throne in a swirling of cloak and robes.

"My lord and Prince. Thou have spoken fairly and with earnest eloquence. For this, we offer thee all amenities and courtesy that are the Christian due of us to such an ambassador. We bid thee good rest and comfort, and will give thee our reply three days hence!" The King finished and glanced toward Lord Ganelon in silent instruction. The Lord High Councillor bowed, then made a summoning gesture to the guards flanking the great airy hall, and stepped forward to indicate to the Emir that he was to follow.

Blancandrin offered a slow and much greater obeisance and, rising, let his eyes flit across the Franks that surrounded him. His gaze paused as it alighted on a tall man who stood a little apart from the rest. Golden-haired with amber gleaming through his locks, his feet apart, his hands before him, resting lightly on the eagle-winged cross pieces of a monstrous dark sword. Golden eyes locked with his for an instant, and a slight frown crossed his face. The Emir found mastery over himself and turned to follow the older Frankish Lord into whose hands he had been given.

So—that was the Djinn of the Dark Sword, he thought. His eyes flitted again, and paused as they alighted on another, more elusively familiar figure. Garbed in white, priestly vestments over armor, he stood near the King's left hand. Remarkable eyes, large—birdlike.

Allowing himself to be led to well-guarded quarters in his own palace, the Emir frowned a little as he wrestled with other haunting suggestions of memory.

That was the priest known to flank the hated Djinn in battle, he knew. Yet—yet, he had seen that face before.

Exactly the same, surely, but younger then. Aye, he *had* encountered him long ago.

Long ago, on the eve of that disastrous battle that had cost him the avaricious and manipulable instrument of the Lombard King Desiderius. Aye—it was the face of the traitor who had sought him out, giving information about the Frankish forces of the young King Charlemagne.

Who, encountered briefly during the battle, had offered a route to escape from that impossible, brutal gorge. And he had followed it, drawing the Lombard Prince with him when defeat was apparent.

But they had been pursued by a fierce and unkempt sapling boy who had, to Blancandrin's astonishment, killed Desiderius, and would have managed to do the same to him. Unnatural golden gaze that boy had possessed. And he had fled knowing that the tenuous foothold in the Italian peninsula was lost.

This Charlemagne, who used sorceries and devils to triumph. Blancandrin allowed his eyes to pass about the familiar chamber to which he had been led, then turned to face the dark Frankish Lord whose eyes studied him with a combination of cunning and interest.

"I am troubled, my lord," he said smoothly, again, in flawless Latin. "For I would seek instruction in this Christian faith and thereby acquire a greater understanding concerning the one Creator who made us all."

Surprise flickered across Lord Ganelon's face at this overture, quickly replaced by caution. "How so, my lord?"

Blancandrin spread his hands and allowed consternation to slip across his features. "I am not blessed by the visions that point the way for my lord, the Emir Marsilla, and know only my own faith that is the worship of Allah, and the keeping of the laws of Mohammed, His Prophet. And we who are followers of Allah, the Most High, shun all traffic with the dark powers of the great Djinn who is called by Christians Satan." Not sure where this was leading, Lord Ganelon inclined his head tersely. "Yet my trust in the wisdom of the Emir Marsilla is uncertain, for I see among thee, and close to the Great Charles of the Franks, one who is known to us as the Djinn of the Dark Sword." Ganelon's mouth tightened. Blancandrin stepped a little closer. "It is this same Djinn who employs most vile magics to our defeat, yet, for all his powers, is found in the company of thy own most Holy King of Kings?'' A gleam in the dark Frank's eyes told Blancandrin he had found the one who was the instrument Marsilla had spoken of.

"It is the very purity of our King, my lord," Lord Ganelon said carefully after a moment, "that enables him to trust such a one as this—Devil of whom thou make mention.'' He crossed himself, allowing a similarly troubled look to cross his face. ''I too have wondered at the defeat of Ferragus, and at the same invulnerability of this lord whose deeds are surely fraught with magic. Yet the King, in his innocence, believes Lord Roland's service to be honest blessing rather than the vile sorceries of his blood. Lord Roland was got of witches, not men . . .'' Their eyes met.

"Truely," Blancandrin murmured. "The path of true and righteous faith is fraught with dangers for even the most conscientious of souls! And for princes?" He left the thought unfinished as Lord Ganelon searched his face. ''To that understanding, I would request of thee a courtesy, my lord. While I am here, I would have discourse with a holy man, a Christian priest such as thou would choose, and pursue the enlightenment that I seek.'' The Frank understood.

"It shall be arranged, my lord," Ganelon murmured softly and bowed. Blancandrin turned away, and with a cursory gesture signaled to the nine faithful he had brought to attend him. Skilled in all manner of service, and brilliant fighters, their silence was assured. Each one had been stripped of his tongue.

Behind him, he listened to the departure of the Frank.

Ferocious discussion seemed endless and without resolution in the long council meetings of the two days that followed. Attentive to every detail of what was said before the King, Roland kept his silence and listened with somber preoccupation as he thought of the look he had seen on the Infidel Emir's face. A fierce scouring of his memory brought him at last to know why the man was familiar. Blancandrin was the very same Infidel lord he had seen guarding Desiderius in his flight from ignominious defeat so many years before—the one who had fled.

The King listened to his lords with the same unreadable silence as ever, and, Roland noted, the Lord High Councillor

likewise kept his thoughts to himself as hot debate passed
among the rest. The lords vacillated between mistrust for the
terms of treaty and surrender proposed by the Infidel, and
the hope that the very same could bring a final halt to such a
brutal and enduring war. It was on the afternoon of the second day that Lord Ganelon's opinions were finally solicited.
He stepped forward and, with a bow, half faced the King,
half faced the rest.

"Majesty." He spoke slowly and with care. "I have wrestled with my wits most arduously upon this matter, and have
been brought to some conclusions, and thereby a route of
solution.

"For the present the major part of Spain is firmly in thy
fist, my liege, and although our losses are great and the war
is costly, we are not so weakened as to be required to desist
until the Infidel are swept entirely from the land. However"—
his look became fraught with consternation—"it is not known
how much more must need be stripped from our lands to
conclude the conquest to thy absolute triumph." Roland's
frown deepened. Beside him, Lord Oliver glanced curiously
at his friend. "Or if such victory is absolutely assured.

"Such proposal of treaty and gifts," Lord Ganelon continued in the same moderate tone, "as was brought by this Emir
Blancandrin, suggest that the Emir Marsilla is much weakened and may be near defeat."

"With the coasts and ports still open and in his grasp?
Nay!" Roland muttered under his breath.

"I consider, Majesty, that the Emir Marsilla sues for honest peace and is willing to forswear his heathen belief and
undertake the True Faith by honest token of the same. In this
petition, I perceive twofold reasoning. Firstly, he does not
wish to lose the fiefs he holds and is willing to become thy
vassal to the keeping of the same. Secondly, if he is a conscientious lord as he would appear to be for the loyalty he
invokes, then he has no wish to see his lands destroyed, nor
the populace thereon, by the long and arduous continuation
of this war.

"Nay, Majesty. I think he offers honest treaty and surrender, and proof of it by giving up great treasure and, more
importantly, highborn hostages. To thy own interest, I would
advise acceptance of the same." Lord Ganelon bowed, then
offered a last thought. "If, as has been likewise proposed, a

strong man was set to rule what is so far won here, then such treaty may easily be enforced.''

''Aaah! So that is the way of it!'' Roland murmured very softly. Oliver glanced at him as silence fell over the court and all eyes were turned to await Charlemagne's decisions.

''How so?'' Oliver whispered. Roland quirked the corners of his mouth, eyes scanning the company watchfully, alighting on Sir Thierry's rather pale face across the hall. His eyes watched Lord Ganelon, not the King . . .

''Wait,'' Roland muttered just as the King settled back in his chair, his cold blue eyes passing across them all.

''Well and wisely spoken, my lord.'' Charlemagne spoke with clear deliberation. ''It is indeed folly to pursue the course of war when triumph may be wrought by more peaceable and fruitful means to the betterment of all. And our decisions must encompass the welfare of the entirety of western Christendom, not only a part thereof.'' He leaned forward. ''To that end, this we will do.

''We will accept the Emir Marsilla's proposal for surrender. We will require immediate proof of him by such as he hath offered to us in the persons of those hostages and such treasure as may be used to further the cause of Christian enlightenment, and will require him to ride to Aix for that baptism he seeks.

''If we are received of these proofs of his honest intent, then we shall accord him such fiefs as he may dutifully hold, lands that have been his.'' Roland's breath hissed as he inhaled. Charlemagne stood.

''To further assure our interest in bringing a secure Christian faith to the whole of this land, we will give the ruling of Spain to one who is proven both strong and loyal enough to hold the same of us.'' Lord Ganelon, who had been looking down with a thoughtful frown, now raised his gaze to Charlemagne's face. ''We will make a single kingdom here, and for the ruling of it, a King,'' Charlemagne continued. His eyes shifted across the company and came to rest on Count Roland. Roland felt his breathing pause, his heart hover in his breast. Nay—surely?

''To the assurance of a Christian peace in this land, we will endow Roland, Count of Brittany and our puissant Champion, with all entitlement as will make him King of all fiefs south of the Pyrenees!'' Absolute silence filled the hall as all eyes turned toward Roland. He felt a peculiar rising of heat along his neck, an appalled sense of discomfiture. He looked from one face to the next and saw black pools of indecipherable expression in the sudden pallor of Lord Ganelon's face, a slight smile, of a sudden, on Sir Thierry's.

"Majesty!" was all he could whisper.

"For the rest." Charlemagne's voice sliced neatly across the silence as gazes, especially of the older men, returned to study Lord Ganelon. "On the morrow, we will dispatch our Infidel ambassador to the Emir Marsilla with these words. He will convey our acceptance of his terms and will require both the yielding of hostages and treasure to us before we may depart for the north. He will also require that the Emir Marsilla ride unarmed to rendezvous with us at Foix that he may accompany us to Aix for that same baptism he requests." Duke Naimes stepped forward then, and the King glanced at him, arching a silver brow. "My lord?"

"One among us should be appointed to go with this Emir to confirm and convey these terms, Majesty," he said.

The King inclined his head. "Just so, my lord. One who understands that it is our chief duty to win souls for Christendom."

Roland strode forward at once, eyes fixed on the King. "Majesty? Let me carry thy staff . . ." He bowed, gaze lowering to catch a gleam in Lord Ganelon's eyes.

"Nay, my liege," Duke Naimes interposed at once. "Lord Roland is not the best suited to such a task."

"Am I not?" Roland turned briskly to face the older man. "If there be treachery, then who better may warrant the Emir Marsilla's fate?" he demanded.

The aged Duke shook his head. "Is that thy intent, my lord? To seal the same?" he asked slowly. Roland inhaled sharply. "It will not serve. Better a man who is more skilled in diplomacy than in battle for this instant."

"I must accede to thy wisdom, my lord . . ." Roland said reluctantly. Then he looked up, filled with that peculiar clarity he experienced in dangerous situations. "Majesty," he said slowly, thoughtfully. "Who is there better suited to the task of negotiation than thy own Lord High Councillor? Let Lord Ganelon, who is greatly experienced in dealing for peace, be sent to Marsilla to contract on thy behalf the specifics here proposed. Surely, none may forget that which he wrought on the northern frontier with the Saxon." Lowering his gaze, he caught the lightning stab of purest venom that vanished as soon as it was released, and knew he had struck deep.

Above them all, Charlemagne inclined his head. "So it shall be done, my lords!" he said clearly. "Who better indeed could we trust to such duty?" Roland stepped back. Duke Naimes did likewise. "Lord Ganelon"—Charlemagne drew a glove from his belt—"do thou come forward and receive from us this gauntlet of our duty in this matter."

Stepping back, Roland knew the Lord High Councillor had no choice but to kneel graciously before the King, bowing his head to receive the proffered emblem.

Straightening, he offered a peculiar remark. "Into thy hands, Majesty, my life is given!" Melting back to rejoin Lord Oliver, Roland listened to the murmured approval of the highborn lords gathered in the hall. It was a remark he was inclined to interpret differently.

He glanced up, across the company, and caught a troubled look on Sir Thierry's face. Aye, he knew of a sudden. That one was the gauge. Had not Leon been given to him from Lord Ganelon's service? He turned, Oliver beside him with a thoughtful expression, and sought the main portal to the hall. He hovered there a pace or two beyond his friend as Lord Ganelon strode briskly in his direction.

The dark lord's eyes had a trapped look as they locked with his. His face was harshly etched.

"I will be avenged for this—my lord—Bastard!" he murmured very softly as he swept past. Roland answered with a slight smile.

"He is sincere, I consider . . ." Oliver said slowly sometime later as the two stood alone together in one of the multitude courtyards of the palace.

"I doubt it not!" Roland said calmly.

Oliver looked at him. "I have never understood this enmity between thee," he pursued. "Or, more accurately, why it is that Lord Ganelon holds thee in such hatred? And it has always been so, I perceive."

"Aye," Roland murmured. "He is private about it. The King does not know."

"Nay," Oliver agreed. " 'Tis another peculiarity. What possessed thee to offer thyself for this embassy?"

Roland grinned, glad to change the subject. "I would see Marsilla dead!" he said simply. "That is our best chance of peace!"

Oliver gave him a sardonic look. "Knowing what the Infidel call thee, it was but invitation to suicide, my friend!" he commented dryly.

Roland shrugged. "Who knows? Now there is a different mischief afoot!"

"How so?"

Roland shifted from leaning against the parapet and faced the other man. "Simply this. Hast thou not wondered, as we marched south, why it was that the Infidel were so hard to overcome?"

"I presumed the Emir Blancandrin . . ." Oliver began, then frowned.

"Nay. They were with us all the way, and better prepared than in the campaigns before," Roland went on. "They knew our numbers, and our weaknesses. The losses were terrible. We would have yielded from attrition alone in the end. And then—this Blancandrin fled Cordoba as we prepared to lay siege. Nay, there are deep and murky waters here!"

"Do thou say this city was given to us?" Oliver half whispered, his eyes searching Roland's.

Roland nodded. "Aye. I do."

"Why . . . ?" Oliver breathed after a moment.

"That is what I am beginning to determine," he said tautly. "Think on this. The Lord High Councillor hath been secure in Pamplona for some time and hath held Navarre more easily than the rest of it. He rides in triumph with the King, and practices great discretion and wisdom in council . . ."

"Aye?" Lord Oliver's brows closed in a perplexed frown. "He hath ever been most astute . . . ."

"Just so!" Roland cut in. "And what was concluded of all this?" he asked brutally, then continued without waiting for an answer. "Who would better serve to rule Spain as King than that same Lord Ganelon? Thou hast heard . . ."

"But his loyalty and brilliance are long established and proven . . ." Oliver began again. "Who better?"

"Just so!" Roland hissed. "Mayhap that is what he hath

sought for himself all along? Consider—Spain is vast enough to become a powerful realm of its own!''

Oliver stared. Then shook his head. ''Nay. I cannot credit . . . '' he half whispered.

''Thou did not see the venom of his look when it was given to me!'' Roland insisted.

''We were all taken aback, I concede!'' Oliver responded.

''None more than myself,'' Roland whispered. ''I cannot see myself a prince. War is all I know . . .'' Then, in harder tones, ''But, as I pursue this in my mind, I conclude one thing. The King knows I will not rest until I have driven the Infidel from this land entirely, and given it to Christendom. Lord Ganelon—well, he was clear enough willing to take a more moderate route.''

''If this treaty with Marsilla is achieved, then that is reasonable!'' Oliver pointed out.

Roland shook his head. ''I mistrust it!'' he said flatly.

Oliver gave him a long look, then sighed. ''The Emir surrenders a great deal!'' he said.

''So it would appear!'' Roland countered, then turned to lean over the parapet once more. ''This Blancandrin who is lord of so much beyond the sea, and who hath yielded up this city without so much as a whisper—he is the same Infidel who I near killed when I pursued the Lombard King Desiderius all those years past!''

''Nay?'' Oliver's eyes went wide.

Roland nodded without looking at him. ''They are cunning, these heathen!'' he said. ''Their schemes transcend the interests of one man, I am convinced of it. They intended a great conquest of the north, and I cannot believe them to have reversed themselves so. Lord Ganelon is somehow embroiled in it. Which is why I proposed as I did! I have not forgot that the lords Basan and Basil were sent as embassy to Saragossa. Nor have I forgot how they were butchered and even their corpses desecrated!'' He smiled a little. ''I think Lord Ganelon hath not forgot it either!'' He glanced at Oliver whose face still showed astonishment. ''It will interest me greatly to see the condition in which he is returned to our liege!'' he drawled.

''Mother of God!'' Oliver breathed, understanding completely. Roland looked away, down to the court below him, a rectangular garden with an empty fountain and hibernating plants. A solitary figure stood there, shadowed in the dusk.

"Aaaah!" Roland murmured. "Sir Thierry of Leon!" An instant later, he was striding away, cloak swirling in gleaming folds about his ankles. Oliver frowned after his friend, then moved to the parapet to look down as well.

The cold wind blew against him with refreshing honesty as Thierry sought the shreds of peace to be found in solitude. Much as he mistrusted his uncle's violent rages, sly enterprises, and scathing contempt, he misliked this mood he had been privately subjected to for the greater part of the past two days.

"When I am King here . . ." Lord Ganelon had stared at him, murmuring suggestions of promises to be fulfilled in the past weeks during those times when they were alone. But this evening had been different. Worse in the entrapment he felt.

Lord Ganelon's mood had been peculiarly cold and constrained. Hate hung like an aura about him as he coolly subjected his nephew to his will concerning the disposition of his affairs and properties. Thierry had attempted to protest this self-induced proclamation of death sentence, and Ganelon had looked up at him with penetrating bitterness and had spoken in splintering tones.

"Aye! This is my death warrant, and I know it! Marsilla will never bear the knowledge that Lord Roland is to be King here. Thou cannot know how well he is hated." Lord Ganelon's voice dropped to a venomous whisper. "And he near did as I wished, as was planned, his own arrogance delivering him into Marsilla's hands! But—God plague that Bastard witch, he hath made of me a dead man by this sorcery that hath persuaded the King to send me instead!

"How much have I wrought? Even this possibility of peace is my own manipulation—and its cost is but the life of one man. Pah! Charlemagne is not fit. I swear I see that he will elevate this Roland above us all now. Mark me well, nephew," he growled. "One day Christendom will be given into the hands of one born into mortal sin, this incest-got bastard!" Thierry swallowed, confusion and horror drawing the blood from his face. What was his uncle saying . . . ?

"Sir Thierry?" Thoroughly startled, Thierry spun about as a clear deep voice shattered his reverie. He bowed abruptly,

seeing Count Roland, of all people, before him, face stern,
eyes penetratingly clear in the darkness . . .

"My lord?" Lord Roland moved a step closer, as impos-
ing, Thierry thought suddenly, in his own way, as Charlemagne . . . Incest?

"I observed thee closely this day in council," Lord Roland said. Thierry felt his stomach clench. "And I am aware
of thy years of intimate service to the Lord High Councillor,
who is likewise thy kinsman. As thou are now sworn to me,
and I pursue the King's interest, I inquire of thee whether
there is some difficulty that His Majesty is not aware of?"

"None, my lord," Thierry managed, eyes widening a little. Lord Roland frowned, golden eyes staring into him.

"Yet my lord Ganelon was most displeased concerning the
honor and trust that were bestowed upon him," Lord Roland
pursued. "I had thought, being of his blood, thou might have
knowledge of the reason?" Highly civil, highly lethal . . .

"Nay, my lord! In truth—I have not—save . . ." Thierry
heard himself respond to that clear gaze he could not elude.
Shrugged. "I think my uncle fears for the honor of his name,
and would not suffer the same disgrace as those other lords
who were sent to serve in a like manner before him."

The Count was silent for a moment. "He has naught to
fear—if the Emir Marsilla's embassy be an honest one!" Lord
Roland's point was made emphatic by the quietness with
which it was uttered. Unanswerable, Thierry thought. Lord
Roland's frown deepened. "Moreover," he added after a moment, "what true Christian knight can fear his own death?
As we are given to serve our honor, and our King, who is
God's champion, so, too, we are given to serve God. Death
cannot but bring glory and blessing to honorable men . . ."
His tone softened somewhat, and Thierry stared, caught by
some fervent personal conviction. Lord Roland's golden eyes
found his and reached something inside him. "Only one who
is bent on treachery and malice need fear the death that holds
the danger of damnation to his immortal soul!"

"Is it so simple, my lord?" Thierry whispered bitterly.

"Thou hast but to look upon the unstained virtue of Lord
Oliver De Montglave to perceive the answer, sir knight,"
Lord Roland said softly. It was another sort of scouring,
Thierry thought. "For myself, that thou may know me fully,

being bastard got, and born able to hear only the eternal silence that is the absence of God's presence, there is naught of hope save that same honor. Know this. My life and mine efforts are given to one single thing—the service of our liege lord, Charlemagne!'' He stared at Thierry for another moment, searching . . .

"I know nothing, my lord," Thierry half whispered at last. Lord Roland drew back.

"God pity thy ignorance then," he murmured, and strode away.

His lie had been read, Thierry knew as he watched the Count disappear, then turned to face the descending darkness.

Wind whistled around corners and bit like ice into the flesh of his face. And the shadows haunted him. The winter cold was bitter, endless tension.

What did Lord Ganelon know . . . ?

Where was the truth?

SIXTEEN

A.D. 778

It was a morning of still, quiet air filled with snow that tumbled gently from a heavy-laden grey sky when Lord Ganelon, resplendent in the finest armor and accoutrements, riding his great destrier beside the slighter, delicate white beast of the Emir Blancandrin, left the gates of Cordoba behind him. Like nine shadows, the white-shrouded servants of the Infidel Emir glided silently after the pair.

They slipped east, then north across the winter landscape, traveling in a moderate manner, and, after two days, were joined by a magnificently furnished company of several hundred Infidel warriors and slaves who had awaited the return of their lord. Blancandrin resumed the normal luxury to which he was accustomed in his traveling and began to indulge in another sort of game.

Like fishing—with the lure of civility and the line of an educated and facile mind, he played the uneasy carp of the Frankish lord he had hooked. A fair fish to be sure, useful. But one intended to serve as bait to catch others, greater than he.

And like the fisherman, he plumbed the strengths of the Lord Ganelon, played upon the weaknesses, then dissected and probed until the Frank fully exposed his ambitions and passions, the roots of his capacity for treason. And when they reached Saragossa and Blancandrin brought Lord Ganelon into the Emir Marsilla's presence, he knew that the bargains to be proposed would be gladly met.

* * *

The first suggestions of spring brought Lord Ganelon's triumphant return from the Infidel stronghold of Saragossa. He rode into the city of Cordoba at the head of a train of mules, each well burdened with riches of all kinds, managed by an entourage of Nubian slaves in gorgeous and exotic attire. Beyond these were stallions of that refined and hot-blooded Infidel breed, muzzled lions and great, spotted hunting cats from distant lands. There were hawks of purest white and camels, of which the Franks had only heard. And at the back, there rode twenty Infidel princes on the same fine, desert-bred horses, each garbed in silks and brocades, each with his hands bound before him by silver chains around a Cross, likewise wrought of purest silver.

A hero's welcome was accorded the Lord High Councillor as he entered the city, then came before the King, his accomplishment splendidly apparent. Even the King showed his satisfaction with all that had been achieved as he listened to Lord Ganelon's reports, with a softening of the stern cast of his features.

Likewise, he manifested his pleasure later by giving praise of his own as Lord Ganelon bowed before him, reports concluded. And the gathering of lords also offered a resounding applause as they thought of homelands and families long left behind for these arduous wars. Others were pleased, foreseeing new fiefs in the new-won lands, confident of keeping them under the leadership of the one who was to be their new prince.

Only Lord Roland remained silent and watchful through the whole.

"As I thought," he muttered softly to Lord Oliver later, before striding from the hall, "he is returned entire!"

Lord Oliver watched his friend leave the buoyant gathering, and stepped to one side to lean against a pillar of spiraling marble, and surveyed the company. He found only one other sober face among the whole. Sir Thierry of Leon watched his kinsman without pleasure of any sort. Only a peculiar wariness. Then Oliver too turned and left the hall.

A few days later the council assembled before the King to hear his will concerning the disposing of forces as was agreed upon in the terms of treaty.

"My lords, we require thee to prepare for the long march

north,'' Charlemagne addressed them all. ''We require that the greater part of our armies undertake to return with us to the heartland of our realm at Aix La Chapelle. The hostage princes shall be brought with us, and will be used with courtesy, that they too may come to seek the light of the True Faith. Likewise, as agreed, we will rendezvous with the Emir Marsilla at Foix, which is just north of the mountains, and there will see him brought to Aix for baptism as he hath consented.

''For the rest, my lords, we require a seventh of our force to remain here to serve the new lord of this land, Roland, Count of Brittany.'' Charlemagne continued, ''When all is accomplished at Aix, and the Emir Marsilla hath undertaken the True Faith and is disposed to such vassalage as we will bestow, then we will require our Champion, the Count of Brittany, to come to Aix, there to receive of us and of Holy Church the anointing and crown that will endow him prince of these new realms of Christendom.''

All eyes were turned upon him, and Roland felt a sense of being suspended. Unimaginable, that the King should elevate him so, but this was the second statement of his intent. His own eyes meeting Charlemagne's, he stepped slowly forward until he was at the foot of the dais. Then, with equal care, he dropped to one knee, still looking up into eyes that seemed to hold a fleeting softness for him alone.

''And there, at Aix, Majesty,'' he heard himself say, ''to swear again eternal fealty to thee!''

Charlemagne smiled, and a resounding cheer issued from the gathering. ''Gladly to be received, my lord!'' the King responded. ''Thy loyalty is not a thing to be doubted.''

Roland stood again and stepped back. Aix—it struck him of a sudden. More than a crown awaited him there. A bride. The Lady Aude to whom he was betrothed, and whom he had near managed to put from his mind. Surely, he thought abruptly, the future that loomed before him was more hazardous than any battlefield.

He hardly noticed that the King raised a hand and extended invitation to his lords to offer further thoughts upon the details of the return.

Lord Roger of Roncesvalles was the first to step forward. ''Majesty, the way is clear and easily attained, but I perceive a point for concern,'' he said with a slight frown. Roland abandoned his private thoughts to listen.

"Speak, my lord."

"I have spent much of the winter past near the mountains north of Pamplona, engaged in struggles to establish dominion over the Basque tribes there. Not an easy task, my liege, nor one as yet resolved. Majesty, my concern is this. I foresee but one difficulty that lies with the march ahead. As the Emir Marsilla hath yielded up so much treasure to the cause of Our Savior, so too, likewise, he hath encumbered our forces with the same. I cannot think there is hazard to be found in traversing these conquered realms, nor even from the Infidel who clearly mean to honor this truce. But, the tribesmen of the mountains, of the Basque country through which we must, of necessity, pass, are fierce and avaricious, skilled in both fighting and eager for all manner of thievery!" Lord Ganelon stepped forward then, frowning with consternation.

"Aye, Majesty. This is true enough. We have been beset by the task of keeping these same barbarians from their usual traffic with the Vikings that seek to plunder the northern shores," he offered slowly.

" 'Tis a point well taken, my lords," Charlemagne began.

"Majesty . . . ?" Roland broke in.

Charlemagne arched a silver brow. "My lord?"

"It may be simply managed, my liege!" Roland spoke with the same clear intensity that marked all of his planning.

Charlemagne sat back. "Is that so, my lord?" he inquired dryly.

Roland nodded. "Aye, Majesty! Let those who are given to remain with me here be entrusted to the duty of providing a rearguard for the army. Give us the escort of those treasures the Emir Marsilla hath surrendered, and we will see them safe across the mountains, then return!"

"This is folly!" Lord Ganelon began.

Roland rounded on him. "Not so, my lord!" he said sternly. "It is the best assurance of the King's own safety! I recall the treachery of those same mountain passes. A greater force would be crippled in its efforts to defense by reason of its size alone in those narrow gorges!"

Lord Ganelon turned to the King, frowning, intent on protest. "Majesty, this is mad arrogance!" he began.

But Duke Naimes strode forward then. "Majesty," the older man broke in. "Lord Roland is correct in this. I concur with the wisdom of such a plan. Let Lord Roland take the rearguard and the treasure. With a force selected from those peers so valiantly proved these past few years, he cannot but succeed.''

''Just so, Majesty,'' Roland broke in eagerly. Lord Ganelon shrugged and stepped back.

Charlemagne's eyes passed from one to the other of the four before him. ''So,'' he said after a moment. ''It shall be done!'' Roland bowed with the rest, then straightened and glanced in the direction of Lord Ganelon, whose face was curiously bland.

''If there be mischief in this''—Lord Oliver looked directly at his friend much later—''then thou are like a ripe plum fallen from the tree into the maiden's lap!'' Roland's golden eyes locked in consternation with the sea-blue depths of Oliver's. ''Thy own arrogance hath made the fruit!'' he added more sharply.

''Arrogance?'' Roland whispered very softly. ''May be, it is that I know exactly what I do . . . ?''

''I was specific,'' Oliver countered clearly. ''I said 'if' . . .'' He inhaled deeply. ''I have racked my wits over this, Roland,'' he continued more slowly. ''And although the enmity between thyself and Lord Ganelon is become apparent to me, I find no substance upon which to hang the rest of thy suppositions concerning any treason he may undertake against the King! Jesu! His service speaks for itself. He is long proved loyal and his accomplishments glorious! I consider that thou are compelled by boyhood resentments of his misuse of thee.''

Roland shook his head. ''Nay!'' he denied promptly. ''There is more to it than that. I grant, I know not what precisely, but my convictions have become absolute.'' Roland sighed deeply and, shifting restlessly, raked long fingers through the thick hair that tumbled at an angle across his brow. ''As for this proposal to undertake both rearguard and the escort of the treasure that the Emir Marsilla hath yielded up, I was motivated by no greater concern than for the certain safety of the King!''

Oliver frowned. ''I cannot think,'' he said dryly, ''that a few wild Basque tribesmen can do more than slightly impede the return.''

Roland looked at him. ''They constitute little threat to such as we," he said clearly. "But I think Marsilla means to recover that which he hath surrendered."

Oliver's eyes widened. "Thou anticipate Infidel treachery?" he asked in surprise.

Again, Roland nodded. "I am convinced of it!"

"Nay!" Oliver shook his head. "There is no sense in that! What of the hostage princes that will be with the King—and the rest?"

Roland turned away. "Do we know these heathen lords?" he half whispered. "And what are twenty lives for a kingdom as vast as this?" Roland turned back, and their eyes locked once more.

Oliver's face grew sterner. "Naught!" he breathed at last.

Roland nodded. "Just so," he said grimly. He stiffened and stared across the room. "If the Emir means to honor this treaty, then there will be little to concern us. If not, and there be treachery afoot . . ." His voice deepened, hardened. "Then I will spit these heathen upon Durandal's unmatched blade once and for all!"

Familiar promises, Oliver thought, watching his friend, that were as good as the deed done. Roland reached out with one hand to touch his shoulder lightly. His face had become young, searching.

"I know thou are to guard the van, Oliver," he said softly. "But I would pray thee—ride with me? The King would grant it, if thou would?"

Oliver probed golden depths, half-wild places, and much more he had come to know most intimately. A slow smile softened his own features and curved his lips. He nodded. "Aye, Roland!" he said gently. "I will ride with thee!" The fingers that clasped his shoulder softened their grip. "What are we if not brethren made to undertake all endeavor together!"

Roland smiled. "Thou are the heart of me . . ." he said softly. They both knew it was true.

The golden stallion, Veillantif, tensed abruptly under Roland's hand and raised its head from the hay before it to snort. Roland stopped his grooming. No one else was allowed to tend his precious destrier. He spun about. Sir Thierry of Leon stood watching him from a few paces away. Roland waited.

"My lord?" Thierry stepped forward to the back of the stall.

"Sir Thierry?" Roland continued to watch the other.

"My lord Roland . . ." Thierry began again. "I am come to request that I may serve thee with the others who compose the rearguard." Roland continued to look at him for a long time, seeing his taut mouth and pallor.

"It is an interesting request, sir knight," he said softly. Thierry looked oddly hopeful. "But," Roland caught him before he could speak, "I understand thou are given to the vanguard."

"Aye, my lord."

"Then I will not change thy duty. There thou will stay," Roland said firmly, and watched as Thierry's face whitened further, something shifting in his eyes just before he bowed and turned away.

A moment later he was gone. Roland stared after him thoughtfully.

"Thou hast learned much from thy friendship with Lord Oliver!" A dry, melodious voice murmured to one side of him.

Roland spun and saw Turpin leaning near the stallion's manger. He scowled. "I mislike this stealth of thine, priest!" he said bluntly.

Turpin grinned and shrugged in that particular way of his. "No matter!" he dismissed it. "Wise decision, I consider."

"Not to grant Sir Thierry's request?"

"Aye." Turpin nodded.

Roland frowned a little. "I sensed motives more complex than simple attention to duty."

"His is a troubled soul. As I have said, thou hast learned much from this friendship with Lord Oliver."

Roland searched those large brown eyes. "There is no better man," he said firmly.

Turpin nodded. "Aye . . ." The priest closed the matter. "I ride with thee, by the King's order. That is what I came to tell thee." Continuing to look at the priest, Roland felt the corners of his mouth tug in a rueful smile.

"I consider," he said quietly, "that our company would not be complete without thee!" Turpin nodded once more and, patting Veillantif's golden neck, slipped away as silently as he had come.

* * *

Pleasant spring warmth yielded prematurely to sweltering arid Spanish summer as Charlemagne's great armies came together and began their northward march. Behind a van of war-proven knights and men, the King and the elder lords of the High Council rode at the head of the main body of the army. In the midst of this vast force were large numbers of burdened pack animals that carried the bulk of the army's baggage and, carefully guarded, the hostage Infidel princes. And, as planned, Lord Roland, with those peers who were to remain with him in Spain, and a force of some five thousand men, rode something less than half a day's distance to the rear, guarding the vast and priceless treasures that had been entrusted to them.

Like a great steel serpent, the army wound north across arid, high plateaus, through deep, fertile river valleys, past the silent manifestations of all their hard-won triumphs. Past grey and silent Pamplona, where common folk stood to watch them pass, making the sign of the Cross, up into the rugged country of northern Navarre, the armies veered straight north to seek passage through the Pyrenees by way of deep, barren gorges.

And, as had been foretold, raids began then. Half-wild and wolf-elusive Basque tribesmen harried the flanks of the army, scenting for loot until they discovered where the greatest riches were to be found. Easily dealt with, for the most part, but tiresome, they became a major preoccupation for Roland's force.

They delay us, Roland thought to himself as they rode along a valley near to Roncesvalles, then veered past the mouth of a high-walled gorge to follow the signs of the passage of the greater part of the army. Horse droppings and scraped rocks revealed they had gone through near a full day's ride before, and to the east, high ground rose up toward the haze that overhung the mountain peaks, rendering them invisible. Barren land, scoured by extremes of climate, filled with shattered rocks and great boulders, gnarled shrubs and trees, and little else . . .

"I am regretful of one thing in all this," Oliver spoke gently beside him. "For my part, I would prefer thee to be no more than the Count of Brittany." His lips quirked, and Roland looked at him. "I fancied summers together fighting Viking raiders!"

"Aye!" Roland grinned. Iron-shod hooves made an eerie,

isolated clattering that echoed off the surrounding walls of the gorge.

"And raising strong sons . . ." Oliver murmured. Roland's smile faded and he stiffened. "And hunting . . ." Roland rose in his stirrups to stand poised and stern, nostrils flaring. "What is it?" Oliver asked in a different tone.

Roland raised a hand to signal a halt. "Do thou not hear the silence?" he asked softly. His right hand slipped up to his shoulder and found the hilt of the dark sword. He drew her. Glancing about him, Oliver set his shield and hefted lance. "We are surrounded!" Roland hissed. "This—this is the treachery of which I was suspicious!"

Oliver shot his friend a look. "Basque, surely?" he began, but Roland shook his head and raised Durandal high over his head in a signal to arms.

"Infidel!" he grated brutally, and as he did so, an insidious pulsing began, such as only heathen drums could make. "Haaarrrgh!" He spurred the golden horse and spun it about to race along the flanks of his men, barking orders that were nearly obliterated by the terrible swelling of that same ominous thunder that seemed to come from all about them. Horses squealed as they were spurred into abrupt readiness, and from every rock and crevice near the walls about them, Infidel warriors emerged into view, each armed to bristling with bow and quiver, spear and scimitar.

"Mother of God!" Oliver muttered as he swung his own destrier about and set it to gallop toward the other flank of their company.

Then the sky rained heathen arrows as uncountable numbers of mounted Infidel emerged as though from the air itself, to line the precipices that walled the gorge, and to fill its northern mouth, and, like a great tide, to swell across the wider, southern end.

Horses screamed as arrows bit into flanks and shoulders, and the earth trembled beneath the roaring of multitude hooves and feet that pounded dirt and shattered rock as the Infidel advanced across the valley floor.

Roland fought as one possessed, knowing in an instant how much lesser were the numbers of Christian men against the surrounding foe. Durandal sang a high-pitched keening hum that was the only sound to pierce that terrible, unrelenting heathen drumming that came from the cliff walls about them.

And the rest answered his example with their own grimly unyielding efforts.

The ground was soon littered with the dead and dying. Blood flowed to ooze down between the stones, sinking into the ground to make a dark and sinister mud of the dust. Horses stumbled or, with white rolling eyes, tried to leap or plunge to avoid such treacherous footing. Froth spewing from mouths and flanks, they answered spurs and fists that spun them about, or sent them hurtling toward another hazard.

The sheen of bright clean armor and arms soon disappeared beneath layers of gore, and the emblems that adorned each painted shield or were broidered upon cloaks and surcoats were lost beneath the same debris. Time became meaningless as the Infidel were slaughtered, and yet seemed to be constantly replaced.

Then, suddenly, after some unmeasurable eternity of time, the Infidel bowmen and foot soldiers melted abruptly away. Horsemen and the rest vanished, leaving corpses.

And silence . . .

Slowly, Roland lowered the sword to which he seemed to have become irrevocably affixed, and turned his heaving, lathered stallion about to survey the valley that was now hideous with destruction. His heart pounded against his ribs and his breathing came in dry-mouthed rasping gulps for air. Sweat trickled down the sides of his face and drenched the clothing beneath his mail.

Among the expanse of dead, there were little more than a thousand men who moved now to gather together near the remaining live mules that carried the King's treasure. Beyond them, the valiant peers sat exhausted on wounded warhorses.

Roland saw Bishop Turpin, still erect on his white horse that stood, head drooping, flanks heaving, one foreleg bent to favor the wound made by an arrow in its shoulder. Sword in right hand, axe in left . . . It was a shock to see the scarlet rents that despoiled the white purity of the priest's cloak and surcoat.

Oliver, lance long discarded, half-shattered shield upon one arm and bloodied sword in his hand, offered a grim salute as Roland pressed his beast to the other man, then drew rein beside.

"I cannot think we have a victory, my friend," he said quietly.

Roland met his look, then shifted to scan the high, craggy escarpments around them. "Nay . . ." he whispered agreement.

"Then do thou make a blast upon the horn," Oliver said more firmly. "There is a fair enough chance that it will be heard, and the King will come to our aid!"

Roland looked at his friend, his own face grim. "Nay, Oliver . . ." he said softly, after a moment. "Not even for this will I put our liege at risk!" He looked about him again, feeling Oliver's stare, and as he did so, lines of Infidel horsemen appeared along the precipices of the gorge, melted forward as though by sorcery, to fill its southern and northern ends once more. "In any event—it is too late for that," he added, and turned to meet his friend's eyes. How bright they were . . . Oliver, who understood . . .

Just then, beyond them both, the Bishop Turpin put a horn to his lips and wound a blast that made the very stones of the gorge reverberate as it swept up to echo high and vanish on the hot wind.

Beloved Oliver, Roland thought, seeing the other search his own face.

"We are dead men!" Oliver said quietly, and, raising his sword once more in a salute, spurred his horse away, leaping tangled corpses and carcasses as he bellowed orders to those remaining. Roland did not attempt to answer, for the Infidel loosed their own horses to plummet down vertical embankments, uttering a high, resonating wave of cries as they swept forward to engulf the remaining Christians.

"Nay," Roland whispered, setting his teeth. "Thou shall not win over us!" He spurred Veillantif as his eyes hunted for the Infidel leader, then loosed the beast, raising Durandal, to charge alone toward the Emir who had perpetrated this treachery.

The gallant stallion struggled to respond, bolting up the valley in pursuit of Marsilla's fresh animal. Seconds later, the great destrier had catapulted Roland through the first wave of Infidel horsemen to slam broadside into the Emir's much lighter beast. He swung as Marsilla's horse tried to recover, another young heathen lord reaching from his own mount to jerk the animal's head up, and as though of her own volition, Durandal sought and found the Emir's upraised right arm, scimitar in hand, and passed on to sever the neck of the other. Arm and weapon tumbled away as Marsilla's mount bolted

with him, blood gushing from the stump, and Roland caught
a fleeting glimpse of surprise on the face as the head tumbled
away, to bounce across the ground before exploding like a
piece of ripe fruit under an iron-shod hoof.

Roland hardly felt the scimitar that caught him in the side,
or the axe that ripped through chain mail to shatter his right
thigh as he swung the golden stallion about to see Infidel
horsemen ride over the remaining stand of Christian foot soldiers, engulfing them completely with flashing blades and
screams of triumph.

Then, as the gold destrier galloped toward them, he saw
Bishop Turpin tumble from his white warhorse as it fell lifeless among the dead. The Bishop tried to pick himself up,
and Roland spurred frantically, but Turpin took a spear
through his belly and fell . . .

The others died then. One by one . . . Roland saw them
all as he fought on, trying to reach, to give aid—almost overwhelmed himself, uncaring of the blows he took across legs
and thighs, ribs and shoulders, only feeling Durandal in his
hand, carving her way through the foe beyond any strength
left in him to guide her . . . All else was lost.

All was lost . . . But Oliver. Where was Oliver . . . ?

The golden horse stumbled badly, then found its footing to
heave onto a ridge as Roland slashed about him with the total
desperation of an unfamiliar and agonizing panic as he sought
his friend. Oliver, last glimpsed astride his own wounded
mount. Still alive . . . Pray God, Oliver was still alive . . .
for Roland knew that was the single thing left to him, the
saving of Oliver.

His stallion lurched as something smashed against its hind-
quarters and went to its knees. It staggered up and turned a
little. Oliver—to his right. Roland felt the dark sword carry
his hands up, then it swung down to slice across a heathen
face and belly. Oliver . . . Then into a sweeping arc that
sought the air with malicious humming. Oliver saw him then.
Roland caught a welcoming gleam in the other man's eyes
and then the dark sword swept down and lunged—slow, it
seemed, and with scalding vicious intent, point first into the
breast of Oliver who stood so close.

''Nay!'' Roland knew it was his own scream this time. And
Oliver looked at him with surprise, standing there, his own
sword falling from fingers gone limp. ''Nay!'' Roland

shrieked again, and tried to jerk the dark sword loose. But it clung obsidian-hued and hideous with malice, erupting finally from Oliver's breast to cling like some noxious venom to his own hand that could not bear to feel it. "Oliver . . . ?" It was a grating, rasping bellow of fear. Blood appeared on Oliver's lips, bloody froth from shattered lungs bubbled through mail and surcoat. Incredibly, Oliver still stood, looking up. He smiled a little, blood trickling down from the corners of his mouth.

"Roland?" he gasped. Simple, welcoming recognition. Did he not know . . . ?

Roland tried to dismount from the stallion that had, somehow, managed to find its feet and stood trembling beneath him, but he could not, his right leg was gone somehow. "God forgive me . . ." he found voice enough to utter.

Oliver's smile widened a little as he dropped slowly to his knees. "No matter . . ." he said around the blood that came from his mouth. "We die honorably . . . That—is the—main thing . . ." he gasped. "Shall—I greet thee—in Heaven— then?" His breath was lost in a clumsy gurgling as he slipped smoothly to one side, his body going limp to lie on the sod, eyes loosing their focus as they stared upward.

Roland shuddered in horror. "Nay! Not thee . . ."

"It is bright, beloved friend . . ." He caught a note of wonder in Oliver's voice as the other's eyes went wide, staring up into the unknown. "I see angels . . . God—keep thee . . ." And then, Oliver vanished from the ruined thing that had been his body.

"Nay . . . NAY!" Roland shrieked and lashed the golden stallion with the single spur he could still feel, sent it in a reeling charge along the side of the ridge into one of the last remaining company of heathen.

He tried to shake loose the murderous clinging of the dark sword, loathing her—loathing himself. Witch blood . . . He did not care when he saw a scimitar come toward him, so close, piercing through tattered surcoat and hauberk and slicing upward before disappearing again.

He heard Veillantif scream and felt the scattered collection of things that he had become tumble through the air, smash down against brutal stone, the dark sword Durandal at last leaping away from his hand to vanish . . .

He cared not where.

And the golden stallion staggered above him, its throat slit, its gleaming coat reduced to wounds and pink froth, then sank slowly to the ground beyond. Faithful beast . . .

Roland tried to raise himself, managed it awkwardly, feeling an unfamiliar weakness as he propped himself on his right elbow. A final clattering echoed across his senses as the last of the Infidel galloped southward, away from the gorge.

Then there was naught—save silence. And the dead.

So weak . . . Roland frowned a little and stared about him. He had, he realized with a strangely remote surprise, lost this battle.

His right hand was empty, fingers half splayed and limp. The dark sword was gone. He saw a mangled thing, that extended before him, a mess of flesh and cloth and armor. Something that might have been a leg and, most curiously, spewing forth from his belly, a blood-streaked array of pink coils.

He had been disemboweled then, he thought without interest. Was he dying . . . ? Durandal—where had she got to? God pity the soul that next raised her. He felt a gentle sinking as his arm gave out and he lay back limp upon the hard earth. Oliver. Mother of God, Oliver . . .

Where was the pain? Was this what it felt like to die? he wondered. This gentle slipping back—the familiar voice that murmured close by.

"Sweet Jesu, I pray—for absolution—from my sins. And—for the salvation of—my soul . . ." Light faded into something grey. Murderer, he knew, and there was a rattling sound close by. The sweltering heat dissipated into a pervasive chill such as he had never felt before. The grey became misty, soft, and deepening . . . and he was sinking through that enveloping fog, toward a most terrible, engulfing darkness. A sickening, spiraling downward plummeting toward a dark void that reached up like the talons of chaos.

No angels for him . . . Oliver. No bright, radiant welcoming light . . . Oliver . . . Roland felt a surge of purest terror and screamed as the last of the shadows vanished, and he was swept down into the damnation that had been his preordained fate . . .

Witch-got bastard . . . and now, got of the same . . . murderer.

* * *

A poignant keening echoed with the wind that swept up along the mountainside, deep and mournful, to touch the ears of all in the slowly moving mass of Charlemagne's army. The King heard it too and drew rein at once, instinct making him rigid in the saddle.

From the south. From the south. He turned, eyes widening a little. Roland. The rearguard . . .

"Majesty?" Duke Naimes had heard it too, he saw.

"We thought to hear the winding of a horn," Charlemagne said softly. Lord Ganelon, close by as well, looked perplexed. "From the rear," the King added.

"I heard no such sound, my liege?" Lord Ganelon offered doubtfully. But Charlemagne looked past him, back to where the slow-moving train of men and beasts had come to an obedient halt, and listened to the subtle whistlings made by the wind as it slipped through the trees on either side of them.

"Aye—it was a horn, we heard!" Charlemagne said firmly, and swung his destrier about to face south.

"An illusion, surely, my liege . . ." Lord Ganelon began.

"I think not, my lord!" Duke Naimes cut in harshly. "For I heard it as well!"

"The rearguard," Charlemagne murmured, then swung his horse about, become in an instant silver vigor. Blue eyes sparked ice as they stared through Lord Ganelon. "Do thou take the van and the baggage and proceed, my lord!" the King barked. "My lord duke, rally the main force. We ride south this instant!"

"My liege!" With a slight bow, the aging Duke spurred his beast away and began shouting the necessary orders.

Lord Ganelon stared after the King who was already galloping through his troops to the southernmost extent of the line. His lips tightened grimly.

"Let it be finished!" he hissed very softly under his breath. He glanced at the hazy skies. "Let it be finished . . ." Charlemagne could not hope to reach them in time.

He spurred his own horse and began, yet again, the appearance of unflagging duty.

SEVENTEEN

Not the least movement was discernable among the thousands of corpses and carcasses that lay entangled across the rugged basin of the valley. The silence was absolute.

Heavy clouds, hanging like shrouds in the sky, brought somber grey tones to the gloom of evening. Even the winds were still.

The dust did not stir by so much as a particle, and those hardy trees and shrubs that struggled to grow amid the rocks did not move, but seemed sinister and contorted like the grotesque dead scattered among them.

The last internal shreds of fleshly life melted away. Bodies began to dry and bloat in the dense, pervasive heat that overhung and simmered across the valley. Tissue erupted through gashes in clothing and armor. Bellies swelled . . . And the silence changed to a somber, muted humming as flies emerged in swarming multitudes from unknown places to settle among the dead. And, as though in final protest, rigor froze flesh into ugly, morbid poses. Limbs rose like hard, carven things into the air once more to make despairing, violent silhouettes . . .

And, with the flies that had begun to scavenge in their millions upon the stench that seeped from mouths and bellies and other places, came crows and buzzards, more cautiously to investigate the silent dead. To pick at first, along the openings of wounds. Or, at eyeballs.

Creatures who understood the uses of active decay.

In one place, its surface clean of gore, the sword Durandal lay against a piece of jutting granite. Its blade shimmered dark and pristine in the deepening gloom. And then the woman hilt began to move, loosing her arms from their place of concealment to stretch herself, engulfing the blade and point, hair shifting down to embrace the winged cross pieces, until she lay in the midnight filament cloud of her own hair.

Slowly, drawing hair and arms about her, she raised herself to stand upon the rocky ground. Erect and proud at first, she shifted, hunching over, becoming ambiguous with shadows until she had become a gaunt and ageless witch of a woman creature. And like a shade of death gaining presence, her darkness changed its quality, loosing translucent depths and the delicate, elusive threads of lightning to become opaque and textured, until, finally, she stood, a crone enshrouded in dark robes of mixed earthen hues.

Then she began to walk like a scavenging hag among the dead.

In another place, deeper in the gorge, upon rubble of stone and dust, another figure lay sprawled among the multitude, a broken lance rising at a skewed angle from his upper belly. The eyes of the one who had been the Bishop Turpin opened abruptly . . .

He shook his head a little and brought up one hand to free himself of the helm and coif that were still upon his head and let them tumble away. Then, with both hands, he found the spear and wrenched it loose, dropping it to clatter among the stones.

He sat up and looked down at himself with a grimace of distaste. In a single, fluid movement, he got to his feet and, with both hands, began to rip and tear at armor and clothing which he discarded in a limp heap near the swelling carcass of the white stallion. Naked now, bloody and begrimed, he reached into the hole in his abdomen. Tore, twisted, and struggled until he drew the skin away from flesh and freed each leg. Then, with bloody human hands, he reached up to pull the rest away from his head and face, finally peeling the

last of it from his hands like a pair of gauntlets. He dropped
the thin, shapeless, tawny skin on top of the rest, letting it
lie like so many rags upon the ground, and stood looking
about him, a sleek, unblemished, delicately radiant figure.

He bent once, with the same fluid grace, and scooping up
a handful of dust, let it trail through the fingers of one hand
into the palm of the other, becoming as it did so a delicate
white material that he then brought about his loins and tossed
over one shoulder in a semblance of a cloak.

Then he stood very still, looking about him at the dead.
His face, wily, cleverly handsome, grew somber beneath hair
that curled in lush abundance with all the hues and tones of
polished woods. Great dark bird eyes stared with liquid clarity at the destruction, pausing at length as they alighted on a
solitary, ragged figure winding its way through the corpses
on the far side of the valley where the ground rose sharply
up toward the bluffs.

Spreading arms and fingers, his garment flowing delicately
about him, the young man jumped a little to walk the air,
avoiding any contact with the bloody contorted ground as he
pursued the other figure.

The crone ceased her prowling to stand over one body,
features twisting with venomous triumph at the sight of dry-
staring blue eyes in a grey, blood-spattered face. Light brown
hair, ugly and matted, was exposed by the helm and coif that
had been knocked to one side, and flies probed the lips of
the open mouth.

"That be an end to thee!" she hissed.

"Lord Oliver De Montglave." A melodious voice, potent
with regret, sounded beside her, and the crone turned to stare
vengefully at the young man. He ignored the look and
crouched down slowly, reaching to draw the lids of those
staring eyes down, shields of dignity for that particularly generous face. Then he shifted, fingers moving to probe the breast
wound and the seared places in its depths, and turned to look
at her.

"This is thy doing," he said.

The crone shrugged. "It had to be!" she retorted.

The young man straightened, shaking his head and frowning at her. "Nay. It did not!" he said sharply. "Roland would
have saved him, and thou know it!" She glowered at him.

"Nay, Durandal, this was no more than thy own intemperate jealousy."

"Enough!" she growled, her voice rumbling like rocks loosed upon a mountainside, and turned away to walk along the ridge toward another place among the dead.

Where the carcass of a golden horse lay sprawled and massive, legs outstretched and rigid in the air—all traces of its power and beauty gone.

The young man continued to frown as he watched the crone and, glancing about him with unrelieved distaste, followed her as she turned from the dead animal and climbed up toward several large boulders close by.

Then she bent over another unmoving body.

The figure was grotesque. Eyes closed in an ashen face gone hideous with fear, the body a shambled thing with multiple and hideous wounds. Gutted . . . Flies swarmed about, buzzing with hunger and frustration, but for some unknown reason, never quite managing to alight. And the right leg and hip were a mangled blend of blood and chain mail, meat and cloth, through which the faintest suggestions of gleaming bone could be seen.

The crone sank down beside the ruin of Lord Roland. She reached to touch the coils of intestine that protruded with a hand that seemed more talons than fingers.

"Were it not for the blood, he would be dead long before so much damage." The crone looked up to see the young man kneel delicately on the other side of Roland's body. He reached with one hand to lightly touch that tormented and unmoving face.

"He will heal," the crone murmured simple assurance.

The young man looked up, his wily brown eyes locking with her midnight ones, widening slightly. "Will he so?" he said in the same peculiarly soft voice. He stood once more.

The crone looked up, hints of distant lightning sparking in the depths of her eyes. "He will heal. The blood will not be denied!" Her voice rumbled a thunderous certainty. The young man did not look at her. Instead, frown melting into pure calm, he looked out across the desolate valley of so many dead, then toward that other place, a little to the south, where the corpse of De Montglave lay.

"Nay, Durandal," he said gently. "Thou are correct in that. The blood will not be denied. He will not die. He cannot die.'' He shifted abruptly, a ruffling movement that seemed a disruption of the direction of his thoughts, and turned to look down at her. ''What he is, and what thou will have him be are not the same,'' he said more sternly. ''I tell thee now, Daughter of Thunder, that this murder of Lord Oliver will be neither forgiven, nor forgot. It will rebound on thee.''

She rose, darkening. ''Thou hast played the part of priest overlong, I think!'' She snarled her retort.

He shook his head. ''Priest or God, it matters not! I do not disguise intemperate virgin passions as a battlefield, or tempest!'' She scowled. ''But thou are weapon wrought, and I am given to deal in subtler things!''

She raised an arm and pointed a finger. ''What hast thou done?'' she demanded with screeching undertones. ''Tell me. What hast thou done?''

The young man shook his head again as he danced out of reach of the lightning bolt that shot from her fingertip to shatter the stone where his feet had been. His look became fey, regretful. ''What else but serve?'' he countered, and stepped back another pace.

''Why do I mistrust thee?'' she hissed, power shimmering like thunder shadows across her robes and the gnarled distortions of her face. He made another ruffling movement and stepped back again, looking down at the corpselike thing that was Roland. He winced visibly.

''Because I speak the truth!'' he said softly and pointed toward the body. ''That is what thou hast wrought, maiden! Yet, this is a different world, with different Gods, and I tell thee again, what thou hast done will rebound on thee. He is not the same!'' A dim gleaming shimmered across him and he began to condense, reduce—legs melting into a body that shrank and became more generalized, sprouted feathers of a snowy color. He stretched out his arms and they became large, broad wings of radiant plumage. His face changed, mouth and nose vanishing into a neatly hooked beak, and hair disappearing to become twin rings of feathers about eyes that did not change.

An instant later, a large white owl rose into the air, beating its wings with steady assurance until it found a thermal far aloft. It soared in a single arc over the battlefield, then disappeared into the deep gloom of settling nightfall.

* * *

The crone stared after it for a time, then bent down once more to take the splayed loops of gut and stuff them back into the gaping pit that had been made of Roland's belly. Then she began to strip the body, shifting it as she did so, until it lay, bloody, naked, and torn in the folds of a cloak taken from another corpse.

"This human meat!" she muttered contemptuously, then turned to seek among the dead for another human carcass. She found one whose head had been crushed beyond recognition and dragged it back to let it sprawl beside the armor and garments that had belonged to the King's Champion.

That done, she drew the corners of the cloak together and wound them around the body of the Count, then picked up the whole and carried it away, half dangling from her arms. Hag and body made their way up the treacherous hill, through a narrow gap in the cliffs, up toward the mountain ridges that offered another path to the north.

He had not known they had fallen so far behind. Aaah, Sweet Jesu! Charlemagne slumped in his saddle as his eyes passed across the desolate valley before him. The stench of death rose in a shifting miasma from that barren place, and seeped through his nostrils to his soul. Crows and buzzards looked up from their feasting, and vultures were everywhere, their haglike plumage ruffling as they fed.

It was beyond the hope of burial, or of any decency, this incredible morass of Christian and Infidel corpses. Beside him, the King saw Duke Naimes' face, more aged than he had ever seen it. Ashen pale . . .

"It was a slaughter, Majesty," the old man half whispered. "See how vastly they were outnumbered." Charlemagne did not respond. Instead, he nudged his stallion and set the beast to slither down over a rubble-laden incline into the worst.

So many dead. And the lie of the bodies, the proportions of Christian to Infidel told most clearly the hideous tale of the relentless struggle that had occurred. Charlemagne did not press his horse when it chose to halt, ears flicking restlessly, upon a bare spot near the center of the valley. Instead, he sat very still, uncaring of the crows that cawed protest or the other sinister birds that took unsettled flight, and listened

to orders barked by some of his lords as they sent men among
the dead to search for those that could be identified.

Eyes bleaker than an ice storm, Charlemagne straightened
slowly in his saddle as a granite weight of permanent grief
settled inside him, a desolation equal to those pitiful and shattered remains brought before him, one by one . . .

He knew each name, each face, the man that each had
been. Now they were contorted, already decaying corpses.

Count Gautier of Hum, Count Berenger—Lord Gerin, Sir
Gerier, and more—

Of the Bishop Turpin, naught was found but his armor and
attire, and a twisted drying human skin that was poignant
and brutal testimony to the sacrilegious flaying the heathen
had done.

Lord Oliver De Montglave's rigid corpse, the only one serene of feature, was brought before him, laid gently down.

Then Charlemagne saw them carry forward yet another
from the far rise. After picking their way through the debris
of dead, his men laid down what was left of Roland, Count
of Brittany.

Naked, mangled flesh that, like its armor, had been pil-
laged and left without dignity—without even a face to recognize. Only shards of bone and meat and tawny hair dangling
from what had been a neck.

Charlemagne felt himself shudder, ice that cracked, as he
stared at that unrecognizable thing. Roland—his son. His most
private and greatest pride. His promise for the future.

Dead.

"Let these bodies be wrapped and spiced and carried to
Aix!" The King's voice was a hoarse, ugly rasping as he
grated the order. "There, they shall be entombed in fitting
splendor that none may forget these gallant and honorable
men, now brought to the sanctity of God's Blessed Presence
after this most terrible trial!"

Then, he turned his horse about, able to bear no more,
and, spurring it, raced the animal back through the valley
toward the trail of the north.

Fury rose, like the wind against his face, and the stench it
bore seeped into his nostrils, and further, into the roots of
his soul.

The Infidel had done this. Treachery. Unspeakable treachery. It did not need any other expression, this knowledge

inside him that they would pay. Hostages and those who were
still free would suffer for the crimes they had wrought.

Forged not of any steel, nor of obsidian, but of the essence
of tempests, the crone that was a form of Durandal walked
on without pause or respite, one footfall at a time, relentlessly carrying that silent, dangling thing that was more surely
a corpse than anything else.

She trod the dark times, and the shadows. North across the
mountains. Down into the valleys and hardwood forests of
southern France. Ever northward, eluding any place of human
habitation, slipping across brooks and rivers, across nocturnal meadows where wild creatures watched, and through deep
thickets and over hills.

Still northbound, she passed along the coast at last, where
the sea whispered moon-got rhythms to the shore, and gulls
soared far above the waves, uttering their melancholy cries.
And as autumn winds stripped the trees of their withering
foliage, she came to that desolate, craggy peninsula that was
the western tip of Brittany . . .

Came to the time-shattered, lost, and overgrown temple
made of witchcraft and stone eons before. Hidden from any
common discovery, it was the last shadowed sanctuary of a
race long vanished, a repository for the artifacts of very different powers.

Up rubble-covered stone steps she trod, across a court half
buried by briars and vines, toward a dark place in the concealing vines beside the smooth suggestions of a wall where
temple and gorge became united, through plants that yielded
to the lightning that shimmered through her robes, and from
her eyes, through the concealed portal behind into the darkness of a cavern deep within the granite.

There, upon a bed of old dried leaves, she set down the
thing she carried and laid it out in a sort of order upon the
tattered folds of the dead man's cloak. Then she stood very
still and stared at it with eyes untroubled by the darkness.

Not a single movement was discernible in the corpselike
being that lay naked and mutilated below her. No slight rise
and fall of ribs in breathing. No faint pulsing of blood at the
throat. No heart beat. Only absolute stillness.

She frowned as she continued to stare at the hideous dis-
tortion of what was left of Roland. The gaping wounds, one

mangled leg and hip, the other broken about the knee. Hair filthy with gore. She bent and touched, fingers tracing across a brow purely cold.

Skin that was dried to tawny leather hue, withering, like the rest.

"This vile human meat!" She rose, frown deepening, metallic glints warring with dark clouds of frustration in the depths of her eyes.

"Thou cannot die . . ." Her voice rumbled thunder across the cavern. "Thou will never die . . . !" The last was a wind howling of power that flitted from wall to wall, splitting into reverberations that slowly died away. But from the body of Roland, there was only the same, utter stillness.

"It is not possible . . ." She breathed a distant keening and spun in a swirl of robes to flow from the cavern, passing into the court of the ruined temple.

She looked up at a sky grey and slumberous, burdened with the promise of coming snowfalls. Her face lost its leathery wrinkles and lines, becoming youthful, tinged, not with the color of blood, but, rather, with the hues of thunderclouds and steel. Vague formless robes condensed into filaments of midnight hair that tumbled about a body smooth and vibrant with power. Suggestions of blue lightning shimmered through the weaving tresses that were her only garb.

"The blood will not be denied . . ." She whispered hollow breeze sounds and turned slowly to stare toward the temple wall, and the figure that lay unblemished, and partially concealed by vines before it on a block of purest white stone. "My lord?" Agile as air, she moved toward it, then paused before the perfect, recumbent figure. "My lord . . ." Voice softened to husky passion, she reached and touched the binding vegetation, scorching it away with blue heat from her fingertips, until the figure was completely exposed.

"My lord," she whispered like traceries of smoke. "It is done. Whyfore do thou continue thus? Let flesh and blood be brought together at last . . ." She reached to touch the pristine marble figure, determination in her voice. "Thou will become that which thou are made to be . . ." Fingertips found his flawless surface and felt—ice.

Bitter, incredible cold. She gasped, darkening, recoiling, for, where she had touched, fine, hairline fractures appeared

and spread across the statue, over his torso, down limbs, up
his neck and face even to the forms of his hair.

"What is this?" She rasped metallic horror. But, like rapidly growing roots, the fractures spread and multiplied and
deepened. The statue of the man shifted insidiously, eroding
to become an exact reflection of that other mortal body she
could not bear to look upon. Flawless, perfect muscling became skeletal emaciation. The right leg shriveled into twisted
deformity, and the left lay against it with the semblance of a
broken knee. Scar forms appeared, and pits where there were
sores. And other, unhealed wounds were reiterated in stone.
Only the lyre remained intact, falling from the grasp of a
hand that had become little more than marble bones, to lie
in the vines about the base of the statue.

"Nay!" She shrieked protest in a high-pitched howling of
pain.

Beads of liquid appeared along each threaded fracture in
the stone. Like sweat. Or some strange kind of blood. "Nay,
thou cannot destroy . . ." The storm woman plunged forward
in an attempt to grasp the remains of the statue, but stone
crumbled, then melted into a clear fluid that seeped forth
between her fingers and flowed like molten diamonds off the
marble base to pool on the ground below. Lightning flashed
in her eyes, her hair swirling about her with thunder and
winds of desperate temper, she pursued the fluid, trying to
clutch it.

But the liquid flowed away, and evaporated into a facile
mist that slipped through the entangled undergrowth to waft
up against the temple wall, then vanish completely around a
corner.

She went after it, hurling herself through the portal by the
recesses of the temple wall into the dark spaces of the cavern.

But there was nothing beyond silence, and the musty odor
of old leaves. The still, damp, stone-flavored air.

And the unmoving body of Roland . . .

She lunged toward it, bent, and crouched down, lavender
hues dancing with storm dark blues across her form. She
reached to touch that shriveled thing.

"Thou are mine . . ." she muttered. "Thou are mine that
I have fought for. Killed for . . ." But the corpse did not
respond. It lay bitter still, cold and distant as ice. "Thou—
why must I be bound to thee?"

She rose, a tempest gathering on her face, in her eyes, sifting across hair and flesh.

"This cannot be!" she screeched. "The blood cannot be denied!" But only silence answered her outcry, drowning it slowly.

So in keeping with what she was, she rose up to occupy the still dark air and condensed.

Wings sprouted forth from hair that melted against her shrinking body, and from her feet, the long and lethal blade of her nature erupted and stretched down. Then, with another screeching of incalculable fury, the sword Durandal plunged down violently to pierce the granite floor of the cave. The stone yielded to absorb the point and the sword hung there, reverberations fading into opaque and dark immobility.

Still—the body of Roland did not stir.

EIGHTEEN

A.D. 778–779

Hell was not a place of fire at all. Nor was it filled with long-tailed demons. Nor was Satan apparent in all his malice, enthroned in some eternal violent conflagration.

Rather, it was an odyssey through myriad and remote shades of grey. Multilayered tones that swept like diffuse clouds across the craggy landscapes of agony. A relentless passage through places where upthrusting rocks pierced, yet could not break the threads of mist blown across them to swirl a little, or dance. Or, sometimes, to part enough to reveal faint and distant images of a discarded world.

And the Devil was a woman thing. Gnarled and hideous, with eyes that held all the nightmares of origin. A crone that enveloped the mists—held, somehow, and carried. Aye, the landscape of pain with all its brutal rubble was a carcass of flesh that sought to dry and wither, to shrivel. Sought to complete the decay that marked absolute death . . .

But, between the mists, thin, delicate rivulets of liquid appeared and ran to trace fine lines, minuscule rippling brooks that wound intricate paths across the arid bitter places. Liquid that flowed into each brutal crevasse and touched to moisten every raw edge.

Fluid that came from no apparent wellspring, yet condensed as though of the very mists. Fluid that increased to spread and saturate the shattered dust.

The rest was shades. Miragelike—illusions in the shifting

245

mists. Glimpses of things beyond, seen for an instant, then lost in grey once more.

Lighter . . . Darker . . . The ribs of uncountable men, still held together by scraps of weathered hard black meat, reached up to claw the air like desperate gruesome hands. And there were skulls that grinned, eye sockets barren. Some with shreds of brown tissue wrapped like soiled rags to make grotesque facsimiles of human faces.

There were horses too, sprawled like haggard and exhausted death steeds at rest between the scattered limb bones of men and broken reminders of rusted weapons and armor. And between the boulders, there was the dismal fluttering of tattered rags that had once been more than suggestions of clothing, distinguishable from dark scraps of flesh only by a faint response to the wind. Death was total desolation. There were no ghosts. Murdered Oliver . . .

Even the crows had abandoned this place.

But, the mists moved in once more, grey clouds that drifted softly across numbness. Defined, yet unfeeling. Like stone . . .

Like stone that lay in an open place with the unmoving patience of the eternally quiescent. Being that was part of, yet distinct from, that other saturated and excruciating clay, forever probed by the restless ebb and flow of vigorously intrusive liquid streams.

Then through the mists, a shadowed form emerged. Moved closer—to what? It was uncertain. Then the figure became familiar somehow. A stormy-hued woman composed of lightning and steel, she reached—toward . . .

Toward? Aye, the stone-frozen form of flesh that was in some peculiarly dichotomous manner, himself. She touched. And from her fingertips came sudden lines of violent heat that sheared across the ice and defined a body, with sensations akin to fire. And her voice was an ominous thunder.

"Whyfore do thou continue thus . . . ? Let flesh and blood be brought together at last . . ." What flesh and blood? This was death, beyond the realm of such things. And her will was a tempest of power. He recoiled, shrinking back from that which he felt in her, and dreaded, seeking even the familiarity of human ordeal as he fled from this intrusive vision, and from the implications of things he had no wish to know.

And the ice form that he was retreated likewise, shattering

into myriad pieces and then into the dust of incorporate mist that evaporated away, unconfined by the blend of soil and fluid that was this other, unreachable flesh.

As the mists darkened to some illusion of quiet, he heard her shrieks of fury, felt them fade, and knew a fleeting sense of triumph. Even in death, it was possible to have victory.

A.D. 779

All was peace then. A suspension in a dark and hollow place where the only movements were the insidious rippling of liquid brooks across the ragged and cavernous arid landscape. Time was irrelevant.

But in time, that dust that he had become was caught and made to settle in the nooks and crannies, in deep places, where it vanished into the emerging recognition of a body grotesquely changed. A body that was not relinquishing him after all.

Roland knew at last, as he felt the familiar pulsing of a heartbeat, felt ribs that creaked to move in response to cycles of forgotten breathing as though they had never ceased. The chill damp air laden with the scents of stone, and earth, and old leaves, of tangible things passed in and out, in and out once again.

He was no ghost. No shade at all. Not even privileged to wander that ghastly barren battlefield of Roncesvalles in search of—in search of some remembrance of the spirits who had died there . . . Of Oliver.

They were all gone. Vanished to other spheres, while he had been left behind without even the dignity of dying with them.

Corporate being became increasingly apparent with the growing strength of each fist-clenching heartbeat and the blood that found all his parts. He felt the body that lay half-twisted and protesting with pain amid the litter of dead leaves. Felt the confusion of a broken knee trying to sort itself into a functional joint, felt the other, twisted leg, damaged beyond repair, simply tighten and wither.

Felt the edges of the canyon where his middle had once been smooth and flat, slowly coming together to form a puckered, brutal ridge over ruined organs below.

The rest, arms and hands, peripherally damaged, but slowly restored to some semblance of familiar form. And a head, with features. An arid cavern of a mouth where his tongue lay furled and dry behind indifferent stone teeth. A nose that breathed damp air, chill air, burdened with mists of substance. And ears that heard the echoes of the silence, then, sometimes, faint rustlings from some place beyond. Wind movements, and creature sounds.

And eyes that he did not wish to open, shielded by lids that were another description of darkness.

Hunger? Thirst? They were forgotten things as the beating of his heart continued and compelled him slowly toward fuller awareness. Nudged him toward the opening of reluctant eyes, so that he might see more than the grief that was beyond absolution.

Oliver . . . And the accursed witch sword Durandal that impaled both stone and the darkness of the cave in which he lay. Durandal that had brought him to glory . . .

And murder. Who stood with silent and vindictive temper but a few feet from him.

Beyond were unending cycles of day and night reflected through a portal on the far side of the cave. Reminders of a world as persistent as his own relentlessly enduring body. He lay there, reluctant to otherwise stir, staring at the light that passed across the portal, watching it change.

Little clumps of white snow hung heavy and moist upon the tangled mesh of slumbering plants at the entrance to the cave. Or rain that fell whispering, to heighten contrasts between blacks and browns. Some days were radiant with brilliant sunlight. Others, grey-dull like the ugliness of the battlefield of Roncesvalles. Sometimes, moonlight sent silver quietly gleaming across the black lines of undergrowth to fill the cave with echoes of stillness. Sometimes, there was only darkness.

Movement was a command that he was reluctant to obey. Yet, his hands groped to find the scabs of healing, minor wounds, or that which sealed the seam where his belly had been slit, now reduced to a basin between jutting prominences of bones, lined with dry, thin skin. The remains of his right leg shrank and twisted further, shriveling up toward a shattered, grating hip, the bones yielding to withered cords of muscle grown short and immobile from disuse. His other leg could move a little, the knee grating like a horseshoe upon an anvil, and the foot flexed with memories of standing, or being seated in a stirrup.

Then he began to turn himself a little amid the bed of leaves and rancid, twisted cloth. It was a way to elude the sight of the dark sword that stood nearby, waiting—haunting the dark spaces of the cave that could have been a tomb instead of another reflection of damnation. Waiting.

For what? His hand upon the hilt?

Never . . .

The tenuous scraps of snow dissolved and dripped away, melding with rains that came more often to whisper liquid sounds through the portal, beckoning.

And, upon the withered vines, buds swelled, then erupted into astonishing green. Infant, virgin leaves of renewal. Days lengthened slowly, and beyond, the music of bird calls reflected a quickening conversation among the wild things.

Unable to bear his proximity to the dark sword, Roland rummaged through the discoordinate pieces of his body, twisting and jerking to lie half on one side, half on his belly. Walking a forgotten skill, so laboriously he dug elbows into stone and struggled to drag the rest across the ground. Before him, rain fell across the cave entrance, and he watched the drops touch new leaves, then tumble down to merge and trickle across the dust.

The portal grew gradually larger as he lurched awkwardly toward it. He felt his heart pound grimly, and air rushed in and out of lungs that did nothing to ease the difficulty. Then, of a sudden, it seemed, he lay in a pool of grey light.

Drops of rain tumbled from a soft, brightly grey sky trickled across his back and sides and wandered down the forgotten strands of his hair, touched nose tip and lashes and fingers that were dug like claws into the sod.

He stared at a world become visible and complete. Sparkling with color after the gloom of the cave. Infant leaves sprouted upon every twig, and grasses were well grown up to cover the dull litter of the previous winter. And briars had opened their first frail blossoms amid protective thorns.

How long had it been since . . . ?

It seemed so callous, this continuity—this freshly contented renewal. Roland rasped a tongue that felt withered and

cracked across the stones of his teeth, and across lips that
were ill-cured leather, and tasted the rain moisture.

It was astonishingly sweet, entirely unlike that other fluid
inside that churned and compelled the mud of his body, and
now felt more like scalding, molten metal than blood.

He dragged himself farther, away from the cave where the
dark sword lingered, relieved to feel it recede behind him.
Fitting place for that murderous and enchanted weapon . . .

Aye, he thought with brutal clarity. Let her remain
there, entombed as he could not be. Enshrouded in an obscure, dank cave, beyond the view of men and living things.
He struggled on through tangled undergrowth, ceasing only
when he reached a patch of soft and open turf. Then he looked
up, looked about him, he felt his eyes widen with astonished
recognition.

He knew this place . . . He knew this place.

It was that same ruined, ancient heathen temple near the
tip of Brittany where he had camped for a night with Oliver—
was it now a pair of years past?

Oliver . . . The name echoed across his mind, and Roland
collapsed to lie half on one side, uncaring of his surroundings. Uncaring of anything else. Oliver . . . Not Oliver.

But truth was bleak and hard. Irrefutable . . . Inescapable.
How gladly he would have yielded up his own life to save
Oliver. It could have been so . . . It could have been. Not
this . . . murder.

And the rain pattered imperviously upon leaves and
branches, upon stone and between blades of grass, whispering to itself of other things. Slipping across his body in little
runnels that wandered between ribs, or flowed down the
channel of his neck.

Roland stared at the hand that lay beside him, close to his
face. Hand? It was a skeletal thing, withered in the manner
of a dead beast preserved in an arid place. And the arm was
the same. Muscles mere cords upon hinges and angles of
bone, covered by skin that was shrunken, dark, tawny, and
brittle-looking. He glanced farther and saw his own ribs, jutting like leather-covered beams beyond the concavity of a
belly that had long forgot how to contain sustenance. And
below, hip bones and—legs.

Had he died then? Roland wondered. For, surely, flesh
could not be in such condition and yet still harbor life. But

the taloned fingers near his face moved when he bade them, spreading out to touch wet sod.

It was his witch blood, Roland knew then. His witch blood that condemned him, not to dissolution with the rest at Roncesvalles, nor to the eternal mysteries of Heaven and Hell such as was given to be the fate of men with souls.

But, rather, to another fate. Some manner of unknown perpetuity that was inextricably bound into the earth. Beyond the sight of God, or Satan.

Or Satan? He felt confused, uncertain. Had he already found the Devil in that accursed and spiteful weapon that he had bound himself to for so long? The memory of Oliver's last melting smile was answer of a kind.

Roland let his head sink into the wet turf, let the rain whisper down around and over him. He felt his flesh, the ruined carcass to which he seemed inextricably bound, and felt raindrops touch his parched lips, a trickle passing from one lock of hair that lay across a cheekbone, slip between his teeth, moisten, fill . . .

Sweet-tasting. Smooth in the manner with which it slithered down his throat.

He closed his eyes, yielding, and, in time, found the silent void of sleep.

Nestled in the branches of an ancient and contorted giant oak some short distance from the temple, a white owl blinked and ruffled feathers into disarray as the rainfall became more determined. Its head hunched down closer to loosely folded wings with a peculiar resignation, and its large brown eyes continued to watch the angular, ruined man thing that lay in the sod amid broken columns visible through a gap in dark green oak leaves.

It was a creature that understood the consequences of patience.

As Roland lay sleeping, the parched and withered flesh welcomed the rain, absorbing that simple fluid essential to its component parts.

Gradually, shrunken cords of meat swelled to pliant and flexible muscle. Gradually, crumpled brown parchment skin softened and expanded, lightened to reflect the hues of living flesh once more. The rhythms of breathing became quietly

synchronous. And the desperate clenching cycles of a beating
heart eased to simpler, confident effort.

Within the cave, the dark sword tried to rise from the stone
in which she had seated herself, and found she could not.
More firmly rooted than any mature tree in soil, she was
caught in the granite. Hilt wings beat the air in furious effort,
and, above them, the woman form of Durandal writhed to
loose herself and undertake another, more mobile form. But,
even the thunder of her voice was confined, and the scorching fire of her will and touch. Nothing loosed her. She was
bound . . .

Fury that had never before been leashed proved entirely
worthless as lightning temper was held from flashing outward
to rend, and, instead, turned inward, becoming, after a fashion, bitter, self-inflicted wounds.

Like a tempest that could be silenced for the forces that it
contained, Durandal, for the first time, experienced futility
in struggling against entrapment. Nor were the means of her
bondage obvious. There were no cords of tangible power to
resist, no vindictive currents in the air. Only the darkness of
the cave. Only dense, unmoving stone without temperament
of any sort. And air that hung still and dank, without mood
or disposition.

How . . . ? How . . . ? He was incomplete, his powers not
yet attained, or even realized in their potential.

And Durandal thought of the other body that had cracked,
then melted at her touch, evaporated into a mist she could
not reach or hope to hold, slipping away to vanish.

Nay? He could not, surely, have wrought this? Have inhaled the atmosphere of that dormant corporate entity into
himself and remained so—hideously—mortal of appearance.
So withered and distorted . . .

Slowly, the dark sword ceased her movements and became
still. How could he have eluded her so completely? And how
else could he have confined her thus?

The owl's words of warning echoed insidious promise.

"He is not the same . . ."

It was the heat of sunlight that Roland first felt as he found
consciousness. Then pain . . . Raw pain that pulsed along
one contorted leg and ascended into the hip. Pain that

throbbed in circles about his one knee and across places where other wounds had been inflicted. Roland opened his eyes to brilliant morning light. Radiant, contented greens—and the sight of his own hand beside him.

Changed somewhat. Still thin, aye, but not that withered, mummified thing that he had last seen. It was flesh now, most clearly. Living meat . . .

He saw then his own body—the body of a man. Damaged, aye. Gaunt and crippled as would be normal. But, beyond refutation, alive.

He pulled himself up on his elbows to glance about him, seeing the eroded columns and the deep, concealed gorge around the temple, clothed in brilliant, lush green foliage. Alive . . . He blinked, pain easing back as he discovered a new clarity to his perception.

Nothing was blurred. Nothing melded. Every detail was astonishingly clear, even the smallest leaf fluttering upon a branch many yards away. Every blade of grass, every pore and crack in the ancient stone of the ruined temple. And the edges of the soft, small white clouds that scudded overhead, driven by high winds such as only eagles were made to feel.

A mouse scurrying through the undergrowth some fifty yards away was easily seen, brown fur and shimmering whiskers. Again, Roland struggled, jerking himself to sit upright, propped on one arm, on the hip that was still entire. He looked down at his bent and twisted right leg and the scars that traced across knee and hip and thigh.

The toes moved a little. Nothing else. And the other leg answered stiffly, knee grating as he bent it. He was alive—and crippled.

A cripple? Aye. For surely this was damage beyond hope of repair? He shifted himself again, pulling on his arms, watched the grotesque leg follow, and felt irrelevant pain.

He had walked and run, jumped, and clutched a warhorse's ribs with unconsidered ease once . . . Such was beyond the capabilities of this contorted flesh. Crippled . . .

Was this his damnation then, for the murder he had wrought through the dark sword? He looked away from his body, across the temple court to that place where tangled vines spread their leaves as they climbed up to conceal the wall where the heathen place joined with the cliffs. Oliver . . . Unblemished even in death . . . His eyes lingered on the long, narrow dark oval of the cave entrance. Where the dark sword still reposed.

Durandal . . . His mouth tightened. Durandal, who had brought him to untold glory—to even the illusion of honor. Then, this . . .

Which of the pair of them was instrument to the other? he wondered coldly. He shifted and felt his crippled leg against the other.

"My hand cannot serve thee now!" he growled.

"Such loathing!" There was amusement in the melodious voice that sounded above him, and Roland jerked around to stare up at a figure swathed in a long, cream-colored wool cloak, the hood of which was drawn so far over the head as to make the face naught but shadows. Naked, little more than a collection of bones and skin, Roland knew his own disadvantage at once.

"Who art thou?" he grated. The figure moved a little closer, dropped down gracefully to sit cross-legged upon the turf, then reached up to slip the hood back a little. Roland gasped, and felt the blood abandon his face.

"My lord Bishop . . . ?" he breathed. "But I saw thee fall . . ."

"I fell, aye," Turpin said quietly. "But I did not die! Thou, I perceive, have not faired so well."

Roland swallowed then, and stared hungrily into those familiar, great eyes. "What of the rest, my lord . . . ?" he rasped unsteadily.

Turpin's eyes gleamed from the shadows beneath his hood, and the answer was as Roland knew it had to be, as he had dreamed. "They are all dead. Every soul . . ."

Roland winced and closed his eyes for a moment. Not even a shred of hope, however fleeting. "So should I be!" he whispered after a moment. Turpin leaned closer, extending a hand to gently set it on the bones and skin of Roland's shoulder. Roland flinched away. "Nay!" he rasped. "Do not despoil thyself. For I am cursed, and thou are a man of God!"

"Am I, my lord?" Turpin asked, and Roland, startled, stared with widening eyes as the priest put back his hood completely to reveal a face most well remembered, yet—aye, remarkably changed.

The eyes were the same, and the construct of the features. But the weathered look was vanished and, with it, all the lines of experience and expression. Instead, Turpin's face was astonishingly smooth, vibrantly youthful.

Roland jerked back, his body taut. "I am mad, or thou are indeed dead!" he exclaimed.

"Nay . . ." The other shook rich brown hair.

"What are thou then?" Roland whispered harshly, his own face vulnerable. "I felt sometimes . . . ?"

"And rightly!" Turpin inclined his head and settled himself more comfortably, his cloak opening farther to reveal a tan-colored, knee-length tunic over cross-gartered brown chausses and soft leather shoes and, against his belly, a rumpled leather pack bag. "I am not human," he continued. "I have discarded the manlike shell that I undertook for a time."

"But, thou are a priest? A man of God, anointed and ordained to holiness!" Roland's voice was husky with shock and disbelief.

"The rituals of disguise," Turpin murmured, unperturbed. Roland stared, then shuddered and drew back in revulsion.

"How many times did I receive the sacrament from thy hands?" he hissed bitterly. "Mother of God. How many times . . ." Then, "Thou art a warlock?"

Turpin grimaced a little and shook his head. "Nay, my lord," he said in the same measured tones. "I am nothing so simple as that!"

"What then?"

Turpin shrugged a little and cocked his head. "Mayhap it is sufficient to say that I am thy friend?" he offered evenly, and looked away to survey the temple court. A suspicious hissing was Roland's sole response to this. Turpin looked back at him. "The King, Charlemagne, grieves most fiercely for his fallen Champion," he went on quietly. "And for the gallant peers who died at Roncesvalles. Daily, Mass is said over the tombs of those proud and noble men." He rose to his feet. "And beside the King, the Lord High Councillor sits in growing power. Lord Ganelon becomes, in truth, the very staff upon which thy liege lord, Charlemagne, leans . . ." He looked away across the clearing and shrugged. "Such is justice, my lord! Such is justice!" Roland flinched, but did not answer. Nor did he move as Turpin looked at him again, then loosed the cloak from his shoulders and dropped it to the turf, along with the satchel that was slung by a strap over one shoulder. "As friends may," he finished softly, "I have brought thee that which thou may find useful.'' Then he turned and walked lightly away.

Roland watched, staring at the young man's airy gait, and the supple perfection of his lightly clad body. Then his eyes widened as, upon reaching the farthest edge of the temple court, the man abruptly spread out his arms to the air, sprouted feathers—snowy feathers—and shrank away to become a white bird that took flight, then vanished into the trees beyond the gorge.

The white owl . . . Aye, the white owl, that same unnatural bird that had haunted him in the past. Turpin who he had thought to be a priest. Priest . . . ? Archbishop. Roland swallowed and shivered.

His own honest efforts to find God through adhering to the rituals of faith went sour before so much illusion. Little wonder that, for him, witch-got, there was only silence . . .

He gave up and let himself sink down to lie in the grass once again.

Justice, Turpin had murmured. This was beyond justice. And as he lay there on the turf, Roland felt the tug of other comments that the owl man had made, summoning thoughts on matters human and of such nature as had been among his chief concerns before this—before Roncesvalles.

Charlemagne—beloved liege who grieved for the gallant dead. For him. Though it was never openly expressed, Roland had felt and understood the wonder of that love that Charlemagne reserved most particularly for him. How much it had motivated him . . . Aye, it was still there, deep within him, his own love and reverence for the great silver King. Justice . . . ?

They had accomplished, at least—the King's safety. But at brutal and bitter cost. And Lord Ganelon? Lord Ganelon, who had perpetrated the whole, hideous treachery, was now seated entire at the King's right hand? Secure in Charlemagne's favor and trust by very reason of the King's innocence of Ganelon's capacity for treason. His ambition. Ganelon, who, Roland understood in an instant of brilliant clarity, did not love his liege at all. Who hated the very King he was bound to serve.

Nay, that was not justice at all.

Roland shifted to prop himself up once more and stared down at the body that extended before him. Unrecognizable.

Condemned to live. Bastard and witchling. And King's Champion . . .

That was a jest now. He was a cripple. He could crawl, or drag himself.

He could not ride a horse, or walk. Or wield a sword. Had he damned himself then? he wondered bitterly as he recalled how he had undertaken possession of the sorcerous dark sword to his own ambition.

Oliver—who need not have died. The rest, unavenged.

How to bring balance to the scales of intemperate grief?

A.D. 779

Days followed, and nights, passing in a smooth progression as spring matured into the onset of summer. Roland did not see the owl man called Turpin again. Nor the white owl that lurked nearby, watching still.

Nor did Roland go near the cave behind the temple where the dark sword lay confined by the force of his passionate revulsion for the murder he had wrought through her. Instead, he used the cloak that Turpin had left to cover himself, and rummaged with hesitation through the empty-seeming satchel to find all manner of practical things. A simple, stoppered flagon that held fluid that was a blend of water and wine and honey, sweetly nurturing to drink, and ever full. Witchcraft, he knew bitterly, yet compelled by new-risen appetites to ease his thirst. And bread endlessly supplied in small, crisply succulent loaves that melted his hunger.

He found clothing as well. Simple, finely woven, yet unadorned attire. A linen undertunic and a soft, green wool tunic for outer garb. There were, as well, chausses and shoes and garters that seemed a mockery to don, pulled over one reluctant but mobile limb, and the other that was gone rigid, twisted to a contorted, grotesque semblance of what it should have been. Yet the clothing gave him dignity, a feeling of having, in some fashion, restored at least a fragment of humanity.

Roland's thoughts turned back to all he had known before. To the King that had brought him from bastard beggary to high estate and nobility. To Oliver—and all that the brother-

hood between them had brought him to know. To other things.
The campaigns. To goals composed of honor and ambition
that seemed meaningless now. And to those moments of clarity that had brought him brilliant achievement.

War—that single thing above all else that he understood.
Kept alive by his witch blood, it was a futile thing to think
on now. He was crippled beyond any such usefulness.

And Lord Ganelon was beside the King, secure in his
treachery. Pity the unavenged dead . . . It was that single
piece of knowledge that drove Roland to drag himself across
the temple court, down the steps, and across the clearing to
drink from the small brook that flowed across one end. To
hunt for roots and berries for sustenance, seeking to avoid
the mysterious, self-replenishing supplies of the satchel. And
it was the same knowledge that drove him to find a staff, to
attempt to stand, then hobble a little.

Stick and limb—unwilling flesh that responded with sour
pain. He was at war with himself, to learn to get about at all.
Then, in the temple court, one morning, as he looked toward
the cave and the white stone wall beside it, he recognized a
stone oblong, familiar, somehow, despite the foliage that covered it.

He dragged himself toward it, struggling through undergrowth that sought to tangle arms and legs that could not step
freely, and, after much effort, jerked to sit upright and stare.

There had been a statue here . . . ? Aye. His eyes widened.
Aye, he remembered. Apollo, Oliver had said then. The statue
of a recumbent man, an image of an ancient and heathen God
long abandoned in the spreading light of Christendom. Still
worshipped by the Infidel, he had heard.

Stone. Nothing more—and he had felt . . . ? He shivered
a little at the recollection of that peculiar unease. Oliver had
dispelled his fancies with well-ordered sensibilities.

But the statue was vanished. And the surface of the slab on
which the figure had reclined was smooth and unblemished.
How . . . ? Foolish question for one who had known the
powers of such as the sword Durandal. Roland pulled and
twisted at himself, drawing closer to reach up, touch smooth
marble, and found a purchase on his left knee. The joint
protested, but he ignored it, feeling the stone, and a sense of
relief at perceiving nothing else.

The statue was gone, and it was better so. Nothing left to

haunt his present mind, or memory, sufficiently tormented by other things. His eyes slid along the slab, then down, gaze freezing as he caught sight of something entangled in the vegetation at its base. He moved toward it, half falling, and tugged to expose . . .

A white stone lyre.

Seemingly of the same marble as the slab to which he held, it was as finely made as any real instrument. And it was the same as that which he had seen before, in the hand of the statue.

Roland stiffened, then, with a grim expression, reached for the thing and pulled it toward him.

Neither hot nor cold, like the air about him, it was uncannily smooth, textured like the finest polished woods. Yet, aye—it was stone.

Roland let his fingertips pass along the two elegantly curved arms that reached from a compact and oval-shaped box, reminiscent in form of a tortoise shell. And in the space between the arms of the instrument were twelve strings of the same impossible material. So fine, and yet—stone? Roland touched, then started violently, for, with the slightest contact of his fingertips, the strings began to hum. To resonate . . .

Rich tones that permeated the air about him with undertones of pain. Then of a sudden, the lyre—changed—in his hands. He flinched back and stared as, like dew yielding to the power of sunbeams, white stone became molten and vanished to reveal hues of interwoven gold and brown beneath. The twelve strings sparkled gold and brilliant in the sunlight, the rest exquisite beyond belief with incomprehensible craftsmanship.

Magic, Roland knew as the notes faded away to meld with the air. He shifted to thrust the thing from him, then saw an image of Oliver in his mind. The pair of them before a campfire . . . and Oliver, plucking sweet melodies from another such instrument. He swallowed, and felt his fingers find the strings again. Touched softly, remembering, likewise, other aspects of his friend.

Gentleness . . . and peace.

And the lyre answered with tones that hummed softly, like insect wings, or the shimmering of sunlight upon still water. Throat tangled with raw feeling, Roland closed his eyes and

bent his fingers to pluck as Oliver had taught him. Beloved
Oliver.

He found whisper-soft breeze tones that danced through
willows, caressing sensually. And complex, multilayered harmonies that were like the calls of birds in the woodlands. So
much to remember . . . And the hawk that floated free upon
a high thermal, confident of the buoyancy of the air . . .

It was a potent agony to understand the extent of sharing
that had grown up between them. And a like clarity was palpable in the voice of the instrument. Magic . . . ?

It did not matter. Roland let himself sink back to recline
against the stone slab, and drew the lyre closer. He felt, like
the new depth and precision in his eyesight, that there was a
new knowledge in his fingertips as they stroked and plucked
the strings.

Talent, Oliver had said to him, and he had feared it, sensing implications of witchcraft. Now, that was irrelevant in the
face of the feelings that this lyre, seemingly without a will of
its own, yet with a power of another kind, obediently expressed and amplified.

For a long time, Roland sat there, eyes still closed as his
fingertips probed the strings, explored the capacities of the
lyre, and sought and found the reach of its voice. Each isolated note, then sequences and harmonies.

A peaceable occupation, Oliver had likewise commented. But
there was naught of peace in all the details of gentle, honorable
humanity he saw in the memories of his friend. Nor in the
poignant combinations of notes that began to emerge, to reflect
in sounds that haunted the settling twilight that gathered about
the temple.

Clinging to the lyre in the days and nights that followed,
Roland found a single, tragic, haunting melody upon the instrument. Repeated, it grew like a will bent to conjuring, and
words began to form. At first, singly, then as phrases isolated
in his mind, and, later, coming together to form descriptive
patterns.

Roncesvalles . . .

Memory and melody became inextricably intertwined and
the words issued forth through a voice richly capable.

Details became lines, then verses. Order evolved in the

suggestions of a song that became both preoccupation and compulsion.

Roncesvalles . . .

Only resolution proved elusive, like a sword held high overhead and poised for the final sweep of execution that could not seem to find its downward path. Melody and words hovered there, compelling repetition of all the details that led up to and surrounded that defeat, and haunted his mind like the restless cries of the unavenged and wasted dead.

Oliver, who, perhaps, would not have been so hideously slain after all. And the rest. And himself, now crippled and stripped from a lifetime of knowledge and ability. Dishonored . . .

Now there was only the song, Roland thought. The song and himself.

Resolution could never be found here, in this abandoned ruin that had become a retreat for his reclusive existence. It lay elsewhere.

It lay at Charlemagne's court. At Aix La Chapelle.

NINETEEN

Summer, A.D. 779

"Aaah, Sir Thierry! I bid thee welcome!" Lord Ganelon smiled a little as he spoke, dark eyes glinting reflections of the light of several candles that flickered from their place at one end of the document-littered table before him.

"My lord?" Thierry bowed and remained standing, preferring the protection of formality as he wondered uneasily why he should have been so discreetly summoned from the evening's feasting to attend the Lord High Councillor in this private ante-chamber. But Lord Ganelon chuckled a little, evidently in high good humor.

"Such exquisite courtesy, Thierry!" he commented, standing himself. "It is both a reflection of breeding, and an instrument useful in the attaining of power!" Thierry, all wariness, forbore response. Lord Ganelon gave his nephew a sharp look as he passed around the end of the table to walk across the chamber and place himself near the hearth fire on the other side. "The business of empire becomes cumbersome," he added, almost as though to himself. "Many things to accomplish . . ."

"Aye, my lord," Thierry offered.

Lord Ganelon looked at him closely. "Thou have demonstrated loyalty and discretion and patience beyond my expectations, nephew," he said. "I am well pleased." Thierry allowed a puzzled flicker of his brows. "We spoke once—of reward."

"I do not understand, my lord." Lord Ganelon gave him a tolerant look. Am I such a fool to thee, then? Thierry wondered silently.

"Thou hast served me well, as, I pray, thou will continue to do."

Skin prickling in unease, Thierry understood the trap. "I am thy blood, and thy liegeman, my lord." It was the only answer, simply uttered.

Lord Ganelon nodded. "Just so! I tend to mine own." Lord Ganelon went on, "As is common known, the King hath been without a Champion since the death of Lord Roland—and the rest." His face expressed regret that, Thierry knew, was entirely false. "The number of worthy knights and lords for such duty is grimly reduced, and the King hath given unto me the endowment of this high office to the most worthy man that may be found.

"The King hath likewise remarked thy gallantry and leadership against the Infidel this season past when he avenged the slaughter of Roncesvalles, and the heathen treachery that wrought the same, with the sacking of Saragossa and the destruction of the deceased Emir Marsilla's ally, the Infidel Baligant." Thierry was genuinely surprised at that. Again, Lord Ganelon nodded, then began to pace a little.

"I have made my choice for that—and," he added clearly, "for other things. Thou, Sir Thierry of Leon, are hereby appointed to be King's Champion!"

Thierry's eyes went round with astonishment. "My lord!" he managed.

Lord Ganelon smiled broadly, well pleased by this reaction. "There is more beside," he said softly.

"Nay?"

"Aye, so!" Lord Ganelon inclined his head in a regal manner. "The King undertook my suggestion that the office of King's Champion be, likewise, endowed with all the fiefs and entitlements that were the Count of Brittany's! Thus," he added in a slightly drier tone, "we may honor a tradition of glory brought to this office by the late Lord Roland!"

Thierry stared at his feet, encased in soft blue leather shoes, as he digested this, trying to absorb the implications. He well knew how much his uncle still hated that butchered knight. "Well—my lord?" the Lord High Councillor prodded.

Thierry looked up. "I am—overwhelmed, my lord!" he managed, not untruthfully.

Lord Ganelon nodded. "Good!" he said bluntly, eyes keen and probing. Thierry bowed. "Good. So be it!" Lord Ganelon repeated, very softly. It was a dismissal, Thierry knew, straightening. He bowed again and turned away, feeling his uncle's dark gaze upon his back until he had passed through the oak door into the large hall beyond.

Nay, he thought, walking across the council chamber, he was reluctant now to rejoin the evening meal and the entertainment of minstrels and jugglers in the great hall where the greater population of the court was still occupied. He needed solitude.

He veered abruptly and strode from the council chamber, finding his way along corridors and up stairs that led to the great battlements of Aix La Chapelle. There, he found a spot that faced west, away from guards or any other soul, and stared out, beyond the castle walls, beyond the woods and hills that comprised the horizon, to watch the fading evening light.

The sun was new vanished, and the sky was a weaving of quiet golds and ambers that brought a last fleeting warmth to view before melting into chill blues that foretold the cold of the night to follow.

There was no sense of elation in him, Thierry knew as he leaned against a crenellation. No satisfaction in what had just been given him. Only a feeling of deepened entrapment, of honor become purest illusion.

He remembered Roncesvalles. Riding at his uncle's flank, he had stolen time to see the desecration of that high mountain gorge, watched as a few priests wound their way among the rigid dead to offer the sign of the Cross and futile blessing for the treachery that had been wrought there.

So many, burial was not even possible. Save for the few— the peers, whose corpses now lay enshrined in the new chapel that the King had caused to be erected near the keep of Aix.

And Saragossa. A futile exercise of vengeance in which he himself had played no small part. There were few enough left to lead. Lord Ganelon, ever methodical, had been the staff upon which the King had come to lean for that. Thierry recalled full well how the Lord High Councillor had summarily dispatched the highborn Infidel hostages. Had led the

King's army, and had given no quarter at the siege and sacking of that Infidel city. And it had been Thierry, with Lord Roger of Roncesvalles, who had been given the task of destroying the large, terrified household of the dead Emir Marsilla—even the women.

Butchery, to prevent a few revealing words, now strangled forever in the gurgling of throats slit from ear to ear. Women, children, eunuchs—people who knew naught of fighting. And Marsilla . . . ? That Emir was already dead from the infection of some wound got at Roncesvalles. Thierry could not forget Lord Roger's triumphant and knowing grin when they stood before Lord Ganelon later.

Thierry looked down at his strong hands. Like Pilate's, they were unclean for what he had learned, what he knew. He looked up at the last fading, deep amber streaks above the black edges of summer trees. Blood was on them.

How he regretted that Lord Roland had declined his request to join the rearguard before that fateful march, a request born of the unclear hope that there was a way to loose himself from the stranglehold Lord Ganelon had on his life—his honor. He would have died there as well. And, he thought bitterly, mayhap it would have been better so. Some shred of honor, at least.

Spain had been abandoned entirely, after Saragossa. The King's fury had dissipated in much the same manner as the fires that had gutted that city, leaving it a charred and smoldering ruin. Charlemagne had turned north, toward Aix, his mood of sober and unrelenting grief shifting, it seemed, into a preoccupation with priests and scholars, with the construction of churches, and the establishment of other forms of enlightenment to spread across the corners of Christendom.

Aye, Spain was lost. Forever, Thierry thought. The King would never undertake another southern campaign. That much was evident. And with it his uncle's hopes of a crown. Or. . . ?

It was likewise true that Lord Ganelon had risen steadily in power since their return. The staff become a rock, it seemed. His power rose from attending to matters of the other frontiers, and from rebuilding the depleted council.

Thierry splayed his fingers, then slowly closed his hands into taut fists.

"Am I thy sword now, Uncle? Or the King's?" he whis-

pered to the still air. The folly of such a question! He knew
the answer, he thought bitterly, for he knew, likewise, the
reach and grasp of Lord Ganelon's blood upon the fiefs that
were so large a part of the realm, power, seemingly, come
from the King.

King's Champion and Count of Brittany. It was a dead
man's cloak that was given him. His fingertips dug into palms,
knuckles whitening. What price was the bondage of gratitude
for such elevation to cost him?

And could he elude the paying of it? His hands unclasped
helplessly, and his expression became drawn, unhappy. Truly,
Thierry realized grimly, only Charlemagne's own life stood
between Lord Ganelon and the throne. A single thread.

A single thread . . .

A triad of limbs, Roland thought, staring down at himself
as he hung suspended by the armpits between two stout and
crudely fashioned crutches whose blunt points dug brief holes
in the sod. A single leg to thrust and brace . . . the other
curled and dangling uselessly beneath the skirts of his tunic.
It had taken him some time, and no inconsiderable effort to
make the crutches, to wrestle saplings stout enough, then,
with chips of stone, to saw and smooth.

Jerking awkwardly, he swung himself about in a half turn,
then lurched the few paces needful to reach the marble slab
upon which he had set the rest of his belongings. He had
little doubt that, given the distance from Brittany to Aix, he
would learn all that was possible of agility with crutches long
before he got there.

Belongings? They were simple enough. The cloak that Turpin had dropped by him, and the satchel that appeared slack
and empty, yet, when opened and probed, was a constant and
unnatural source of provender. And the lyre . . . It was a
wonder how it caught the sun to reflect perfect wood tones
and golden hues.

It was a month since he had come upon it and first plucked
the strings to discover the unnatural qualities of music that it
wrought. Powerful tones, pure and compelling. Magic.

Like the song that had arisen in him, melodies and verses
yet unconcluded. The lyre was another kind of enchanted
thing for him to wield. He looked toward the dark space of
the cave entrance, his expression hardening.

Not the same as the dark sword at all. It was most essentially an instrument.

The song was his own. Got of him . . . Explanation and question, purpose and—he sensed—impending justice. It held within it all that was left to him of his honor and of all the things he had known in his life. For it seemed that when he played upon the lyre, he could hear the purest empathy expressed in each note, each harmony—as if the instrument knew him . . .

Still staring toward the cave, Roland turned again and jerked his way through the surrounding undergrowth toward it. Upon reaching the entrance, he paused to stare through the surrounding vines to the gloom of the cavern beyond. Aye—she was still there.

Durandal. Mouth drawn to the same bitter hardness that had been his unthinking expression in battle, Roland entered the gloom completely, his eyes never wavering from the weapon that stood, tip down, dark and sinister, point imbedded in the granite.

Eagle-winged cross pieces that had seemed to fly of their own volition in innumerable encounters, as blood had dripped away from that flawless obsidian, lightning-laced blade. Another pace, and he stood within a hand's reach of her. And the woman hilt. Lithe and perfect, amid the illusion of restless locks of hair. A seduction against his palm. How well his hands remembered . . .

"Did I swear faithfulness to thee once?" he asked with soft menace. There was no apparent response. Nor did he expect any, beyond the seething interplay of hues that was Durandal's own color. "Or," he pursued in the same tone, "did I forswear my soul in undertaking the use of thee?" Ambition proven bitter and futile. He had been a boy then. Had not understood . . .

How clearly he saw her, now. Each detail of a face that before had been so small as to be indistinct. He stiffened, eyes narrowing. Was it but another illusion of her sorcerous nature that he sensed familiarity in those perfect features, such as might have been seen in a dream?

"Nay!" he grated. "I'll not be owned by thee again!" He drew back. "Murderer, thou art, and damned for it!"

He jerked himself about and swung recklessly through the portal into the sunlight beyond the cave. He sought the marble slab and braced himself as he snatched up lyre and satchel, then seized the cloak and caught it about his shoulders. He grasped his crutches firmly and struck out across the temple court, down the traces of steps into the depths of the clearing.

There, near the brook, he paused, turned, and stared back at the ancient ruin. Half smothered by vegetation, it was indeed lost—rightly abandoned, even by such a creature as he.

Roland jerked himself about and carefully negotiated the steep banks and difficult terrain, the entangling thickets, that lay before him, which he had once traversed with thoughtless ease astride his golden stallion, Veillantif.

East, he knew. That was the way the song impelled him to go, although, toward exactly what, he could not attempt to guess.

And, within the cavern behind the temple, the dark sword felt a shift in the power that held her. Like a change in mood, it was a moment of flight. Sufficient. He had fled. She slipped upward to loose herself from the grip of the stone that bound her, and stretched to engulf the blade and winged cross pieces of her sword form until her feet were set upon the cool floor. Then, with the sweep of a hand, she conjured a garment for herself. A chiton of deep blues and shifting purples that fell in lush, delicate folds about her from a clasp on her left shoulder, exposing her right breast, gathered about her slender waist by a simple girdle. Tempest in her eyes, her hair swirling about her like windstorms, she stepped toward the cave entrance in pursuit.

"Nay, Durandal, thou shall not!" In an instant, Turpin appeared within the portal.

The stormy-hued woman paused and glowered. "Remove thyself!" she ordered. Turpin, relaxed and youthful, shook his head and moved a pace toward her. "Nay, maiden. I shall not," he said quietly. "Nor shall thou undertake to pursue Roland at this time!"

"He is mine!" she began, with undertones of thunder.

Again Turpin shook his head, his wily, clear brown gaze never leaving her face. "I think he is not thine at all!" he said with melodious quiet. "Or do thou misunderstand how cunningly he eludes thee? What use hath a cripple for a sword?" She stood before him like the calm before a terrible storm. "Did I not caution thee, Durandal? Hast thou not already known a consequence of his power?'' he asked softly. Her eyes held sinister midnight tones, seething in waves across the hues of a winter sea. He cocked his head a little. ''Aye, I see thou hast!'' he added before she could speak. ''So. It is as I have understood! That which thou have done is not forgiven!''

''A mere human!'' She spoke in contempt. ''A nothing! It was time to dispose of him. His influence . . .''

''Just so, Durandal!'' Turpin seemed to grow a little, his tone stern. ''His influence . . . A mere man! Pity De Montglave for that! Or hast thou forgot that these humans are the children got of our kind upon those hairy beasts of long ago? Protest as thou will, the world is theirs now, and, I consider, they are creatures who belong better to it than we, being as mortal and transient as the rest! Even I, in my trafficking with them, these ages past, have seen the rightness of it, for their heritage from us is well confined by that same frail mortality that thou hold in such unwarranted contempt!''

''They are like flies that breed and spread, and desecrate!'' she growled.

Turpin's eyes widened. ''Do they so? Such is their heritage, maiden. And I consider that those attributes have served us well enough to the accomplishment of this resurrection of the blood over which we were given stewardship all these ages past! But, do thou mark me well. He is not the same as that other who fathered me and forged thee. He is new-got for all that composes him. And he is the last of us to be entire.'' He shifted, a ruffling movement. ''Even the Gods must answer to the consequences of time,'' he said softly, his ingenious gaze passing around the gloomy silence of the cavern. ''Such is the result of our congress with these children we have derived. Do thou not perceive the silence, Durandal? Even in the sanctuary, only ghosts remain.

''And for the rest, sometimes witches who are humans are given to little more than a greater sensitivity of the mind, but are otherwise powerless. Our other flesh is vanished likewise, eroded and crumbled into rubble. Statues of Gods that are vanished, maiden. There is naught else, save we three. Thou, who are a sword, and I. Only Roland is pure . . .''

''And he is mine!'' she reiterated, sharply.

Turpin sighed. ''That is the nature of thy bondage, Durandal. Not his!'' he said with definitive clarity. ''His powers are beyond any management of thine. Know that. Be assured of it!'' He stepped back a pace, and the stormy-hued woman shifted, in accompaniment to the streaks of lightning that flitted across her form. For her, it was pain.

"Nay!'' she breathed. "How much I have wrought for him. How much I have done . . .'' Then, eyes darkening, lightning fading from their depths, she stared at him. "This is not love!''

"Nor was the murder of Lord Oliver!'' Turpin's voice was certain as he stepped back again to occupy the space of the cave entrance. "Intemperate weapon that thou art, think on it!'' And in an instant, he had vanished into the daylight beyond.

With a howl Durandal flung herself after him. But as she reached the entrance to the cavern, the blend of sunlight and air seemed to solidify against her. She recoiled and stared. Nay. Nay! He could not hold her so! Again, she hurled herself at the portal and, again, was rebuffed.

Her screeches of fury reverberated through the cavern. Nay . . . Nay . . .

She was held as surely as by the hands that had forged her eons before, hands whose power was incalculable in their ability to touch, to mold, to confine, and to fit, most perfectly against her. In an instant, become a sword again, Durandal found the air, as echoed screechings died away into the gloom, and danced the blade and point of herself toward that same resolute barrier. But she was flung away, this time to clatter against granite.

She melted again into her woman form. The hands were gone—but the power was there. Intact . . .

This time, she did not arise from the floor of the cave for a long, long time.

What horses could accomplish with fluid power and rhythmical speed became an arduous, careful plodding effort over all manner of terrain. Every detail of the earth was felt through the swing and planting of crutches and underneath his functional left foot. Every rock, or rise. Dip and gully, slippery places and firm, and the resistance of all manner of vegetation to the destruction of passage.

From the first hints of dawn until the last suggestions of evening, Roland pursued his course each day, forcing the

miles to pass away behind him in much the same manner as
he had pursued each victory he had found for Charlemagne.
Moving ever eastward, Roland likewise found himself avoiding places of human habitation, the villages and manors that
were scattered through the forested land. Instead, ever conscious of his deformed condition, he kept to the woods and
copses, the wild places between areas of human encroach-
ment.

At night, he slept huddled on the ground, sometimes beneath bushes, or trees, or in the tall, flourishing grasses of
mid-summer, in much the fashion of the deer.

He did not hunt, nor grow hungry, for reluctantly aware of
the witchcraft that replenished the owl man's satchel, he ate
of the sweet bread it offered and drank from the flask that
never emptied. He needed the sustenance for flesh that ever,
pained him.

Another consequence of crippling, he thought. Of surviv-
ing that which should have destroyed him but for the witch
blood he could not escape.

Or had his life been retained for the intent of the song that
possessed him, it's incompleteness becoming more potent
with promise because of that which lay ahead. He, who was
the sum of all that had been lost at Roncesvalles. Now, no
more than a voice for the dead.

The land crawled slowly past him as Roland trudged relentlessly onward.

Late flowers bloomed, touching the edges of glades and
hills with a delicate brilliance of lavenders and whites and
golds that faded shortly, yielding to the first suggestion of
brown in the vegetation.

Roland went on, more nimble now, as he had known he
would become. Across the low and gentle valleys about Paris,
then upward, into the higher, rugged lands that surrounded
the southern regions about Aix La Chapelle.

Autumn, A.D. 779

Roland emerged from thicket and woods into a large clearing
on the hillsides immediately to the south of the great castle

of Aix, and stopped his uneven, swinging gait to hang wearily upon his crutches.

Pain rippled up the thing—he no longer thought of it as a leg—that hung from his right hip. He winced at aches that wandered beneath his skin.

Before him, about a mile distant, at last, the towers of that enormous and complex castle stood up gleaming golden in the glow of autumn's late afternoon. He saw in fastidious detail, even from such a distance, sparkling bright colors and lively designs of banners that flapped slowly in the breeze, testament to the King's presence at his court. In the woodland and broad meadows about the castle were the shadows of small cottages, and the like. He had not paid much attention, if any, before, he thought, to this evidence of the serfs that farmed the land thereabouts . . .

But then, adjusting to the new clarity and range of his vision, he had learned to attend to the most minute of details. Slowly, in keeping with his exhaustion, Roland lowered himself and his crutches to the ground and shifted awkwardly amid the new-fallen leaves to accommodate his painfully contorted right leg. Then, with a sigh of relief, he slipped the baggage he carried from his shoulders. Satchel and lyre, neither were particularly heavy, but of sufficient bulk to be burdensome.

He shifted his gaze toward the sun to stare at that ruddy orb as it hung just above the trees to the west of him. It was strange, likewise, to have discovered that he could tolerate the full force of that violent light. It was another of the subtle changes he seemed to be discovering in himself. He turned to look again at Charlemagne's great castle, and felt a curiously disturbing sense of remoteness—of alienation.

"It is not the same, I consider." A voice sounded softly behind him. Roland jerked around quickly and stared at the cloaked figure that crouched down nearby, then raised hands to thrust back the hood of his cloak.

"Thou!" Roland whispered.

Turpin smiled. "Aye!" he acknowledged with a nod.

"Thou—thou art the same white owl I have seen since my boyhood," Roland said harshly.

"That I am."

"Thou are not human!"

"As I have said," he acknowledged gently. "I am something more than human!"

"Thou art a witch—or warlock!" Roland pursued. "I saw thee change form."

Turpin ruffled his shoulders a little, ignoring Roland's belligerence. "I am not a warlock," he replied clearly. "Though, I must seem much as thou would imagine such to be!"

Roland frowned. "Thou are magical!" he said roughly. "Such is the province of witches and the like."

"Magic?" Turpin's voice softened. " 'Tis a simpleton term for abilities and knowledge beyond the perceptions of mortal men." Roland continued to stare. Turpin's youth, he perceived suddenly, was an illusion. Yet there were timeless things in those great bird eyes. An inexhaustible fund of experience lurked there—and cunning—and knowledge of things beyond human understanding. Even his movements manifested an elegant patience that suggested time had a different mode of passage for him.

"And I am a bastard," Roland said brutally. "Got of witch and human. Like the blood in me that I despise, it is a condition that seems ever to summon magical, witching things . . ." He glanced down at his twisted and shriveled right leg. "They are damnation . . ." His tone grew husky, abrupt. "Ever, I have tried to find honor, and faith, and manhood. Now I am a man who cannot die. A murderer. Mayhap, because of that self-same blood, I am without a soul . . ." He looked up. Turpin sighed heavily and glided to his feet, shifting restlessly. Roland's golden eyes followed his every move. "But," he stressed in the same vehement tone. "For all of that, I am a man! Crippled or nay, I am a man!" His voice died away.

Turpin's gaze did not waver at this determined declaration. Instead, his large eyes gleamed dark with knowledge. "Thou are whatsoever thou will to be, Roland," he said quietly after a time. "That is thy power . . ."

Roland stiffened further at the suggestiveness of the comment. "I am a man!" he affirmed again with a deadly quiet of his own. "I am a man!" Then, with the suddenness of a sword blow, *"What art thou?"* Turpin gathered his cloak about him, gaze unwavering. "What art thou?" Roland demanded.

"I am thy father!" Turpin said clearly, then turning on his

heel, he strode away to disappear in the deep embrace of surrounding trees.

Father . . . ? Shaken to his innermost depths, Roland stared after the vanished owl man. His father . . . ?

He did not move for a long time.

Darkness came and the air grew cold. Frost hovered above the ground like a restless spirit, touching branches and those few crumpled leaves still upon them, and the tips of tall, withering grasses.

The moon rose from the east to glow, round and full with its own silver luminescence as it pursued its elusive dance with the sun.

And the great castle of Aix, still and unmoving in the night, gleamed with a chill radiance in the distance.

Roland sat there, huddled in the folds of the cloak, staring. Turpin—his father? The shock of that was devastating. He had long ceased to think of who was his male parent. His mother, clear in his memory, had been all the witch-source he had needed to explain himself. And he hated her for her cruelties and spite.

The moon rose high overhead, and the night became as another sort of day, brilliant with silvers and blacks. His father . . . ? Slowly, Roland moved past shock, even disbelief, into an acceptance that had little to do with logic and reason, but was something felt as explanation for the increasing evidence of his inhuman blood and deathless existence.

It could be of little wonder to him now that the trust and convictions of Christian faith had ever eluded him. But . . . he frowned ferociously as he stared at distant banners gone slack and dark in the windless night, and remembered Oliver—other things had not. Honor . . .

Justice . . .

Aix beckoned.

"On the morrow, it will be resolved," he whispered after a time, and reached for the lyre, held it close against him, his fingertips delicately caressing the arms of the instrument.

TWENTY

How very different it was Roland thought as he struggled to keep from being toppled by an impatient serf with a load of firewood, to hobble across the drawbridge of Aix La Chapelle, then to enter that magnificent castle as he had before.

Gone was the nobility. And the high office that had scattered humbler folk without his notice. Gone, likewise, was Veillantif, the gallant stallion that had served him so faithfully.

A guard glowered suspiciously at him, unable, in the afternoon light and the shadows of the portcullis, to see Roland's face beneath the hood he had drawn over his head, then relaxed his expression as he caught sight of the lyre against Roland's hip, half concealed by the folds of his cloak.

Roland hobbled slowly on. There was little need to hurry, and paused in the middle of the great outer bailey to lean for a moment and look about him. Familiar activity surrounded him. Things he had long forgot to notice were now intriguingly clear. Groomsmen tending horses. Other servants preoccupied with the tasks of butchering and salting meat for winter storage. Or stacking fodder for the priceless warhorses stabled within the castle walls.

A bailiff, mounted on lathered palfrey, paused to exchange words with a monk whose arms were filled with scrolls of recorded business. A blacksmith hammered red-hot iron in one corner.

Roland set his crutches and swung himself onward, making his unhurried way across the outer court, shabby and ignored by busy folk, through the gates that led to the large and well-remembered expanse of the inner bailey. He paused again to hang upon his crutches. He stared up at the intricate structure that was the great keep of Aix, cold stone that glowed warm in the afternoon sun.

Someone went past him, hesitating to stare, then shifting away to give him a wide berth. Roland stiffened, conscious suddenly that he was no longer a part of this. He turned to watch knights and squires to his right. The highborn, playing at the skills of war. As he had.

He looked away from that part of the court, his eyes coming to rest on the large chapel where he had spent well-remembered, troubled hours of futile prayer.

But that structure was gone, and in its place stood a new building. High-reaching and elegant, this new chapel was round, and solid.

Roland hobbled slowly across the court toward the chapel, up steps difficult to negotiate, and through a vast oaken door, partly opened, as though in invitation.

Crutches that seated well on turf, or woodland sod, now slithered upon the smooth, polished stone floor of the chapel. Roland stopped carefully under a flawless arching of stone that separated the aisle from the large central choir beyond.

Gone were the nave and transepts of his memory, and the choir and altar he had known. This new chapel was completely different from the one it replaced. Above the lowest aisle that encircled the whole was another contained by an elegant tracery of worked bronze. Slim, elegant columns rose up from this, toward a third and narrower balcony that underlay the high, vaulted roof that reached across to cover the open space of the choir itself.

Gone, as well, were the pews of polished wood. Instead, the floor of the choir was bare of any furnishing or ornament. An open silent place.

Daylight came through the glazing that filled the single, arched window high above the altar, and scattered into soft rainbow filaments as it touched silent columns and dusted the stone floor. Like ghosts, shadows of the Cross angled to lie like illusions, caught in reflective patterns of diffused sunlight. And above the altar, an ornately carved wooden figure hung.

Christ, Roland thought as he stared at it—who had, at least, died.

He looked away, feeling the chill of the air. This was not a chapel to the glory of God, he thought. It was a place for the remembrance of death. He looked at the floor of the aisle that passed in a wide curve around the choir to his left, and saw that there were marked stones set in the floor. Moving carefully, he swung himself on his crutches in that direction, pausing to look at each one.

Tombs. Each with a single name engraved in clear relief and, below it, the arms of the man whose remains lay beneath. Roland knew them all. The peers. Those lords and gallant knights who had fought with him at Roncesvalles.

Slowly, he passed along the curve of the aisle, pausing to offer silence to each one. As he reached the last, his eyes widened. This one was set beside a pair of high, long tombs such as were made for Kings in the final bay of the aisle that adjoined the sanctuary.

The name upon this stone was that of a woman.

"Aude the Fair," the inscription read. "Blessed in Death for a most Faithful Love." Roland flinched. Nay. Yet it was clear enough. Oliver's sister, and his own betrothed lady. How could this be . . . ? He had barely seen her, had endeavored to avoid her. He flinched again at the memory of awe-filled woman eyes that had frightened him so thoroughly, and felt a leaden, miserable weight in the pit of his belly. Nay. Had she died for him? He swallowed, troubled, and shifted away to stare at the final pair of tombs.

Waist high and made of the whitest marble, they were set in perfectly parallel alignment, illuminated by the fireglow of sconces set in high bronze holders. Intricately carved with all manner of ornamentation, each bore the effigy of a man, likewise engraved in flawless detail. Compelled now, Roland swallowed awkwardly as he lurched to stare down at the first.

A knight, with all the accoutrements of high estate. Roland's breathing became harshly uneven as his eyes traveled up the figure. Past spurred feet that rested on a shield with the arms of Brittany inscribed delicately into the surface. Past the folds of a surcoat, and the ingenious rendering of chain mail, to the left hand that lay loosely holding a familiar helm.

And the right—that was clasped about the hilt of a mighty eagle-winged sword.

Durandal. Roland leaned forward and felt cold shock as he stared at the white carven head that lay amid cunningly wrought waves of hair.

To see his own lips—his own strong jaw, clear, straight nose, and high, defined cheeks. The eyes that were so peacefully closed . . .

Unblemished . . . Roland reached up with his fingers to touch the few inches of beard that he had long forgot.

Is this my corpse then? he thought. My grave that I cannot occupy? And what forgotten man lay entombed and decaying in his place beneath so much exquisite workmanship? Roland frowned and touched his own cheek, shadowed by the hood of the cloak he wore.

Beneath his fingers, his skin moved like some thin illusion over—nay. Not bones at all, but—something else.

His eyes widened as he stared at his own effigy and felt the contours of his flesh. And he fleetingly recalled another carven face, much the same, belonging to a statue that had lain on a marble altar, bound beneath multitude briars . . .

An ancient heathen God that had held a lyre against one hip. Roland gasped, his fingers touching the instrument suspended against his own flank.

A lyre . . . This lyre.

"What am I?" he rasped, close to terror, clutching at the crutches as pain surged through him. "What am I?"

Only echoes answered as he swung violently toward the other tomb.

Oliver, he knew at once . . . And looked down at that equally perfect effigy. Oliver turned to stone. He gasped again. Oliver . . . Not even a shade to haunt. Neatly and eternally asleep—his beloved marble face serene.

Absolutely dead.

Grief welled up in Roland as he reached to touch the image of his friend's face, then drew his hand away with an awkward jerk. Stone and Oliver . . . ?

They were not the same. Oliver had been a man.

Roland clasped his crutches and pulled himself away, uncaring of clumsiness or the smooth treachery of the chapel floor as he sought exit from the unresolvable doom of that place.

Like pain, the song inside him was welling a clarion summons. He must needs find the great hall—the King.

"How fares our young liege, Majesty?" A gentle question, and Charlemagne removed his gaze from the roast grouse and venison in their rich sauces of herbs and apples, and looked at his right where Lord Ganelon sat, face concerned.

"He is frail, as ever," the King answered quietly. Lord Ganelon sighed and looked toward his wine cup.

"I pray . . ." he offered. Charlemagne's hard mouth shifted to suggest the fleeting hints of a smile.

"For that, we are grateful, old friend," he replied, then let his eyes travel across the great hall, across the lords and ladies that comprised his court, many, the officers of government. They were all settled to indulge their appetites for both the evening's feasting, and the entertainment that was more oft than not, mere accompaniment to conversation. Interestingly, the King noticed, his new Champion, Lord Thierry, also sat with a manner of quiet and sober brooding.

Sons . . . Charlemagne shifted a little. This new child got of his year-old marriage was unhealthy and fretful. Charlot did not have the look of a boy who would reach manhood, and yet, this was his legitimate firstborn. His entitled heir . . . Nay, young Charlot was not at all like that first, incest-got seed. Now dead, struck down at the gates of full manhood by Infidel treachery.

Roland . . . His grief was worse for its absolute privacy. A bitter cup to drink from, Charlemagne had come to know full well. How carefully he had paved the way for kingship, relying on time to temper ferocity into experienced strength. How he had loved the beauty of his unknowing child, and the temperament he understood so thoroughly. Aye, Roland would have had it all . . .

Now, there was only the weak, thin infant Charlot to bring reason to the future, and Charlemagne, well aware that he was past his own first youth, knew that the time to prepare would be increasingly precarious.

The reality of kingship bore little resemblance to the expectations of ambitious princehood . . .

He let his eyes settle on a familiar minstrel, perched in his usual manner on a footstool to one side of the central area between the heavy oak tables. He was wisely contriving an assortment of light and pleasant melodies upon his harp to accompany the feasting in progress. Charlemagne, dagger in hand, speared a capon and raised it toward his mouth.

"Ho! What is this?" he heard Lord Ganelon murmur beside him, and looked up to see a tall, bedraggled figure hobble clumsily upon a pair of crutches from behind one of the stone columns at the far end of the hall. Others began to notice as well, conversation melting away as the cripple lurched forward to a place some fifteen feet before the King. Not displeased by the distraction, Charlemagne set down the capon and leaned back in his chair. The cripple attempted an awkward bow, his face shrouded entirely by the hood of his unkempt cloak. Curious murmurs rippled through a diverted gathering . . .

"There is charity for beggars in the kitchens!" Lord Ganelon pronounced sternly as he leaned forward. The cripple did not respond, but hung upon his crutches and drew from the folds of his cloak a lyre of brilliant and astonishing craftsmanship. A golden thing, priceless. His head moved, and the gleam of a tawny beard showed below his hood.

"I am a jongleur, Great Charlemagne . . ." The cripple's voice was likewise astonishing, deeply melodious and strong. "I am come from distant parts to offer a song for the King's pleasure!"

Intrigued, Charlemagne leaned forward, quelling Lord Ganelon's intended intervention with a glance.

"What is thy name, minstrel?" he asked.

"I am nameless, Majesty."

"Let us behold thy face then?" But the cripple shook his head.

"I am deformed, my liege. The sight of my face . . ." Charlemagne frowned, there was an elusive familiarity about that voice . . . Then he inclined his head in acceptance as he noted a hideously twisted right leg, the hunched stance of the man.

"So be it, minstrel," he said clearly. "Do thou sing for us then." Again, the beggarly man tried to bow. Then he moved back, lurching to his former place at the back of the hall. Why so far distant? Charlemagne wondered. The court minstrel, offended, sat still and rigid with indignation, his own instrument rendered silent by the King's will.

Curious eyes followed the cripple as he set himself to lean

between his crutches, propped against a stone column, then drew his lyre farther forward, setting it against his left hip . . .

Am I dead then, after all? Roland wondered. To feel this way? To feel this frozen bitter hardness inside? This strange form of consciousness, where all is perceived, and all is remote.

He felt power gathering—the song held feelings in thrall, awaiting release.

Tucked against a far column in the great hall, his fingers found the strings of the lyre and began to pluck them as, inside him, the song swelled, rose up. The first threads of haunting and tragic melody began to find their way across the hall, filling spaces, demanding attention.

From the shadowed protection of his hood, Roland saw the faces of the highborn turn toward him. So many. Some familiar. Others new, filling the voids left by the ambushed dead of Roncesvalles.

And Lord Ganelon, beside the King whose features were more sharply etched than he remembered, his expression as ever carefully arranged. Nearby, along the high table, Roland recognized Lord Thierry. Richly attired over his hauberk, wearing the broidered arms of Brittany upon his breast.

So, have thou my place now? Roland wondered, seeing changes in that well-remembered face. Unhappiness, and a new sternness that had not been present before.

Voices stilled one by one as attention became fixed upon the deformed minstrel caught by strains of purest music that wove richly poignant spells in the senses of every soul present. Even the court minstrel relaxed, and bent his attention to learning that which was about to be sung.

Roland closed his eyes. He had no need, or wish, to see any of them who made the warp and weave of a tapestry to which he no longer belonged. There was only the song to slip upon the shuttle of his voice into the whole. He surrendered himself to the rising power of it, yielding with the instruments of his hands and voice.

This time, he knew, the song would find its own course. This time, it would move toward resolution with the very conviction of a fate that it alone would define.

* * *

Food was forgot as the cripple began to sing. The court grew still, losing even the awareness of breathing as they listened, then recognized.

Names. Places. Reality.

Lord Ganelon sat in rigid silence, and glanced once at the King. Charlemagne was a silent silver giant, his face marble hard, eyes the clearest blue ice.

A little farther away, Lord Thierry bowed his head as the color drained from his face. He listened to the truth, now become lyrics and music. That which he knew at last being revealed.

The crippled minstrel sang the triumph of Charlemagne over Cordoba, sang of Marsilla and the embassy of Blancandrin. The appointing of Lord Ganelon. And more. Like a spell, the song wove exquisite specifics on the discourses of treachery between Christian lord and heathen princes, clarified motives of jealousy and hate . . .

And then there were passages of that vile and irreparable massacre of so many valiant and loyal vassals. Names again . . . There was none who did not recognize the accomplishments and tragic end of each one of those gallant dead whose struggles and achievements were expounded with such clarity.

Even the King, whose face had gone as silver as his hair as he listened . . .

How strange it was, Roland thought from some remote and watchful place in his mind, as the words slipped from his throat of their own volition—how vague the ambush at Roncesvalles had become in his memory until now.

Had he seen so much then . . . ? Each triumph that made of them a formidable, if outnumbered, force. Each death . . .

But the song had him in its service now, and he was startled to feel it shift as Oliver's death became yet another struggle with the Infidel, and not the murder he knew it to be. Why not this truth as well?

Then the song led him to his own dying, and of a sudden Roland understood that, bound into melody and verse, it was all that made of him a normal, human man. There was no place for witching things in the song. Or spirits. Only men . . .

In a fashion, he felt himself depart that corpse he had not

become upon that bleak and abandoned battlefield. Now the song was free of him as it told truths he could not know . . .

Of Charlemagne's bitter grief. Of the bodies that were brought to Aix for entombment . . . And the bloody vengeance that leveled Saragossa . . . and the abandonment of Spain.

Even the death of his own betrothed, the Lady Aude.

Then, like an eagle high upon the air, the song paused. Roland opened his eyes as the phrases gathered themselves in his throat like updrafts held beneath the knowing wings of a bird as it prepared, with full conviction, to dive. His gaze focused on Lord Ganelon. The dark lord . . .

With unwavering vision of absolute clarity, the eagle verses plunged, plummeting like destiny toward the moments that lay before them all.

Roland saw Lord Ganelon's face gone grey with horror as he sang of accusation—and a trial.

Lord Thierry's face changed likewise, becoming youthful and relaxed, as though relieved of a profound burden. His lips even curved into a slight smile.

With the same pure certainty, still staring at the new King's Champion, Roland sang, for the last, of combat.

And, almost softly . . . of execution.

The words were gone. Roland's hands stilled upon the lyre, silencing it, letting it slip to its resting place against his body.

It was done.

"This is witchcraft!" Lord Ganelon roared violently. "It is treason and malice to so defile our lost and glorious dead who sought to defend our liege lord and Christendom against Infidel dishonor!" Charlemagne did not move. Instead, he stared at the crippled jongleur, caught between a brutal resurgence of his grief and sheer incredulity.

"Not so!" Lord Thierry rose from his place, his voice clarion-strong. He nimbly moved around the table to stand before the King. "Let no man forget the justice that God hath brought here today through the voice of this minstrel! I, Thierry, Lord of Leon and Brittany, do bear witness of mine own knowledge to the absolute truth contained in this Song of Roland. For my office of King's Champion, and to the defense of the honor of our most Christian liege, Charlemagne, thereby, I accuse thee, Lord Ganelon de Maganze, of highest and most vile treason!''

Lord Ganelon lunged to his feet, hand going to the hilt of his sword, face contorting with rage.

"Nay!" he bellowed. "I will not bear my loyalty, nor my honor to be so impugned!" Moving with startling speed, he strode across the hall, unsheathing his sword as he went, then raising it as he advanced upon the unmoving cripple. "Let there be an end to the mischief this—thing wreaks among us!" he roared. But Lord Thierry moved with lightning speed as well, his own sword screeching as he loosed it, then brought it up to strike Lord Ganelon's weapon away.

"Thou shall not murder the truth, my lord!" he barked loudly, quickly stepping between the two. "This jongleur is in my own custody!" He turned the point of his sword toward his uncle's breast and looked toward the King. "Majesty . . . ?"

So—this is the way of it, Roland thought as he stared into the face of Lord Ganelon from the concealment of his hood. Then he too looked toward the silver King.

Charlemagne rose slowly to his feet, gigantic in his sternness and the icy penetration of his stare as it traveled about the hall, then settled upon the Lord High Councillor. Not a soul stirred, each caught in the realization that the concluding verses of the song were already becoming events . . .

The King removed from his place and walked with the same stern demeanor until he too stood before the cripple. Lord Ganelon's color faded slowly to grim pallor as he met Charlemagne's gaze. And Roland shifted a little, sufficient to change the shadows that concealed his face as the King glanced toward him.

Charlemagne saw—his eyes went wide—then terrible with pain as Roland bowed his head once more.

The King spun on his heel, shifting to once again confront Lord Ganelon, and to block any view the other might have of Roland.

"My lord," he said in frigid tones. "We mark the force of thy distemper in this—unusual circumstance. Likewise, we are compelled to notice that unhealthy hue upon thy features that speaks beyond any refutation of fears and secrets held against us in thy duties.'' Lord Ganelon's face lost the last remnants of color and became brutal, eyes glinted as his brows gathered. But the King continued. "My lord," he thundered. "We must think thou are found out! And by our will, these murders will, before God, have their just due!"

Charlemagne turned a little, subjecting Thierry to a penetrating stare, then murmured softly, "Do thou remove this minstrel to the safety of our chambers, my lord." Then he strode back the way he had come, seeking his place upon the dais.

"So be it!" Lord Ganelon growled, his dark eyes fixed venomously upon his nephew's face. "I, who have ever been the King's most loyal servant, am now condemned by the fantasies of a crippled man's ballad!" This time, Thierry met his uncle's look with assurance.

"Wasted words, my lord!" he said crisply. "We know the truth, we two. And it is past time for the rest of Christendom to be enlightened on the same!" He raised an arm, curtly summoning guardsmen, and turned to the cripple, attempting to give aid by taking one of his arms. But Roland shrugged away the offer and shifted on his crutches. "Come with me," Lord Thierry told him quietly, and began walking, slowly, with a particular courtesy, just ahead of him. A slight smile flickered across the corners of Roland's mouth as he swung his crutches and obediently followed. He felt the stares of the court touch his back. Now, he knew, pandemonium would ensue. Argument, and defense . . .

It did not matter. Lord Ganelon was doomed. Dark lord, he thought—into darkness, I dispatch thee.

A look was sufficient to move the guard to open the oak door that led to the King's private antechamber. Thierry stepped aside to make way for the cripple.

"As the King wills, do thou stay here," he said quietly, then followed that ungainly and bedraggled man as the cripple hobbled to the center of the richly appointed room and stopped. His head made a slight, nodding movement. Thierry's brows flickered at the lack of words, then he stepped forward, wondering what the King had seen to make such determined pronouncement. Something, he thought by instinct, beyond his own accusations that had yet to be given the endorsement of testimony. He stepped closer still, then reached suddenly to jerk back the cripple's hood.

"Nay!" he breathed, the blood draining from his face. Shivering violently as he stared at that unmistakable countenance . . . "My lord—Roland!"

Roland flinched and jerked back as Thierry's shocked eyes stared into his, then moved down the wreckage of his body. Nay, not like this, he thought. Not like this . . . But Thierry's eyes rose again to meet his own.

"So—the King knew thee!" he half whispered. "And thou art alive!" Again Roland winced, then reached clumsily for his hood, pulling it over his head once more.

"Roland, Count of Brittany, is dead, my lord!" he grated. Lord Thierry froze, hesitated. His eyes went soft, confused and searching. "Lord Roland is dead!" Roland repeated harshly. "All that remains of him is a song!" Still the new King's Champion did not move, but continued to search the shadows beneath Roland's hood. Then he looked again at the rest, the leg, especially.

At last he looked up, his face changed markedly from all that Roland remembered of him.

"I understand," he said with unfamiliar gentleness. Then, with a cautious hesitation, "I cannot forget this day. For by thy song, minstrel, thou hast given me my honor at last." He shifted away, and Roland stared after him. Lord Thierry turned again as he reached the door, his demeanor marked by a new dignity.

"Do thou await the King's will here, minstrel," he said, and then he was gone. The door closed by the hand of the guard beyond it.

Roland stared for a moment, then slumped to hang on his crutches. He closed his eyes for a time, then opened them abruptly. As the song had said—Lord Roland, Count of Brittany, was indeed—a dead man.

What was he now . . . ? A ghost? Fate that had spun the silk of destiny with infinitely greater intricacy than any spider could manage had stripped from him all that had been the sum of his life. He bowed his head, and breathed an excruciating sigh.

TWENTY-ONE

A rippling passed through the company of lords as Lord Thierry reentered the hall and strode with newly-found efficiency toward the King. He stopped, then bowed, turned on one heel and raised a hand to point direct at Lord Ganelon's breast.

"Majesty, again, for my office of King's Champion, I accuse Lord Ganelon De Maganze of highest treason!" Those assembled shifted restlessly in their seats, some rising to fill the space in the center of the hall. Factions were evolving. And in the midst of it, Lord Ganelon stood with furious pride, his dignity, as with his sword, stripped away by the four guards that flanked him. His dark eyes glinted in outrage as, abruptly, he spoke.

"It is not treason, Majesty, to seek vengeance for injury wrought!" His response rang across the hall. "Ever, this Lord Roland was bent to seek my destruction. To injure me for some imagined boyhood resentment!" Charlemagne's blue eyes were unreadably cold, and Lord Ganelon's glowering became more baleful as he looked about him to the lords and knights gathered closer. "It was I who was sent by his contriving among the Infidel. And, it was I who was compelled to purchase that offer of peace to thee, my liege, by the promise of his life that they sought above all else! Devil, they called him. The Djinn of the Dark Sword! Even the Infidel knew that Lord Roland's prowess was unnatural!

"What treason have I wrought that I am accused by a song? By witchcraft of a most unchristian kind?"

Thierry turned to the King then. "Majesty," he said clearly, "the very duties of my service to Lord Ganelon are sufficient testament to my convictions in this matter, and I will verify that God's own truth was heard here. This man hath indeed wrought the death of Lord Roland and the rest at Roncesvalles by treasonous conspiracy." He spun to face his uncle. "That Lord Roland was the King's own good vassal, pledged and proven in loyalty to serve high office, Lord Ganelon, was sufficient to warrant his safety from any spite of thine! Do thou mark me, for the Infidel feared Lord Roland because he so ably served our liege and our Christian cause. Nay, my lord! It will not stand. Should such vengeance as thou hast wrought to the cost of so many good lives be right or just, then who among us, with such license as thou did exercise, should remain alive to serve the King, and our Christian duty?

"I say again—thou are traitor!" There was silence in the hall as the echoes of that word died away. Then, from among the company, Lord Pinnabel of Sorence strode forward and bowed before the King. Straightening, he turned a little to scowl at Lord Thierry. Another, Thierry knew, who was risen high because of the Lord High Councillor's favor.

"I proclaim it is not so, Majesty!" Lord Pinnabel stated. "Or if there be some warrant to the charge, I pray that Lord Ganelon's good repute and honest service for all these years past is not forgot or dispatched by this singular error. Lord Roland and the rest are dead. Let there be an end to this! I say, that for the same good service that hath long been given, let Lord Ganelon's honor be restored and these charges forgot—"

"Nay, my liege!" Thierry cut across the other's speech. "Lord Roland and the rest were good and loyal men all to thee. To betray them into slaughter was, indeed, treason. Nor will I recant my charge against the King's interest. That which was wrought with such disgrace to the honor of Christendom may well be contrived again. The traitor"—he turned to frown at Lord Ganelon—"like the fox, may not change his fundamental nature." Lord Ganelon's eyes locked with those of his nephew, and he paled further. The weapon he had forged was now turned upon him. Never had he seen or imagined his nephew so strong or powerful.

"Liar!" Lord Pinnabel retorted promptly, drawing a gauntlet from the pair at his belt. This he flung down at Thierry's feet. "I say thou lie, my lord, and will contest this matter with thee to final resolution!" To the surprise of all, Lord Thierry, never known for boldness, smiled and bent, gracefully scooping up the glove. He turned to the King.

"So be it decided!" Charlemagne's voice was a frigid wind across the gathering, his quickness of response suggesting that he took private part with his Champion. He stood. "God's will shall decide this matter with the rising of the new sun! Let those who fight for this resolution prepare themselves with honest vigil and open soul to the revelation of the truth!" He nodded his head to the guards about Lord Ganelon, and they moved to bind him. Lord Ganelon shuddered with rage and indignation, his dark eyes still upon the King's cold face as he was dragged roughly away.

Lord Pinnabel and Lord Thierry looked at each other, then bowed in unison before Charlemagne. One of them would die—and they both knew it. They watched him nod, before he rose, then, in a sweeping of cloak and robes, strode across the hall and out of the great hall, dismissing his guard as they moved to follow him.

How much he had seen upon that harsh, swarthy face, Charlemagne thought as he continued along shadowed corridors, up winding steps. Kings may have no friends . . . Thou knew . . . I saw it in thee. All this time, thou hast known, and have fought my will by subversion.

What had become of boyhood bonds? Roland . . .

The sentry on duty beside the door to the King's private quarters struggled to conceal a look of surprise as Charlemagne hesitated before that portal, then proceeded through it with uncharacteristic caution. He closed the door, aware of the bedraggled cripple that waited for the King within.

With a bitter sense of tragedy, Charlemagne paused and looked across the luxury of his apartment chambers to the figure of the cripple who stood some three or four paces from the hearth fire that warmed the room. Slowly, he walked toward the other man.

"Thou are here . . ." he said quietly.

"As thou did command, Majesty!" The response was calm, and the voice richer than he remembered, coming from the shadow-hidden face. Closer, and the King raised a hand and reached for the hood. Roland flinched, moved back.

"I must know the truth!" Charlemagne grated harshly, discarding the royal prerogative. Again he jerked the hood back to reveal that which he had glimpsed before . . .

Golden eyes stared warily back at him. And the face was the same though terribly gaunt. Still—vibrantly alive. Bearded now. Hair no different, as thick as ever, and as tawny gold, with the same amber lights flickering through it.

"Roland . . ." Charlemagne whispered unevenly, his eyes traveling lower to the crippled leg that hung from the right hip and protruded below the shabby tunic. Roland winced visibly as the King's eyes came back to meet his own, filled with something he had never seen before—a grief that was far worse to witness than to hear about.

"Roland—Kingslayer—is dead, Majesty!" he tried awkwardly. But Charlemagne's eyes deepened as they continued to stare into his own.

"Not so." A quiet contradiction. Heart pounding unhappily, Roland tightened his grasp upon his crutches and looked down at himself.

"What else, then, my liege?" he asked, painfully brutal. "The rest are dead. I alone did not receive that singular honor—or relief!" He looked up into Charlemagne's unwavering gaze.

"I am thankful!" the King whispered. "I am thankful . . ." he repeated more softly.

"Whyfore?" Roland rasped. "I am no longer capable of those knightly things that are useful to thy service." Charlemagne turned away—paced a little, restlessly.

"Thou have served me again, for thou have wrought justice." He spoke quietly. "Living justice—the truth of thy song is beyond any refutation!" The King turned then to face Roland once more. "Such a song may never be forgot . . ." Roland tried again.

"It is my final service, my liege, to render just vengeance for the dead of Roncesvalles, and to keep Lord Ganelon from stealing that which rightfully is only thine." Charlemagne nodded. He had begun to suspect that was Ganelon's purpose. He had not cared. And Roland, irreparably damaged, still was before him, hanging on those repellent crutches, still regarding him with that same devotion. "The song was another death warrant for me, my liege," Roland tried. "Mayhap, through it, my service may continue in some fashion." He shrugged clumsily. Charlemagne did not move. Roland inhaled awkwardly, his face revealing pain, and acceptance. "At least by it, I am given an honorable death—as befits—an honorable man . . . There is no place here for me, such as I have become. And, I *am* witch-got . . ." Charlemagne's face tightened at this last.

"Not so!" he grated abruptly, striding closer. Roland stiffened. "Not so!" Roland's eyes widened. "Roland the Bastard . . ." the King spoke on. "That appellation is true enough, God forgive me! But witch-gotten thou are not, nor were thou ever so!"

"Aye, Majesty," he countered in a hard voice. "I am witch-got. I know it true." Charlemagne shook his silver head.

"Nay, Roland, thou are not." He felt taut with pain, with a depth of feeling he had long sensed, but had never felt in full before. "I know far better than thou the truth. Thou are the firstborn son of my loins."

Roland froze, even his breathing becoming suspended. "Aye," the King continued, his voice reflecting profound, unshared burdens. "Thou are my son, got of my loins upon the body of my own sister—a child of temptation and the most tragic sin of incest!"

"Nay!" Roland rasped, feeling that peculiar painful tautness in his skin again. "Nay . . . ?" he repeated. "It is not possible?"

"Is it not?" Charlemagne whispered, suddenly seeming to be an aging, lonely man, not at all a prince. "Nonetheless, it is God's own truth!" He shifted, aimlessly, then held out a hand that found Roland's shoulder. "The sins of intemperate youth . . ." he breathed. "Thou cannot know how well I watched thee all these years. Or of the pride I have known in thee, seeing thee grow to strong, if willful, manhood. Or how I have made use of every opportunity thou have brought me to give thee such honor as is due the prince thou are surely bred to be. Some redemption in that, I pray . . ." His hand fell away. "I would have made a king of thee. Christendom

would have come to thee in the end, for I have known thou
were strong enough to hold it . . .''

Roland could not answer. Instead, racked with brutal feeling, he stood unmoving, hardly breathing. Truths that he had
somehow known—had felt, without ever understanding. He
drooped, head bowing, eyes on the stone floor.

Impossible . . . It was impossible? Turpin the owl—Turpin
the witch—had claimed his paternity likewise. How could he
be got of two men? But the one was not a man at all. Long
distant memories flitted across his mind. His first encounter
with this silver King. The hag who had mothered him . . .
Things she had shrieked at him . . .

Slowly, his face haggard, Roland looked up again. Charlemagne, the man, waited with unfamiliar and humble patience. Roland swallowed raggedly.

"There is only one," he whispered, "that I have loved so
well as thee." As he said this, he knew he was irreparably
removed. Dead, in another fashion. Charlemagne inclined his
head. He had known that too . . .

"Aye—Roncesvalles," he murmured grief and bitterness.

Roland stiffened. "That Roland is gone, my liege," he said
more clearly, feeling the echoes of the song pass through
him. "This creature before thee now cannot be the same."

Frigid blue eyes locked with gold as silence held them both
for a time. Gone were the boundaries between King and vassal. Gone were all the confused devotion and defiance that
had compelled Roland's life. Gone like Oliver, irretrievably
deceased.

And, Lord Ganelon—had he known the whole? He, too,
was a dead man. Roland's fingers clasped about the hafts of
his crutches. He moved slowly, lurching past Charlemagne
toward the door of the chamber. He paused then, and glanced
back at the silver King who stood—isolated as ever. He inhaled deeply, feeling something ease within him.

His love for his King was still there, deep within him.
Roland smiled a little, then passed through the door into the
night.

Charlemagne stared at the space where the crippled Roland
had been, then found a chair and sank into it with the hesi-
tance of an old man. Like the song that had brought definition
to everything, so many years were likewise brought to irrev-

ocable conclusion. Griefs? Ancient, private guilts were meaningless now, discarded by Roland himself. But so were his feelings and hopes for the future.

He spread his capable and long-fingered hands. Stared at them. The power of kingship was still firmly clasped therein, and—Charlemagne looked up again, his face composed to its usual remoteness—that was the sum of it.

Both resolution, and a tale that could not be forgotten by men, Roland's song was as eternal as the future itself. An apt memorial . . .

A deafening ringing shot across his skull, and Lord Thierry shook his head, aware of wetness as Lord Pinnabel's sword swept away to prepare for another blow. Thierry staggered and blinked away the dark spots before his eyes, catching a glimpse of Pinnabel's triumphant grin amid a world that skewed with sudden violence and tried to spin about him.

"Yield!" he heard the other man bark. Death . . . ? Nay.

"Aaaaarrrrgh!" Thierry roared as he lunged forward and brought his sword up into a powerful arc that swept across Pinnabel's guard, then down, through the other man's surprised counterstroke, to feel his weapon slam into the crest of his foe's helm. The casque split. Lord Pinnabel stared in astonishment and began to fold as blood gushed, and the steel covering for his skull fell away. Unbalanced, Thierry barely kept his own footing, feeling a dim surprise as he watched his opponent fall.

Before him, blood and brains erupted through sweat-matted hair. He had won. He jerked his sword loose and stared for a moment, breath coming in great, heaving gulps. He had won . . .

Slowly, realizing the moisture trickling down the sides of his face was his own blood, Lord Thierry turned to look at the King.

The crowd of highborn people, gathered about to witness God's will through this trial of strength, was silent to a man. Only Charlemagne spoke.

"God's will be done!" the King said with a somber absence of expression. "Let the punishment for proven treason be worthy of the crime!"

Smothering a surge of weakness that was a combination of both injury and exhaustion from what had been a long and arduously intense battle, Lord Thierry turned to look at the former Lord High Councillor.

Bound in manacles of iron, his clothing in disarray, his face grimly ashen, Lord Ganelon was without a shred of his former power or dignity. He was abruptly seized by his guards, then hauled roughly across the trampled meadow toward the four restless warhorses that had been brought forth. Thierry felt no pity as he shifted to watch his uncle being flung down and stripped to naked vulnerability. Ropes were bound about each ankle and wrist . . .

Nor had he any wish to witness this, Thierry knew as well. He turned away and, sword still in hand, walked carefully away, toward the King who acknowledged him with a grim nod. The warhorses snorted and squealed, and began to pull. Thierry did not flinch at the first of Lord Ganelon's screams, clearly audible above the grunts of the warhorses who lunged with all their considerable strength in four different directions.

Screams that reverberated off the impassive stone purity of Aix La Chapelle. He looked up, feeling honor at last, staring at the King.

Unknowable Charlemagne who watched . . .

Screams that carried out toward the quiet woods and hills beyond . . .

Roland, crouched down upon his left haunch amid the grasses and shrubs of his previous campsite, watched the valley far below and listened. Trial, then execution were but flecks of color in the distance. He had no wish to see. He knew, for the song wove threads of conclusion through the wild air.

Slowly, as the last sounds died away, Roland reached for his crutches and pulled himself up to hang upon them. It was done.

They were all avenged. His mouth tautened. Oliver . . . ? He turned toward the radiant morning sunglow that was melting the last traces of frost from the tips of grasses and bushes.

There was nothing for him here. Ruffling sounds behind, and he turned to see Turpin, his cloak thrust back, staring toward that distant meadow below Aix with a bland expression.

"What do thou here?" Roland grated.

Turpin looked at him in surprise. "Should I not be with thee?" he inquired with melodious calm. "As friends may . . ."

Roland frowned, his nostrils flaring. "Or, fathers . . . ?" Turpin inclined his head. Witch creature, Roland stiffened. Unknowable for the powers that lurked behind those eyes, and within that youthful, elusive flesh. It was not the same as he had found the night so recently past.

"Nay," he said, after a moment, and pulled himself back. This warlock who had haunted him, even to claiming paternity? "Nay, thou should not!" he said harshly. Curiosity rippled across Turpin's wily face, and his eyes deepened, seeming to grow as they searched. Roland looked away toward the brightness of the castle of Aix. Turpin's presence was another unhappy twist to a past that had naught to do with whatever lay before him.

He felt totally alone.

He looked back toward the owl man who was continuing to watch him. He raised one hand to his shoulder and slipped the satchel that Turpin had given him from it, then flung it toward the other.

"I am a man," he said roughly. "I have no use for such as this! Or thee!" Turpin seemed to flinch a little. Then he gracefully reached for the pack bag, letting it vanish beneath the folds of his cloak.

Memories . . . Oliver. Roland glowered, watching Turpin step back slowly, slipping away to disappear into the trees. Then, inhaling deeply, he looked away, finding a view far from Aix La Chapelle, and began to swing upon his crutches toward it.

Oliver, who had disposed of witching things by simple human clarity . . . Somehow, Roland thought, he would be a man . . .

A human man.

CLASSIC SCIENCE FICTION AND FANTASY

___ **DUNE Frank Herbert** 0-441-17266-0/$4.95
The bestselling novel of an awesome world where gods and
adventurers clash, mile-long sandworms rule the desert, and
the ancient dream of immortality comes true.

___ **STRANGER IN A STRANGE LAND Robert A. Heinlein**
0-441-79034-8/$4.95
From the *New York Times* bestselling author—the science
fiction masterpiece of a man from Mars who teaches
humankind the art of grokking, watersharing and love.

___ **THE ONCE AND FUTURE KING T.H. White**
0-441-62740-4/$5.50
The world's greatest fantasy classic! A magical epic of King
Arthur in Camelot, romance, wizardry and war. By the author
of *The Book of Merlyn*.

___ **THE LEFT HAND OF DARKNESS Ursula K. LeGuin**
0-441-47812-3/$3.95
Winner of the Hugo and Nebula awards for best science fiction
novel of the year. "SF masterpiece!"—*Newsweek* "A Jewel of
a story."—Frank Herbert

___ **MAN IN A HIGH CASTLE Philip K. Dick** 0-441-51809-5/$3.95
"Philip K. Dick's best novel, a masterfully detailed alternate
world peopled by superbly realized characters."
—Harry Harrison

279